1637
Dr. Gribbleflotz and the Soul of Stoner

THE RING OF FIRE SERIES

1632 by Eric Flint
1633 with David Weber
1634: The Baltic War with David Weber
1634: The Galileo Affair with Andrew Dennis
1634: The Bavarian Crisis with Virginia DeMarce
1634: The Ram Rebellion with Virginia DeMarce et al.
1635: The Cannon Law with Andrew Dennis
1635: The Dreeson Incident with Virginia DeMarce
1635: The Eastern Front
1635: The Papal Stakes with Charles E. Gannon
1636: The Saxon Uprising
1636: The Kremlin Games with Gorg Huff & Paula Goodlett
1636: The Devil's Opera with David Carrico
1636: Commander Cantrell in the West Indies with Charles E. Gannon
1636: The Viennese Waltz with Gorg Huff & Paula Goodlett
1636: The Cardinal Virtues with Walter Hunt
1635: A Parcel of Rogues with Andrew Dennis
1636: The Ottoman Onslaught by Eric Flint
1636: Mission to the Mughals by Eric Flint & Griffin Barber
1636: The Vatican Sanction by Eric Flint & Charles E. Gannon
1637: The Volga Rules by Eric Flint, Gorg Huff & Paula Goodlett
1637: The Polish Maelstrom by Eric Flint
1636: The China Venture by Eric Flint & Iver P. Cooper
1636: The Atlantic Encounter by Eric Flint & Walter H. Hunt
1637: No Peace Beyond the Line by Eric Flint & Charles E. Gannon
1637: The Peacock Throne by Eric Flint & Griffin Barber
1635: The Tangled Web by Virginia DeMarce
1635: The Wars for the Rhine by Anette Pedersen
1636: Seas of Fortune by Iver P. Cooper
1636: The Chronicles of Dr. Gribbleflotz by Kerryn Offord & Rick Boatright
1636: Flight of the Nightingale by David Carrico
1636: Calabar's War by Charles E. Gannon & Robert E. Waters
1637: Dr. Gribbleflotz and the Soul of Stoner by Kerryn Offord & Rick Boatright

Time Spike with Marilyn Kosmatka
The Alexander Inheritance by Eric Flint, Gorg Huff & Paula Goodlett
The Macedonian Hazard by Eric Flint, Gorg Huff & Paula Goodlett

Ring of Fire I-IV, ed. by Eric Flint
Grantville Gazette volumes I-V, ed. by Eric Flint
Grantville Gazette VI-VII, ed. by Eric Flint & Paula Goodlett
Grantville Gazette VIII, ed. by Eric Flint & Walt Boyes
Grantville Gazette IX, ed. by Eric Flint, Walt Boyes & Joy Ward

1637
Dr. Gribbleflotz and the Soul of Stoner

KERRYN OFFORD
RICK BOATRIGHT

BAEN

1637: Dr. Gribbleflotz and the Soul of Stoner

This is a work of fiction. All the characters and events portrayed in this book are fictional, and any resemblance to real people or incidents is purely coincidental.

A Baen Books Original

Baen Publishing Enterprises
P.O. Box 1403
Riverdale, NY 10471
www.baen.com

ISBN: 978-1-9821-2560-8

Cover art by Tom Kidd

First printing, September 2021

Distributed by Simon & Schuster
1230 Avenue of the Americas
New York, NY 10020

Library of Congress Cataloging-in-Publication Data

Names: Offord, Kerryn, author. | Boatright, Rick, author.
Title: 1637 : Dr. Gribbleflotz and the soul of Stoner / Kerryn Offord and Rick Boatright.
Description: Riverdale, New York : Baen, [2021] | Series: The ring of fire ; volume 33
Identifiers: LCCN 2021029312 | ISBN 9781982125608 (trade paperback)
Subjects: GSAFD: Science fiction.
Classification: LCC PR9639.3.O325 A146 2021 | DDC 823/.914—dc23
LC record available at https://lccn.loc.gov/2021029312

10 9 8 7 6 5 4 3 2 1

Pages by Joy Freeman (www.pagesbyjoy.com)
Printed in the United States of America

1637
Dr. Gribbleflotz and the Soul of Stoner

Prologue

May 1636, Prague

Dr. Phillip Theophrastus Gribbleflotz stood back while his patron, King Venceslas V Adalbertus—formerly known as Albrecht Wenzel Eusebius von Wallenstein—was helped back into his bed by his valet.

"Enough!" the king roared, waving away the man who was trying to drape a blanket over his shoulders. He looked pointedly at the cloth-covered item on the three-legged easel a couple of servants had carried into the room when Phillip arrived. "What do you have to show me?" he demanded.

Phillip allowed himself a quick smile of satisfaction as he gazed at the cloth-covered item. "I have recently achieved an advance in the science of color photography." He gestured for one of the servants to remove the cloth. "Your Majesty, I give you the GribbleChrome."

King Venceslas leaned forward to get a better look. "Amazing." He looked at Phillip. "That is your good wife and your children?"

"Yes," Phillip said as he cast his eyes over the GribbleChrome image of Dina, Jon, and Salome. The color needed more work, but the image was a good proof of concept. He was just about to say that, suitably rephrased for the ear of his patron, when the doors burst open.

Phillip's initial reaction was one of abject terror. He knew his patron's up-time history. On February 25, 1634, in the up-timers' universe, assassins burst into Wallenstein's (as the king was then known) bed chamber and murdered him. Was this an assassination?

Terror turned to relief when Phillip spotted the massive turban with its equally enormous gemstone brooch worn by the great Dr. Thomas Stone. It was not assassins after all.

With his heart rate returning to normal, Phillip allowed himself to be distracted by the costume Dr. Stone was wearing. How was it possible that the man responsible for some of the great colors that he personally wore would wear something so drab as a black turban, even if it did sport silver threads?

"Thanks be to the Lord Jesus!" Dr. Stone bellowed. "I am here in time! Guptah! The violet ray! This is an emergency!"

They should have made for the king—this was, after all, the king's chamber—but they did not. Instead, both made for Phillip. His heart rate started to spike again.

"Doctor, God save us!" Dr. Stone shouted.

Dr. Stone started spraying Phillip with something from a bottle. There was renewed panic as Phillip put up his hands to protect his finery.

"Your Chakras," Dr. Stone said, "are fluctuating so dangerously that we felt the effects in the antechambers!"

Phillip swallowed. That comment, plus the obvious urgency in Dr. Stone's manner, scared him. He was distracted when Dr. Stone's companion, Guptah Rai Singh, shone a light into his eyes.

Off to his right, Phillip could hear Dr. Stone saying something to the king as he waved something over Phillip's torso, but he could not follow what was being said. There was something about his Mishawaka being drained and his Sheboygan being enlarged. He knew they were Chakra energies and he got the impression that there was something seriously wrong with them. "They are?" he managed to ask. "It is?"

"When you drink wine at dinner, do you sometimes feel dizzy when you rise, sahib?" Guptah asked in mangled German. "Do you find yourself waking in the night with a terrible need to relieve yourself? Do you find yourself stumbling over nothing? Do you sometimes forget a word or a name that you know as well as your own?"

Phillip paled as he wondered what was wrong with him. He could tell from the way Guptah Rai Singh was looking at him that it had to be bad. He shot a glance at the GribbleChrome of Dina and the children. Could this be the last time his eyes set upon them?

Guptah thrust a hand at Phillip's belly, and it started flashing, as if it had a light inside the hand that was flashing. "Sahib! Dr. Thomas!" he screamed. "The Mishawaka! There is no time! I must operate!"

Phillip barely had time to take in Herr Singh's last word before Dr. Stone shoved him into a chair, and ruthlessly yanked up and tore open his clothing, probably damaging his fine lime green linen shirt beyond repair. And then, Herr Singh plunged his fingers into his belly. Phillip stared at the hand that was digging around inside his body, and then Herr Singh pulled out something bloody and sticky. Herr Singh opened his hand to reveal a mass of what looked like bloody hair and things best left unidentified.

"You see!" Guptah shouted as he waved his prize for all to see. "You see! It was almost too late!"

That was the last Phillip took in as his traumatized mind decided it had had enough and let him sink into unconsciousness.

Part One

September 1636

Chapter 1

September 1636, Prague Hospital, Prague, Kingdom of Bohemia

Sheboygan, Mishawaka, Muskogee, Oskaloosa, Chillicothe, Oologah, Austin.

Doctor Phillip Theophrastus Gribbleflotz, M.D. (Amsterdam), M.D. (Prague), M.D. (Olmütz), M.D. (Karolinum), and president for life of the Royal Academy of Science (Bohemia), chewed on the hairs of his mustache as he looked at the list. The mustache was quite tasty, or at least the temporary mustache of hot chocolate made with full cream milk and Dutched cocoa powder with a sprinkling of marshmallows and freshly grated nutmeg currently coating it was tasty. He reached for his mug and took another sip before checking the list on the report from Grantville once more.

Muladhara, Svadhisthana, Manipura, Anahata, Vishuddha, Ajna, Sahasrara.

Phillip sighed. One list was not like the other. And that was a problem. The first list was attributed to Dr. Thomas Stone, master of Akashic Magick and scholar of the Chakras. The second list was the result of qualified researchers checking the libraries of Grantville for information on the Chakras. "Why are they different?" he wondered.

"Herr President Dr. Gribbleflotz."

Phillip lowered his mug of hot chocolate to the cafeteria table. He spared it a mournful look. It was still more than half full or, for one who was enjoying drinking it, nearly half empty. It was, however, still steaming hot. Something he hoped he would still be able to say about it when he finished with Samuel Hartlib, secretary of the Royal Academy of Science (Bohemia). Samuel only used the full complement of his titles when he wanted to talk about the Royal Academy. "What is it now, Samuel?" he asked as he finally looked up.

Samuel was a stocky man in his mid-thirties, with wavy brown hair down to his shoulders and a Greek nose over a thin mustache. He was wearing an old-style—as in, not tailored to fit—white linen shirt with gathered cuffs and plain black trousers. Over this, he wore a black silk academic robe. Phillip, with his fondness for color, could not understand how Samuel could enjoy looking so drab. However, at least the black academic robe was of the finest silk, suggesting that there was still hope for the man.

"Zacharias Held has failed to produce his promised article for the Royal Academy's October issue, and we are now over three thousand words short."

"And?" Phillip prompted. There was, of course, always an "and."

"Someone needs to produce a suitable article of not less than three thousand words by Friday."

Phillip glared at Samuel. There was no doubt in his mind who Samuel expected to be that "someone." "And what am I supposed to write about?"

Samuel pointed to the notes Phillip had been looking at. "You have already started research on Dr. Stone's Chakras."

In answer, Phillip pushed the two lists over so Samuel could read them. "How do I explain that?" he demanded.

Samuel spared the lists a quick glance before shrugging. "I'm sure there is a perfectly logical explanation."

Phillip snorted. "Of course there is. However, Dr. Stone isn't available to give it."

Samuel sighed. "What about your experiment into the efficacy of vibrating beds in the acceleration of patient recovery?"

Phillip shook his head. "We don't have conclusive results yet."

Samuel ran a hand through his flowing locks. "There must be something you can write about."

"Maybe you could write about the special surgical techniques used by Dr. Stone's strange colleague?"

Both Phillip and Samuel looked toward the man who had approached Phillip's table while they were speaking.

"Unfortunately, Dr. Handsch," Samuel said, "we have been

unable to contact Dr. Stone's colleague. We believe he has returned home, to India."

"That is terribly inconvenient," Dr. Georg Handsch said. "The guild is most interested in learning how he was able to perform abdominal surgery on Dr. Gribbleflotz without benefit of anesthetic, and without leaving a scar."

The guild in question was the Prague surgeons' guild and they had been pestering Phillip to get Dr. Stone and his colleague to present a course of lectures on their techniques ever since the incident back in May. "Yes," Phillip agreed, "it is a grave pity that we have been unable to talk to Herr Singh." It was not just the surgeons' guild who wanted to learn how to operate on the human body like Herr Singh had done. Phillip too wanted to know.

"We are still short three thousand words for the October edition of the *Proceedings of the Royal Academy*," Samuel prompted.

"Maybe Dr. Gribbleflotz could write a description of my new surgical procedure," Dr. Handsch suggested.

Phillip licked his lips, once again coated in a thin layer of hot chocolate and marshmallow, as he considered Georg's suggestion. The man was a uroscopist—a physician who used a patient's urine as a diagnostic tool—and had recently returned from a trip to Grantville where he had learned a new, minimally invasive, surgical treatment for bladder stones. "Unfortunately, I would need hands-on experience of the procedure before I could write about it properly."

"That's not a problem," Georg said. "I have such an operation scheduled for tomorrow, and I would be delighted, Dr. Gribbleflotz, if you were to assist me."

Phillip nodded. "Thank you. I accept your offer. Who will be your anesthetist?"

"Dr. de le Boë."

Phillip nodded again. He had expected nothing less. Dr. Franz de le Boë was a recent graduate from the Grantville-Jena medical program, where he had learned all about things like anesthetics. "I need to drop in on Dr. de le Boë anyway, to see how the vibrating beds experiment is progressing. Maybe you could fill me in on the procedure on the way over to the ward?"

"I would be delighted, Dr. Gribbleflotz."

Phillip smiled. "I'll just finish my chocolate and be right with you."

Georg nodded vigorously. "Please, don't rush. I need to have a short word with a colleague about something. You take your time and enjoy your hot chocolate and I'll be right back."

Samuel kept his eyes on Dr. Handsch as he hurried off. Phillip made eye contact with Samuel. "Bathroom?" he asked, guessing where Dr. Handsch was heading in such a hurry.

Samuel nodded. "If the operation isn't until tomorrow, will you be able to have the article in the typesetter's hands by Friday?"

Phillip picked up his still-steaming mug of hot chocolate. He held it in both hands just below his nose, so he could appreciate the aroma as he gently shook his head. "Samuel, I am wounded by your lack of faith in me."

"Just don't mention Dr. Handsch's name too often," Samuel warned. "You know why he is so willing to help you write an article?"

Phillip nodded. "It's not advertising if it appears in a learned article in the *Proceedings of the Royal Academy*."

"Precisely," Samuel said. "Well, as long as you know why he is so willing to help, that's my business with you complete, Phillip. I'll see you later."

Phillip smiled and saluted Samuel with his mug of chocolate before taking another sip. It was just the right temperature. He sighed contently as he took another, larger sip.

Chapter 2

Prague Hospital, Prague, Bohemia

Diana Cheng was in Prague under protest. She could have been back in Grantville studying, but no, her parents had insisted that she abandon her studies—apparently because she was too far ahead of the rest of her intake—and take a short break in Prague while her father and brother examined something that had failed at the city's new radio station. She sighed. She was happy for her brother, who could visit his girlfriend whom he hadn't seen since she graduated from the State Technical College with an Electrical Trades Certificate back in May, but there wasn't much to keep her interested, not when her parents had insisted that she leave her medical textbooks behind. Her brother had suggested that she could check up on Dr. Gribbleflotz's vibrating bed experiment—something she had screwed her nose up at, believing it was nothing more than the usual fake science Dr. Gribbleflotz seemed to unerringly latch onto. She was visiting the wards where Dr. Gribbleflotz was running his experiment for one reason only: She was so bored that anything had to be better than nothing.

"And this," said Nurse Gertraud Kaufmann as she led Diana into a ward, "is Dr. Gribbleflotz's number one experimental ward."

"But everyone knows Dr. Gribbleflotz's number two ward is the place to be if you want to get better faster," one of the patients called out.

This sally was met with mutters of agreement from several of the other patients lying in beds.

"Hey, Nurse, what do I have to do to be moved to Ward Two?" one of them called out.

"Does Ward Two have the vibrating beds?" Diana asked. She knew that Dr. Gribbleflotz was testing a hypothesis that beds vibrating at a certain frequency, based on a cat's purr, would increase the speed of healing for muscular and skeletal injuries.

Nurse Kaufmann nodded.

"Is there really a difference in recovery rate between this ward and Ward Two?" Diana tried not to show how skeptical she was about the whole idea, but a glance at Nurse Kaufmann told her she'd failed.

"The results are very convincing," Gertraud said. "Maybe you should talk to Dr. de le Boë, Frau Cheng. He's responsible for the day-to-day running of the experiment."

The name rang a bell with Diana. "Would Dr. de le Boë have recently completed his medical training at Jena and Grantville?" she asked. If he was who she thought he might be, some of her fellow students back in Grantville were going to be extremely jealous when she got back and told them who she had met.

Gertraud nodded. "Please, come this way."

Diana followed Gertraud through the ward toward a door at the end. Gertraud knocked and entered. "Dr. de le Boë. This is Frau Cheng, a visitor from Grantville. She is interested in learning more about Dr. Gribbleflotz's vibrating bed experiment."

Franz de le Boë's head swung around at hearing his name. "Frau Cheng?" He tilted his head as he stared at Diana. "Do I know you from somewhere?"

"Maybe," Diana said. "I was a student nurse working on the wards when you were doing your practical assessment." She wanted to reassure him that she was not one of the silly girls who had haunted his every step but did not know how to bring it up without embarrassing everyone.

Franz nodded. "I thought you looked familiar." He grinned. "There aren't that many people of Chinese descent in Grantville."

"No, there aren't," Diana agreed with a silly smile on her face.

Franz smiled back. "So, you want to know more about Dr. Gribbleflotz's vibrating bed experiment? How did you hear about it?"

"Magdalena Rutilius is my brother's betrothed," she said. That was not official yet, but with Mags' latest invention—a way of using a small Alexanderson alternator to create an audio amplifier—likely to make her filthy rich, her parents had dropped the last of their objections.

"Ah! The original cat woman," Franz said. He shook his head ruefully. "Her arm is healing much faster than one would expect." He grinned. "Probably because she has a natural source of vibration at the correct frequency."

"Liova," Diana confirmed, naming Mags' cat. Mags had broken the arm several weeks ago when she disturbed a couple of housebreakers trying to steal Dr. Gribbleflotz's lucky crystal. "Is there really something in the theory?" she asked.

Franz answered by pointing to a chart on the wall. "See for yourself."

Diana looked at the chart. It was straightforward. For each diagnosis in each ward, it showed the length of stay. A quick scan of the data suggested that patients in the vibrating bed ward had shorter stays than those in the control ward. "Are the differences statistically significant?" she asked.

"Pardon?"

Diana stared at Franz. "Surely you understand the importance of results being or not being statistically significant?" she asked. "How else will you know if the results are due to the treatment, rather than to chance alone?"

Franz stared blankly at Diana. "Was that part of the medical curriculum?"

Diana had to think hard about that. She'd been taught statistics, but that had been early in the undergraduate portion of her medical training. Dr. de le Boë had turned up in 1634 and was awarded his Doctor of Osteopathic Medicine earlier this year. To earn his D.O. in barely two years, he must have had significant medical training before arriving in Grantville. That would have allowed him to test out on much of the program without ever attending a statistics class. "Medical statistics are taught in the undergraduate BSN, so it's possible you missed it."

"I must have," Franz confirmed. "Maybe you could examine the data and tell me if the results are statistically significant?" he asked.

Diana ran her tongue over her lips. "I don't have my books with me," she warned. "But my mother knows a lot about mathematics." That last was a massive understatement. Her mother held graduate and postgraduate degrees in mathematics and had, on several occasions over the years, seriously considered going back to school to do a doctorate. "And she brought her laptop to Prague with her." That was important because there were several statistics packages installed on it.

"So, you'll be able to look at the data and tell me if the results are *statistically significant*?" Franz asked.

"Probably." Diana did not wish to seem too eager, so she punctuated the word with a nonchalant shrug.

A smile burst across Franz's face. "Then let's get the records," he said, reaching for a couple of folders on a shelf.

There was a serious look on Franz's face when he handed the folders to Diana.

"Is there something that troubles you?" she asked.

Franz chewed his lip for a moment. "Do you know much about up-time medical practices from before the Ring of Fire?"

"A bit," Diana said. "I've been dreaming of becoming a doctor since I was in junior high."

"Good. Good," Franz nodded. "And are you aware of any surgical techniques that don't leave scars?" he asked.

Diana nodded.

Franz's eyes lit up with pleasure. "Do you know how they do it?" he asked. "And why wasn't it covered in my training?"

Diana sighed. People never asked the simple questions. She really did not have much more than a vague idea of how the operations were performed, but she could answer the other part of the question. "The reason they don't currently teach the techniques is because they need pretty advanced equipment we just don't have," she said.

"But I've heard that Dr. Stone's colleague from India operated on Dr. Gribbleflotz with just his bare hands!"

Diana's brows shot up. "What sort of operation?" she demanded. Normally she wouldn't be so aggressive, but she was her mother's daughter and back up-time her mother had been a card-carrying supporter of James Randi, the great skeptic. She had her suspicions about the operation, but she needed more information to be sure.

"Herr Singh removed a *Mishawaka* from Dr. Gribbleflotz's abdomen. The witnesses I've spoken to say there was a lot of blood."

"I bet there was," Diana muttered. She had no idea what a *Mishawaka* was supposed to be, but she was pretty sure the word was not Latin. Which meant it was not a proper medical term.

Which in turn told her that someone had been playing games. And pretty nasty games at that. "I'm sorry, but your witnesses are mistaken. There is no way someone can perform surgery on the abdomen with just their bare hands." She held her hand up to stop the utterance she could see Franz wanted to make. "I'm pretty sure I know what was done. It's all sleight of hand. The *surgeon*, and I use that term loosely, will have used previously prepared props to suggest that he has entered the abdomen and removed something. In the cases I've read about, the people who do this kind of surgery—it was called *psychic surgery* back up-time—usually claimed to remove cancerous growths—probably because that was where the money was. Only for those same cancerous growths to still be present when the patient died and an autopsy performed." There was some heat in those last few words. Back when she was in junior high, back when they lived in North Carolina, the mother of her best friend had been taken in by one such practitioner. Her mother's death had just about destroyed her friend.

"Are you saying the surgery Dr. Stone's colleague performed on me didn't actually happen?" Dr. Phillip Gribbleflotz asked from the doorway.

Diana spun round at the sound of another person's voice. She had never seen Dr. Gribbleflotz before, but she had little doubt that the man she was facing was him. The orange-and-yellow-brocade waistcoat, purple pantaloons, and lime green socks he was wearing just about screamed his identity. She noticed Dr. Gribbleflotz was looking at her expectantly. That reminded her of the question he had asked. "Yes," she said.

Phillip stepped into the office and closed the door behind him. "You seem very sure."

Diana backed away a couple of steps. "I am. There is no way you can get through the epidermal layers of the abdomen with just your bare hands. Nor is it possible to make an opening in the abdomen large enough to stick a hand into the abdominal cavity without leaving a scar."

Phillip rubbed a hand over his abdomen as he stared at Diana. "But that is exactly what they tell me happened," he said.

Diana shrugged. "Whoever *they* are, they're wrong," she said. "What they think they saw is physically impossible. They only think that's what they saw, Dr. Gribbleflotz. I'm afraid that Dr.

Stone's colleague was using sleight of hand to make it look like he was operating on you."

"But why would he pretend to perform surgery on me?" Phillip asked.

Diana swallowed. This had the potential to become very messy. "I don't know." She clamped the folders Franz had given her protectively against her chest as she edged away from the obviously distressed Dr. Gribbleflotz.

"Why would the Great Stoner do such a thing?" Phillip cried.

Diana grabbed the first moment Dr. Gribbleflotz was not looking at her to escape. She did not exactly run for it, but she was out of the room before anyone could call her back. Behind her, she could hear Dr. Gribbleflotz repeating the same word time and time again. "Why?" As she made good her escape, she too started to wonder why Mr. Stone would want to perform psychic surgery on Dr. Gribbleflotz.

When she got home from the hospital, Diana found her mother alone in the apartment the family was renting while they were in Prague. "Where's everyone?" she asked.

"Your father and the boys are helping Mags with something," Jennie Lee Cheng said. She looked at the folders in Diana's arms. "What do you have there?"

Diana glanced down and realized she was still carrying the folders Dr. de le Boë had given her. "They're the clinical records of the patients involved in Dr. Gribbleflotz's vibrating bed experiment."

Jennie Lee's brow lifted. "The hospital just let you walk out with them?"

"No," Diana said. "Dr. de le Boë, the doctor responsible for the day-to-day running of the experiment, asked me to have a look at them to determine if the results they are seeing are statistically significant."

"Why would he do that?"

Diana grinned. "Because he has absolutely no idea about the statistical design of experiments. Nor does he know how to perform a statistical analysis of the results. I was hoping I could use your laptop to do that."

Jennie Lee smiled. "Bring it over here," she said, gesturing to the dining table she was using as a desk, "and we can work on it together."

Meanwhile, back at the hospital

"Why?" Phillip demanded of no one in particular.

Franz shrugged. "I don't know, Dr. Gribbleflotz. Maybe Frau Cheng is wrong? She is, after all, just a young woman."

Phillip swung round, expecting to see the young up-timer. "Where is she?" he demanded. "Where did she go?"

"I don't know, Dr. Gribbleflotz. Maybe she has returned to her lodgings."

Phillip sighed. He had thought he was starting to understand the up-timers, but then something like this happened. "If you need me, I will be in my laboratory reading my up-time sources to see what they have to say about *psychic surgery*."

"Of course, Dr. Gribbleflotz."

Phillip waved to Franz before leaving the office. He made his way back to his laboratory at the top of the Mihulka Tower lost in his thoughts. "Why?" he kept asking himself. "Why would the Great Stoner do such a thing to me?"

Chapter 3

Next day, Prague, the Mihulka Tower

Magdalena Rutilius resided and, since leaving her job with Radio Prague to work on her invention full time, worked in rooms attached to the Mihulka Tower—the top level of which was Dr. Gribbleflotz's personal laboratory. Jason Cheng Jr. was walking toward the HDG Laboratories workshops and apartments with his friend and fellow mechanical engineering apprentice, David Kitt. They were intent on joining Mags to help her produce more of the new Alexanderson alternator–based amplifier units she had invented when his eyes fell on two men leaving the tower. One of them was wearing a heavily embroidered floor-length vest over what looked like a plain knee-length dress, even though he was pretty sure down-timer men did not wear dresses. Peeking out from under the man's skirts were red boots. But the pièce de résistance was the massive yellow turban he was wearing wrapped around a gold-and-orange hat. It was simply huge, and just to cap everything off, it was adorned with an equally enormous brooch with an equally enormous yellow-faceted crystal set in it.

The other man was a symphony in red. From his red turban wrapped around his gold-and-orange hat, to his red-leather fringe vest over a red shirt, and what looked like red-silk skin-tight pants. The ensemble was completed by red boots that reminded Jason of a court jester's upcurled boots. The only thing missing were the little bells dangling from the tips of the upcurled toes.

"Is today fancy-dress day and no one thought to tell us?" David asked.

Jason had been so stunned by the vision of the two men that he had forgotten that he was not alone. With David's prompting he glanced around. "No, they're the only ones in fancy dress. But who the heck are they?"

"No idea," David said, shaking his head.

"That's Martin Zänkel of the Prague Chapter of the Society of Aural Investigators and his assistant," a sweet feminine voice said from the doorway.

Jason recognized the voice immediately and swung round. "Mags!" he said when his eyes lightened on his girlfriend. "How are you?"

"The better for seeing you," she said.

"What's with the fancy costumes?" Jason asked, gesturing toward the departing backs of Martin and his assistant.

"They are each wearing the ceremonial dress of the society appropriate to their rank. I assume there's some important event they have to attend, although I'm sure Dr. Gribbleflotz won't be attending."

With an opening like that, Jason could not help himself. "What color are Dr. Gribbleflotz's ceremonial robes?"

Mags glared at him. "Don't be ridiculous. Dr. Gribbleflotz wouldn't be seen dead in those fashion crimes the society calls their ceremonial robes."

"No. Of course not," Jason said, shooting David a quick smile. "What was I thinking of? Dr. Gribbleflotz is always the epitome of sartorial elegance."

That earned Jason a snort from David and a fiery glare from Mags. Dr. Gribbleflotz was a bit of a hero to her, having saved her from a life of poverty when she was originally recruited to work at his laboratory in Jena. Jason knew he should not twit her but Dr. Gribbleflotz was a self-confessed alchemist—actually, the self-proclaimed world's greatest alchemist—and, like most Americans, Jason had no respect for a group of people who pursued the philosopher's stone and hoped to use it to transmute lead into gold.

In an effort to restore Mags' good humor, Jason changed the topic, a little. "How on earth did they dream up that collection of fashion crimes?" he asked.

"They didn't dream them up," Mags said. "Except for the colors, which are used to define rank, they're supposed to be faithful copies of the costumes Dr. Stone and his colleague wore when they were in Prague to do Chakra readings for the king."

"Chakra readings?" Jason glanced at David, who appeared equally lost. "What're they?"

"It's the use of crystals to scry for an individual's aural energy."

Jason stared at Mags. "Why would Dr. Stone be scrying the king for aural energy?" he demanded. "Surely he doesn't believe in that sort of nonsense?"

Mags shrugged. "How should I know? I'm just telling you what I've heard."

Jason turned to look down the street. Martin and his assistant had already disappeared, but Jason was not really seeing the street anyway. He was reviewing the outfits the men had been wearing. He had never seen Mr. Stone that outlandishly dressed. There had been some funny color combinations in his choice of tie-dyed T-shirts, and he might have favored open sandals, even in winter, but other than that, he had always seemed pretty normal. So, he wondered, why did Mr. Stone and his associate—whoever that might be—dress up in fancy dress to visit the king? For that matter, why would he want to give the king a Chakra reading?

"Are you coming in?" Mags asked.

Jason let Mags drag him into the tower.

Meanwhile

Diana had not so much forgotten to tell her parents about the revelations of the previous day as she became so involved in interpreting the data from Dr. Gribbleflotz's vibrating bed experiment that her encounter with him completely slipped her mind. So, it was a particularly unsuspecting young up-timer who made her way to the experimental wards in the hospital with her neatly handwritten notes.

The first person she met was the ward nurse. "Is Dr. de le Boë available?" she asked Nurse Gertraud Kaufmann.

"Dr. de le Boë is in the operating room this morning, Frau Cheng."

"Oh!" Diana looked around randomly, not sure what she should do. She had expected, rather foolishly she now realized, that Dr. de le Boë would be in the ward.

"You're quite welcome to observe the operation, Frau Cheng," Gertraud said. "I can call an orderly to guide you to the operating room if you wish."

"Yes, please," Diana said. It was not so much that she desperately wanted to watch Dr. de le Boë at work, but more that she didn't have anything better to do while she waited for him, and anyway, she might learn something new.

The hospital had been built with funds from the Roths, who had dictated that it be built according to the best practices from Grantville and Jena. That meant the operating room was well lit, with a skylight and several chandeliers to ensure that the surgeons could see what they were doing. The walls, floors, and ceiling were tiled in white porcelain, so they could be easily cleaned, and spectators watched proceedings from a viewing gallery that was separated from the operating room by glazed windows.

Diana was led into the viewing gallery and abandoned by the orderly. She glanced around, taking in the number of men who had turned to look at her as she entered. Some of them returned to looking through the windows she could see, while others continued to stare at her. She tried to ignore the stares she was getting as she made her way to an empty spot by one of the viewing windows.

Down below, she could see half a dozen men in white surgical gowns, caps, and masks. She had no idea what procedure they were going to perform, so she tried instead to work out which of them was Franz. The first man she identified was Dr. Gribbleflotz. Not that she was one hundred percent sure she had properly identified him, but who else would be wearing purple pantaloons with that particular shade of orange stockings?

With Dr. Gribbleflotz as a metric, she decided the surgeon was not Dr. de le Boë. Franz was taller than both of them. So, she thought to herself, if Franz were not the surgeon, what role would he have in this procedure? Her eyes fell on the anesthetist. With ether the current anesthetic of choice, someone with Franz's Grantville training would be the logical person for that important role. She studied the anesthetist for a few seconds before smiling. Found him.

The surgeon turned and spoke to the audience in the viewing gallery, and Diana discovered why her spot had been empty. It was, apparently, the only window overlooking the operating table that did not open.

A quick glance at the men gathered around the other, open, windows told Diana that none of them were likely to make space for her. She sighed in resignation and turned her attention to what was unfolding below. It was, she realized when the surgeon displayed an instrument that she recognized to Dr. Gribbleflotz and the rest of his audience, a mechanical (rather than sonic) transurethral lithotripsy—in layman's terms, an operation to remove bladder stones by sticking a medical instrument down the penis to break up the stone. To amuse herself, she created her own commentary as the operation unfolded.

Diana walked out of the viewing gallery while the surgeon was still giving his final address to his audience. No doubt, she thought, the man was telling everyone what a good job he'd done. She snorted as she walked down the stairs. Even Dr. Gribbleflotz could not muck up a transurethral lithotripsy.

She walked over to the surgical theater's doors and picked a section of wall to lean against while she waited for Franz. When the surgical team finally walked out—in their normal civilian dress—Franz was one of the last. Diana waved when she saw him looking around. That caught his attention. He waved back and headed in her direction.

"Frau Cheng." Franz smiled. "I thought I saw you in the viewing gallery, but it was difficult to be sure with all those men crowded around you. I hope they weren't bothering you."

The last was almost a question. Diana smiled. "They were asking me about the operation."

"Oh!" Franz's eyes widened as his brow furrowed. "Why would they do that?"

"I couldn't hear what the surgeon was saying, so I made up my own commentary." Diana shrugged and grinned. "It must have been better than the surgeon's, because the guys kept asking me to speak up."

"But how could you give a commentary?"

"It wasn't the first transurethral lithotripsy I've seen and provided a commentary to."

"It wasn't?" Franz shook his head. "Why would you do that?" he asked.

"My father designed the lithotrite they were using today. Back when he was first designing it, he needed my help."

"And that involved attending a transurethral lithotripsy?" Franz asked.

Diana grinned. "It was more than one, and Dad needed a detailed description of what was going on."

Franz's wince was something to behold. Diana nodded. "Yep. Totally embarrassed. But that's Dad for you. He didn't even notice."

Franz smiled. "I assume you didn't turn up today just to watch another transurethral lithotripsy..."

"No, I didn't." Diana patted the satchel she had slung across her chest. "I've got the results of the statistical analysis of the vibrating beds data if you'd like to look at them."

"Frau Cheng," Dr. Gribbleflotz called out. "A moment of your time," he said as he hurried over.

Diana sighed, quietly, and folded her arms as she stood and waited for Dr. Gribbleflotz to catch up. It would not do to allow people to think she hadn't wanted their twosome disturbed.

"Frau Cheng," Dr. Gribbleflotz repeated when he joined Diana and Franz. He glanced around to check that no one was close enough to overhear. "Would it be possible to discuss my operation with you in more detail?"

Diana knew immediately that Dr. Gribbleflotz wasn't talking about the transurethral lithotripsy he had just assisted with. "My mother knows more about psychic surgery than I do."

"Oh." Dr. Gribbleflotz looked slightly disappointed.

"But she should be home right now if it is convenient."

"Good. Good," Dr. Gribbleflotz said. "And Franz, would you be able to join us?"

"Of course, Dr. Gribbleflotz," Franz said. "And maybe, while we walk over, Frau Cheng can tell us what she discovered when she analyzed the vibrating bed data."

Chapter 4

Diana used a key to open the door to the apartment she and her family were staying in during their time in Prague. "Mom, I'm home," she called out as she stepped into the apartment. "I've got Dr. Gribbleflotz and Dr. de le Boë with me. They want to talk to you about something."

Diana led Franz and Dr. Gribbleflotz into the apartment and waited for her mother to turn up. It did not take long. In less than a minute Jennie Lee appeared at a door into the entry hall.

"Mom, this is Dr. Gribbleflotz and Dr. de le Boë," Diana said.

"Jennie Lee Cheng," Jennie Lee said as she offered the two men her hand. She smiled at Franz. "How are you finding Diana's analysis?" she asked.

"It was quite enlightening, Frau Cheng," Franz said as he bowed over Jennie Lee's hand. "I had thought that random assignment of patients with similar injuries to the treatment or control groups would have sufficed. However, I now accept that I would've gained more information on the benefits of the treatment if I'd assigned a fourteen-year-old boy with a broken arm to the control group and the forty-year-old with a similar injury to the treatment group."

"They aren't here about the vibrating bed experiment, Mom," Diana said.

Her mother turned her attention to Diana. "They aren't?"

Diana nodded. "Something's come up that they need to talk to you about."

"Can't you tell me?" Jennie Lee asked.

Diana shook her head. "I think you need to hear what Drs. Gribbleflotz and de le Boë have to say without any input from me."

Jennie Lee glanced over to Franz and Dr. Phillip Gribbleflotz.

"Your daughter is correct, Frau Cheng," Phillip said. "She has made a claim that is rather staggering in its potential to cause problems if it is true."

"You have?" Jennie Lee asked Diana. "And, is it true?"

Diana nodded. "That's why we are here. They want a second opinion."

"Well, then, please, take a seat," Jennie Lee invited as they entered the study. She waited until everyone was seated before continuing. "So, what is it you need a second opinion about?"

Franz started by describing the conversation he had had with Diana, with Phillip adding details he was familiar with. Jennie Lee listened carefully, interjecting occasionally to ask for clarification as they described what Dr. Thomas Stone and his companion, Guptah Rai Singh, got up to while they were in Prague.

Diana kept an eye on her mother throughout. She was, as Diana had fully expected, completely outraged.

"George. It must have been him. No one else would have the knowledge and skills to carry it off," Jennie Lee muttered furiously.

"George?" Phillip asked.

"George Mundell," Jennie Lee answered. "He's a stage magician. Dammit!" she said with force. "I would have expected him to be totally against psychic surgery."

Phillip sighed. "So, it was psychic surgery?" he asked. "Franz and I were hoping your daughter might have been mistaken."

Jennie Lee nodded. "Oh, yes. It was definitely psychic surgery. But I can't understand why George would lower himself to doing it, nor why Tom Stone would let him get away with it."

The four of them were sitting in silence when the main entrance to the apartment could be heard to open. Jason Jr. called out, "Mom, Dad, we're home." This was followed by the thuds of heavy outdoor footwear being removed, to be replaced with slippers.

"Is there anything to eat?" This latest request from Jason was punctuated by the opening of cupboards and drawers in the kitchen. Naturally, being teenagers, there was no sound of said cupboards and drawers being closed.

Jennie Lee sighed. "We're in the study."

"You wouldn't believe what we saw today," Jason called out. There was the clatter of a knife on the wooden kitchen table and soon after, Jason, Magdalena, and David appeared at the door, each holding a thick sandwich and a mug or glass of something. "We arrived at Mags' place just as a couple of guys dressed like characters from a Christmas pantomime were leaving," Jason said as he stepped into the study.

"I told you, they were members of the local chapter of the Society of Aural Investigators and that they were wearing their ceremonial dress," Magdalena said as she followed Jason into the study.

It was about this time that Jason spotted Franz and Phillip. "Hello. I'm sorry. We didn't know Mom had visitors."

Phillip waved away the apology. "What is a Christmas pantomime?" he asked.

Jason shot a glance in his mother's direction for permission before answering. "It's a sort of comedy theater for children that was usually televised on Christmas day."

Phillip's tongue slipped out and ran along his lips. "Theater," he muttered before turning toward Franz. "Do you think..."

Franz nodded. "From what I've heard, the Chakra readings Dr. Stone and his colleague gave the king was very theatrical. It would have provided the perfect cover for them to administer a number of simple diagnostic tests without the king noticing."

"Excuse me!" Jennie Lee called out. "Chakra readings? Diagnostic tests?"

Phillip nodded. "Back in May, Dr. Stone and his colleague, Herr Singh, examined the king using the new science of the Chakras. They did, as your son suggests, wear clothing that would have been out of place in Grantville. Franz and I think that the costumes may have been part of a performance intended to divert the king's attention from what they were actually doing."

"They could easily have given the king a full physical examination while he was distracted by the 'smoke and mirrors' of the Chakra reading," Franz said.

"Why did they need 'smoke and mirrors'?" Diana asked. "Couldn't they just do a normal physical?"

Franz shook his head. "There is no way they could have got the king to willingly submit to a full physical. He doesn't trust physicians. Not even those trained in the up-time medicine."

"Especially not them," Phillip said.

"True," Franz agreed with a grin. "Maybe you should try the same technique. Do you think you know enough about the Chakras to put on a suitable show while giving the king a physical?" he asked.

"I've already added Chakra readings to Kirlian imaging and use of the Gribbleflotz Magneto-Etheric Aural Aura Detector."

Franz looked at Phillip with wide eyes. "The king let you near him with the imaging equipment and an aural detector?"

Phillip sat up and, with a straight face, said, "Naturally. I am, after all, his personal aural investigator, and they are the acknowledged tools of the trade."

Franz smiled at Phillip before turning his attention to Diana. "Would it be possible to set up a Gribbleflotz Magneto-Etheric Aural Aura Detector to perform some standard tests?"

Diana pointed to Jason and Mags. "Ask them, not me. I don't understand electronics."

Franz turned his attention onto Jason. "Could you connect, say, a sphygmomanometer to the Magneto-Etheric Aural Aura Detector?" Franz asked.

"What's a sphygmomanometer?" Jason asked.

"A blood pressure gauge," Diana answered. "You know. Like Dr. Shipley uses to measure your blood pressure."

"Ahhh!" The tip of Jason's tongue poked out as he thought for a while. "That's a three-stage project. You have the cuff, the mercury column thingy, and then there's the stethoscope the doctor uses to listen to the blood pumping through the veins."

"Arteries," Diana said.

"What? Pardon?" Jason demanded.

Diana shook her head in dismay at her brother. "A sphygmomanometer measures arterial blood pressure. Veins have valves to stop blood flowing backwards, as they operate at much lower pressures."

Jason waved off her explanation. "Never mind that. As I was saying, doctors use a stethoscope to listen to the blood pumping through the artery." He glanced over his audience. "That sort of leaves the patient out of the loop. What if, instead of using a stethoscope, the doctor used a microphone connected to the amplifier in an aural detector. That way, both he and the patient can hear."

"What about modifying the detector to give a paper trace,"

an enthusiastic David suggested. "A red line showing jumps with each heartbeat would surely be something to show the king."

"Green," Phillip said. "The Chakra color of the heart is green, so it needs to be green ink."

"Hey, no problem," David said. "I'm sure they can do green ink too."

"Are you talking about an electrocardiograph?" Franz asked.

Jason shook his head. "Just a simple heartbeat counter. An ECG would be much more complicated." He glanced across to David. "Could your father help?"

David shrugged. "The paper trace, sure. No problem. But getting the signals? That's electrical."

Jason smiled. "Me and Mags can handle that."

"With a bit of help from Herr Haygood," Mags added.

"Who is Herr Haygood?" Franz asked.

"He was my electrical technology teacher at the State Technical College in Grantville," Mags answered.

"This is all very good and interesting," Jennie Lee said, "but we still haven't found an explanation for the psychic surgery."

"For that," Phillip said, "I imagine we will need to talk to Dr. Stone. Unfortunately, he is currently in Padua."

"We could ask George," Jennie Lee suggested. "I know he's still in Grantville."

"Oh?" Phillip prompted.

Jennie Lee grinned. "His wife works for our company. Believe me, I would have heard about it if George had left Grantville."

"Yes." Phillip smiled. "I would like to ask Herr Mundell." His grin was evil. "Please, don't warn him that I wish to speak with him."

"Why all the fuss about psychic surgery?" David asked. "I mean, it wasn't a nice thing to do to Dr. Gribbleflotz, but in the great scheme of things, what does it matter?"

"The Prague surgeons' guild has already asked me to get Herr Singh to return to Prague to teach them his techniques," Phillip explained.

"Oh!" David said. "They've been taken in?" he asked. Then, before anyone could answer, he continued, "What happens when they discover that they were taken in?" He shook his head ruefully. "That's not going to go down well. No one likes being made a fool of."

"It could get messy," Diana said. She looked to her mother. "So, what are you going to do about it?"

"Talk to your father, and see what he thinks we should do," Jennie Lee replied.

"Why is it up to us?" Jason demanded. "Why do we have to clean up after Herr Stone and Herr Mundell?"

"Because we want to stop the idea of psychic surgery dead in the water before it gains any headway," Jennie Lee said. She looked around, just in case any of the others might disagree. None of them did. She nodded in satisfaction. "So, when will your father be home?" she asked Jason.

Chapter 5

Volta Mantovana, 12 miles northwest of Mantua, Duchy of Mantua, northern Italy

Bernardo Ponzi mopped the sweat from his forehead as he paused to take a breather. Fire and brimstone evangelism required a lot of effort, but looking out at his congregation, Bernardo knew that it was worth it.

"Ready to cue music."

That was his wife speaking to him via one of the children's walkie-talkie radios the up-timers had sourced. He had an earpiece taped to his right ear connected to the receiver from another one hidden in his turban. Bernardo lifted his left hand, the hand holding the microphone for the public-address system that allowed him to broadcast his words to everyone in his congregation, to show he was ready to proceed.

"Cueing music in three, two, one."

On Elisabetta's count of one, the music started. It was a recent recording of a hymn played on the pipe organ in the new opera house in Magdeburg. A few bars later, angels started singing.

Okay, so maybe calling Crescenzo and Angelo angels might be a bit over the top, but their voices—trained by the choir master of Milan's cathedral—could easily have graced angels.

With Crescenzo and Angelo to lead them, the congregation slowly joined in, giving Bernardo a chance to set the stage for his next act.

Two men brought forward the cloth-draped table that had

occupied the rear of the stage. Once it was in position, they helped Bernardo change out of his colorful evangelical robe into a glaringly white lab coat, the working uniform of the Society of Aural Investigators.

While the hymn continued, Bernardo opened the elaborately decorated wooden box that graced the top of the table and carefully removed the seven colored crystals within and laid them in order along the centerline of the table. With everything ready for the next stage of the revival meeting, Bernardo stood and waited for the hymn to finish.

The doge's palace, Venice, Republic of Venice

Doctor Tom Stone stood back and watched as Dr. Johann Vesling palpated the abdomen of His Serenity Francesco Erizzo, the 98th doge of Venice. There was obviously something wrong with the man, otherwise Dr. Sanctorio Sanctorius would not have sent all the way to Padua for Tom and Johann.

"What is it?" Tom asked.

"Bladder stones. And they seem to be getting worse," Dr. Sanctorius said. He invited Tom to palpate the doge's abdomen for himself.

"No thanks," Tom said. "I'll take your word for it. But why am I here? What is it you want me to do?"

"Use your science of the Chakras to cure me," His Serenity demanded.

Tom winced. His chickens were certainly coming home to roost. "I'm sorry, Your Serenity, but the Chakras are diagnostic rather than therapeutic, and *dottori* Vesling and Sanctorius seem pretty sure what the problem is."

"So, your Science of the Chakras cannot help?" Dr. Vesling rubbed his hands together in anticipation. "Then, I'll have to operate."

"No!" Francesco said as he tried to crawl backwards on his bed. "You are not operating on me." He pointed at Tom. "You can operate on me. Like you operated on *Dottore* Gribbleflotz. He was up and about, without even a scar, within days."

Tom winced once more. Lori Drahuta had hoped he enjoyed his just deserts over the psychic surgery conducted on Dr. Gribbleflotz.

He was sure that she would be happy to know that he was not enjoying them. Still, there had been one thing that came out of that meeting that was useful—a lie. "It wasn't me who operated on *Dottore* Gribbleflotz, Your Serenity. I'm afraid that I am unskilled in the techniques my colleague used. And, unfortunately, a death in the family necessitated *Signore* Singh returning home, to India." He added the last to be sure of killing off any hope that he could contact *Signore* Singh.

Francesco looked desperately at Tom. "Surely there is some up-time technique..."

Tom shrugged. "I'm sure there is," he said, "but I'm not familiar with them. I trained as a pharmacist. If you want drugs, I'm your man. But for surgery..." He shook his head regretfully.

"Send a request to Magdeburg," Francesco called out to his secretary.

"Of course, Your Serenity."

Part Two

October 1636

Chapter 6

The doge's palace, Venice, Republic of Venice

Valerio Diacono skidded to a halt as he reached the doors to the doge's chamber. He took a few moments to regather his breath before straightening his garments and nodding to the senior guard at the door. The two guards then pulled open the massive double doors.

"Your Serenity, I bring great news," Valerio announced as he stepped into the doge's chamber.

His Serenity Francesco Erizzo looked up from the little escritoire where he was writing and cocked an eyebrow. "Please, Valerio, come in and tell me this news that had you running through the halls to bring it to me."

"I didn't run, Your Serenity," Valerio protested as he advanced toward the doge. He flipped open the journal he was carrying and offered it to the doge. "The president of the Bohemian Royal Academy of Science himself, *Dottore* Gribbleflotz, has written an article about a procedure he has performed to remove bladder stones." He proffered the open journal to Francesco. "He says the patient felt no pain and was back on his feet the next day."

"No pain?" Francesco asked as he took the open journal.

Valerio nodded. "Yes, Your Serenity." He gestured to the journal. "The patient was rendered unconscious by the use of ether."

Francesco started reading the article. At one point he looked up. "He calls sticking something down a man's penis 'minimally invasive'?"

"I believe it is a medical term, Your Serenity, meaning that the procedure does not involve cutting an opening into the patient."

Francesco nodded and got back to reading. When he finished, he dropped the copy of the *Proceedings of the Royal Academy of Science of Bohemia* onto the writing surface of his escritoire. "We need to get *Dottore* Gribbleflotz here to perform this operation." The doge looked at Valerio. "See to it!"

"*Dottore* Gribbleflotz is a member of the court of the king of Bohemia," Valerio said with a slight warning tone.

"So?"

A wry smile accompanied Valerio's expressive shrug. "We may have to offer His Majesty King Venceslas something to encourage him to lend us his courtier."

Francesco waved a hand. "I'm sure there is something we can supply that Venceslas wants."

Valerio nodded. "Yes, Your Serenity, there are many things the Republic of Venice can supply that King Venceslas wants. However, in order to get the best deal..."

"What are you quibbling about, Valerio? This is important." Francesco stared at Valerio. "In fact, there is nothing more important than my health. Contact the Bohemian ambassador and tell him I want *Dottore* Gribbleflotz here as soon as possible to perform a..." He paused to check the article. "A transurethral lithotripsy on me."

"I will get right onto it, Your Serenity." Valerio reached toward the journal of the *Proceedings of the Royal Academy of Science of Bohemia*. "If I might have the journal?"

Francesco shook his head. "Not right now; I wish to learn more about my upcoming operation." He waved Valerio off with his free hand and settled down to read.

A few days later, Prague

Doctor Phillip Gribbleflotz could hear the footfalls making their way up the steps to his laboratory at the top of the Mihulka Tower. He had heard those particular footfalls often enough that he knew who it was even before Samuel Hartlib, secretary of the Bohemian Royal Academy of Science, stepped into his laboratory. As such, he had his reply to whatever Samuel wanted ready to fire off the moment he appeared.

"No!" Phillip said a split second after the door to his laboratory opened and before Samuel could take a step into the room. However, that did not stop Samuel, and judging by the smile on his face, Phillip was not going to like what he had to say.

"The king needs you..."

Phillip released a set-upon sigh that would have done a teenager proud. He glanced back toward the project he was currently working on. With resentment visible in his every movement, Phillip started taking off his lab coat.

"...to go to Venice."

"What?" Phillip all but shouted the question at Samuel as he dropped his lab coat. He blinked a few times—on the off chance that maybe he was dreaming. "Venice? Why would Venceslas need me to go to Venice?" he asked as he bent to pick his lab coat up off the floor.

"It seems that the doge of Venice has bladder stones. It also seems that his advisors have read your article in the latest issue in the proceedings and decided it would be a good idea for you to perform a transurethral lithotripsy on the doge."

"But why me?" Phillip protested. He waved toward the equipment set up on the various benches in his laboratory. "I have things I need to be working on."

Samuel shook his head slowly in, Phillip was sure, totally insincere sympathy.

"You are going because the king has decided that you are going." Samuel stared hard at Phillip. "You are not going to endanger the position of the Royal Academy of Science with the king on a whim."

"But he gets to send me to the other side of the world on a whim?"

Phillip's response reeked of childish petulance. Something that Samuel easily picked up on. He smiled. "Venice is not the other side of the world, Phillip. And, besides, it's not a whim when a king does it." His next smile was a bit more sympathetic. "There is a trade deal in the offering."

Phillip sighed. "Why can't the king send Dr. Handsch? Surely he would be more suitable. He's fully trained in the procedure, whereas I have only assisted in a single operation."

"They asked for you, Phillip. So it is you they will get. Now, I need you to put together a list of what you need before you can fly out."

"Fly?" Phillip stumbled back a few steps in horror. "You mean I'm supposed to fly to Venice? In one of those rickety flying machines?"

"The latest aircraft aren't that rickety," Samuel said at his most reassuring.

Phillip snorted. "It was only recently that one crashed on the runway at Magdeburg."

"It didn't crash, Phillip. The pilot failed to take a corner properly while taxiing and ran off the taxiway and got stuck in mud."

"What about that airplane with the duke and duchess of Saxe-Altenburg aboard? You can't tell me that one didn't crash."

"It crashed because of sabotage, Phillip. And only the pilot died. Now, why don't you just accept that you are going and start making plans."

Phillip glared at Samuel. "Obviously my first step will be to visit my lawyer to ensure my affairs are in order."

Samuel rolled his eyes. "Don't be such a drama queen, Phillip. I need a list of what you need to take with you."

Phillip slumped down into his chair and searched for paper and a pencil. "You need to get in touch with Dr. Handsch. I'll need to borrow his lithotrite. And I'll need Dr. de le Boë to accompany me as the anesthetist. I'll also need at least one nurse familiar with the procedure."

"You can't have Dr. de le Boë, Phillip. Given the state of the king's health, he, as the only fully certified Grantville-trained physician in Prague, needs to stay here. As for Dr. Handsch's lithotrite, I'm afraid he has a number of operations scheduled and he will need it himself."

"I suppose that also applies to his surgical team?" Phillip muttered.

"Probably."

Phillip sighed mightily. "Then I need to visit Frau Cheng's father and see about him making me my own lithotrite. And while I'm in Grantville, it might be a good idea for me to receive some formal training in the procedure, and to recruit a team." He looked sternly at Samuel, or at least he hoped he appeared stern. "See to it," he said with a nod of dismissal.

It came as no surprise to Phillip that Samuel completely ignored his dismissal. "You can go," Phillip said with a wave of his hand.

"Now, Phillip. You should look on the bright side of things."

Phillip glared at Samuel. "Bright side?" he all but shouted. He waved toward his apparatus-loaded benches. "I have projects to finish, and the king sends me to Venice to perform an operation someone else could do just as easily."

"But they aren't Dr. Gribbleflotz, the president of the Royal Academy of Science."

"You just want good publicity for the Royal Academy," Phillip accused.

"Naturally," Samuel said. "After all, it helps to ensure our continued funding." He looked past Phillip to the loaded benches rather pointedly—everything there had been paid for by the Royal Academy. "And think, you could take your family to Venice. You could take an extended holiday and visit your friends in Padua."

Phillip's eyes lit up at the mention of Padua. He had spent three years there learning medicine under the watchful eye of the great Dr. Giulio Casseri. He had lived with a local family and still corresponded with them twenty years later. However, his eyes had not lit up at the thought of seeing them again. That is not to say that he did not want to see them, but there was someone else he really wanted to see—Dr. Thomas Stone. He was currently based in Padua, and there was a question Phillip wanted to ask him. It was not a complicated question. In fact, it could be expressed in a single word: Why?

Chapter 7

A few days later, Leahy Medical Center, Grantville

Dr. Johannes Schultes waited for the last of the six men he had called into his office to find a seat and settle down. "I have a job for an anesthetist," he announced. That caused raised brows from the two Medical Department advanced medics. "Yes, both of you are suitably qualified," he told them before returning his attention back to the group.

"I require a single volunteer willing to join a small team, to be led by Dr. Gribbleflotz, that will travel to Venice to perform a transurethral lithotripsy on a Very Important Personage."

"Gribbleflotz?" Dr. Daniel Ettmüller all but demanded. "I won't be a part of anything he is associated with."

"Scared of upsetting Dr. Rolfinck?" Dr. Konrad Schneider asked in a snarky tone.

"Yes," Daniel said, "and you'd be too if you were smart. You'll never become a professor if he takes against you."

Konrad glanced over to the other doctors. "Either of you two afraid of Dr. Rolfinck?"

Dr. Anton Deusing shook his head. "I'm not scared of Dr. Rolfinck, but I have patients to worry about." He turned to Johannes. "How long would we be away, Dr. Schultes?" he asked.

"Plan on a week to ten days."

"But it will take more than ten days just to get to Venice," Dr. Andreas Schamberger protested.

Johannes smiled. "The team will be flying..."

"Flying?" the group roared.

Johannes nodded. "Yes, flying. In an air-o-plane." He passed his gaze over the six men. "Will that be a problem?" Judging by the looks on their faces, Johannes thought that for most of them it might be. "Could I have a show of hands. Would everyone still interested please raise their right hand?"

Only one hand went up. It was the hand of one of the Medical Department's advanced medics. The one attached to the USEMC 1st Marine Reconnaissance Company. "Thank you, Corporal Böhm." He smiled at the others. "The rest of you may go. I need to brief Corporal Böhm on what will be involved."

A few days later, Leahy Medical Center

A rap on the door of Dr. Schultes's office had him looking up from the patient file he was examining. "Yes?" he called.

The door opened to reveal Wilhelm, his secretary. "Dr. Gribbleflotz is here, Dr. Schultes."

Johannes dropped the papers he was holding onto his desk—one of the up-time-inspired desks with a large flat working surface rather than a tiny, and therefore next to useless for dropping papers onto, escritoire—and got to his feet. "Show him in."

Johannes studied Dr. Gribbleflotz as he entered. He was, as expected, gaudily dressed. Still, the colors seemed to work for him. Johannes stepped forward with his hands outstretched. "It is good to see you, Dr. Gribbleflotz. I understand you have been invited to perform a transurethral lithotripsy on the doge of Venice?"

Phillip gave Johannes a wry grin as they shook hands. "I don't think 'invited' is the right word."

"Commanded?" Johannes suggested. "Certainly Emperor Gustavus has been throwing his not inconsiderable weight about, ordering the medical faculty to give you all possible assistance."

"Sorry about that."

Johannes waved his hands. "Don't let it bother you, Dr. Gribbleflotz. A few feathers might have been ruffled back in Jena, but that's no skin off my nose.

"Now, how familiar are you with the procedure?" Johannes asked.

"I assisted Dr. Handsch in the operation I described in the latest proceedings of the Royal Academy."

"When you say you assisted . . . ?"

"I mean, Dr. Handsch allowed me to insert the lithotrite and break up a bladder stone."

"That's good," Johannes said. "And what about aspirating the resulting fragments? Did Dr. Handsch allow you to do that?"

Phillip shook his head. "No. Dr. Handsch said the fragments were sufficiently small that they would be excreted during normal urinary function."

Johannes nodded. "Then we will have to make sure you are taught how to aspirate any fragments." He nodded again. "I have a couple of patients lined up for you to practice on. Would you like to meet them?"

Phillip glanced down at his clothes. "Now?"

Johannes grinned. "Yes, now. Wilhelm," he called out to his secretary, "could we have a lab coat for Dr. Gribbleflotz?"

There was a gaggle of white lab coats already gathered around a bed in the six-bed room into which the ward nurse led them. However, she did not lead them to that bed. Instead, she led Phillip and Johannes to the bed in the far corner. Before anything else was done, she pulled a curtain around the bed.

"This is Mr. Diemer. He has volunteered to allow Dr. Gribbleflotz to operate on him under your supervision, Dr. Schultes."

"It's the only way I can afford to have it done," Michel Diemer said. "The pain is so bad sometimes that I can't hold down a job."

Johannes reached out and patted Michel's hand. "Don't worry, Mr. Diemer, we'll soon have you fixed." He glanced at the ward nurse and raised his brows in question.

"An operating room has been booked for 5:00 p.m., Dr. Schultes."

"Good. Good."

"It won't be painful?" Michel asked. His hands were noticeably shaking.

Johannes reached out and gripped Michel's hands. "You won't feel a thing, Mr. Diemer. You will be sleeping while Herr Dr. Gribbleflotz and myself are hard at work."

"Really?" Michel asked.

"Really," Johannes confirmed.

Before he could say anything more the curtain was pulled aside, and Diana Cheng poked her head through the gap. "Sorry to disturb you, Dr. Schultes, but Dr. Paulli would appreciate it if you would have a look at Mr. Berst."

Johannes glanced over to his patient. "I'll just be a couple of minutes." He turned to Phillip. "Would you care to join me?"

Phillip nodded, and trailed Johannes as Diana led them to another curtained-off bed.

"What seems to be the problem?" Johannes asked as he passed through the curtain.

One of the students, a Frenchman in his mid- to late twenties, pointed an accusing finger at Diana and, in heavily accented Latin, complained that she seemed to think that she knew better than a qualified doctor.

Johannes turned to Diana and raised an eyebrow, inviting her to explain.

"He," Diana said, waving in her accuser's direction, "maintains that, despite the test results, the description of the pain from the patient, and palpating of Mr. Berst's abdomen, that Mr. Berst has a urinary infection." Diana shrugged. "I said it was more likely appendicitis."

"There! You heard her," Dr. Pierre Bourdelot said. "She questions my diagnosis. What does she, a mere nurse, know about diagnosing a medical condition?"

Johannes held out his hand to the supervising physician, Dr. Paulli, for the patient notes he was holding. A quick perusal of them found all the evidence Diana had described. He quickly palpated Mr. Berst to confirm the diagnosis before turning to Dr. Bourdelot. "One of the advantages of people coming to the medical program via the nursing program is that they have spent time in the wards and have had personal contact with a number of different conditions." Johannes looked over at Diana. "How many cases of appendicitis have you encountered during your studies?"

Diana shrugged. "A dozen or so."

Johannes smiled and turned his attention back to Dr. Bourdelot. "And how many cases of appendicitis have you encountered?"

Dr. Bourdelot muttered something.

"What was that, Dr. Bourdelot? I didn't hear."

Dr. Bourdelot glared at Johannes. "None."

"So, isn't it possible that Frau Cheng might know what she is talking about?" Johannes did not wait for an answer. Instead, he turned to the ward sister, who had joined them. "We need to schedule Mr. Berst for immediate surgery," he said, switching from the Latin they had been using to German.

"Someone will have to be rescheduled," the sister warned.

"Of course someone will have to be rescheduled," Johannes muttered. "Just call admissions and tell them Mr. Berst needs to be operated on immediately."

"Immediately?" Mr. Berst squeaked.

Johannes laid a calming hand on Mr. Berst's shoulder. "There is nothing for you to worry about, Mr. Berst. For admissions, 'immediately' means sometime today."

"Oh, that's good," Mr. Berst said as he let Johannes settle him back on his bed.

Johannes nodded reassuringly before turning to Phillip and switching back to Latin. "Dr. Gribbleflotz, would you like to examine the patient? The swelling of the appendix is nicely pronounced. A textbook example of acute appendicitis if ever I have seen one."

Phillip nodded. "What am I looking for?"

Johannes guided Phillip's hands around Mr. Berst's abdomen. Pointing out the pain response from Mr. Berst as the swollen appendix was palpated.

While Johannes was guiding Phillip's examination of Mr. Berst, the ward sister returned. "Dr. Schultes, the only opening this afternoon is at five."

"Five?" Johannes turned to stare at the sister. "But I have Mr. Diemer scheduled for five this evening."

The ward sister shook her head. "You *had* Mr. Diemer scheduled for five, Dr. Schultes. He has been rescheduled to eleven tomorrow, freeing up your five o'clock for Mr. Berst."

Johannes sighed. "Would you be good enough to inform Mr. Diemer that his operation has been rescheduled?" The sister nodded and walked off. "Dr. Gribbleflotz, it appears that I will not be guiding you through a transurethral lithotripsy today, but maybe I can make up for it. How would you like to assist in an appendectomy?"

"I would be delighted to assist," Phillip said. "What is an appendectomy?"

Next day, 10:45 hours, Leahy Medical Center

Dr. Phillip Gribbleflotz followed Dr. Johannes Schultes into the surgical preparation room. There were already two people there, a man and a woman.

"Corporal Böhm, Nurse Gebauer. I'd like you to meet Dr. Gribbleflotz. Dr. Gribbleflotz, these are the rest of the team that will be accompanying you to Venice. Nurse Gebauer will be your surgical assistant while Corporal Böhm of the military's Medical Department will be your anesthetist."

Lise Gebauer and Stephan Böhm approached and offered Phillip their hands to shake. "A pleasure to meet you, Dr. Gribbleflotz," Lise said. "I look forward to working with you in Venice."

"Likewise," Stephan said.

"It is a pleasure to meet you both," Phillip said.

"Right! Now all the pleasantries are done, let us get started." Johannes turned to Lise. "Do you have the equipment laid out?"

Lise gestured toward a shiny metal tray on a bench. The equipment on it was covered by a pristine white cloth.

"Good. Good," Johannes said as he approached the tray. He flipped back the cloth to expose a lithotrite. He pointed to it. "You might want to try the lithotrite. It's probably a later model than the one you used in Prague."

Phillip looked at the lithotrite. It looked very similar to the one he had used in Prague. He picked it up. "What might be different?" he asked as he tried to activate the jaws.

"That one is supposed to have superior-quality jaws."

Phillip nodded. Not that he was really paying attention. He was still trying to manipulate the jaws. "They are very stiff," he said.

"Stiff?" Johannes asked. "How do you mean?"

"I can't get the jaws to close," Phillip said. He demonstrated as he tried to squeeze the hand grips.

Johannes reached for the lithotrite. "That shouldn't happen. Let me try it."

Phillip was happy to hand over the lithotrite, and he was even happier to see Dr. Schultes having the same trouble he had had.

Johannes held up the lithotrite. "Nurse Gebauer, call for a technician. We need this fixed for Mr. Diemer's surgery, and he is not going to be happy if it has to be delayed again."

"Immediately, Dr. Schultes." Lise dashed off.

Johannes laid the lithotrite down on the tray and covered it before turning to Phillip. He had a wry smile on his face. "Sorry about this."

Phillip waved away the apology. "No need to apologize, Dr. Schultes." He stared at the covered lithotrite. "Does that kind of problem happen often?" he asked.

Johannes shook his head. "Hardly ever."

"Still," Phillip said, "it might be a good idea to add someone familiar with the equipment to the team just in case."

Johannes nodded. "Yes. It wouldn't look good for the lithotrite to fail just when you are about to operate on the doge."

Phillip winced at that image. It certainly would not look good, and it would reflect badly on his reputation. "I definitely need to add a suitable technician to my team. Can you recommend someone?" he asked.

Johannes shrugged. "You could ask whoever turns up in answer to Nurse Gebauer's call."

Phillip made up his mind to do just that.

A few minutes later, Phillip was surprised when Diana Cheng walked in with a backpack over a shoulder and a toolbox in her hand.

"I hear you have a problem with a lithotrite," she said.

"That's right," Johannes said. He gestured to the tray the lithotrite sat on. "Though, I am surprised to see you instead of a technician."

"Mr. Wurtz did a disappearing act when the call came in."

"Will you be able to fix it?" Phillip asked. "I mean. I know you helped your father develop Dr. Handsch's lithotrite..."

"Never fear, Dr. Gribbleflotz. If anyone at Leahy can fix what is wrong, it is Frau Cheng. That," Johannes said pointing to the lithotrite, "is one her father made for me a couple of months ago."

Phillip watched as Diana laid open her toolbox and started to fiddle with the lithotrite. After trying to operate the levers, she started to disassemble it, checking the components as she did so. It was not long before she looked up, an expression of satisfaction on her face.

"I think I've found the problem. The last person to clean it didn't do a good enough job."

"The missing Mr. Wurtz," Johannes muttered.

"No doubt," Diana said as she removed a bottle of clear liquid from her toolbox and poured some onto a clean cloth. She then rubbed the lithotrite components with the cloth.

"What are you doing?" Phillip asked.

"The last person to clean this did a lousy job, and left a residue of calcium," Diana said. She examined the component she had been rubbing. "I'm using white vinegar to dissolve that residue."

"I'm scheduled to be operating on Mr. Diemer at eleven," Johannes said in a hopeful tone.

Diana glanced up at the clock on the preparation room's wall. "If you're happy to sterilize it with a wash rather than using the autoclave, then you should be able to make your eleven o'clock schedule, Dr. Schultes."

Phillip watched as Diana expertly—or at least he thought she was doing it expertly—cleaned the various components of the lithotrite and reassembled it. "Frau Cheng," he said to attract her attention. "You may be aware that I am supposed to be taking a surgical team to Venice to operate on the doge."

"You're to perform a transurethral lithotripsy," Diana said, shooting Phillip a smile. "Although, I don't remember ever reading that the ninety-eighth doge of Venice had a problem with bladder stones. Not like Samuel Pepys. I wonder what he's been doing differently this time."

Phillip had no idea who Samuel Pepys might be, or might have been, nor did he have any interest in learning the information. He was more interested in a more pressing issue. "How would you like to join my team?"

"And go to Venice?" Diana dropped her hands and looked at Phillip. Her tongue slipped out and moistened her lips. "I'd love to go." A moment later she shook her head. "But Mom and Dad would never let me go."

Johannes waved a nonchalant hand. "Let me deal with your parents." He smiled. "By the time I finish with them, they'll be begging you to take advantage of this marvelous opportunity."

Diana looked skeptically at Johannes. "You really think you can do that?" She shook her head. "Looking after the lithotrite is a technician's job. They're going to wonder why I need to go."

Johannes stared into the distance for a while. And then he clapped his hands. "*Scheiss drauf!* I'll do it." Johannes turned to Diana. "You can go as a surgical assistant to Dr. Gribbleflotz." He smiled smugly. "Even the best surgeon needs a qualified assistant." He turned to Phillip. "Do you object to Frau Cheng learning the procedure with you?"

Phillip shook his head. "No. I have no problem with that. Anything to ensure Frau Cheng and her skills with the lithotrite will accompany me to Venice."

"There you are then. Frau Cheng. I will teach you how to perform the procedure. Actually"—he quirked a wry smile at Diana—"given how many times you have watched the procedure, maybe you should be teaching *me*."

Color flooded Diana's face as she hastened to deny her ability to teach Dr. Schultes anything.

Chapter 8

Phillip might not have been skipping as he made his way from Leahy Medical Center to his hotel, but the thought was definitely there. Everything was coming together for the trip to Venice, making for an unbeatable day.

His eyes darted around as he took in the changes that had occurred since he was last in Grantville. They were considerable. And then his eyes passed over a familiar profile. He stopped in his tracks and concentrated on the man on the other side of the street. He took off his spectacles and polished them before looking again. The skin color was whiter than he remembered, but if what Frau Jennie Lee Cheng had told him was true, it was nothing a little walnut juice couldn't correct. He changed direction and set off on an intercept course.

As he got closer, Phillip became more and more convinced that this was the man who had performed psychic surgery on him in Prague. The man who had, effectively, publicly humiliated him. It was time for a little payback. Phillip accelerated and got in front of the man and the woman he was with.

"Herr Guptah Rai Singh. It is you," Phillip said as he reached out with both hands and took a strong grip of Guptah's right hand and started to pump it. "They said you'd returned to India. But here you are, in Grantville." Phillip shot the woman with Guptah a smile. "Herr Singh saved my life." He nodded vigorously in response to her blank look. "Yes. He did. In Prague, where I was living.

"He removed a . . ." Phillip moved his gaze to the shell-shocked man. "What was it you removed, Herr Singh? I never did get to examine it. Do you still have it?"

Herr Singh managed to free his hand and backed away a couple of paces. "I'm sorry, but I have absolutely no idea what you are talking about."

Phillip turned to Herr Singh's companion. "Can you imagine, Herr Singh operated on me with his bare hands, and I didn't feel a thing." He nodded to reinforce what he had just said. "And without leaving a scar. The Prague Guild of Surgeons have been after me ever since to get Herr Singh to return to Prague to teach their members his special technique.

"And then there is Dr. Stone's Science of the Chakras, which the Prague Chapter of the Society of Aural Investigators was hoping he would present a short series of seminars on. However, he is currently in Padua."

Phillip opened his eyes wide, as if he had just had a brilliant idea. "But surely you, Herr Singh, are also familiar with the Science of the Chakras?" He nodded to himself, as if the answer was obvious. "Of course you are. Perhaps you could visit Prague to give a series of seminars to the Society of Aural Investigators? Money is no object."

The man Phillip was calling Guptah Rai Singh shot Phillip a dirty look, grabbed his companion's hand and, essentially, ran away.

"If Prague is too much trouble, Herr Singh," Phillip called out, "I'm sure the University of Jena would be only too happy to host a series of seminars on your surgical technique."

The woman with Herr Singh looked back at Phillip as she was dragged away. She was an innocent party, and he was sorry if he had done anything to upset her, but Herr Guptah Rai Singh deserved everything he had done.

With a final smile at the memory of Herr Singh's face, Phillip set off once more for his hotel. This time he was humming one of the new hymns his wife liked so much—"Awake, My Heart, with Gladness." Meeting Guptah Rai Singh, also known as George Mundell, had capped off the perfect day.

Lorrie Mundell pulled her hand free from her husband's grasp. "Who was that?" she demanded.

"No one important," George Mundell muttered, even as he shot another glance over his shoulder. Gribbleflotz seemed to have given up on holding his attention and was heading off. Fortunately, in the opposite direction to the one George had taken.

"He seemed to know you," Lorrie said. "And what was it you did in Prague? He said something about you performing surgery on him. With your bare hands.

"George, just what did you get up to in Prague?"

George ignored his wife's questions. He had enough to deal with already without adding his wife's reaction to him performing psychic surgery. He needed to think. He also needed to contact the prime minister. Maybe he could intervene before the shit hit the fan.

Next day, Kitt and Cheng Engineering

The dining area at Kitt and Cheng Engineering was a fairly intimate space. One might even call it cramped, even if there were only four employees currently sitting at the table.

Lorrie Mundell picked out a spot beside Rosina Trempling and sat down. Across the table sat Mr. and Mrs. Cheng. "Jason, Jennie Lee, you were both in Prague recently?" It was a purely rhetorical question, so she continued without waiting for an answer. "Does the name Guptar Rising mean anything to either of you?

"No, wait," Lorrie said. "He called George 'Herr Sing,' so I guess it should be 'Guptar Rye Sing.'" She looked hopefully at Jennie Lee and Jason.

"He?" Jennie Lee asked.

Lorrie nodded. "It was the strangest thing. George and I were leaving the Higgins, where George had just done a show, when this down-timer leapt in front of George and started shaking his hand and calling him 'Guptar Rye Sing.' He claimed that George had saved his life." She looked expectantly at Jennie Lee.

"Dr. Gribbleflotz?" Jason suggested.

Jennie Lee nodded. "It couldn't have been anyone else."

"What're you talking about?" Lorrie demanded. "What does Dr. Gribbleflotz have to do with anything?"

Rosina's significant other, Barry Thompson, humphed. "One might imagine the down-timer you met might have been Dr. Gribbleflotz," he suggested. "Was the man 'colorfully dressed'?"

"Oh!" Lorrie pictured the man in question. "Yes. He was rather colorfully dressed."

Jennie Lee slapped her hands on the table. "Rats!"

"What?" The question erupted spontaneously from Lorrie.

"I wanted to be there when he confronted George," Jennie Lee said by way of explanation.

"Whoa!" Lorrie starred at Jennie Lee. "What are you saying? What's George been up to? And, is he in trouble?"

Jennie Lee licked her lips. "Where to start," she muttered. Then she smiled. "George isn't in any trouble."

Lorrie was not buying it. Jennie Lee was trying too hard to be reassuring. "But?" she prompted, because there had to be a "but."

"But that's the best we can say about the situation," Jason answered.

And that choice of words did not inspire Lorrie with any degree of confidence. "What situation?" She passed a full-powered glare over both Jennie Lee and Jason. "Could you both just stop prevaricating and tell me what George got up to in Prague?"

Jennie Lee met Lorrie's gaze. "What do you know about why George was in Prague?"

Lorrie shrugged. "Nothing. One day he got a phone call from Ed Piazza and the next thing I knew he was off to Prague."

Jennie Lee nodded. "Right then." She cast a look over Barry and Rosina. "This doesn't leave the shop. Understand?"

"Understood," Rosina answered.

Barry mimed zipping his lips closed.

Lorrie glanced from Barry and Rosina to Jennie Lee and Jason. "Just how bad is this?"

"Pretty bad," Jason said.

Lorrie sighed and concentrated on Jennie Lee. "Give it to me straight."

The prime minister's office, Magdeburg

George Mundell was pacing. At the rate he was going, he would soon be wearing a track in the hardwood floor. Ed Piazza, the prime minister of the USE, was sitting back in his chair, his eyes following George as he paced. At a nearby escritoire, Ed's secretary, David Zimmermann, sat waiting for something to be said that he could transcribe onto paper using the latest and greatest of multilingual typewriters.

"So, what you're saying," Ed said, "is that Gribbleflotz knows you performed psychic surgery on him."

"No!" George was emphatic. "The twit believes I really operated on him, and now he wants me to teach my surgical technique to the Prague Guild of Surgeons." He stamped along for a few paces before stopping and turning to face Ed and David. "Tom's solution was for Guptah to just disappear, but that won't work. Not now."

"Why not?" Ed asked.

David flicked the paper sticking out of his typewriter with his hand. "Herr Mundell has already told you, Herr Piazza. Dr. Gribbleflotz recognized him. He knows Guptah Rai Singh is alive and well, and living in Grantville." He turned to George. "Are you sure Dr. Gribbleflotz is not aware that the surgery was fake?" he asked. "I mean, he recognized you out of costume and with a significantly lighter complexion."

"We met in passing a few times in Prague before the last encounter," George muttered.

There was a clatter of keys. "That last encounter, that would be when you performed psychic surgery on Dr. Gribbleflotz?"

"Yes." George's response was surly. Having his every word recorded was getting to him. He turned to Ed. "Does he have to take down everything I say?"

David paused in his typing. "I am not taking down everything you say," he protested. "For example, I have not transcribed that question. I am limiting my note-taking to things pertinent to the situation." He smiled at George. "So, would you say that it is likely Dr. Gribbleflotz saw you often enough to distinguish your features?"

"Yes."

There was a clatter of keys from David's typewriter.

George cursed under his breath at the distraction. "Couldn't you at least just use a pencil? The clatter of your typing is getting on my nerves."

David patted his typewriter with a gentle hand. "I don't do shorthand. I could, however..." The pause was, George thought, overly dramatic. "...call in a girl from the typing pool to record this meeting and type it up."

George met David's pointed look with a glare. "The story would be all over the building by morning tea and spreading through the city by lunchtime."

David nodded. "If not sooner. So, would you like me to call for someone from the typing pool?"

George breathed out heavily and waved his hand. "Keep typing," he muttered.

"I thought you might see it my way." David smiled serenely. "Now, where were we?" He glanced down at the paper protruding from his typewriter. "Ah. I see. We had just determined that Dr. Gribbleflotz had recognized you as Guptah Rai Singh." He looked inquiringly at George. "I assume you believe Dr. Gribbleflotz, having determined that Guptah Rai Singh has not returned home to India, will make a concerted effort to recruit your services to teach the members of the Prague Guild of Surgeons how to perform 'psychic surgery.'"

"At some point, Gribbleflotz is going to discover that George Mundell and Guptah Rai Singh are one and the same," Ed muttered.

"That's what I've been trying to tell you," George thundered. "That fool could cause everything to unravel."

"Then we need to talk to Dr. Gribbleflotz and beg his assistance in preventing things from unraveling."

Both Ed and George stared at David. "Tell Gribbleflotz that I faked the surgery?" George demanded.

David nodded. "It is better than the alternative."

"What alternative?" Ed asked.

David riffled through some of his carefully typed notes. Finding the sheet he wanted, he passed it across to Ed. He left a finger pointing to a line as he did so.

Ed took possession of the paper. He stared at it and shook his head. "That was just a joke."

David sighed. "Do you think King Venceslas V Adalbertus of Bohemia is going to appreciate having been the butt of a joke?"

George walked over to see what they were talking about. He smiled when he saw the passage David had been pointing to. "It wasn't his butt Tom painted blue," he joked.

Kitt and Cheng Engineering, Grantville

"They painted his balls blue?" Barry roared with laughter.

Jennie Lee aimed a glare at Barry. "I'm sure you think it is hilarious, but I doubt King Venceslas will agree if he finds out he was the butt of a joke."

"Come on," Barry said. "What's the worst that could happen?"

"You mean, other than King Venceslas suing the pants off of Tom?" Jennie Lee raised her brows, inviting a response. When there was none, she continued. "Or, maybe, the king will just issue an arrest warrant for Tom and George." She looked hard at Barry. "Give them both fair trials, and then execute them."

"Execute George?" Lorrie was outraged.

Jennie Lee just nodded. "A king can't afford to become a figure of ridicule," she said. "Imagine what the emperor would have wanted to do to the tailors in Hans Christian Anderson's 'The Emperor's New Clothes' when he realized they had made him a laughingstock." She gestured toward Barry. "And if Barry is any example, once stories start circulating about what Tom and George did to him . . ." She did not bother finishing the sentence.

"The king will be after blood," Lorrie whispered.

"And then," Jason said, "there is the flow-on effect as down-timers start to question anything and everything Tom Stone has said about modern medicine."

"It's a matter of faith, trust, and credibility," Jennie Lee explained. "And what Tom and George have done threatens the acceptance of up-time medicine and medical theory."

"All because George performed psychic surgery on Dr. Gribbleflotz?" Lorrie asked.

Jennie Lee nodded. "If we let George's psychic surgery stand, it'll become the new plague on society as every con man with good sleight-of-hand skills tries their hand at it. And people will die.

"And if the wrong people discover that what was done to Dr. Gribbleflotz was a fraud, then . . ." Jennie Lee shrugged.

"The shit hits the fan," Jason said. "Tom Stone gets pilloried in the media. And everything he has ever said about modern medicine comes into question."

"Diana thinks people will even start questioning germ theory," Jennie Lee said.

"And people will die," Lorrie muttered.

Jennie Lee nodded. "And people will die."

"So, what is being done about it?" Barry asked.

"Dr. Gribbleflotz hopes to talk to Tom while he's in the Republic of Venice. We're hoping that if they can get together, that they will be able to construct a story that explains everything."

"Gribbleflotz is going to help?" Barry demanded.

Jennie Lee and Jason nodded. "He understands the seriousness of the situation."

The prime minister's office, Magdeburg

There was an unnerving look on David's face as he smiled at George. "King Venceslas will, of course, demand both your and Dr. Stone's heads on a platter. But that is not the worst that can happen."

George tugged at the collar of his shirt as he glared at David. "Speak for yourself," he muttered. He turned to Ed. "You can stop that happening, can't you?"

David took in Prime Minister Piazza's pained expression as confirmation of his own belief. "The government may have little choice but to allow you to be extradited to face charges of..." He paused to consider just what the charges might be. As he was a former professor of languages and not a lawyer, his knowledge of certain aspects of law was rather limited. "Treason, or at least being a party to a treasonable act."

"Treason!" George was outraged. "I haven't committed treason."

David ran a finger across his mustache before answering. "What do you call painting the king's nether regions blue?"

That silenced George, and he turned to Ed in mute appeal. Ed, in turn, looked to David. "Any appeal from King Venceslas is likely to be addressed directly to Gustav?"

David nodded. "And I'm sure the emperor will consider that making a laughingstock of a fellow monarch is an extraditable offense, if only to discourage anyone from doing the same to him."

David turned back to George. "And lest you think Dr. Stone is safe in Padua, I can inform you that King Venceslas has sent his personal physician to Venice to perform a life-changing operation upon the doge."

That stopped George in his tracks. Or it would have if he had still been pacing. "Personal physician? But Venceslas doesn't have a personal physician. He doesn't trust the medical profession. That's why this whole mess happened."

"True. True." David nodded his head. "However, he does trust Dr. Gribbleflotz, and it is he whom the doge requested."

George snorted. "And what kind of operation is that charlatan going to perform?" He backed into one of the armchairs populating Ed's office and sat down.

David slowly shook his head. "I don't know where you get this idea that Dr. Gribbleflotz is a charlatan." He paused, giving George time to reply. George did not.

"In addition to three years of study at Padua under the great Dr. Casseri, Dr. Gribbleflotz served as a military physician and surgeon for more than four years. He is, I assure you, more than capable of performing the operation in question." David stopped and smiled before adding, "And just to make sure, Dr. Schultes has been asked to train and certify him in the procedure."

"Well, that's a relief," George muttered. He took a deep breath. "So, Tom's just as likely to be extradited as me?"

"More likely," David said. "He is, after all, a very wealthy man." That statement was met with blank looks from both the prime minister and Herr Mundell. "It would be an application of the 'deep-pocket rule.'"

George laughed. It was not a particularly happy laugh. "I guess I should be glad I don't have Tom's money."

"So, back to your earlier statement," Ed said. "What is the worst that can happen?"

David looked down at his hands as he slowly hyperextended his fingers a couple of times. He was, of course, procrastinating. He did not think the prime minister would appreciate what he was about to say. He took a deep breath and slowly released it.

"Nothing can be that bad," George muttered.

That was a challenge David could not let go past. He stared at George. "How about the complete collapse of faith in anything Dr. Stone is associated with?" He looked at Ed. "Dr. Stone isn't just associated with medicine, although the impact of a loss of faith in modern medicine could be catastrophic enough. He is also closely linked to the paper dollars and, well, the paper dollars are only backed by the faith people have in them. If that faith is damaged..." David shrugged.

"Whoa!" George protested. "How do you connect painting King Venceslas' balls blue with the loss of faith in the USE dollar?"

"Both used dyes and Dr. Stone was responsible for the design, and the sole supplier of the special dyes used to print the paper dollars." David checked to see if George and the prime minister were following his line of thought. Their blank looks suggested that the answer was no. "The *Kipper und Wipper* years are not yet a distant memory. Too many ordinary people suffered as they were expected to exchange their goods and services for worthless money while the rich got richer. Rather than suffer a repeat, they will refuse to accept worthless paper money. Trade and business will stagnate, and the economy of the USE will collapse. And, as we are in the middle of a war against Poland and the Ottoman Empire, such a collapse could cause the disintegration of the USE."

David smiled at Ed's and George's horrified looks. "You did want to know what was the worst that could happen."

Ed exhaled noisily. "So, what do you really think could happen?"

David steepled his fingers. "Well, at a minimum, Herr Mundell and Dr. Stone will have to answer to King Venceslas for their actions." He shrugged. "Their punishment could be sufficient. But one never really knows how the public might react when their heroes are found to have feet of clay."

Ed slammed his hands onto his desk. "David. You obviously see a solution to the problem, so how about cutting to the chase and enlightening us?"

David smiled. "It is simple, Herr Piazza. Dr. Stone needs to confess all to Dr. Gribbleflotz and beg his aid in creating a plausible explanation for everything that happened in Prague."

George snorted. "I can just see that happening. They'll be at each other's throats as soon as they meet."

"I really hope that is not the result of a meeting between the two men, Herr Mundell. Because Dr. Stone and Dr. Gribbleflotz need to talk."

"I can see that." Ed sighed. "We'll need to send someone along with Gribbleflotz to keep them from killing each other."

David smiled. "I know just the man. He is already a member of Dr. Gribbleflotz's party. He just needs to be briefed as to what is going on."

Chapter 9

A few days later, Grantville airfield

Corporal Stephan Böhm of the Medical Department of the USE military passed his eyes over the Royal Dutch Airlines Jupiter sitting on the tarmac. He read the airplane's serial number and smiled. She was an old friend, except this time he expected to be sitting on a proper seat and not on the floor with his back resting against the fuselage waiting to arrive over the drop zone. This flight, he fully expected to step off the plane straight onto the ground rather than parachute down to it.

"Corporal Böhm. Ernst Schreiber. The *Grantville Times.* I was wondering if I could have a moment of your time, if you please?"

Stephan turned toward the voice. He did not recognize the man, but Lieutenant Dauth of the Grantville office of the Joint Armed Services Press Division had warned him about Mr. Schreiber. He was, as he claimed, a reporter. However, he was not just any reporter. Mr. Schreiber also wrote under the Roger Rude byline—a byline famous for delivering stories about things people didn't want to get into the public domain. "How can I be of assistance?"

Ernst pulled out a spiral-bound notebook and pencil. "I'm wondering why you are being sent on this mission. Is there something we, the public, aren't being told?"

Stephan smiled. Of course there was something the public wasn't being told. "Of course not," he said. "What makes you ask?"

Ernst raised his eyebrows and pointed the end of his pencil

at Stephan. "When the government sends a Special Forces soldier on what is ostensibly a simple medical mission, one can't help but ask questions."

Stephan grinned. "I am not a Special Forces soldier. I'm just a simple medic with the Medical Department."

Ernst snorted. "There is nothing simple about any of the 'Men from M.A.R.S.'"

"They're just Marines," Stephan protested. Although he was with the Medical Department, he was usually assigned to the USEMC 1st Marine Reconnaissance Company as a combat medic. He had only been in Grantville to attend an advanced training course. "Marines who have been trained to reconnoiter beaches looking for suitable landing sites and clear obstacles." He grinned. "We spend most of our training time on or in the water."

"Yeah, right!" Ernst muttered. "Next you'll be telling me you aren't a crack shot, and nor are you an expert at unarmed combat."

Stephan slowly shook his head. "You've been watching too many movies," he said. "Yes, we all qualified as 'expert' with our service small arms. That was a requirement for graduating from the Marine Advanced Reconnaissance School. But none of us are going to be running around dropping the bad guys like Commander Erik Zeetrell in *On His Majesty's Secret Service*, and as for being experts at unarmed combat . . ." Stephan laughed. He took some time to regather himself. "You need a lot more than the three-hours-a-week close-quarters battle drill we get to rate as an expert."

"Three hours a week?"

There was a pained look on his face as Ernst said that. No doubt, Stephan was sure, at having his illusions shattered. "If we're lucky," Stephan said. "There are too many other demands on our training time to justify spending more of it on CQB training."

Ernst sighed. "Do you expect our readers to believe there is no significance in the fact the government is sending one of the Men from M.A.R.S. to Venice?"

Stephan shrugged. "I can't do anything about what your readers do or don't believe. But the truth is, I am going to Venice because the surgery Dr. Gribbleflotz is to perform has to be done under anesthesia and I've recently completed a course to give ether as an anesthetist."

"So," Ernst said, "there is no significance in the fact that you are one of the *Men from M.A.R.S.*"

"I wouldn't say that," Stephan said. He paused as Ernst's face lit up. He waited until Ernst's face achieved maximum wattage, and then he shot him down. "Of the six certified anesthetists Dr. Schultes considered for the mission, I was the only one willing to fly." Stephan gestured toward the plane sitting on the tarmac to illustrate his point.

Ernst glared at Stephan. He appeared ready to say something when someone called out.

"Corporal Böhm. Over here!"

Stephan followed the voice to a young woman who was waving. He waved, and then turned back to Ernst. "Sorry, but I have to go."

Ernst looked in the direction of the woman. "Frau Cheng?" He turned back to Stephan. "And why is a green nurse going on this trip?"

"Well, she is a Registered Nurse, even if a newly minted one, and we do need a second nurse. However, the reason why it is Frau Cheng and not a more experienced nurse is because she helped her father develop the lithotrite Dr. Gribbleflotz will be using. If anything goes wrong with it, she knows how to fix it."

A loud, piercing whistle sounded. Stephan checked. Yes, it had come from Frau Cheng, and now he was looking her way, she was waving him over again. "I'm sorry, but I really must go."

"Yes. Yes." Ernst waved Stephan off. "Thank you for your time."

Stephan picked up the kit bag at his feet and hurried over to Frau Cheng.

"You're late," she said by way of a greeting.

Stephan looked pointedly at the group of coverall-clad men with RDA embossed on their backs milling around the aircraft. Then, just to reinforce matters, he looked at his Medical Department–issue wristwatch. There was, he was happy to see, plenty of time until their scheduled departure.

"Lise and I have already spoken with Frau Mittelhausen," Diana said by way of explanation.

Stephan caught on immediately. The three of them had hit upon the idea of making a little money on the side by performing transurethral lithotripsies on anyone willing to pay them. Their problem was that they had no idea how to go about arranging such operations. "And she is willing to help?" he asked. As soon as he said it, he realized what the answer had to be. "How much is she charging for her help?"

"Nothing."

"Nothing?" Stephan was immediately wary. "The Frau Mittelhausen I've heard so much about wouldn't do anything for nothing."

Diana grinned. "And you'd be right. She's just not asking for money."

Stephan sighed. "What is it she wants?"

"Hey," Diana protested. "If you'd been here when you were supposed to arrive, you could have hammered out the agreement yourself."

Stephan sighed a second time. Only this time it was laden with foreboding. "What have you and Lise committed me to doing?"

"Nothing too difficult. In return for her help finding us suitable patients, she wants you to use Dad's new all-dancing, all-singing theremin during the surgery."

Stephan stared at Diana. He had thought she was smarter than this. "What use is a musical instrument during surgery?" he demanded.

Diana smiled. She was not smiling up at him. It was more of a smiling down—she being a little taller than him even when she was not wearing raised heels. "One of the new features is a microphone. You can use it to amplify the patient's heartbeat."

"What's wrong with a simple stethoscope?" Stephan asked. "It has the virtue of being a simple and proven technology."

"You can use a stethoscope as well if you like, but the modified theremin will allow everyone to hear the heartbeat."

Stephan gave a reluctant nod. "That seems almost reasonable."

"And then you get to promote it to anyone who looks interested."

"That's not reasonable," Stephan protested. "I'm not a salesperson."

Diana slapped him on the shoulder. "Don't worry, we'll soon have you spouting the specifications on cue."

Stephan grunted his lack of appreciation of the offer and stepped around Diana as a precursor to carting himself and his gear over to the Jupiter. He cast an eye over the passengers already gathered there. Dr. Gribbleflotz and his wife were there, as were their two young children, but one very important person was absent. He stopped and looked back at Diana. "Where's the kids' nursery maid? Because there is no way I'm looking after them."

"As if we'd ask you to," Diana said. "Weight limits mean she has to be left behind."

"What?" Stephan stared at Diana. "We're well within the weight limits the airline gave us."

Diana nodded. "We are. However, the airline decided they wanted to send him along too." She punctuated the statement by pointing to a young man standing over a couple of large trunks. "That's Sebastian Jones, and Royal Dutch Airlines have commissioned him to take photographs to promote their air link with Venice."

Stephan stared hard at the youth. "Should I know him?" he asked.

"If you don't, you will by the time we get to Venice."

Part Three

November 1636

Chapter 10

Venice, the Republic of Venice

Carlo Contarini stood at the window of the small office on the second level of the doge's palace. He gazed absentmindedly at St. Mark's Square down below, lost in his thoughts. Even in these few precious moments of relaxation his mind still insisted on thinking about all the little problems that were part and parcel of his job. He was one of the three State Inquisitors for the duration of his eight months of service with the Ducal Council. He was also the senior member. The wearer of the scarlet robe—*Il Rosso*. His colleagues had to settle for robes in a very good-quality black. They, the *Tre Inquisitori di Stato*—the three Inquisitors of the State—were responsible for all aspects of state security, including conspiracies, betrayals, public order, and espionage. The health and well-being of the doge was a matter of state security. For that reason, he had learned everything he could about the operation *Dottore* Gribbleflotz would be performing.

There was a rattle of knuckles on wood and the door to the chamber opened to admit a single man. Carlo kept track of the familiar footfalls as they approached. "What's the news, Domenico?" he asked as he turned to face his secretary.

Domenico Molin bowed. "*Dottore* Gribbleflotz and his team have almost finished setting up their equipment, Your Excellency."

"Equipment?" Carlo asked. "What equipment do they need to set up? My understanding is that the only equipment they need is a handheld lithotrite."

"They have a new model of the Gribbleflotz Magneto-Etheric Aural Aura Detector that they intend using during the operation."

"They what?" Carlo demanded. He mentally reviewed what he knew about the piece of equipment, which wasn't much. "What good is an aura detector during an operation?" He shook his head. "This I have to see."

"They will be ready for your inspection soon," Domenico said as he stepped up beside Carlo and joined him in looking out at the scene below. "Naturally, I have made some inquiries about the Gribbleflotz Magneto-Etheric Aural Aura Detector and..."

Carlo took in the look on Domenico's face and hastily waved away the explanation he was sure Domenico was ready to give him, in excruciating detail. Domenico's attention to detail was usually one of the many traits that made Carlo's senior secretary so indispensable. However, it sometimes had its downside. Like just now. "Have your written report on my desk by tomorrow," he said to foreshorten any explanation. The sigh of disappointment from Domenico almost brought a smile to Carlo's face. However, he was able, though only barely, to hold it back. Such an action would only have encouraged Domenico.

"What other news do you have?" Carlo asked as he turned his attention back at the square below.

"There are reports from western Veneto of a group of traveling showmen purporting to be from Grantville, the Miracle City from the Future, performing before large crowds."

"I know of that group already, Domenico," Carlo interrupted. "They are sponsored by the USE's equivalent of the *Sanità*." He smiled at Domenico. "Your brother wrote a report and I have already asked that they be granted the necessary licenses for their traveling roadshow."

Domenico shook his head. "This is a different group of charlatans, Your Excellency. Their leader performs under the *nome d'arte* of 'The Magnificent Ponzi.' And it's what he is doing that I found interesting. The reports say that he claims to perform faith healing and perform surgery on members of the audience with his bare hands."

"Didn't *Dottore* Stone say that the only surgeon capable of doing that had returned to India?" Carlo demanded. A moment later he shook his head. "Never mind. An investigation of this Magnificent Ponzi's operations is clearly in the purview of the *Sanità*. Have..."

A knock on the door caused Carlo to pause. It opened and a young man entered. "Your Excellency, they are ready."

Carlo nodded in acknowledgment. The page bowed and exited the room.

"Advise the *Sanità* to send someone suitable to observe their activities and report back," Carlo said. With the command for action given, Carlo departed his office and made his way to the doge's private apartment.

Carlo's junior secretary and two guards were standing attentively outside the room—a room that, in the up-timers' world, would take the name of the man to be operated on. "Has everyone assembled?" he asked his junior secretary.

"Everyone has assembled, Your Excellency. And *Dottore* Gribbleflotz's team is eagerly awaiting your inspection," Alvise Molin said as he indicated to the guards to open the door.

Carlo stepped into the room and immediately noted how crowded it was. Apart from *Dottore* Gribbleflotz's party and the patient—the doge; there was also *Dottore* Sanctorio Sanctorius, the personal physician of His Serenity, and with his assistant; two secretaries; and three servants. Also, custom demanded that members of the patriciate be present at such times. However, because of the limited space, Carlo had decided to limit the number of patrician witnesses to two. There had been an outcry against his decision. Demand to be present—the operation was to be performed by the famous *Dottore* Gribbleflotz after all—had been so great that they had been forced to hold a ballot to allocate the two slots available to the members of the patriciate.

"Francesco, Giovanni," he acknowledged them and proceeded to pay his respects to the patient. "Your Serenity," he bowed as the doge returned his greeting.

"Your Excellency," *Dottore* Sanctorius interrupted. "May I introduce you to *Dottore* Gribbleflotz and his assistants, *Signore* Böhm, *Signora* Gebauer, and *Signora* Cheng."

Carlo glared at Sanctorius. His interruption, as well as the quality of the introduction, was a major breach of protocol. Such a breach needed to be reprimanded, but it could wait until they could talk privately—public reprimands too often created a feeling of grievance amongst the reprimanded. He pointed to the big box on legs that *Dottore* Gribbleflotz, the female up-timer, and the soldier were working on. "Is that a Gribbleflotz Magneto-Etheric Aural Aura Detector?" he asked them.

"It is one of the new improved Gribbleflotz Magneto-Etheric Aural Aura Detectors, Your Excellency," Phillip said.

"I thought it might be," Carlo muttered. "And how are you planning on using it?" he asked. "Surely His Serenity will be unconscious during the operation?"

"I will be," His Serenity Francesco Erizzo said. "However, the machine is very interesting." He held up a strip of paper about three inches wide. "This is a record of the beating of my heart made by the machine. *Signora* Cheng was just explaining its capabilities to me. Did you know that it contains an Alexanderson alternator just like those used by the Voice of Luther and Radio Prague, only a lot smaller?"

"No, Your Serenity."

"Ha!" Francesco crowed. "I discovered something before the State's Inquisitors." He turned to Diana. "Would it be possible to build a broadcast radio using the Alexanderson alternator in the aura detector?"

Diana shrugged. "It's not my field, Your Serenity. I could send a message to Grantville to ask my father."

"It is theoretically possible," Stephan Böhm said in stumbling Latin.

"Carlo," Francesco called out. "I wish to know if it is truly possible. Could you make inquiries?"

"I will attend to it as soon as your operation is safely over, Your Serenity," Carlo said.

Francesco groaned. "You would have to remind me of that." He shook himself before turning to Phillip. "It's not going to hurt?"

"You won't feel a thing, Your Serenity. The ether Corporal Böhm will administer will render you completely unconscious. When you next awaken, the operation will be over, and you will be in your own bed. It will be as if you have awoken from a restful sleep."

"You're sure?" Francesco asked. "Will I feel pain when I wake up?"

"None of the patients I have worked on have reported any residual pain on waking, Your Serenity."

Francesco released a reluctant sign. It was immediately followed by a twinge of pain from his abdomen. He clasped the area with a hand. "Argh! Do it. Start now!"

Phillip hurried over to Francesco. "Just lie back, Your Serenity. Corporal Böhm will start administering the ether, and the pain will have disappeared when you wake."

Meanwhile, at the Provveditori alla Sanità (Public Health Board of Venice), Venice

"Let me see it, Paolo."

Paolo Molin handed his report to Pietro Gradenico, his boss, and waited. Poor eyesight, among other maladies, had taken its toll on the frail old patrician, so he had learned to keep his reports short and succinct. This one was only two pages long.

"Another excellent job, Paolo," the Commissioner of Health said as he removed his reading spectacles.

"You are very kind, sir," Paolo replied.

And he meant it. When the Senate, acknowledging Pietro's failing health, granted him an assistant for the duration of his tenure, he chose Paolo from among the many—some of them better-qualified—candidates. Paolo knew it was an act of kindness to the son of a dear old friend. But it was appreciated, and he tried hard to live up to Pietro's expectations. Paolo might be a lot of things, but he was neither lazy nor ungrateful.

"I have a new assignment for you," Pietro said as he reached for a piece of paper sticking out of a pigeonhole in his escritoire. "A request from the State Inquisitors. They want us to investigate a group of charlatans purporting to be from the City from the Future."

"Grantville?" Paolo asked as he accepted the paper. "But, sir, the *Sanità* gave them permission for their performances and the sale of their medical products following a request from their embassy in Venice. Why would the Inquisitors of the State want us to investigate them again?"

"It is not that group," Pietro said. "There is, apparently, a second group that neither the *Sanità* nor the State Inquisitors have previously heard of that is drawing crowds in the west of the Republic, near Verona. This second group also claims to be from Grantville. We have been asked to investigate and report back. You will lead the investigation."

Paolo did not need to ask why he had been chosen. His mother and her parents had been English, so he spoke the language of the up-timers. He was also fluent in German, having worked at the *Fontego dei Tedeschi*—the trading house in Venice where merchants from Germany were required to live and trade—for several years before he secured the position as Pietro's assistant. Those qualifications made him ideal for the assignment. "When do I have to leave?"

Pietro shrugged. "If it were urgent or serious, Contarini could have handled it himself. It's not as if he doesn't have the resources to do so. So, not that urgent, I suppose," he said. "Let's play it safe. See if the health authorities beyond Verona have reported anything. If not, send messages asking them to do so. Write a report to Contarini explaining our actions. This will leave you enough time, a few days at least, to prepare for the journey should it prove necessary for you to interview the group in person."

"As you wish." Paolo bowed and started to leave.

"Paolo!" Paolo stopped. "Could you stop by the Chair to pick up my medicine?"

"Of course, sir."

The Chair Apothecary, St. Mark's Square, Venice

Apart from selling medicines and other remedies, the pharmacies of the Republic offered a place where people could socialize in safety and comfort. People, from patricians to the lowest fishmonger, could gather to converse, read the latest *avvisi*—local handwritten newsletters—and newspapers from all around Europe, discuss the affairs of the world, exchange news . . . and gossip. Paolo, in his role as Pietro's assistant (after all, checking the qualities of the medicines the apothecaries sold was a job for the *Provveditori alla Sanità*), took advantage of every opportunity to visit any of them he could, to learn the news and maybe—if he was lucky—gather useful tidbits of gossip that he could use to supplement his meagre salary.

His favorite was the apothecary with the sign of Chair. On the ground floor of *Procuratie Vecchie* at St. Mark's square—just a stone's throw from the Ducal Palace. Matteo Bamboni, the apothecary at the pharmacy, and an old family friend, was one of the finest accumulators of gossip in the city.

He walked into the sign of the Chair and almost collided with his past.

"Paolo? Paolo Molin? Where have you been, you old rascal?"

That was all the warning Paolo had before Luigi Corner wrapped him in a bear hug. "You haven't changed a bit," Paolo said as he fought his way free of Luigi's hug. "How long has it been? Four, nearly five years since we were together in Candia?"

Luigi had been a fellow classmate at the *Collegio dei giovani nobili*. As luck would have it, upon their graduation, they had both been posted to Candia, where they served in the naval squadron of the *Capitano alla guardia di Candia*, the naval commander of Crete. It was a time that held fond memories for Paolo. It was a time before...

"Indeed, since then," Luigi replied. "You left to see your family and then you disappeared. We all wondered what happened to you."

After five years the pain had dulled, just a little. "My family perished in the plague. All except for my little sister, Marietta, who survived relatively unscathed. We are the last of the Molin of S. Samuel." He sighed sadly. His family had been neither rich nor influential. Just a junior branch of the prominent Molin patrician family, but he had loved and now missed them all.

"I am sorry, my friend," Luigi said solemnly. "We all lost dear ones. And then?"

Paolo shrugged. "I had to take care of Marietta. She was eleven, almost twelve, and the loss of our parents, sister, and brother affected her badly. I wasn't much good for her. I had little time for her. I had to save the family fortune. Which wasn't that easy. Giovanni..."

Giovanni, his oldest brother, was supposed to take over the management of the family fortune when Father retired. That had been the plan. Giovanni had been sent to Padua. Not to excel academically—although a law degree was always useful—but to make friends with and establish connections with the scions of other prominent families studying there. For Paolo, his father took advantage of some Senate decree and enrolled him to train as a naval officer. His sisters would either be profitably married off or stay at home to care for their parents. It was a good plan... and then God laughed.

Paolo gathered his thoughts. "Lawyers, contracts, creditors, debtors, obligations. It took time and money. I've sold my family house and rented an apartment in S. Barnaba." He saw Luigi cringe a little. "Yes, I know. Not the best of places, but the rent is cheap. With the proceeds from the sale of the house as a dowry, I was able to secure a good marriage for Marietta with the son of an old associate of my grandfather."

He was stretching the truth, and he knew it. But the truth was not something he could share with Luigi. A man needs to have some pride. Admitting to living in S. Barnaba had been bad enough. The truth was that he had been lucky. Marietta had caught the eye of a distant cousin from another branch of the family that had also suffered from the plague. The young man had been a third son of a large family. Normally he would have remained unmarried to preserve the family fortune. However, Marietta's dowry, small as it was, had made a marriage possible. The marriage was flourishing. Being in public with the two of them together, Marietta and her Martino, could be embarrassing. He told Luigi this, adding that he was soon to be a proud uncle.

"Oh, the married life," Luigi replied. "My sweet Julietta. Are you married also?" Paolo stared at him. "I guess not. So, except for securing a suitable marriage for your sister—which is commendable given the circumstances—what else did you do?"

"Papa's colleagues at the *Fontego dei Tedeschi* found me a position. I worked there until . . ." Something clicked in Paolo's mind. He stared at Luigi. "Julietta? As in Julietta Morosini? Our capitano's daughter?"

"The one and the same," Luigi laughed. "But now she is Julietta Corner, mother of Ippolyto and Maria and daughter of the next *Provveditore Generale da Mar*."

Paolo raised his eyebrow. "When did that happen? Last I heard, Giovanni Venier had been nominated."

"Venier developed a severe case of gout a couple of days ago and had to withdraw," Luigi replied. "My father-in-law was the next available choice. Thus, I have to inform my dear wife that a trip to Corfu is definitely in our plans now. I am my father-in-law's assistant after all, and I have to follow him wherever he goes." He looked at Paolo speculatively. "We can always use good and competent naval officers," he said. "I remember that the capitano was impressed by your professionalism and courage when we were in Candia." Luigi grinned. "If he has forgotten, I can always remind him, if you are interested in joining us."

"Thank you, Luigi, for your consideration. Let me think

about it. Currently I am working for the *Sanità*, assisting Pietro Gradenico . . ."

"Is that old goat still alive?"

"He still is, but I don't know for how much longer," Paolo replied. "Let me think about it."

"As you wish," Luigi replied. "We won't leave for quite some time. And the offer stands."

The clock at the *Torre dell'orologio*, the clock tower in St. Mark's Square, struck the hour. "Oh my," Luigi said. "I must be going. Paolo, don't be a stranger. Visit us. We live at my parents' house, Ca' Corner, near the American Embassy. *Ciao*," he called over his shoulder as he hurried away.

Paolo's eyes followed Luigi as he made his way to the gondola stanzas at the other side of the square. His offer was tempting. It needed due consideration. He would have to talk it over with Marietta and Martino. Pietro Gradenico's hold on life was tenuous. At any time Paolo could find himself without a job. A return to the navy would give him some security. It was, he realized as he saw Luigi clamber aboard a gondola, something to think about. In the meantime, he had Pietro Gradenico's medicine to collect.

"Paolo, are you daydreaming again?" Matteo said with a smile brightening his face as he walked up to him. "The privilege of youth is to be able to dream."

"So true, my friend. But at thirty-three, I can hardly consider myself young," Paolo said. At that moment something caught his eye. A man. A young man. A young man in clothing in the style of the up-timers. A young man who was holding some strange object up to his face. He raised his hand to forestall Matteo's reply. "Who is that man?" He pointed toward the man. "And what is he doing?"

Matteo followed Paolo's pointing arm. "Ah, *Signore* Sebastian Jones," Matteo replied. "He is an American commissioned by Royal Dutch Airlines to take photographs of Venice for tourist brochures. That is what he is doing now, with one of his up-time cameras. He arrived a few days ago."

Paolo raised an eyebrow.

"He came here earlier to ask about the availability of photographic papers and chemicals," Matteo replied to the unanswered question. "I stock them for the Society of Aural Investigators. They use Kirlian photography to detect the auras they interpret," he quickly added. "Come, I can show you the photographs he took of his flight from Grantville."

Paolo followed Matteo to a back room. Hanging from a cord suspended across the room were a number of photographs. On the floor below them, water puddled. He walked along the line, admiring what he saw, and then he came to the last photo. He turned to Matteo. "He took your photograph?"

Matteo nodded as he too looked at the ten-inch by twelve-inch photograph. "He's a handsome devil, isn't he?"

Paolo laughed. "How did you get him to take your photograph?"

"I didn't have to do anything. He actually asked *me* if he could take my photograph. Of course, I have to pay if I want a print I can keep."

"Do you think he would be willing to take my photograph? For Marietta?"

"We can only ask. Come, I will introduce you to him."

Sebastian Jones lifted his Speed Graphic camera, framed the shot, and gently squeezed the shutter button.

"*Signore* Jones!"

He lowered the camera and flipped the film holder as he turned to the source of the call. He recognized the apothecary from the Chair Apothecary who had rented him some space to process the photographs he'd taken on the trip to Venice. *Signore* Matteo Bamboni—commercial photographers made it a habit to remember names; a photograph with a name was worth more to the newspapers than one without—was waddling toward him at some pace, but it was the contrast with the man accompanying him that caught Sebastian's attention. His camera came up.

Click.

He lowered the camera and replaced the double-dark with a fresh film holder. He would have to get the man to sign a release, because the contrast between Matteo's bulk and his lithe form was almost comical. Definitely something his agent could sell.

"*Signore* Jones!" Matteo called once more.

"*Signore* Bamboni." Sebastian waved to indicate he had heard. "How can I help you? And who is your companion?"

"This is an old family friend, *Signore* Paolo Molin. I showed him your photographs, and he is wondering if you might be so good as to take his photograph."

"Mr. Jones, I am hopeful that you would be willing to take my photograph. It would be a gift for my sister," Paolo said in fluent, but not American, English. He held his hand for a handshake.

Sebastian grasped the hand. The grip was strong, but the skin was smooth and uncalloused. That suggested a "soft" occupation. Sebastian let his photographer's eye float over Paolo. The clothes were not top quality—Sebastian had been around Dr. Gribbleflotz long enough to learn the signs—but their quality was superior to that of Matteo's, and they were better tailored. Taking everything together, it screamed "impoverished nobility." He smiled. "I would be happy to take your photograph, just as long as you're willing to sign a release."

Paolo stared at him. "A release? What is a release?"

"It is paper that gives me permission to sell copies of your image to other people."

Paolo ran a hand through his hair. He looked over to Matteo, who shrugged. "I am confused," Paolo told Sebastian, stating the obvious. "Why would someone I don't know want a photograph of me?"

Sebastian quickly glanced behind him. Yes, there was a clear path of retreat. He smiled at Paolo. "Royal Dutch Airlines might be interested in buying a photograph of you." He held up his hand—the free one not holding on to his Speed Graphic—to stop Paolo before he could ask the obvious question. "I am taking photographs that are intended to appear in tourist brochures encouraging people to travel, by air, to Venice. And tourist brochures don't just need to show attractive scenery; they need to also show people. Real people. Locals. Preferably aesthetically pleasing locals."

Sebastian had his eyes on Paolo as he said it. Ready to bolt if he seemed offended.

"You think I am aesthetically pleasing?"

Sebastian backed up a couple of steps. "You have the kind of face and physique that would make a great cover for a romance." He winced even as he said it. He was just glad he had not mentioned the option of him being bare-chested.

"A romance?"

"Romantic fiction," Sebastian clarified. "Boy meets girl. They have some kind of conflict, and then they get married and live happily ever after." He saw the look of disbelief on Paolo's face. "They sell really well. Mostly to a female audience," he added. "They usually have a handsome hero and a beautiful heroine. Covers depicting beautiful people sell better than covers without."

Sebastian looked hopefully at Paolo. "I don't suppose you are married or have a girlfriend who would be willing to be photographed with you in romantic locations. I will pay."

Paolo laughed. "No, but I have a young sister. I am sure she and her husband would be interested in what you are suggesting."

"Is he handsome and she beautiful?"

"Yes," Paolo said.

Sebastian ran his tongue over suddenly dry lips. This might be just what he needed to add that something special that he felt was missing from the photographs of Venice he had taken so far. Not that there was anything wrong with the photographs he had already taken. Royal Dutch Airlines would be very happy with what he had already done, but a series of photographs featuring the same couple in different locations around Venice, that could be gold. Also, literal gold, in his pocket or bank account. "Would they be willing to be photographed at various romantic locations around Venice?"

Paolo smiled. "We can only ask, but I'm sure they would enjoy the experience."

"Now?" Sebastian asked as he picked up the camera bag at his feet.

"I have to pick up some medicine for my boss, but as soon as we do that, and deliver it, we can head over to their home."

"Boss?" Sebastian said it carefully. That implied work. He had thought Paolo was a noble of some sort, even if he was a poor one. "Won't he object? Don't you have to report back to work?"

Paolo laughed. "I have to drop off his medicine. Why don't you come with me? I'm sure he will love an opportunity to converse with someone from the City from the Future."

Sebastian suddenly realized where Paolo was taking him. He laid a hand on Paolo's shoulder and brought him to a halt a dozen paces from the door Paolo had been leading him toward. "Who exactly is it you work for?" he asked. He thought it a fair question, considering that they were right outside an entrance into the doge's palace.

"I'm an assistant to *Signore* Pietro Gradenico, an official in the *Provveditori alla Sanità*."

Sebastian, with the benefit of having survived four years of Latin at school and six weeks of intensive Italian just before this trip to Venice, mentally translated that as "providers of sanitation."

Which, he was sure, was probably wrong. "Is that something like our Sanitation Commission?"

"Something like that," Paolo agreed. "We protect the health of the citizens of the Republic by policing compliance with health regulations with respect to the proper disposal of wastes, water management, the food industry, as well as the supervision of physicians, barbers, and apothecaries."

"Physicians?" Sebastian asked. "You are responsible for supervising physicians?"

"Not me personally," Paolo said. "At most, I only take note of any complaints I might hear as I do my rounds of the apothecaries and food traders and pass the information onto the officials responsible for investigating complaints against physicians."

Sebastian had an idea. It was a great idea. It would give his standing amongst Dr. Gribbleflotz's party a much-needed boost. It was, he thought, less of an idea and more of a brainwave so good was it. "So, Paolo, hypothetically speaking. If, say, a small group of foreigners wanted to perform a minimally invasive medical procedure—say, an operation like *Dottore* Gribbleflotz and his team are supposed to perform on the doge—on paying customers, you would know who they had to see to get the necessary permissions?"

Paolo stared hard at Sebastian. "Just how hypothetically speaking is this group of foreigners?"

"I flew to Venice on the same flight as *Dottore* Gribbleflotz and his party."

"So not very hypothetically speaking." Paolo shook his head. "*Dottore* Gribbleflotz and his party already have permission to operate on His Serenity."

"Yes," Sebastian agreed. "But what if they wanted to operate on people other than the doge?"

"Ah! In that case, *Dottore* Gribbleflotz and his team of medical professionals would have to be properly vetted and licensed to operate." Paolo's eyes brightened. "Do they really wish to do that?" he asked.

"Not *Dottore* Gribbleflotz, but Diana and the others talked a lot about it during the flight. Diana is as qualified as *Dottore* Gribbleflotz to perform the operation, and she has all the necessary equipment. They just need the proper paperwork and somewhere to operate."

"I know a number of places suitable for surgery." Paolo's

tongue slipped out and moistened his lips. "I believe we have an additional topic with which to discuss with my boss."

Later that day

In his bedchamber, His Serenity Francesco Erizzo slowly woke. His first thought was that there was no pain. He tentatively ran his hand over his abdomen. Then he palpated the area over his bladder. Nothing. A smile grew on his face as he sat up. Still no pain. He pulled the covers back and swung his legs out before standing. Again, there was no pain. Driven by curiosity, Francesco pulled up his nightgown to check for any sign of the procedure he had undergone.

"I'm brown!" he exclaimed. He dropped the hem of his nightgown and roared for a servant.

One tentatively poked his head around the door.

"Get me *Dottore* Sanctorius!"

The page hastened away, to return minutes later with *Dottore* Sanctorius.

"Your Serenity..." Sanctorio Sanctorius started to say.

Francesco waved him quiet. "Why are my nether regions brown? What has happened? What has gone wrong?" he demanded.

Sanctorio stuttered as he struggled to answer. After several false starts he shrugged. "I don't know, Your Serenity."

"Well, find out!"

Sanctorio made a hasty getaway, only to be called up short before he escaped through the door. "Get *Dottore* Gribbleflotz. Now!"

A few minutes later, Sanctorio reappeared with *Dottore* Gribbleflotz.

"Is there a problem, Your Serenity?" Phillip asked as they were shown into the doge's bedchamber.

"You tell me," Francesco demanded. He pulled up his nightgown. "Why are my nether regions brown?"

Phillip bent down to examine the area in question. "That'll be the Tincture of Iodine," Phillip said as he straightened. "I had the nurse paint the site prior to surgery," he explained to Francesco.

"I don't remember anything about painting the patient's nether regions brown in your article in the *Proceedings of the Royal Academy of Science of Bohemia*."

"It's there," Phillip said.

Francesco gestured toward *Dottore* Sanctorius, who had a copy of the proceedings open in his hands. Sanctorio passed the journal to Phillip, who skimmed through the text. "Ah. I think I see the problem." He planted a finger beside a paragraph. "Just here, I talk about painting the surgical site with a topical disinfectant solution. And here I name it." He smiled at Francesco as he pointed to another piece of text.

Francesco checked the text *Dottore* Gribbleflotz was pointing to. "Nowhere does it say that it will stain my skin brown."

Phillip shrugged. "It is only temporary, Your Serenity. The brown stain will disappear in a matter of days."

Francesco stared hard at Phillip. "It better."

"It will." Phillip nodded emphatically. "The brown stain was all gone on my previous patient in Prague inside seven days."

"Then we will wait for seven days," Francesco said. "Meanwhile, *Dottore* Gribbleflotz, you and your people will remain in Venice." He waved a hand of dismissal and turned his attention back to *Dottore* Sanctorius.

Next day

Sebastian was standing on the old stone bridge on the *Riva degli Schiavoni* where it crosses the *Rio di Palazzo*. For once, he was not carrying a camera, but only because the camera he was using was so big and cumbersome that it needed a tripod. It was a three-frame color camera able to record three images at once. It used a precision ground prism to split the light so that each of the three negatives were exposed to only red, green, or blue light. You could not print color photographs from the negatives it produced, but you could make three-color printing plates that could be used to print color posters and the like.

Sebastian sighted along the lens's axis. That looked good. Next, he got under the blackout cloth covering the back to adjust the focus of the inverted image on the ground-glass back plate. Perfect.

He removed the blackout cloth and placed the rear double-dark film holder into position. He then pulled the inner slides of each of his three film cassettes and grabbed the cable release. He was ready.

"Okay, give them the signal," he called to Paolo.

Paolo waved to the gondolier farther down the *Riva degli*

Schiavoni. The gondola started moving. His sister and brother-in-law snuggled up together as they approached the Bridge of Sighs.

Sebastian waited until just the right moment before activating the cable release. "Okay, back them up," he called as he started switching the double darks. Less than a minute later, he called for Paolo to signal them to sail under the bridge again.

He tripped the shutter on his large-frame camera and immediately picked up his Olympus OM1-N and rattled off a few frames of the happy couple as they continued down the *Riva degli Schiavoni*. Most of the extra shots were security shots just in case something went wrong. As it was, he was sure that the first shot was a keeper.

He lowered the OM1-N and smiled at Paolo. "Perfect. I'm finished with Marietta and Martino for today."

Paolo had his eyes on the gondola as it approached. "That's good, because I don't think you're going to get much sense out of the pair of them for a while. I'll let them know you've finished with them and pay off the gondolier."

Sebastian felt in a pocket for some coins. He handed them to Paolo. "Give this to the gondolier as a tip. I'm sure his patience must be nearly at an end."

Paolo accepted the coins and trotted over to the steps that led down to the water. Sebastian, meanwhile, started to disassemble the components of his color camera.

"Excuse me, *Signore*. Pardon me for interrupting you, but might you be one of the up-timers who recently arrived in Venice aboard the Jupiter airplane?"

Sebastian stopped what he was doing and turned toward the voice. It was a local. Well dressed, but obviously an employee of some kind. "Yeees," he said cautiously.

He had not been cautious enough. The man immediately erupted into a flood of Italian. He was speaking so fast that Sebastian was struggling to even catch a word here and there. It was not helped by the way the man was slurring his words together. His teachers back in Grantville had never done that.

Fortunately, help was close at hand. Paolo arrived to take over the conversation.

Sebastian continued listening. He was not sure what was being said, but Paolo sure looked happy. "What's he saying?"

Paolo held up a hand to stop the man speaking. "He has been trying all morning to gain access to *Dottore* Gribbleflotz's medical team. He has a client who wishes to engage them to perform the same operation on him as was performed on His Serenity."

Paolo's explanation to Sebastian was in Italian, but it was spoken slower and with the precision Sebastian, who had learned the language in a classroom, required for comprehension. That meant that the man, or as he now suspected, someone's agent, also understood what Paolo was saying. Which would explain his enthusiastic head-nodding.

Sebastian grinned. He now understood Paolo's happy face. Frau Mittelhausen had promised a commission on every patient Paolo referred to them for surgery. "I'll leave you to deal with him then. If you need me, I'll be over at the Chair processing the shots I've taken and reloading the cassettes."

"See you later then," Paolo said before leading the man off.

Sebastian returned to packing up his gear. The three-color camera was heavy and delicate, so it had its very own custom-made carriage-case, with space for additional double darks and lenses. He slid the camera into position and closed the case. That just left carrying it, and the heavy tripod that had supported it, over to the Chair. The combination was too much for Sebastian to carry on his own. Which was why he had hired a couple of men to carry the equipment for him. He looked around until he spotted Luca and Nicolo. His natural reactions came into play as his eyes fell upon them. Up came the OM1-N.

Three shots later he lowered it. He put his fingers to his mouth and whistled.

They did not come running. That would have been too much to expect. However, they did collect their cards and wander over to Sebastian in good time. Shortly thereafter, the three of them set off. Sebastian in the front with a leather camera bag slung across his shoulder and his Speed Graphic to hand. Behind him were the two men; one carried the color camera while the other had the heavy tripod over his shoulder.

At the Chair Apothecary, the men laid down their burdens and looked to Sebastian for further instructions. "That's it for today," Sebastian told them. They did not look happy at that, until he paid them the full promised daily rate.

"Thankee, sir. Will you be wanting us again?" There was a lot of hope in Luca's question. Day labor was a precarious way of earning a living.

Sebastian checked his diary. "Not tomorrow, but I'll need some help on Wednesday. However, it will be an early start. I want to get the sunrise." He looked hopefully at Luca and Nicolo. "I'll pay extra if we can get set up on the point of the island where the Grand Canal meets the Giudecca Canal before the sun appears above the horizon."

"The sun won't rise until about seven." Luca stared consideringly at Sebastian. "Given how long it took you to set up for your last photographs, we'll have to assemble at the dock by six o'clock."

There was a question in the way Luca said that. Sebastian nodded. "I can do that." He looked across St. Mark's Square to the *Torre dell'orologio*. The clock face was visible, but he could not read the time on the clock face from where he was standing. He needed to check its time against his wristwatch, so as not to be late.

"Do you have a boat arranged?" Nicolo asked.

"What?" Sebastian brought himself back to Luca and Nicolo. What had Nicolo asked? Oh, yes. "No. Not yet," Sebastian admitted.

"We'll see to it," Nicolo said. "I know someone reliable."

Of course he did. Sebastian smiled. They expected to earn a gratuity from the boatman. Who would, no doubt, overcharge him so that he could recover the additional expense. Sebastian didn't care. It wasn't his money they were getting. It was Royal Dutch Airlines' money. He had an expense account on this job. "Right then, we'll meet here on Wednesday in time for the Moors to ring the bell for six o'clock."

"Six o'clock." The men nodded as they confirmed they knew when they were supposed to show up.

They left, no doubt to find more work, and Sebastian headed for the room he had rented in which to process his photographs and reload his film cassettes.

A couple of days later

"That young American, *Signore* Jones. Is he a spy?" Carlo asked as he and Domenico walked down the corridor.

"He seems very open about who and what he is," Domenico pointed out.

"Maybe he is being too open," Carlo said. "The contract he

has with Royal Dutch Airlines makes an ideal cover story for him to go around photographing all of our secrets."

"No, not really," Domenico replied. "In fact, according to reliable sources, he takes great care not to photograph anything that might be considered controversial. In fact, he is paranoidly careful. Not to mention, actually paranoid."

Carlo turned and stared at Domenico. "Paranoid? How so?"

"He is constantly asking his guide whether or not it is permitted to photograph something."

"He has a guide? Who is it? Is he reliable?"

Domenico nodded enthusiastically. "Paolo Molin. A distant relative. He is Pietro Gradenico's assistant at the *Sanità*. He is also the man Pietro has assigned to investigate the Verona group. He has attached himself to *Signore* Jones as a friend and guide."

"Interesting . . ." Carlo replied. "Keep me informed, Domenico."

"As you wish." Domenico bowed and excused himself.

Five days later

"Bring me Gribbleflotz and his companions!" His Serenity Francesco Erizzo roared at a servant. "NOW!" he added, just in case the servant was in any doubt as to the urgency of the matter.

The man escaped, scampering out the door in a clatter of leather on polished wooden floors.

With the servant on his way, Francesco turned his attention back to Carlo Contarini. "You are sure?" he demanded.

Carlo gestured to his companion. "Domenico's source saw *Signora* Cheng paint the nether regions of *Signore* Rofari with his own eyes."

Francesco spared Carlo's companion a quick glance. "And the brown stain has faded already?" he asked. "After little more than a day?"

Domenico nodded. "Your Serenity, according to my source, *Signora* Gebauer, the nurse, appeared very excited when she discovered that the stain had faded. She was quite vocal on the matter."

"So, it is not a secret?" Francesco mumbled as he thought about it. "She appeared surprised?" he asked the secretary, just to confirm what he thought he had heard.

Again, Domenico nodded. "She immediately called for *Signora* Cheng and *Signore* Böhm to examine the patient."

"We will wait," Francesco announced. "Where is that servant? He should have been back with *Dottore* Gribbleflotz and his party by now." He was being unreasonable. He knew that. But he wanted to know what was going on. He wanted to know why his nether regions were still stained brown while the nether regions of an insignificant merchant had already returned to their normal color, even though his operation had occurred well after his. Being unreasonable was, after all, one of the privileges of being the doge.

It was some time before the guilty parties assembled. Francesco was, of course, jumping the gun a little here, but aiming for a confession of guilt sharpened the mind.

The servant led in *Dottore* Gribbleflotz, *Signora* Gebauer, *Signore* Böhm, and finally, and most definitely not least—because she was the person who had conducted the operation on Rofari—the up-timer *Signora* Cheng.

Francesco stared at them all as they lined up like guilty children. "It has come to my attention," he said as he paced along the line, "that you have been performing operations like the one *Dottore* Gribbleflotz performed on me."

He paused on the last word and scanned the lineup. "That, in itself, is not an issue. What is an issue is that the brown stain you painted on *Signore* Rofari has already disappeared. Meanwhile, my nether regions are still brown." He walked to the middle of the line, from where he could watch all of *Dottore* Gribbleflotz's party.

"What do you have to say for yourselves?"

Diana Cheng stepped forward. "Your Serenity, back up-time, we used to paint a square inch of skin with an iodine solution as a screening test for iodine deficiency. If it disappeared within a day or so, we said the person suffered from iodine deficiency."

"So, *Signore* Rofari suffers from iodine deficiency?" Francesco asked.

Diana shook her head. "Given that we painted a lot more than just a square inch of skin with the iodine solution, and that it has all been absorbed in little more than a day, I would say he has chronic severe iodine deficiency. We have already started treating him for it."

"Treating him for it?" *Dottore* Sanctorius roared from the doorway. "I am sorry, Your Serenity," he immediately apologized. "But *Signora* Cheng should not be providing treatment she is not trained to provide."

"What would you have me do? Let *Signore* Rofari develop hypothyroidism?" She ran a finger around her throat. "That's when the thyroid glands expand in size."

Francesco ran his hand over his own throat. "Goiter?" he asked.

The girl gave him a smile that had him standing straighter. It was like being patted on the head by his father for being a bright little boy. As that thought charged through his mind, he frowned. "You can treat goiter?"

"We already know how to treat goiter," *Dottore* Sanctorius protested. "It requires a dangerous surgical procedure—although, with the new method of anesthesia, it should be a little safer."

"You can treat it before it gets that bad," Diana said. "All you have to do is give the patient iodine. Either paint it on, mix it with water and let them drink it, or add it to food."

Francesco stared at the girl. "Let me see if I understand you correctly. *Signore* Rofari suffers from *iodine deficiency*. That is why the brown stain disappeared so quickly?"

"Chronic severe iodine deficiency," Diana corrected. "He's very lucky we treated him for bladder stones," she said. "Judging by how quickly his body absorbed the iodine on his skin, he was *this* close to developing acute hypothyroidism." She held her thumb and forefinger a hairsbreadth apart to illustrate just how close he had been.

"So, he almost had goiter?" Francesco asked.

Diana shook her head. "He has goiter, just not bad enough that his thyroid had grown large enough for the swelling to be noticeable."

Francesco swallowed and rubbed his neck around the thyroid glands. "Do I have goiter?"

"Given how long it is taking for your body to absorb the iodine in the solution we painted on your skin, it's highly unlikely, Your Serenity," Diana said. She held up a hand to stop Francesco before he could question her comment. "Living in Venice, I'm guessing you eat a lot of seafood?"

Francesco nodded. "Of course. Why?" he asked.

"All seafood contains iodine, whereas not all food sourced from land contains iodine.

"That's kind of why *Signore* Rofari has chronic severe iodine deficiency," Diana said. "He comes from Bergamo, and I'm guessing that he doesn't eat much seafood."

"Probably not," Francesco said. Bergamo was, after all, nearly a hundred and thirty miles west of Venice and a hundred miles north of Genoa. In Italy, one could hardly get farther away from the sea.

"Then we need to start giving our people iodine." Francesco turned to Carlo. "See to it!"

"Your Serenity," Phillip interrupted. "It is true that up-time, they managed to reduce levels of iodine deficiency by giving them iodine, but they gave it to them in the form of iodized salt. You could do the same; but a word of caution. While a lack of iodine can lead to goiter, too much iodine can be dangerous." He turned to Diana. "*Signora* Cheng, what are the symptoms of *iodine poisoning*?" he asked.

"It depends on how much iodine is in your body," she said. "The mild symptoms include diarrhea, burning sensation in your mouth, nausea and vomiting."

"And the severe symptoms?" Phillip probed.

Diana gulped as everybody stared at her. "Swelling of your airways, turning blue, weak pulse and coma," she said. "Too much iodine can also lead to *iodine-induced hyperthyroidism*," she added.

"Iodine-induced hyperthyroidism?" Francesco asked.

"Too much iodine sometimes can also produce a form of goiter, Your Serenity," Diana clarified. There were some gasps in the room.

Carlo turned to Phillip. "You brought this to our attention, so I assume you have a solution you wish to suggest."

Phillip gave his audience a modest nod. "Of course," he said, equally modestly. "Iodine can be beneficial in the right dosages, but dangerous if the dosage given is incorrect. For this reason, it must be treated as a medicine. Its production and supply must be regulated.

"If you grant me the required licenses to produce iodized salt, that can then be sold to apothecaries. I could also produce enough iodine for testing purposes or as a disinfectant." He could see both the doge and Carlo nodding affirmatively. He smiled. He had them in the palm of his hand. Now to work on getting the physicians on board.

He turned to the nearest member of the Republic's medical

profession. "If *Dottore* Sanctorius is willing," he said, "we could join together to write the procedure for the new treatment of goiter. With smaller contributions from both *Signora* Cheng and *Signore* Böhm, of course," he added.

He stopped as a thought struck him. Samuel Hartlib would be proud of him. "In fact," he said, "I shall write an article describing the treatment of goiter with iodine and iodized salt for the *Proceedings of the Royal Academy of Science of Bohemia*. *Dottore* Sanctorius, I would consider it a great honor if you were to join me in authoring the article."

"I would be honored to co-author an article with the great *Dottore* Gribbleflotz for such an august publication," a beaming Sanctorius replied.

"In the meantime," Phillip added, moving his gaze to Carlo and the doge, "we need to organize seminars here, at the Colleges of Surgeons and Physicians, and in Padua teaching the new procedures to our esteemed colleagues." He glanced at Sanctorius, who nodded his agreement.

"Your Serenity, Your Excellency, dear colleagues, ladies and gentlemen, with our efforts, and God's help"—Venice was after all a pious state—"Venice can become the leader in goiter treatment in Italy and, perhaps, the world."

Phillip looked expectantly at his audience. Diana was the first to start clapping. Hers was a slow clap. Stephan joined in, also clapping slowly. The others, excluding Carlo, chimed in with more appreciative applause. Carlo just watched Phillip.

The applause petered out after a couple of minutes. Or more correctly, once the doge stopped clapping.

"*Dottore* Gribbleflotz. The licenses you are asking for could be granted, but only if you can guarantee that the iodized salt won't be too expensive for the common people to afford," Carlo said.

"Yes," Francesco said. "Carlo, I believe we are all in agreement. Please see to it."

Nobody moved. Francesco stared at them. Then, with a heavy sigh, he waved at them. "Go. Off you go. Now. You are dismissed."

Everyone got.

"And that's how one does business in Venice!" Phillip said to his awestruck companions as they walked away from the doge's apartment. "Now who knows how to make iodized salt?"

"No idea," Diana offered.

"That's not particularly useful," Phillip muttered. He mentally reviewed what he knew about iodine. It didn't take long. "I need to get to Padua. I have contacts there who can help me."

"You know people in Padua?" Diana asked.

Phillip nodded. "From when I attended the university. There is also an alchemist I knew. If he is still there, he will let me use his laboratory to experiment with adding iodine to salt."

"We could just radio Grantville and ask for help," Stephan Böhm suggested.

Diana swung around. "You have a radio?"

"No, but the embassy does."

"That would be much better than trying to develop a technique myself," Phillip said. "Please, send your message."

Phillip led them into the apartment assigned to his family. He gestured toward the chairs and sofas in the room before collapsing into a comfortable sofa. The others followed suit. Moments later, his wife and Frau Mittelhausen walked out of the children's room.

"What did the doge want?" Dina asked as she snuggled down beside Phillip.

Phillip waved vaguely at Diana, Stephan, and Lise. "One of their patients absorbed all the iodine they painted him with in less than twenty-four hours."

Dina's brows shot up. "Isn't that bad?"

"Very bad," Phillip agreed. "It signifies acute chronic iodine deficiency."

"Is there a lot of that around in Italy?" Ursula Mittelhausen asked. There was a special glint in her eyes that signified an economic interest.

"Maybe not chronic-level iodine deficiency," Diana said, "but I bet there are a lot of people suffering from some level of iodine deficiency."

Ursula smiled and rubbed her hands together. "I sense an opportunity. They add iodine to the salt in Grantville. Do we know how to add iodine to salt?"

Phillip, Diana, Lise, and Stephan all shook their heads.

"Why not?" Ursula asked.

"It's never come up," Diana said. "However, Stephan thinks we can radio Grantville for a cheat sheet."

"You've already thought about starting a business supplying the Republic with iodized salt? I'm impressed." Ursula smiled. "Dr. Gribbleflotz, do you know who we have to see about setting up a business to make and sell iodized salt?"

"We don't have to see anyone, Frau Mittelhausen," Lise said. "His Serenity has already promised Dr. Gribbleflotz a nonexclusive license to supply iodized salt to the Republic."

"Well technically that isn't true," Phillip replied. "We still need to provide the necessary papers to the proper authorities, but with the backing we have, that is a mere formality. Any competent lawyer can prepare the necessary papers."

"Not a monopoly?" Ursula asked.

"No," Phillip confirmed.

"A pity," Ursula muttered. And then she shook her daydreams of impossible wealth from her head.

Phillip smirked. "Actually, my dear Ursula, this is even better," he said. "Much better than a monopoly."

Ursula's eyes narrowed. "Even better than a monopoly?" she said. "Dr. Gribbleflotz, have you lost your mind?"

Phillip looked around and saw the curious faces of everyone in the room. Up-timer and down-timers alike seemed to agree with Ursula's assessment. He sighed.

"It is obvious that none of you understand Venice," he said.

"What's there to understand?" Diana asked. "A monopoly is a monopoly."

"Not in Venice," Phillip said. "In Venice, there are monopolies, and then there are State Monopolies.

"Salt is probably the most important of all the state's monopolies. There are a million committees that regulate the salt market, whereas with medicines, which is what iodine and iodized salt is to be classified as, we are dealing mostly with two or three."

Ursula nodded slowly. "Having to deal with so many regulatory committees and their regulations could severely dent our profits." She sighed mightily. "At least no one else will have a monopoly on iodized salt.

"That means we have a free market, and that means we need to organize an advertising campaign. And..."

Phillip smiled. It was one of his more superior smiles. Not one that he would ever display to a patron, but among friends, it could be forgiven. "There is no need to advertise, Frau Mittelhausen.

I, Phillip Theophrastus Gribbleflotz, great-grandson of the great Paracelsus, have achieved the impossible.

"Soon, every doctor and apothecary in the Republic will be prescribing an iodine or iodized-salt treatment for goiter." He raised his hand toward Ursula to forestall whatever it was she appeared to want to say. "There is no need to thank me." He turned to Diana. "Frau Cheng, tell us what you know about iodine deficiency and iodized salt."

All eyes turned to Diana. As a top medical student, she probably knew more about goiter and how to treat it than the rest of them combined.

"Well," Diana said, "back up-time, before about 1920, iodine deficiency was pretty bad in what they called the Goiter Belt in the U.S. Then, in response to news of the benefits of iodized table salt coming out of Switzerland, a company in America, the Morton Salt Company, started distributing iodized salt nationally."

"And that cured the problem?" Ursula asked.

"Mostly. According to Dr. Sims, rates of iodine deficiency dropped to the low single digits, and average intelligence rose a whole standard deviation."

"A whole standard deviation?" Phillip asked. He had been exposed to modern statistics when Diana and her mother helped investigate the results from his vibrating bed experiment, so he had a good idea what that meant. "Iodine deficiency is bad for intelligence?" he asked, just to confirm what he thought.

Diana nodded. "It is one of the issues. Iodine is metabolized to make thyroid hormones, and if there are not enough of them, the body can't develop to its full potential."

Phillip glanced toward the room where his children were, hopefully, sleeping. "So, adding iodine to salt can cure that?"

"Mostly," Diana said. "Although Dr. Sims did say that rates of iodine deficiency had been rising steadily by the time of the Ring of Fire."

"How is that possible?" Phillip demanded. "If iodizing the salt can reduce the problem to 'low single digits,' why would it go up again?"

"Changes in eating habits," Diana said. "And companies reducing the proportion of iodine they were adding to the salt."

Phillip nodded. "I can see how reducing the iodine in the salt could cause rates to go up, but eating habits?"

"The health industry demonized salt, encouraging people to cut down on their salt intake." Diana snorted. "Well, some people cut back on their salt intake. Other problems included a move to gourmet salts, which weren't iodized. Such as sea salt, which naturally contains less than the recommended amount of iodine. That impacted a lot of people who actually cooked meals from scratch using fresh meat and produce. There was also a growth in demand for processed foods by people who didn't want to spend the time cooking from scratch. Unfortunately, those people were a little picky over what colors they were prepared to accept when it came to their food."

"All of our salt will have the right amount of iodine," Ursula said. "What does the color of food have to do with anything?"

"Iodine causes various things to change color," Diana explained, "and American consumers won't touch anything they consider to be the wrong color. So, the manufacturers stopped using iodized salt."

"Seriously?" Ursula shook her head in disbelief. "Other than the change in color, there was nothing wrong with the food?" she asked.

"Nothing," Diana confirmed.

"That is so silly," Ursula muttered. "They should have promoted it as a feature. 'Look! You can see that this food was prepared using iodized salt.' That is what we will be doing."

"We?" Stephan asked.

"The Gribbleflotz Iodized Salt Company."

Chapter 11

Near the Castello de Pérgine, Trentino, Republic of Venice

It was a market day, but a market day like no other in recent memory. The difference was the travelers from Grantville, the City from the Future. With the approval of the local priests nearly the entire population of the surrounding villages were making their way to the market set up on a fallow field below the *Castello de Pérgine*. Amongst the crowd lined up to enter the large area the travelers had fenced off with canvas were Alberto de Massimo and his wife, Lucia de Samuele, from the village of Canezza.

Alberto noticed his wife rubbing at the faded mark on her arm. In response, he glanced at the similar mark on his arm. It was not as faded. "They will still allow you in for half price," he informed her.

Lucia, a sensible twenty-year-old woman, snorted. "Of course they will. They have my name on their list. But why has my mark faded more than yours?" she asked.

Alberto, even with the superiority of an extra three years of living, was forced to shrug. "I have no idea." He was, obviously, one of that rare breed: a man who could admit to not knowing something. This was not a natural skill. It was the result of more than twenty years of training by his mother and grandmother—neither of whom had ever found anything they did not know. Or, at least, did not have an opinion on.

A few minutes later it was their turn to pay to enter. After giving their names, Alberto pulled back his sleeve to show his mark. One of the women at the door placed a color wheel against it and called out a number. Then it was Lucia's turn.

She noticed that the wheel had different shades of the brown stain that had marked her arm. From the dark brown of when the solution had been initially applied right down to the almost nonexistent shade barely visible against her sun-kissed skin.

"One," the woman said as she carefully scrutinized Lucia.

Lucia didn't like the intensity with which the woman was staring at her and edged closer to the warmth and security of Alberto. "Why did my mark fade more than my husbands?" she asked.

"All will become clear during the show," the woman said as she handed Alberto a couple of tickets and waved for them to move on.

Lucia wanted to protest, but Alberto put his arm around her and forced her to move on.

The moment they stepped into the enclosure a youth greeted them. He asked to see their tickets before directing them toward the stage set up at the other end of the tent. Lucina's eyes never sat still as she took in the posters decorating the two caravans that bordered the back of the stage. Everything was so exciting.

"What's the holdup with the microwave?" Luchia Odescalchi all but shouted into the cheap two-way radio she was holding. She glanced through the two-way mirror that pretended to be a window on the side of the caravan she was sitting in. Through it she could see her husband and the audience that had paid good money to watch Gio's performance.

"Keep your hair on. We had a minor problem with the generator, but it's been dealt with," Rachel Lynch replied.

Luchia glared at the child's two-way radio in her hand as she ran her free hand through her hair. It was all her own and in no risk of falling out. "Gio needs the microwave." She released the transmit button so she could hear the American woman's excuse.

"And it's ready to go, Luchia," Rachel said. "Gio can start the intro whenever he's ready."

"He's been ready for the last ten minutes," Luchia said. "Are you sure it is going to work?"

"Of course, I'm sure it'll work," Rachel snapped back. "I told you, I've fixed it."

Luchia rolled her eyes. Rachel was always so sure of herself and her capabilities. She keyed her boom microphone.

"Rachel says that the microwave is ready, Gio. Start the intro in your own time."

With her husband advised that the performance could continue, Luchia could not resist a last dig at Rachel. She keyed the two-way radio. "Really, Rachel? So who fixed it last time?" She smiled as she released the transmit button. Without Rachel they would have had to retire the microwave eighteen months ago. They could probably survive without it, but the effects it produced were so far beyond most down-timers' experience that it might as well be magic, or, more favorably for what they were doing, be seen as being the work of God.

Giovanni "Gio" Battista Fasolo could hear the muted rumble of the compression-ignition engine as it wound up to full power. He would have to remember to ask Rachel what the problem had been, as they could not really afford to be without the microwave. The light effects it produced when it ran with the crumpled balls of metal foil inside were usually enough to convince even the greatest of skeptics of just how otherworldly the Americans of Grantville were, and as that was a major selling point of the products they had for sale...

He smiled at his audience. Part of the driving force behind the smile was the fact he could continue with the program. The other part was that the Americans seemed convinced that smiling was an important part of forming a connection with an audience. One never knew, the Americans might even be right. Either way, it did not cost anything to throw the audience an occasional smile.

Gio reached for a glass jug—the blue-tinted water clearly visible through the clear glass. "As you may remember, earlier in the show, I treated this jug of water with five drops of a solution made from the Ethereal Essence of Common Salt infused in Thrice-Blessed Radiated Water.

"And, I'm sure, many of you wondered what was thrice-blessed radiated water?" Gio grinned. Even if they had not wondered, they really should have. "More about that shortly. For now, I need a drink."

He poured some water into a glass mug and drank it down, wiping his mouth on his sleeve when he finished. He held the now empty mug up for all to see. "It wasn't the nicest tasting water I've ever drunk, but it was definitely some of the safest.

"Would anyone else like to try it?" he asked. A few hands went up. Gio signaled to one of his assistants, and she was soon walking around, with the jug in one hand and the glass mug in the other, giving people a taste of the purified water.

Gio waited just long enough for Luchia's cousin to start her round before continuing with the program.

"So, what is thrice-blessed radiated water?" Gio stepped aside to allow the audience a clear view of the microwave oven in pride of place on the table. "It is water prepared in one of these.

"This is an invention of the Americans," Gio said, patting the top of the oven. "It uses *nonionizing electromagnetic radiation* generated by a *cavity magnetron* to exorcize the little devils that make water so dangerous." The English loan words in that explanation would have been virtually unintelligible to the people in the audience, but the sentence sounded suitably otherworldly, which was what his audience expected when he talked about the wonders from the *City from the Future*.

He took another of the glass jugs that had been filled with water from a local creek earlier by members of the audience and placed it in the oven. "Using prayer and the wonders of *nonionizing electromagnetic radiation*, I shall now drive out the devils in this jug of water."

Gio could have continued talking during the next five minutes, but they'd learned quite early in their travels that the light show occurring inside the oven as the microwaves hit the crumpled balls of metal foil hanging from a frame mounted on the glass turntable tray was too much competition.

After five minutes, the microwave binged. Gio did not need to hear it to know the five minutes were up. The loud sighs and other expressions of disappointment that the light show was over was a more than adequate indicator.

He waved his hands over the microwave as he gave it a second blessing. He then laid his hands on top of the microwave and added a silent prayer. They had disabled the turntable so that it did not rotate, but all it took was one small particle or scratch inside the jug large enough to form a nucleation site and the effect he was hoping for would fail.

He took a steadying deep breath before opening his eyes

again and making eye contact with his audience. They were still with him. He straightened and picked up the long wooden spoon that had been sitting on the table. He held it up. "When dealing with the devil, one needs a long spoon," he said as he stepped round to open the microwave. He swung the door open all the way and stood clear so everyone could see. Then, with deliberate care, and standing as far from the jug as he could, he gently tapped it with the spoon.

The superheated water erupted, splashing all over the turntable and onto the table. Only his previous experience with the effect allowed Gio to stand firm in the face of the violence of the reaction. The same could not be said for the audience. Their reaction was everything Gio could have wanted. He shot a quick smile in his wife's direction. Once again, the microwave oven had come up trumps.

Gio moved in front of the microwave and addressed the audience. "As you saw, the evil spirits in the water have been driven off, making it safe to drink." So saying, he poured a little of the remaining water into a clean glass and held one up for everyone to see. He then took a sip. Not a big one, as the water was still nearly boiling hot.

"It's a little hot," he told his audience. "And, like water that has been boiled to make it safe, it lacks taste. However, we can fix that." Gio had a smile on his face as he added a teaspoonful of dark powder from a small pot to the water. He stirred it in, and then sipped it. He licked his lips at the taste. "That is soooo good," he told his audience.

He held up the little pot so people could see it. "Doctor Gribbleflotz's Desiccated Essence of Coffea," he said. "Just add a teaspoon or so, according to taste, to hot water, and you have instant nirvana.

"You can buy it from one of the stalls outside."

Gio finished his drink. While he licked the last traces of coffee from his lips, he contemplated his empty mug. That was the signal to Luchia that he was ready to close the performance.

"Smoke in three from your mark," Luchia said.

Gio showed the audience his empty mug. "And with that, it is time for me to go." He laid the mug on the table and raised his arms.

"Three," Luchia said. "Two. One."

On "one" Gio brought down his hands. There was a flash, and a cloud of white smoke enveloped him. When it cleared, he was gone.

That evening

After a long market-day, the members of the traveling roadshow liked to spend part of the evening sitting around a fire. There they could talk about their day and, if they could persuade Gio to play, sing. Given Gio's love of music, he did not take much persuading.

Edith Lynch lay back in her fully wooded deck chair and enjoyed the music as she sipped her mug of drinking chocolate. Her eyes settled on Gio. The poor man looked lost, even as he played his up-time–style six-string guitar. Suddenly his eyes lit up. That could only mean one thing. Edith looked over her shoulder. Yes, there was the lovely Luchia leaving their caravan. It did not take long for the others to notice Luchia, and they fell silent.

There was an air of expectation as Luchia sat beside Gio. She looked around the group, as if searching for someone. Then her eyes locked onto one man in particular.

"Your sales of iodized salt still haven't recovered," she said.

"It's the radio," Antonio Fossato protested. "Ever since we left the coverage area of Voice of America, sales have been dropping."

"We left Voice of America's coverage area months ago," Luchia said.

"Yes," Giovanna Parini agreed as she laid a comforting arm around her husband's shoulders. "And without the Sanitation Commission's advertising, it is difficult to persuade the ignorant peasants of the benefits of iodized salt." She glared at Luchia. "It's not like the bleach. You have Gio to help sell that."

Edith sighed. Luchia and her cousin were happy to get noisily emotional at the drop of a hat. The company, being made up almost completely of Luchia's extended family, did not seem to have any trouble with these noisy demonstrations of emotion. Maybe that was because they were all Italian. Edith, however, was American, and proud of it. She did not do intense emotions. Or at least, she did not do them with as little justification as these screaming Italians. "What you need is some kind of gimmick," she said, hoping to defuse the argument before it took off.

"Gimmick!" Luchia and Giovanna protested in unison.

"Are you suggesting that my Gio uses gimmicks? That he is some kind of charlatan? Little more than a snake oil salesman?" Luchia demanded.

Edith was tempted to say that she was. After all, what was the thrice-blessed radiated water if it was not a gimmick? "Of course Gio's not a snake oil salesman," she said, picking on the less contentious item. "Snake oil is fake medication. The bleach solution he promotes does exactly what he promises. It's all in the way he promotes it."

While she had been talking, Edith had been watching for her daughter. Rachel had been checking in with Grantville on the radio transceiver the Sanitation Commission had issued them before sending them out to *convert the savages*. She noticed movement from Rachel's caravan, and then her daughter was walking toward the fire.

"Grantville wants us to make our way to Padua as soon as possible to meet up with Dr. Gribbleflotz and his party," Rachel Lynch said as she settled down beside Edith.

"What's Gribbleflotz doing in Padua?" Edith asked.

"Visiting friends, and"—Rachel paused dramatically—"researching how to make iodized salt."

"Why is he researching how to make iodized salt?" Giovanna demanded. "We already know how to make iodized salt."

"We might know," Rachel said. "But Dr. Gribbleflotz doesn't, and apparently he has just been granted a license to supply the Republic of Venice with iodized salt."

Antonio, Giovanna's husband, cursed. Actually, it was more of a rant as he cut loose, calling into question most of Dr. Gribbleflotz's ancestry and personal habits.

Rachel waited until Antonio paused for breath. "Grantville have suggested that we might help set up and run a salt-iodizing facility near Venice. With financial support from Gribbleflotz."

Antonio's jaw moved up and down without anything coming out until Giovanna gently closed it. "Would we be working for Dr. Gribbleflotz?" she asked.

"Technically, yes. However, given that Dr. Gribbleflotz will no doubt return to Prague at some point, I expect you'll be left in charge of the company."

"Nice," Antonio muttered dreamily.

Chapter 12

Padua, the Republic of Venice

Doctor Thomas "Tom" Stone dropped the letter onto his desk and buried his head in his hands.

"What is the matter, Thomas?"

Tom looked up at his wife. Even with her concern for him, she had a glow about her. She was pregnant, again. However, this time the pregnancy had survived beyond the first trimester. He got to his feet and walked over to join her. He wrapped his arms around her, being careful of her little bump. "Gribbleflotz is coming to Padua."

"Is that so bad?"

Tom sighed into her hair. "He's going to insist on being taught the Science of the Chakras. I know it. And he's going to ask about George, and how to perform surgery like he does."

Magda rolled her head back so she could stare into Tom's eyes. "Herr Mundell is a surgeon?" She shook her head. "I didn't know that."

Tom moved his hands to Magda's shoulders and gently pushed her back a bit so he could look at her better. "That's because George isn't a surgeon."

Magda stared at him. "But you said Dr. Gribbleflotz is going to ask you to teach him how to perform surgery like Herr Mundell does."

Tom released Magda and slumped back into his chair. "George performed something called 'psychic surgery' on Dr. Gribbleflotz."

"So teach Dr. Gribbleflotz how to do this 'psychic surgery.'"

"If only." Tom shook his head. "The problem is, 'psychic surgery' isn't real surgery. It's fake surgery that uses sleight of hand to suggest that an operation has been performed."

"Fake surgery?" Magda stared at Tom. "You performed fake surgery on Dr. Gribbleflotz? Why would you do that?"

Tom's shoulders slumped. "It seemed like a good idea at the time." He picked up the letter and waved it at her. "Ed Piazza says that I need to confess everything to him."

Magda's arms tried to wrap around him. "Confessing everything will set you free."

"If only," Tom muttered to himself. In addition to telling Gribbleflotz that he had been played for a fool, he also had to get the fraud to agree to some form of damage limitation exercise. That was going to be so much fun—not.

Chapter 13

Padua, Republic of Venice

As the barge drew up to their last stop, Phillip looked around, trying to locate a familiar face. Of course, it had been more than twenty years since he was last in Padua. So no face was going to be particularly familiar. And then he saw it. A familiar face. It was younger looking than he would have expected. The man looked about his own age . . . and then it clicked. He had to be the son of his old friend Alberto Rovarini. "Carlo!" Phillip bellowed and waved. "Carlo Rovarini. Over here."

The man, in his forties, waved back and hurried over to where the barge was about to dock. "Filippo," Carlo called out. He reached out a hand and helped Phillip onto the dock and hugged him. "It has been too long."

Phillip made space so he could help his wife off the barge. "Dina, I'd like to introduce you to Carlo Rovarini."

"A pleasure to meet you," Dina said in her best Italian.

Carlo beamed as he took her hand and kissed it. He reached out to touch the child Dina was carrying. "And this is?" he asked in German.

There was a hint of relief from Dina as she too switched to German. "Salome." She cleared away the coverings to properly expose her face. "And that," Dina said, gesturing to the baby Ursula Mittelhausen was carrying, "is Jon. Short for Jonathan. He is named for one of our up-timer friends."

Carlo made clucking sounds over Jon, but he slept right

through them. He turned back to Phillip, an enormous grin on his face. "I can see why you chose to travel by barge."

Phillip could only nod. The two-day boat trip from Venice to Padua along the *Naviglio del Brenta* had been both peaceful and restful. Everything that the equivalent road trip would not have been. To call Jon and Salome bad travelers was to do them a gross disservice. They were actually good travelers—if the ride was smooth, and if they did not have to deal with changes in air pressure. "You should be thankful that you're unlikely to find yourself on an airplane with young children."

Carlo's eyes lit up. "You flew? In an airplane? What was it like?"

Phillip gestured to Sebastian Jones. "Ask him to show you some of his photographs."

Carlo cast an eye over Sebastian. "A photographer?"

Sebastian edged closer and held out his hand. "Sebastian Jones, photographer extraordinaire."

That description earned him a snort from Diana.

Sebastian looked at her. "Hey, I'm only quoting my agent."

That earned him another snort. "Typical overblown promotional hype."

"Well, yes," Sebastian admitted, "but it helps get me the commissions, which pays the bills." He waved off Diana and returned to Carlo. "I've been sent by Royal Dutch Airlines to take photographs of things tourists might be interested in seeing. You wouldn't happen to know of..."

Diana groaned. "Sebastian. Can't this wait until after we get settled in our accommodations?"

"Speaking of which, where will we be staying?" Phillip asked Carlo.

"With Mama, where else? Mama would be deeply offended if you were to stay anywhere else." He looked around. "Where has she got to now?" he muttered.

"Where has who got to?" Phillip asked.

"My daughter," Carlo muttered. "She is supposed to be... Ah! There she is." Carlo whistled. In the distance, a young woman waved a hand, but did not leave the young man she was talking to.

Carlo glared in the direction of his daughter. He then placed his little fingers in his mouth and let rip with a piercing whistle. This time the woman turned and glared at him.

"Come here and meet Filippo and his family," he shouted.

The young woman turned back to her companion and said a few words before stomping back toward Carlo.

"I was talking, Papa."

"To some unsuitable young man."

The girl grinned. "Naturally. The suitable ones aren't very interesting." The girl turned her attention to Phillip. "Hello. I am Marianna. I've been told I'm going to help look after the bambinos."

Phillip cast an eye over Carlo to see how he'd taken his daughter's comment about suitable young men. It was all he could do not to laugh. Instead, with a serious look on his face—the ability to create such a look had been cultivated over the years as he dealt with laborants, apprentices, and students in his laboratories—he gestured to the bundles Dina and Ursula were carrying.

"*Signora*. Please. *Signora*, you promised..."

"What did you promise this person?" Carlo demanded of Marianna as the man she had been talking to drew closer.

She sighed—heavily and extremely dramatically, as only a set-upon teenager can. "*Signore* Cristofori heard that we were meeting *Dottore* Gribbleflotz and asked that I introduce him." She turned to Phillip. "*Dottore* Gribbleflotz, this is *Signore* Cristofori of the local chapter of the Society of Aural Investigators."

"President of the local chapter," the young man corrected. He turned to Phillip. "I am Prospero Cesare Giulio Cristofori, and it is an honor to meet the person who discovered the science of Kirlian Image Interpretation." He cast an eye over the luggage still on the barge. "I don't suppose you brought a Gribbleflotz Magneto-Etheric Aural Aura Detector with you?" Prospero looked hopeful. "I've read about how the Prague Chapter has started using them."

Phillip started to reply, but Diana interrupted. "*Dottore* Gribbleflotz has with him the very latest in Gribbleflotz Magneto-Etheric Aural Aura Detectors. It comes with some new features. Now, not only can you hear the difference when you adjust a client's aura, you can also create a graphical representation as the sounds are transcribed onto a moving roll of paper."

"What are you doing?" Phillip whispered his demand right into Diana's ear.

Diana responded by gesturing toward Ursula Mittelhausen. She was looking extremely happy. "Maybe when *Dottore* Gribbleflotz is settled in, *Signora* Rovarini can get in touch and arrange a time for you to meet with the *dottore* and learn how the new and improved Gribbleflotz Magneto-Etheric Aural Aura Detector works."

Prospero smiled and nodded. Marianna smiled happily, and her father, Carlo, threw up his arms. The look he sent her was clearly of the "you can explain this to your mother" variety.

Prospero left his card with Marianna before departing, leaving Carlo to organize various members of his family to load Phillip's party's baggage onto a light wagon. And then, with Dina and Ursula sitting on the wagon holding a baby each, they set off for the Rovarini residence.

There were a lot of people gathered at the Rovarini compound when Phillip and his party arrived. Phillip turned from assessing the waiting crowd to Carlo. "Just family?"

Carlo answered with an enormous grin.

Marianna took it upon herself to verbalize an answer. "We're a big family."

Phillip conceded that point with a nod. And then his stomach rumbled. That made him pay a little more attention to the smells emanating from the compound. There was food. That was expected. However, there was the distinct aroma of meat being roasted. He sniffed loudly. "If that's a fatted calf..."

Carlo looked at him, all innocent appearing. "Would Mama do a thing like that?" There was a discernible lack of sincerity in the way he said it.

Phillip just looked at him. The answer was, of course Paola, Carlo's mother, would do such a thing. And speaking of the devil. Phillip broke away from Dina and ran forward as Paola Rovarini ran toward him.

"Filippo!" Paola cried as she wrapped her arms around him. There were tears in her eyes when she looked into Phillip's. She reached out and ran a hand through his hair. "There's a lot less of this," she noted.

Phillip hugged her before trying to gesture toward his family. Paola was not letting go, until she saw Dina and the babies.

"Your wife and children?" she asked as she broke away.

"Yes," he muttered into thin air as Paola hurried over to

Dina. He stood and watched as Dina received a proper Paola Rovarini welcome.

"Hello, Phillip."

Phillip spun around. He stared at the woman for a few seconds, until memory kicked in. "Francesca. You barely look a day older." He moved in for a hug.

As they broke apart, Phillip noticed Francesca's husband standing just behind him. In his arms was a bundle of books.

"The children need to be entertained while the adults get everything ready for the feast," Giacomo Sedazzari explained as he held out the stack of books.

Phillip looked at the books Giacomo was holding. He glanced back to see what Dina was doing. She was being well taken care of by the womenfolk. He passed his gaze over the gathering crowd of children and smiled. Some things did not change. "I need to send a letter to *Dottore* Stone at the university first," he said.

That statement was greeted by impatient groans from the children. Their disappointment at the delay brought a wince of guilt from Phillip.

"Of course." Giacomo snapped his fingers and a child ran off, to quickly return with a portable writing box.

With impatient eyes burning into his back, Phillip wrote a quick missive to Dr. Thomas Stone. He kept it short, and because there was no way of knowing who might look at the message, he kept the reason why he wanted to meet with Dr. Stone vague.

A cheer rang out when he exchanged the finished letter for the books Giacomo was still holding. "You have somewhere set up?" he asked. Giacomo gestured toward a barn. "And you have the essential supplies laid on?"

Giacomo grinned. "Of course, Filippo. We wouldn't want you to starve, or to lose your voice." He turned to the gathering children. "Filippo will read you stories while your parents get everything ready for the feast." He shoved Phillip's letter under his jacket and clapped his hands. "Off you go!"

There was a cheer from the children, and they gathered around Phillip and escorted him to the barn, where a suitable reader's station had been set up. There was a comfortable chair, with a blanket to wrap around him if he felt cold. There was a good lamp as a source of light, and most importantly, someone was just laying a tray with food and drink on the table set up beside the chair. It was just like old times. He picked up the first book and smiled. It was an old favorite from twenty years ago, when he first started reading to the children of the Rovarini clan to keep them out from underfoot while the adults got things ready for one of the many feasts on the Venetian calendar. He settled down in his chair, sampled some of the cake and sipped on his drink. The children fell into an expectant silence, and then Phillip started to read aloud to them.

Dr. Thomas Stone accepted the letter from the messenger and shut the door of his apartment. He glanced at the back, checking for a sender's address, but it was blank.

"Who was it?" his wife Magda called out.

"A messenger with a letter." He walked into the lounge gently slapping the letter against his hand.

"Who is it from?"

"No idea." Tom stopped by his writing desk and used his letter opener to cut the wafer that held the folded single sheet of paper closed. He opened it and froze. He barely managed to hold back the curse that wanted to escape as he read the short missive. "It's from that fraud Gribbleflotz." He looked up at Magda. "He's in Padua to visit friends and would like to drop around for a few words." Tom snorted. "We know what those few words are going to be about. He wants me to do seminars on the Science of the Chakras and George's surgical technique."

"But you said you had to confess to him that you had made a fool of him."

Tom winced. He had said that. And he did have to confess his various sins to Gribbleflotz. It was just that the necessity to do so stuck in his craw. "I know," he admitted. "That doesn't mean I have to like it." He sighed heavily and pulled his diary from a drawer. He needed to find a suitable time and place for this meeting with Gribbleflotz. He wanted few witnesses. Preferably none.

Next day, University of Padua

Phillip glanced at his watch. He was not lost—Padua hadn't changed that much in the twenty years he had been away. However, there had been sufficient changes that he had become distracted and now he had to hurry, or he would be late for his appointment with Dr. Stone.

He rounded a corner and there it was, the main gate into the University of Padua. Standing to one side, leaning against the wall, was Frau Cheng. She was whittling.

"Frau Cheng," Phillip called out by way of greeting. "Why the whittling?" he asked.

Diana wiped her knife clean before sheathing it and pushed off from the wall. "The wolves tend to keep their distance when a girl is holding a sharp knife in her hand."

Phillip grinned. The wolves in question were university students, and a shapely young woman such as Frau Cheng waiting outside the university gate would normally have been virtually irresistible. The presence of the knife in her hand—and it was a suitably impressive and no doubt very sharp knife—would have rendered her eminently resistible. "Where is Stephan?" He glanced at his watch again. "He said he would be here."

"He will be."

"We don't want to be late." He certainly did not want to be late. Such a thing would put him on the back foot when it came to the upcoming discussion with Dr. Stone. He wanted the high ground, which was why he glanced at his watch again.

"That's not going to make him turn up any sooner."

The squeak of rubber boots on cobbles had them both looking around. "There he is," Diana said.

Phillip studied Stephan as he approached. He was dressed in regulation Medical Department fatigues. An open standard-issue greatcoat showed glimpses of a holstered revolver and a belt pouch. Slung across his chest was a standard medic's satchel. "About time," he announced when Stephan joined them.

"Do you really need that?" Diana asked.

Stephan patted his medical bag. "It's better to have it and not need it than to need it and not have it."

"I was talking about the revolver and . . ." She swept open Stephan's coat so she could better count the speed-loader pouches attached to his webbing. "One, two . . ." She met his eyes. "*Three* speed loaders? Isn't that just a tad excessive?"

Stephan tapped the pouches fondly. "It's better to have it and not need it than to need it and not have it."

"A parrot," Diana muttered. "Is there anything else you're carrying just in case you might need it?"

Stephan nodded. "There's a compass in my belt buckle, some money sewn inside my belt, and I've got some survival gear in the heels of my boots."

"Survival gear in the heels of your boots?" Phillip stared at the footwear in question. The boots were up-time–style rubber-soled combat boots. The type that did not reach much beyond mid-calf, rather like the cowboy-style boots Phillip was wearing. Except, of course, being military issue, they were in a drab brown color and not the multicolored spectacle of his own boots.

"It's a guy thing, Dr. Gribbleflotz," Diana said.

"Hey, one day I might need it."

"Yeah. Yeah. I know," Diana muttered. "It's better to have it and not need it than to need it and not have it."

"Enough," Phillip said. "Are we all ready?"

"As ready as we'll ever be," Diana said.

"Then, let's go." Phillip led the way into the university and along the maze of corridors until they arrived at a door with Dr. Stone's name on it. Stephan slid in between Phillip and the door.

"Now, remember," Stephan said. "We want a quiet and reasoned discussion. No yelling. No swearing, and no violence."

Phillip gave Stephan the glare his reminder deserved. "Yes. Yes. Now, do you mind?"

Stephan stepped aside so Phillip could knock on the door.

Chapter 14

University of Padua

Phillip composed himself as he awaited a response to his knock on the door. He took a deep breath and slowly released it, repeating to himself as he did so, "Keep calm. Keep calm."

The door was opened by Dr. Stone himself. Phillip ran his tongue over suddenly dry lips as he tried to verbalize a greeting suitable to the occasion.

"Gribbleflotz," Tom Stone muttered. He cast a look over Diana and Stephan before stepping back from the door. "You'd better come in."

The less than welcoming reception set Phillip's back up. He forgot all about being conciliating and cut loose with the one question that had been bothering him since that day in Prague. "Why?" he demanded. "Why did you do it?"

"Do what?" Tom asked.

Phillip did not launch himself at Tom, but he did step forward aggressively. At least he tried to. Something latched onto his shoulder before he could take more than a half step toward Dr. Stone. He tried to brush whatever was restraining him off and discovered a hand. He glanced over his shoulder and saw that the hand belonged to Stephan. They exchanged looks. Phillip absorbed the message Stephan's eyes were sending and turned back to face Tom. "You know," he said. "Why did you make me believe that the king's aura really was blue?"

"Well, that was unexpected," Diana said.

Phillip turned to Diana. "What do you mean?"

"Well, I was sort of expecting you to lead with a question about painting the king's scrotum blue, or maybe ask about Guptah Rai Singh and his surgery." Diana shrugged. "Maybe even ask about his brand-new Science of the Chakras, which seems to bear no resemblance to the up-time Chakras."

"That's nothing." Phillip pointed at Tom. "He made me believe there was some truth in Kirlian Aura Interpretation."

"Hang on," Tom protested. "You're the king of Bohemia's personal aura investigator."

Phillip looked at Tom. "So?"

"So, doesn't that mean you believe in that aura rubbish?"

"Aura rubbish?" Phillip's eyebrows climbed. "That's strange coming from a master of the Science of the Chakras."

Tom blushed. "Yeah, well, about that..."

"It too is 'that aura rubbish,'" Phillip suggested. "Yet you used your Science of the Chakras to say that I was correct when I said the king's aura was blue?"

"But I had to do that," Tom protested.

"Why?" Diana asked.

Phillip nodded. "That's a very good question. Just why did you have to say that the king's aura was blue?"

"Because I needed an in." Tom sighed. "I was sent to Prague to perform a medical examination of Wallenstein..."

"Venceslas V Adalbertus, king of Bohemia," Phillip corrected.

Tom stared at him for a few seconds before shaking his head. "Mike and Ed called him Wallenstein."

"That's the title he had before he became king of Bohemia," Phillip said.

"Okay. Okay. I was sent to Prague to perform a medical examination on the king of Bohemia and I needed an in, because he doesn't trust physicians."

"Why didn't you ask for my help?" Phillip asked. "I was there. I already have an in with the king. I could easily have performed any medical examination required."

"But you're an alchemist!" The last word was almost strangled as it escaped Tom's lips.

"So?"

"Alchemists are charlatans who believe in the philosopher's stone and that they can use it to turn lead into gold."

"Not all of us," Phillip said.

Tom glared at him.

"Dr. Stone," Stephan said from the sidelines. "If they had been attending the king, would you have been happy to ask, say, Robert Boyle or Sir Isaac Newton for help?"

Tom stared hard at Stephan. After a few seconds he gave a tentative nod.

"Why?" Stephan asked. "What is it about those two men that makes them better choices than Dr. Gribbleflotz?"

"They were great men of science," Tom said.

Stephan smiled. "They were also both alchemists. Both searched for the secret of the philosopher's stone, and both were interested in turning base metal into gold."

"What?" Tom stared at Stephan. "Where did you hear this?"

"Chemistry class at the technical college in Grantville," Stephan said. "Frau Penzey told us that both Robert Boyle and Sir Isaac Newton were alchemists, and she produced a copy of an old journal article to support her claim."

Tom stared at Stephan. "Seriously? Are you saying Robert Boyle, the father of modern chemistry, pursued transmutation of lead into gold?"

Stephan nodded. "He was so confident of success that he even petitioned the British parliament and succeeded in getting a law against making gold through alchemy repealed."

"Alchemy is a respectable science," Phillip said into the silence that followed Stephan's statement.

Tom snorted. "Respectable? To be that, it needs to be replicable."

"If you follow the directions, most experiments can be replicated."

Tom stared at Phillip for a moment before gesturing for him to follow and stalked off. Phillip glanced first at Stephan and then Diana. Both shrugged and indicated that they should follow, so follow they did. Tom stopped at a bookcase and after a brief search, pulled out a large volume.

"Ah," Phillip said when he saw the title. "Valentine's *The Triumphal Chariot of Antimony.*"

"You're familiar with the book?" Tom asked.

"Of course," Phillip said. "It is probably Basil Valentine's most famous work."

"Famous? You mean infamous. It's a load of rubbish. You

can't make a safe medicine from antimony. Heck, you can't even make his 'sulfur of antimony.' Not from his directions."

"Yes, you can," Phillip protested.

"You can't," Tom said. "I've tried and failed. Heck, I can't even make his glass of antimony."

"You can't?" Phillip stared in disbelief at Tom. "But you're the Great Stoner. The best chemist to come from the future. All you have to do is follow the recipe as written. Any marginally competent alchemist should be able to make sulfur of antimony."

"You think you can succeed where I've failed?" Tom challenged.

"I've already done it."

Tom snorted in disbelief. "You've made Valentine's sulfur of antimony? Impossible. Prove it. I dare you to try and make it right now."

"It takes two to three hours to roast the stibnite," Phillip warned.

"Backing out already?"

Phillip glared at Tom. "If you have the correct ingredients, I will be happy to demonstrate to you how a real alchemist can follow a simple recipe. I was just worried about my companions."

"I don't have anywhere I'd rather be," Diana said.

"Me neither," Stephan said.

"Very well." Phillip turned to Tom. "Do you have a suitably equipped laboratory?"

"I can get access to one." Tom moved toward the door. "Don't go away. I'll be right back."

When the door closed behind Dr. Stone, Diana edged closer to check the book Phillip was holding. "May I?" she asked.

Phillip passed the book to her.

Dr. Stone led them to a typical alchemist's laboratory. The room was larger than most such places, but that was because it was used for teaching iatrochemistry. It had all the usual amenities, just with a lot more room so students could stand and watch. Phillip smiled as he checked the equipment. It was like coming home. There was a row of jars on a shelf. He quickly donned the clean white lab coat Dr. Stone gave him and, with Diana reading off the materials list, he collected what he needed from what was available. When he came to the antimony, he stopped and frowned. "Is this Hungarian antimony?"

Tom edged close enough to read the label. "It says that it's antimony."

"I know it says that it is antimony, but Valentine clearly states that he used Hungarian antimony. Diana, show him."

Diana held the Valentine text out, so Tom could see it. She left a finger pointing to the sentence in question.

"And you need this Hungarian antimony to make sulfur of antimony?"

Phillip raised his brows at Tom. "I need Hungarian antimony because that is what Basil Valentine says to use. One cannot expect to replicate his results if one does not replicate his method."

Tom glared at him.

Phillip smiled as a thought struck him. "Could it be that you didn't use Hungarian antimony when you tried to make Valentine's sulfur of antimony?"

Tom turned up the intensity of his glare for a moment before turning to one of the assistants working in the laboratory. "Roberto. Do we have any *Hungarian antimony*?"

"A moment," Roberto called out before running off. He returned in less than a minute. "What are you making?" he asked as he handed over a jar clearly marked "Hungarian antimony."

Tom gestured to Phillip. "*Dottore* Gribbleflotz here claims he can make Basil Valentine's sulfur of antimony."

"You are?" Roberto asked. "You can?" he asked excitedly.

"Yes."

Roberto licked his lips, nodded, and ran off.

Diana, who had come up beside Phillip, gestured at Roberto's disappearing form. "What's with him?"

"No idea," Phillip said. He carried the Hungarian antimony over to a workbench and poured some into a mortar and, with a stone pestle, started to grind it to a fine powder.

Diana laid down the book and reached for the pestle. "Here, let me do that while you do something else."

"Put on a lab coat first," Phillip said. Once she did that and took over crushing the antimony ore, he set to preparing a crucible for the roasting of the crushed stibnite.

Phillip was gently stirring the slowly roasting ground stibnite when he noticed some students entering the laboratory. He watched them for a few seconds before returning to his task.

A few minutes later, someone nudged him. He glanced up to find Diana standing right beside him.

"How much longer do you have to keep stirring it?" she asked.

Phillip stared at the ground stibnite. There was no sign yet of the light gray color that would indicate the calcination was nearing completion. "A while," he said.

"Then let me stir while you do something to entertain everyone."

"Everyone?" The word was barely out of his mouth before he took in what Diana meant. The few students had grown into quite a crowd. "How should I entertain them?" he whispered to Diana.

"You could describe what you are doing."

Phillip released a gentle snort. "We have to roast the stibnite for at least another two hours before we can move onto the next step."

Diana stuck the tip of her tongue out as she thought. "What about some of your seminar demonstrations?" she suggested.

That appealed to Phillip. He passed the stirrer over to Diana and told her what to look out for. He then gestured to Roberto. He gave the man some brief instructions before he turned to address his audience.

"As I'm sure you all know," he said to the crowd that had gathered, even if he was not sure that they did know. It never hurt to flatter an audience. "Calcination of the ground antimony ore can take a while." He smiled at the few nodding heads. He had been right. Not everyone here knew just how long it could take. "So, while my assistant continues to stir the ground stibnite, she has suggested that I might entertain you with a few of my favorite laboratory demonstrations."

"How long will it be before you can start the next step in the formation of sulfur of antimony?" someone asked.

Phillip checked his watch. "Two hours should do it."

There were a few groans, but more noticeable, at least to Phillip, was the sudden interest in his watch. He proceeded to show off his FrankenWatch—an up-time digital watch fitted into a pocket-watch-size container complete with a down-time-sourced battery. That took fifteen minutes, which was long enough for Roberto to return with the materials he had requested.

"My first demonstration will be something I call the 'Gribbleflotz Candles of the Essence of Light.'" He gestured for the laboratory assistants to wheel in a large tub of sand. They set that up near the furnace chimney. They then provided Phillip with jars of powdered iron oxide and powdered aluminum, a large bucket of water, a metal tripod, a pipe-clay triangle, and a selection of other chemicals and tools Phillip had requested.

He set the bucket on the tub of sand and poured some of the sand into the bucket—enough to give a layer of an inch or two at the bottom. He then set the tripod above the bucket and placed the pipe-clay triangle on top. With the apparatus in place, Phillip described what he was doing as he carefully measured off a small amount of both powdered metals and thoroughly mixed them by repeatedly pouring the mixture to and fro between two pieces of paper.

He poured the resulting mixture into a filter paper folded into a cone and placed the cone into the pipe-clay triangle. He was now ready to initiate the experiment. However, Phillip wasn't stupid. He wanted to be a safe distance off when the reaction started, so he made a small pile of permanganate on top of the thermite and added a few drops of glycerin. He then stepped well back.

There were murmurs of dissatisfaction starting amongst the crowd when the reaction did not begin immediately. He waved to his audience to tell them to have patience. And then the permanganate ignited. That raised excited cries from the audience.

And then the thermite ignited. The levels of excitement hit a new high for the duration of the burn.

Phillip used a magnet to recover the lump of iron from the bucket. He held it up, and then he handed it over to the audience to admire and pass around. As expected, there were cries demanding a repeat. He checked his watch against the progress the stibnite was making and set up for a repeat.

After a second repeat of the "Gribbleflotz Candles of the Essence of Light," Phillip suggested that they should move on to another demonstration.

"This one, my laborants call 'the Alchemist's Fly Trap.'" He smiled as he said that. "What I will be making is called nitrogen triiodide. If you've purchased one of the Gribbleflotz Intermediate Alchemist chemistry sets, then you might have already tried this."

Phillip called on Stephan, who had been quietly standing to one side, to help set up the demonstration. While Phillip prepared the triiodide, Stephan set up a retort stand with four large diameter retort rings set equidistantly apart.

Phillip smeared moist triiodide onto four filter papers and placed one on each retort ring. He then turned to his audience.

"Nitrogen triiodide is what is known as a contact explosive. That means it is extremely sensitive. Much more sensitive than even fulminate of copper. It's just not quite as dangerous." Phillip smiled as he said that. Even triiodide was dangerous if you had enough of it, and enough started at under a gram.

"Now, you might be wondering why we call it the Alchemist's Fly Trap." Phillip cast his eyes over his audience just in case someone wanted to ask a question or suggest why they thought it might have that name. No one seemed willing to say anything. He sighed in disappointment. Phillip liked it when his audience asked questions. It proved that they were listening. Still, he needed to continue. He picked up a long stick that Stephan had tied a feather to.

"Unfortunately, there seem to be no flies willing to assist my demonstration." He held up the stick. "If I could have a volunteer? You just have to pretend that the feather is a fly and land it gently on the compound I smeared on the bottom paper."

Eventually, a less than willing volunteer was pushed in front of Phillip. He handed over the stick and gestured for the young man to proceed.

The man, identified as Alfredo, tentatively advanced on the retort stand. With his arm outstretched, he waved the feather at the triiodide on the bottom retort ring. And then the feather touched the triiodide. There was not so much a flash as an instant cloud of purple smoke with filter papers sent flying.

The reaction received the round of applause Phillip expected. He recovered the stick with the feather and invited the audience to applaud Alfredo before letting him escape back to the anonymity of the crowd.

"Can you make RDX?" a member of the audience called out.

Phillip winced. "Yes. I can make RDX. However, while it is considered one of the safer high explosives"—he put air quotes around *safer*—"that presents a few problems. Whereas you can set nitroglycerin-based dynamite off with a blow from a hammer, you need a detonator containing a primary explosive to set off RDX. And the current primary explosive of choice for detonators is fulminate of mercury. I can make fulminate of mercury, but it is a far from safe compound to make. In fact, in Grantville, people have died making it."

Phillip glanced toward Diana, hoping that the calcination was finished. She shook her head. Phillip sighed as he considered how to hold the attention of his audience. And then he had an idea. "Although I don't intend to prepare any fulminate of mercury, or RDX for that matter, I can give a very simple demonstration of the explosive tendencies of finely ground flour." He saw a few interested looks directed his way.

"I first started investigating what the Americans call a 'dust bomb' after reading about the battle of Wimpfen where, on the sixth of May 1622, a lucky hit from a cannonball is supposed to have caused the Protestant forces' magazine to explode, resulting in their defeat at the hands of the Catholic League." Phillip started pacing as he spoke. "Now, my experience of gunpowder is that hitting it with a hammer won't set it off. You need a proper source of ignition. A spark, or a naked flame. Both of which are lacking in a typical cannonball."

Phillip's pacing had taken him up to a candle mounted in a tall candlestick. He held that up so everyone could see before carrying it back to the open space in front of the furnace where Diana was still dutifully stirring the ground Hungarian antimony. He stood the candlestick on the floor and used his GribbleZippo lighter to light the candle. He used the device surreptitiously, keeping it hidden in his hands to avoid having to interrupt his narrative to explain how the piezoelectric lighter worked. He was totally unaware that, to the audience, it appeared that he lit the candle with his bare hand.

Phillip stood back to assess the lit candle. It was of a good size, with a good flame. "Now, all we need is some fuel." A laboratory was not a place you would normally find flour, but he knew of an alternative that most apothecaries kept for pill-making. He quickly located a jar of starch. "Yes," he announced to his audience. "I know it isn't flour. But this will do just as well. And best of all, we have it to hand." He smiled as he said it, and then he spooned a small amount onto a sheet of parchment, which he rolled into a rough tube, and carefully approached the burning candle.

"Would everyone please take a couple of steps back from the candle." They moved a little. "A little more, please," Phillip said. "This demonstration can become a little too exciting if I misjudge anything." That elicited a couple of steps back from nearly everyone. Phillip gave the holdouts the evil eye. That did not get them to move. He shrugged. He had done his duty. They could not claim he had not warned them.

He crouched down, so that his head was just higher than the flame of the candle. "Is everyone ready?" he asked. Phillip did not actually wait for anyone to answer; he just blew through the tube of parchment, launching the powdery starch into the air. The cloud of starch particles filled the air, until the first bits arrived at the flame.

Whoomph!

It was not an explosion, more of a rapid displacement of air. However, it was certainly impressive as the cloud of starch dust flashed. And it had those who had not moved far enough away jumping with fright.

"And that," Phillip said, "is how I think a cannonball hitting a barrel of gunpowder resulted in the magazine exploding. It wasn't the impact that set it off. No. In my opinion, the cannonball destroyed a barrel of gunpowder creating a cloud of gunpowder dust. Once that happened, it just needed a source of ignition anywhere on the battlefield to set the cloud off, which would have caused any exposed gunpowder to ignite." Phillip waved his hands. "*Boom.* The magazine explodes."

"*Dottore* Gribbleflotz," Diana called out. "I think it's ready."

"Perfect timing," Phillip announced as he hurried over to the furnace where Diana was stirring the ground Hungarian antimony. He took possession of the iron stirrer she had been using and checked the melt. A smile grew on his face. "Perfect," he announced.

Phillip poured the molten material onto a firebrick. "And there we have it, exactly as Basil Valentine described: glass of antimony."

Tom Stone, who had been quiet throughout Phillip's demonstrations, was the first to arrive at the bench. He probed the transparent yellow glass-like substance. "How did you do that?" he demanded of Phillip. "I've tried at least a dozen times without success."

Around him, others nodded and muttered their similar lack of success.

"Did you use Hungarian antimony?" Phillip asked.

"What difference does that make?" Tom demanded. "Antimony's antimony."

"Yes," Phillip agreed. "But we aren't working with pure antimony, we are working with the ore—stibnite. And not all ores are created equal." He reached for the container of Hungarian antimony—which was really stibnite from Hungary—with one hand while pulling a folding jeweler's glass from a pocket with the other. He flicked the lens out of its protective brass cover and offered both to Tom.

Tom tipped a small sample of antimony onto a clean filter paper and used the lens to examine it. A few seconds later he looked up. "There's some kind of clear crystal mixed with it."

Phillip nodded. "Quartz. Or at least, I have found that I get the same result mixing a pinch or two of ground quartz to any sample of stibnite." He turned to his audience. "If anyone happens to have some stibnite from a failed attempt to make glass of antimony, we can melt it and see what happens if we add some ground quartz to it."

"You're saying that the Hungarian antimony is contaminated with quartz, and that it is that which gives the glass of antimony?"

Phillip tried not to appear too smug as he nodded. "The results I have obtained support that hypothesis. But don't take my word for it. All we need is some stibnite from a failed attempt to make glass of antimony and a little ground quartz."

"Why a failed attempt?" Tom demanded.

Phillip looked at Tom. "Would you rather spend the next two or more hours roasting a fresh sample of stibnite?"

"I have some," a man called.

"Me too," said another.

In all, three men departed from the laboratory. While they waited for them to return, the rest of Phillip's audience poked around at his sample of Valentine's glass of antimony.

"All we have to do is melt our samples and add some crushed quartz?" one of the men who had dashed off to get a sample from a failed trial asked as he and the others returned with sample jars in hand.

Phillip nodded. "A pinch or so of quartz should suffice."

The men stared at Phillip for a few moments. Then they stared at each other. And finally, they moved over to the furnace and got to work melting their samples. It was not long before they were pouring out their results.

"It looks like it might be Basil Valentine's glass of antimony," one of the alchemists said.

"It is glass of antimony," Phillip said. "Now, if you would like to move onto the next step?" He gestured for Diana to join the three volunteers. "We need to grind the glass to a fine powder and add vinegar.

"It should produce a red solution."

As each man added vinegar to their ground glass of antimony, the expected red solution failed to eventuate. There were mutterings of discontent. Phillip gestured for Diana to take her turn. The addition of vinegar to her ground glass of antimony resulted in the red solution he had expected.

Phillip stared at the red solution. Then he looked at the three solutions that should have been red. Something had gone wrong. He walked over to the book Diana had brought to the laboratory and checked the recipe. It took a couple of readings, but eventually he found a clue. He turned to his three volunteers. "What did you use to stir your antimony with during calcination?" he asked.

Each man held up the glass rod they had used to stir the molten antimony in front of them.

Phillip smiled. He was now pretty sure he knew what had gone wrong. He collected the container of powdered iron oxide from his thermite demonstration and added a pinch to each of their dissolved glass of antimony. The solutions immediately started to show red. With a little stirring, each sample became red, just like the sample in front of Diana.

"What the heck!" Tom Stone protested. "What did you do?" he demanded of Phillip.

"I added a little iron to the mix."

Tom looked from Phillip to the red solutions and back. "And why would you do that?" he demanded.

"It is really quite simple, *Dottore* Stone." Phillip paused for a moment, wondering if that might have sounded a little too patronizing. He checked his audience. No one seemed worried, so maybe it had not sounded patronizing to them. "In accordance with the procedure laid down by *Signore* Valentine, I had *Signora* Cheng stir the roasting antimony with an iron hook. Meanwhile, these three gentlemen used a glass rod with which to stir their mixes." Phillip shrugged. "*Quod erat demonstrandum*. The reaction needs iron."

"But you didn't add iron to your sample," Tom protested. "All you did was stir the mix with an iron tool."

Phillip stared at Dr. Stone. How could he not realize? He

shook his head at the thought. "*Dottore* Stone, are you not aware of how aggressively stibnite corrodes iron? The simple act of stirring the stibnite with an iron stirrer as it roasts is enough to enrich the mix with iron."

"So it's all just another case of alchemists faking the results," Tom said.

"I protest the use of the word *fake*," Phillip said. "I believe Basil Valentine was a proper scientist."

"Proper scientist?" Tom laughed.

Phillip waited for Dr. Stone to stop laughing before continuing. "Would you agree that the mark of true science is replicability?"

"Yes."

"And do you agree that we are well on the way to duplicating Basil Valentine's production of sulfur of antimony?"

"But it's not real," Tom protested a little defensively. "He got everything wrong."

Phillip grinned. "The interpretation of what occurred may be faulty," he said. "However, you have to agree, the methodology allows replication of his results." That earned him a glare from Dr. Stone.

"Which, I believe," Phillip said, "makes Basil Valentine a true scientist. Which in turn, implies that alchemy has a claim to be a true science."

"*Dottore* Gribbleflotz," one of the three alchemists called out. "Could we go onto the next step, please."

"Of course," Phillip said. He referred to the book for the next instruction. "Please evaporate the vinegar solution."

Phillip walked the line checking on Diana's progress and that of the three alchemists. "Now, dissolve the gummy residue with *spirits of wine* and decant it off."

He smiled as he examined the residues left in the retorts. He pointed to Diana's retort with its solid residue. "This retort contains the poison." He gestured to the retort containing the decanted solution. "And that contains the sulfur of antimony."

There was a resounding round of applause, with a lot of foot-stomping. Phillip took the accolade as his due and returned it with a bow. "Now, is there anything else people would care to have me demonstrate?"

A hand shot up. "*Dottore* Gribbleflotz. Are you familiar with Valentine's third key?"

Phillip smiled. "Are you trying to make Valentine's red dragon's blood?"

"There is no such thing as dragons," Dr. Stone plaintively cried out. "They don't exist."

"It is a purely allegorical dragon, *Dottore* Stone," Phillip replied. He turned his attention back to the speaker. "Would you like me to demonstrate the procedure?"

His answer came in a sea of nodding heads.

"I'll need a sample of gold," he warned. Gold was, naturally, an expensive experimental material and wherever possible he preferred that someone else pay for his demonstrations. "And I'll also need to make some aqua fortis and *acidum salis*."

"We have aqua regia already made up," Roberto, the laboratory assistant, said.

"That is all very nice, but I require acids of uncommonly high purity."

"We have some high-purity aqua fortis and *acidum salis* from the laboratory of Leonardo da Vinci. Would they be suitable?"

Phillip's eyes lit up at the name. "Are you talking about Leonardo di ser Martino da Vinci?"

Roberto nodded.

"Then his acids will do." Phillip smiled as he said it. Leonardo had let Phillip use his laboratory in return for making him high-quality acids back when he was first in Padua—twenty years ago—and he'd taught the old alchemist to make acids almost as good as his own.

While Roberto collected the required acids, Phillip collected the retorts and beakers he was going to need. When Roberto returned, Phillip measured off the required amount of each acid and poured them into the distillation retort. And then he held out his hand. "The gold."

Roberto gave him a couple of beads of gold which Phillip dropped into the retort. Bubbles started to form on the gold and the combination of acids, known as aqua regia, started to turn yellow. To speed up the reaction, Phillip placed the retort over a flame on the furnace. The reaction intensified, and the color tended toward orange as the gold dissolved. Before too long, Phillip was able to hold up the retort to show the gold was fully dissolved. He then returned it to the furnace and started to distill off the acid.

At the end of the distillation, Phillip had a beaker of aqua regia and was left with elemental gold in the retort. He poured the aqua regia back into the retort and dissolved the gold again. He then distilled it once more.

Phillip was into his third repeat of the process when Tom Stone, who had obviously had enough, chose to speak out. "This is madness," he said. "I don't know what you are trying to do, *Dottore* Gribbleflotz, but there is no way you are going to get a different result by constantly repeating the same process."

"I am performing a *cohobation*," Phillip explained to nods of agreement and understanding from the various alchemists gathered around to watch the process. "Eventually the residue will turn into Basil Valentine's red dragon's blood."

Tom Stone snorted. He looked at the apparatus and shook his head. "Impossible," he announced.

"I've got ten ducats that says *Dottore* Gribbleflotz can make Valentine's red dragon's blood," Diana Cheng called out. She tipped coins from a drawstring purse onto her left hand to show just how serious she was. She was immediately "pounced" on by people willing to take her money.

"He'll lose you your money," Tom said.

In the middle of recording bets in a notebook, Diana looked up. "I have utmost faith in *Dottore* Gribbleflotz. If he says he can make it, I believe him." Her attention was taken by yet another individual trying to take her up on her wager.

Tom turned to Phillip. "It's insanity," he said.

"Insanity is doing the same thing over and over again and expecting different results." Phillip smiled. "I believe the quote is attributed to the great up-time scientist, Albert Einstein.

"However," he said as he started yet another cycle of pouring the aqua regia back into the retort and dissolving the gold again, "maybe Basil Valentine knew something *Signore* Einstein didn't, because his instructions are to continue the cohobation until we get his red dragon's blood."

Tom humphed and retreated to a distant corner, well away from everyone.

Phillip watched Dr. Stone walk away. It was as if the man wanted nothing to do with the demonstration. That thought brought a smile to Phillip's face. It would be interesting to see how Dr. Stone reacted when the red dragon's blood formed.

He wandered over to Diana and glanced at the open page of her notebook where she was recording her wagers. He whistled silently. There were several bets for ten ducats. "I thought you were only waging ten ducats."

"Stephan offered to come in with me, and people think our credit is good."

"Can you cover all those bets?" he asked.

"If you fail, we might have to borrow from Frau Mittelhausen, but we won't need to," she said. "Will we?"

"It doesn't always work," Phillip warned.

"For other people," Diana said. "But you are Dr. Gribbleflotz, the world's greatest alchemist."

He stood straighter in the face of her confidence. However, he had to be realistic. "Even I have had my failures."

Diana looked at the numbers in her notebook and licked her lips. "But not once you have learned the correct procedure?" she suggested.

"Not usually."

"Well, stop trying to scare me and get on with making the red dragon's blood." She paused and stared into the distance for a few seconds. "Is that blood from a red dragon, or red blood from a dragon?"

"Get off with you," Phillip said with a smile. The moment Diana stepped clear, he turned his attention back to his retort.

Three cycles later, loud cheers filled the laboratory as the residue from the latest distillation formed as blood-red crystals.

Phillip looked around for Dr. Stone. Their eyes met. Phillip could see the disbelief in Dr. Stone's eyes. He had a choice. He could behave in a modest manner or . . . He blew on his fingernails and burnished them on his white lab coat. Sometimes one just had to admit how good one really was.

Chapter 15

Padua

They filed along the corridor toward Dr. Stone's office. Stephan was a quiet but happy shadow bringing up the rear of the group. Diana had a brilliant smile on her face. No doubt due to all the money she had just won wagering on Dr. Gribbleflotz's skills. Phillip was happy because he had just demonstrated his not inconsiderable skills to the top alchemists at the University of Padua. Not the least of whom was Dr. Thomas Stone. Dr. Stone was the odd one out in the group. He was noticeably unhappy.

"I'll work it out," Tom announced to the world as he stomped along the corridor.

"Work what out?" Diana asked.

Tom pointed to Phillip. "Whatever it was he did."

"But you saw what Dr. Gribbleflotz did. He cohobated the gold and aqua regia until the residue turned red."

"Which is impossible."

"But he did it," Diana said. "That means it wasn't really impossible."

That earned Diana a glare.

She shrugged. "If something can be achieved, then it can't be impossible."

"Once you eliminate the impossible, whatever remains, no matter how improbable, must be the truth," Phillip said, tongue firmly in cheek.

"First you quoted Einstein, now Sherlock Holmes. You're quite the well-read smarty-pants," Tom muttered.

"You're too kind."

"Do you have any idea why it worked, Dr. Gribbleflotz?" Stephan asked.

Phillip shrugged. "Not really. However, if we consider the importance of contaminants in Herr Valentine's other experiments, I wouldn't be surprised if there was something in the retort that changed the direction of the reaction."

"There can't have been a contaminant in the retort," Tom said. "Otherwise it would have affected the reaction the first time you did it.

"Don't worry," an obviously frustrated Tom muttered. "I'll work it out."

"Before you try working out how Dr. Gribbleflotz made Basil Valentine's red dragon's blood, Dr. Stone," Stephan said, "maybe you could start thinking about how to explain away the Science of the Chakras and psychic surgery."

Tom glared at Stephan. "Let's wait until we're in my office before we talk about that."

Tom held the door to his office as his guests filed in. He followed, closing and locking the door behind him. He waved around the room. "Find yourselves somewhere to sit," he said before seeking the sanctuary of his own chair, safely behind his large flat desk.

As he settled into his leather-covered chair, Tom stared at Phillip. After nearly a minute of doing that, he took in a deep breath and let it out in an audible sigh. "Okay, I'm sorry. I should have asked you for help back in Prague."

"There. That wasn't so hard, was it?" Diana said.

"There's no need to pile fuel on the fire, Frau Cheng," Stephan said.

"Thanks!" Tom muttered in Stephan's direction.

Stephan gave a small nod of his head. And then he smiled. "Of course, there is still the small matter of explaining what happened that day in Prague."

"I made a mistake," Tom said a little forcibly. "How many times do I have to say it? I'm sorry."

"Ahh! Herr Dr. Stone. You misunderstand me," Stephan said. "When I talk about explaining what happened, I don't mean explaining to Dr. Gribbleflotz. I mean explaining to everyone who has heard about what happened in Prague and wants to learn how to do it."

Tom stared at Stephan. "What're you talking about?"

"The psychic surgery," Stephan said.

"Yeah," Diana said. "How do we explain away the 'surgery' Herr Mundell performed on Dr. Gribbleflotz?"

Tom winced. "This is making my head hurt. Is there any possibility of having this conversation in English?"

Diana shrugged. "I don't have a problem with that. Dr. Gribbleflotz?"

"My English should be good enough, but what about Corporal Böhm?"

"My listening is better than my speaking," Stephan said. "However, I do think it would be a good idea to hold this conversation in a language anybody overhearing it might have difficulty understanding."

"That's a good point, Stephan." Diana smiled. "If you run into difficulties, just let me know, and I'll translate for you."

"Thank you," Tom said in English. He turned to Phillip. "I'm sorry about the psychic surgery."

"Why did you do it?" Phillip asked. "I have the Prague Guild of Surgeons demanding that I get either you or Mr. Mundell to teach them how to perform scarless surgery with their bare hands and no anesthetic, just like you did."

Tom seemed to shrink in his chair as he answered. "You'd been with the king for a while, and we were scared that you might have been promoting your Kirlian stuff over the Science of the Chakras, which would have cost us our 'in.'"

Phillip gently shook his head. "I was demonstrating the wonders of my latest discovery, the GribbleChrome."

"What's a GribbleChrome?" Stephan asked.

"It's a way of making a color photograph," Phillip said. He turned back to Tom. "The king was most impressed and was just asking about having one made of his family when you and Mr. Mundell burst in."

"We didn't know that," Tom said defensively. "Anyway, that's why we launched straight into the actions that resulted in George performing some psychic surgery."

Phillip, Diana, and Stephan stared at him.

"It seemed like a good idea at the time," Tom protested.

"Well, it wasn't," Diana said. "And now we have to come up with a plausible explanation for what happened before every accomplished sleight-of-hand merchant gets on the bandwagon."

"Come on," Tom protested. "You're exaggerating the problem."

"I hope you're right," Diana said, "because, if you're wrong..."

The group fell silent.

"Botfly," Stephan said suddenly.

"What?" Phillip demanded.

"The thing Mr. Mundell expelled from Dr. Gribbleflotz's body could have been something like a botfly larva," Stephan said.

"Do they have botflies in Prague?" Diana asked.

"No, but Dr. Gribbleflotz could have been examining a specimen someone obtained for him."

Diana glanced at Phillip. "That might work," she suggested.

"What's a botfly?" Phillip asked.

"It's a native of Central and South America," Stephan said. "Their larvae are transmitted to their hosts by mosquitos. They burrow under the skin and feed on the flesh of their host. They breathe through an airhole in the host's skin. We can claim Mr. Mundell squeezed the larva out through the breathing hole, and that is why Dr. Gribbleflotz doesn't have a scar from the 'surgery.'"

Diana clapped her hands. "That's perfect."

"Except for the blood," Phillip said. "I'm sure there was blood. A lot of blood." He looked toward Dr. Stone. "Wasn't there blood?"

Tom nodded.

Diana shrugged. "So the larva ruptured as it was expelled," she said.

"Larvae don't have red blood," Tom said.

Diana glared at him. "You're not helping."

"But it's true," Tom protested. "They have an almost colorless interstitial fluid called hemolymph. The oxygen carrier is hemocyanin instead of hemoglobin."

Phillip's eyes lit up. "You know about insect larvae?" he asked. "What about maggots?"

"Well..." Tom managed to say before Phillip continued.

"Do you know what is in the liquid maggots excrete?" Phillip asked. "I've hypothesized that maggots excrete a liquid that contains an antibacterial agent that protects them from the filth in which they live.

"I've experimented with it in the past and discovered that if

I coat wounds that I've manually debrided with maggot extract, that they heal much faster and with significantly lower rates of secondary infection than if I don't."

"Maggot extract?" Tom asked.

Phillip nodded. "You can get it by washing maggots, or by siphoning it off from a maggot-infested wound."

Tom rubbed his head. "I'm not sure..." He glanced toward a bookcase. "Maybe..." He walked over to the bookcase. Phillip followed.

Diana's eyes met Stephan's. Both smiled. She gestured toward the door and he nodded. They both slipped out quietly.

"Well, that was a bit of a turnup for the books," Stephan said as he and Diana walked away from Dr. Stone's rooms.

Diana nodded. "But it does bode well for getting agreement over the cover story."

Stephan nodded in turn. "Though... I have been wondering... Why did Dr. Stone paint King Venceslas' testicles blue?"

"He probably thought it was a good idea at the time."

Stephan laughed. "Probably. But that's not what I meant. I mean... why blue? The Root Chakras should have been red."

Diana sighed. "Another thing we have to sort out."

They walked in silence for a while, and then, Diana's head shot up. She smiled at Stephan. "Both Drs. Stone and Gribbleflotz claimed the king's aura was blue..."

Stephan smiled back. "And you think we could claim that the blue dye job was supposed to restore his aura." Stephan nodded a few times. "That would work."

Diana offered up her hand for a high five. "Now all we have to do is write up the cover story, so everyone can stay on the same page."

Chapter 16

Verona, the Republic of Venice

Rachel Lynch stopped in front of the poster and worried her way through it. It was written in the local variant of Italian, and although her Italian was progressing well, there were a lot of holes in her vocabulary. The font it was printed in was not particularly helpful either. She looked around the busy thoroughfare for help. Her companions had drifted off. Or, more correctly, Luchia had dragged her husband away to look at clothes. Rachel wandered over to see what she was trying to buy for Gio.

"What do you think?" Luchia asked the moment Rachel turned up. She held the colorful top across Gio's chest.

Rachel took in the pained look in Gio's eyes and smiled. The former Franciscan friar—he left before taking his final vows—preferred colors more in line with his former vestments. However, Luchia was his weakness and he would do anything to keep her happy. Even wear a top that even famous fashion disaster Dr. Gribbleflotz would consider *too loud.* She took pity on the poor man and shook her head. "Put it back and come have a look at a poster for me."

She led them back to the poster and both Luchia and Gio studied it.

"Who is The Magnificent Ponzi?" Gio asked.

"No idea," Rachel said. "So, what kind of show is he putting on?"

Gio read aloud the complete contents of the poster.

"Where did The Magnificent Ponzi learn about the Science of the Chakras?" Luchia asked.

Rachel stared at the poster. Gio's reading of the poster had helped clear up the mysteries of the fancy font it was printed in, making it easier for her to read what it said. "I don't know," she said. She tapped a phrase. "Is that saying Ponzi will reveal secrets from Grantville?"

"He's calling it the Miracle City from the Future," Gio answered.

"I thought we were the only group the Sanitation Commission sent to Italy," Luchia said.

"We are." Rachel tapped the poster. "I think Ponzi is freelance." She sighed. "The others can go on ahead, but we're going to have to delay our departure. We need to attend his performance and discover what lies and misconceptions he is propagating, just in case we have to do some damage mitigation." She studied the poster. "Where is it being held?"

"The old Roman theater," Gio said.

Rachel glanced over her shoulder in the direction of the old Roman amphitheater that dominated the *Piazza Bra*. "They're holding a performance in that?" she demanded. They had walked around it earlier and it was enormous.

"Of course not," Gio said. "That's the amphitheater. The theater is much smaller. It is built into the slope of the hill on which the *Castel San Pietro* stands, just in front of the river."

"Good," Rachel said. "Because if they were holding it there, they'd need a PA system in order that everyone could hear. And that means up-timer involvement."

"We down-timers are quite capable of running a sound system," Luchia said.

Rachel winced. She really should have kept a tighter grip on her tongue. Now Luchia was going to mount her high horse. She sighed and surrendered herself to her fate as Luchia cut loose on how down-timers were just as capable as up-timers.

A couple of days later

Bernardo Ponzi faded off the back of the stage while Crescenzo and Angelo launched into song. The moment he was backstage he pulled off the massive turban he was wearing. It was immediately grabbed by Brent Little, one of the Americans responsible for special effects. Bill Franklin, the other American, handed him a dry towel.

Bernardo dried the sweat from his hair and face. "Why do I have to wear that thing?" he protested as he exchanged the towel for a mug of small beer.

"It's part of the costume," Bill said patiently.

Bernardo glared at Bill over the lip of the mug. "It's heavy and hot. Why can't I just wear it for the Chakra components of the show? Why do I have to wear it for the whole show?"

"The audience don't like costume changes," Brent said. "Remember what happened when you changed into a white lab coat."

Bernardo sighed. In a previous act he had just put on a white lab coat over his normal costume. Unfortunately, there had been an immediate disconnect between him and his audience. "What fool designed this costume anyway?"

"It is a faithful reproduction of what they say *Dottore* Stone wore when he was attending the king of Bohemia," Brent said as he presented the turban for Bernardo to put back on.

"*Dottore* Stone is a fool," Bernardo said as he drank the last of his beer. He swapped it for the towel Bill was still holding and gave his head a final wipe. "This better be worth it," he said.

"It will be," Bill assured Bernardo as he and Brent slipped the turban onto Bernardo's head. "Just look at the size of the audience."

Bernardo did just that. It was easily the biggest he had drawn in more than four months of operations. Of course, the size of the venue might have had something to do with that. The ruins of the old Roman theater at Verona had a capacity of over a thousand people and it looked like they had managed to fill it.

Concession holders were wandering around the crowd selling food and beverages. Unfortunately, Bernardo and his people were not getting any of that action. That went to the people managing the facility. Still, they had provided the bench seating that filled the orchestra area right in front of the stage.

There was a reason why the theater was packed, and it was not just because of his scintillating stage presence. Admission was free. Bernardo had not believed the Americans when they said such a move could fill the theater. But here he stood. Before a crowd easily ten times the size of their previous best. If even as few as a third of them put something into the collection boxes that were being passed around, they would make more from this one performance that they had in their last three performances combined. Bernardo was prepared to be magnanimous and admit that he had been wrong. Or, at least he would be after they tallied up the night's takings. Of course, that was dependent on him doing his job properly, which was not being helped by the current delay.

"Do we have a mark yet?" he asked.

"Elisabetta is still checking," Bill said as he checked that the bulbs in Bernardo's rings worked.

Bernardo glanced at the flashing lights on his hands. "Are you sure they're safe?"

"Relax," Brent Little said as he adjusted the web of wires that fed power to the grain-of-wheat light bulbs set into the hollowed-out plastic crystals mounted on the rings on his fingers. "There's barely enough charge there to give you a tingle."

That did not inspire Bernardo with a lot of confidence, and he worried about the flashing rings.

"Try for a color," Brent called to Bill.

"Going for blue," Bill called.

The rings continued to flash for a few more seconds, then, one by one, they stopped flashing until only the blue one flashed.

"That's good," Brent said. "Go for red this time."

A few seconds later only a single ring flashed. It was flashing red.

"That's good," Brent said. "Now for the turban."

Bernardo sighed and tried to wait patiently while they checked their circuits. Meanwhile, the ever-faithful Crescenzo and Angelo continued to entertain the crowd with their singing.

He tapped the earpiece he was wearing. A signal to his wife that he wanted to hear something. Preferably that they had identified a suitable candidate.

"Hold your horses," Elisabetta's voice sounded in his ear.

He waited impatiently.

"Okay, we have our *mark*. Section four, third row of the orchestra. Seat four. You can't miss him. He's the guy in the loud green collar taking up enough space for two."

Bernardo searched the audience for their mark. As he looked, Elisabetta filled him in on the man's background. There were two important points. The man was rich, and he was a hypochondriac. With the man located, Bernardo indicated that he was ready to begin by tapping the boom microphone he was wearing.

"Sound is good," Bill said. "You are now live."

Bernardo controlled his breathing so the boom microphone by his mouth did not pick up his excitement as he once more stepped out onto the stage.

The moment Crescenzo and Angelo finished their latest hymn a spotlight illuminated him.

Through his hidden earpiece, he heard Elisabetta's cue to start.

He placed his fingertips at his temples and bowed his head slightly. On that cue, the lights behind the massive crystal set into the front of his turban and the lights in the rings on his fingers started to flash. "I can hear a call in the ether. A cry for help. A cry only I, a master of the Chakras, can hear, for help only I can provide."

Chapter 17

Two days later, Padua, the Republic of Venice

"That's when things really turned strange," Edith Lynch said as she lounged back in the divan in Dr. Stone's Padua apartment. Instead of enjoying a well-earned rest after covering the nearly fifty miles from Verona to Padua in just two days, the four of them—Edith, Rachel, Gio, and Luchia—had been dragged off to Dr. Stone's apartment to describe The Magnificent Ponzi's performance to Dr. Stone, Dr. Gribbleflotz, Diana Cheng, and Stephan Böhm.

"Became strange?" Rachel said. "I thought the whole performance was pretty strange."

Edith shook her head. "Other than the constant references to Dr. Stone's Science of the Chakras, The Magnificent Ponzi wasn't doing anything I haven't seen a televangelist do. But performing abdominal surgery live on stage, that's strange."

Phillip was suddenly intensely attentive. "He performed surgery on stage?" he asked.

Edith nodded. "With his bare hands."

"He said he was removing kidney stones, just like you did from the doge," Rachel said.

"There was blood everywhere," Luchia added.

"I bet there was," Diana muttered. She turned to Phillip. "Something's going to have to be done about The Magnificent Ponzi."

"Why?" Luchia asked. "He saved that man's life." She responded to Diana's dubious look by nodding emphatically. "Not only did he remove some kidney stones, but also, he removed some diseased organs that would have been the death of him."

"*Signora* Odescalchi, the surgery was fake," Diana said. "The Magnificent Ponzi didn't operate on anyone. He didn't stick his hands into anyone's abdomen. He didn't pull anything out of that man's body. It was all faked."

"But the blood," Luchia protested.

"A small bladder of animal blood concealed in his hands, which he burst open."

"How can you say that?" Edith demanded. "I was there. I saw The Magnificent Ponzi operate on that man."

"With his bare hands?" Phillip asked.

"Yes," Edith said.

"Have you ever tried to force your fingers into your belly?" Phillip asked.

"Of course not."

Phillip smiled. It was not a particularly pleasant smile, but then, he was dealing with a number of rather unpleasant thoughts. "Why don't you try it right now?"

Edith looked at her hand, and then at her abdomen. She looked back at Phillip, and then toward Dr. Stone. "The Magnificent Ponzi said he received special training from you."

Tom sighed mightily. "I haven't taught anyone how to perform surgery, Frau Lynch. It's not what I do. I'm a pharmacist. I make drugs. Dr. Gribbleflotz is correct. The surgery you think you saw was faked."

"But I saw..."

"A stage magician pretending to operate on someone," Tom said. He turned to Phillip. "I'm sorry about this."

Phillip waved off the apology. "There's no need to apologize. However, we do need to stop Ponzi doing psychic surgery."

"Especially when he is claiming I taught him how to do it," Tom added.

"Yes," Phillip agreed. "That could become extremely inconvenient."

"When do we leave?" Diana said.

"We leave early tomorrow morning," Phillip said. "You, however, will not be going."

"Now, just a minute," Diana protested.

"I'm with Dr. Gribbleflotz on this, Frau Cheng," Stephan said.

"We don't know how dangerous Herr Ponzi and his people might become when their scheme is exposed. It would be best if you stayed in Padua, where it is safe."

Verona

Bernardo Ponzi surveyed the table on which the evening's takings were on display. His hand moved out and toppled over a pile of coins, just for the satisfaction of seeing the coins tumble. He turned his attention to his chief lieutenant. "The takings are down on yesterday."

"It's only to be expected," Bill Franklin said. "We've done three shows in as many days. We've attracted good crowds, but the pool of people able and willing to attend our show is limited. Even here in Verona."

"Then we need to move on. To Padua," Bernardo said. "They have more people. They even have a new amphitheater where I could perform."

"And this time, we get the food and beverages concessions," Elisabetta added.

"Yes," Bernardo said in emphatic agreement with his wife. "Food and beverages sales during a performance take coin that could otherwise have gone into our collection boxes."

Bill released a weary sigh. "Padua also has Tom Stone in residence. And if you think he's just going to stand back when we put on a show including his Chakras, then you have another think coming."

Brent Little nodded morosely. "And he'd be even less happy about the psychic surgery."

Bernardo stared at Bill. "But you said he performed psychic surgery on *Dottore* Gribbleflotz," he protested.

"I said it sounded like psychic surgery," Bill said. "I wasn't there. I'm only guessing what happened based on what information I've managed to pick up over the radio net."

Brent shook his head. "I just can't imagine why he'd do it. Or, more likely, condone George Mundell doing it."

Bernardo stared at Brent as he considered the question he had sort of voiced. "Why was *Dottore* Stone trying to defraud *Dottore* Gribbleflotz?" he asked.

"That's the sixty-four-thousand-dollar question," Brent said. "Stoner's got more money than he knows what to do with. He doesn't have to defraud Gribbleflotz. So, maybe, it wasn't psychic surgery."

"All this is irrelevant," Bill said. "We can't go to Padua, because that's where Stoner is based. So," he asked as he dragged out a map, "where else can we go?"

"We can't go south," Brent said, pointing toward their previous port of call, the Duchy of Mantua. "By now, they've probably noticed that the people Bernardo is supposed to have healed weren't."

Elisabetta tapped the map. "Vicenza. They have the *Teatro Olímpico*. It will be a step up from the old Roman theater in Verona."

"Vicenza is getting awfully close to Padua," Bill said.

"I have family in Vicenza," Elisabetta said.

Bill sighed. "I guess it is at least a day's ride from Padua."

"So, Vicenza it is," Bernardo said.

Chapter 18

Vicenza

Elisabetta Garivaghi had dragged them through the narrow streets of Vicenza as soon as they had secured their baggage. Now, in a typical narrow street near the northern wall of the city, she stopped. "This is it," she said.

Bill Franklin stared at the Palladian-style building. "You know someone who lives here?" There was, he noticed, more than a hint of disbelief in his voice. Well-founded disbelief in his opinion. "It's a fucking palace."

"Palazzo," Elisabetta corrected. "The Palazzo da Porto. My cousin Alessandro is related to the da Porto."

Bill licked his lips. "Okay, so he doesn't own the joint. Is he going to have enough influence to get us into the *Teatro Olimpico*?"

"Alessandro has the ear of the da Porto." Elisabetta glared at Bill. "Trust me."

"Yeah, well," Brent Little muttered. "We've come a long way just to find out we can't get the theater you want."

Elisabetta responded by lashing out with her booted foot.

"That hurt," Brent muttered.

"It was supposed to." Elisabetta surveyed her companions. "Now. Best behavior everyone. We probably won't be invited to speak with the da Porto, but if we do, follow my lead. And don't speak unless spoken to." She stared hard at Bill and Brent. "The da Porto is a count. Treat him as you would your American president if you ever met him."

"Ease off, Elisabetta," Bill said. "Brent and I know how to behave in company."

Elisabetta glared at them intensely. It clearly said that they had better behave, or else. And with Elisabetta, Bill was sure he would not appreciate the "else."

He watched her walk up to the gate and ring a bell. After a short wait, a hatch in the upper section of the heavy wooden gate opened. Elisabetta spoke with someone, gesturing to her party. A head poked out the hatch and stared at them. Bill managed to grab Brent's arm before he could wave at the man. The head ducked back, and the hatch closed.

Elisabetta walked back to Bill and Brent. "We are in luck. Alessandro is here. Someone has been sent to get him, and he should be here shortly."

Simone da Porto, son and heir of the late Iseppo da Porto, sat back as he read the letter from one of his nephews. The boy was studying medicine in Padua and, surprisingly, his latest missive was not a request for more money. Instead, it was full of news about a recent visitor to the university. He lowered the letter to stare at the man in the chair opposite. "How much progress is your pet alchemist making with the philosopher's stone and transmutation of gold?"

Alessandro Garivaghi sighed ruefully. "Not as well as I would have liked."

Simone nodded. He had not really expected anything else. Alchemists were continually promising that they were close to discovering how to transmute lead into gold. Of course, they usually followed that claim with a demand for more funds. "Girolomo writes that a visiting alchemist from Prague demonstrated how to achieve Valentine's third key. He says that he tried it himself and was successful in creating red dragon's blood."

That earned a snort from Alessandro. "That is more than Luigi has done. Who is this alchemist?"

Simone checked the letter. "*Dottore* Phillip Theophrastus Gribbleflotz."

"Gribbleflotz?" Alessandro rubbed his head. "Where have I heard that name before?"

"Drugs. It was being treated with Gribbleflotz Sal Vin Betula that saved the life of Lelio's son."

Alessandro turned his head and sucked in his lips. Seeing

this, and knowing what it portended, Simone called out. "Don't even think of it."

Alessandro swallowed and looked at Simone shamefaced. "I am sorry, da Porto. But the thought of that man's son occupying our estate sticks in my craw."

Simone looked sympathetically upon his companion. "It is unfortunate that the boy didn't die. However, one day, in the fullness of time, we shall recover the Vivaro fief."

Alessandro nodded. "Of course, da Porto. Children often die."

Simone sighed. Alessandro and his family had been amongst the worst affected when the Council of Ten confiscated the property of Count Ludovico da Porto as a part penalty for his criminal activities. The late Lucillo Cereda had been enfeoffed with one of the most important pieces of land in the da Porto portfolio. The fief of Vivaro had been part of the nucleus of the da Porto title of counts. As such, it held a position in the family well beyond its mere economic value. Through the peculiarities of Venetian law, if Lucillo's male line was to die out, then the fief would revert back to the da Porto line. Lelio had been Lucillo's only son. They had been one death from a severe fever away from recovering Vivaro.

"You are not to do anything," he warned. "If you need money, you may call upon my banker."

"I am not a beggar." Alessandro leapt to his feet. "When Luigi starts making gold, I will have the wealth I deserve."

The silence that followed was interrupted by a knock at the door.

"Enter!" Simone called.

A servant poked his head around the door. "I'm sorry to disturb you, milord, but a woman claiming to be a cousin of *Signore* Garivaghi is asking after him." The man paused. "She claims that the two men with her are Americans, from the City from the Future."

Simone's eyes lit up. "From Grantville. In Thuringia?"

The servant shrugged apologetically.

"Never mind," Simone said. "Does the cousin have a name?"

The man nodded. "*Signora* Elisabetta Garivaghi."

Alessandro nodded to Simone. "I know her. I wonder what she wants."

Simone turned, his eyes alight with interest. "Your cousin knows some people from the future?"

Alessandro shrugged. "It is possible. I know she and her husband were intending to try their luck in the USE."

Simone gestured to the servant. "Have them shown in. And bring refreshments," he called as the man backed away from the door.

He steepled his hands and stared at the door. "People from the future. They must have many interesting stories to tell."

Simone and Alessandro rose to their feet as Elisabetta, Bill, and Brent were let into the room. They were invited to be seated and servants appeared with a trolley of food. Simone waved the servants away before sitting himself. "So. You are from the City from the Future?"

Bill and Brent agreed that they were, and Simone started asking questions. It was over an hour before he had satisfied his immediate craving for knowledge. "We must chat again."

Simone next turned his attention to Elisabetta. "I'm sorry, I believe you called to talk with Alessandro."

Elisabetta nodded. "I was hoping he would ask you to use your influence as a member of the *Accademia Olimpico* to persuade them to let us check out the *Teatro Olimpico,* and if it is suitable, let us hire it for a few performances of my Bernardo's act."

Simone smiled. "Such a small thing to ask in reward for bringing me such interesting companions. Consider it done.

"Alessandro. See that your most charming cousin and her American friends are given every assistance."

Simone got to his feet and held out his hand so Elisabetta could kiss his signet ring. He offered his hand to Bill. "Maybe you and *Signore* Little could find time to talk to the academy about the future world?"

"I'm sure they would be delighted." Elisabetta cast both Bill and Brent a look that told them they had better agree.

"It would be no trouble," Bill said as he shook Simone's hand. Brent nodded.

Moments later, they were out the door in the company of Elisabetta's cousin.

Later that day

Their lanterns did their best to fight back the darkness in the cavernous auditorium of the *Teatro Olimpico* as Bill Franklin, Brent Little, and Elisabetta Garivaghi examined the facilities in the company of Valentino Pasini, a member of the *Accademia Olimpico*, the owners of the theater. Bill looked around as best he could in the light cast by the lanterns. "How long's it been since anyone used this place?" he asked as he noticed their footprints in the dust.

"A while," Valentino said. "Most of the academy's business is conducted in the adjoining *Odèo*."

"Is that going to be a problem?" Elisabetta asked.

Bill shook his head. "But the place needs a good clean."

"Are you volunteering?" Elisabetta asked.

"Heck no!" Bill said. "Cleaning's woman's work."

Elisabetta snorted. "No wonder your wife divorced you."

Bill glared at her. "The bitch didn't divorce me because I expected her to keep the house clean."

"No. Of course she didn't." Elisabetta smiled, and it was not a particularly nice smile. "She divorced you for desertion."

"What the hell do you expect?" Bill demanded. "Three kids under five and another one on the way. I couldn't afford to have any fun once she got a support order against my army pay."

"So you quit the army to get out of your obligations."

"Hey," Bill protested. "I left her the house. That's worth a fortune."

"After mortgaging it."

"I only mortgaged my half."

Elisabetta shook her head gently. "You're such a charmer."

"Hey, peace, people," Brent said. "We need to make a decision. I'm happy with this place. Bill?" he asked.

"This is fine," Bill agreed. "It's better than Verona."

"But it is so much smaller than Verona," Elisabetta said.

"Sure, it's smaller, but we're in a building. We can control access, so we don't have to worry about people getting in without paying. And the roof will protect everyone from the elements."

"The wooden seats won't hurt either," Brent said. "Those huge marble slabs people were sitting on in Verona might be okay in summer, but in November . . ." He shivered graphically.

"But will we get enough people coming?" Elisabetta asked. "You said we needed to have free admission to attract a good-sized audience back in Verona and you were right. Surely we need to do the same here?"

Bill shook his head. "Verona was different. The theater was

bigger, and the nights were cold. Free admission got people in who might otherwise have stayed away."

"And a half-empty theater wouldn't have given the impression The Magnificent Ponzi wants to present," Brent added.

Elisabetta looked dubiously at both up-timers. "You're sure?"

Bill nodded.

"Very well." She turned to Valentino. "We'll take it."

Padua

Click!

The knight lowered his visor.

Click!

The knight nudged his horse into a walk, and then a trot.

Click!

The knight lowered his lance and kicked his horse into a lope.

Click!

The knight leaned forward in his high-cantered saddle and kicked his horse into a gallop.

Click! Click! CRASH. Click! Click! Click!

Sebastian Jones took his finger from the shutter button and lowered the camera. He smiled as he let his eyes settle on the man struggling to his feet. Hopefully, and he was very hopeful, he would have caught the moment of impact and the immediate aftermath.

While he watched, a couple of men rushed out to help the knight to his feet. Sebastian realized the need for urgency when he noticed two gangs of warriors grouping at either end of the arena. The moment the knight was clear, there was an almighty roar and the two groups charged at each other.

A quick glance at the counter on top of the motor-drive-equipped Olympus OM1-N warned him that the camera was almost out of film. He rattled off the last few shots on the roll before handing the camera with its long lens to his trusted assistant. He then picked up his Speed Graphic and clambered over the low fence onto the field to get closer to the action.

"Sebastian!" Paolo wailed before he too clambered over the rail onto the hallowed turf in pursuit of his charge.

Clunk! Clang! Clunk! Click!

Sebastian stepped back from the action to flip the double-dark film cassette before returning to the action. He managed to get one more shot before Paolo hauled him back.

"What's the matter?" Sebastian demanded as he changed double-darks.

"We are in the middle of the field," Paolo pointed out.

This was a slight exaggeration. They were actually at one edge of the field. It just happened to be the edge closest to the action, and to the audience that had paid good money to watch the mock combat. Even in his excitement at having action to photograph, Sebastian could see the two bruisers clambering over the rail. "Are they coming for us?" he asked.

"They aren't coming for them," Paolo muttered as he waved toward the performers still bashing at each other with swords and various blunt instruments of mayhem.

"Do something!" Sebastian pleaded. "You're with the *Provveditori alla Sanità*. They'll listen to you."

Paolo rolled his eyes. He also grabbed Sebastian by the arm and marched him back toward the fence. "I'm sorry. He's a foreigner. He got away from me," he announced before the bruisers could say anything.

"He almost interrupted the fighting," Marco Loschi, the larger of the two bruisers, said as he graciously accepted the coins Paolo dropped into his hand.

"I was just photographing the action," Sebastian protested as he tried to fight free of Paolo's grip on his arm.

"Photograph the action?" Zabarella Loschi demanded. "With that?" He pointed to the Speed Graphic Sebastian was holding.

Sebastian nodded.

"It's too small. Tommaso's camera obscura is much bigger." Zabarella used his hands to indicate a full-plate-sized camera.

"And he can't photograph action," Marco said. "His subjects have to hold a pose."

"Your friend is obviously using old stock film. The new stuff is much faster," Sebastian said.

"Friend?" Marco asked. He turned to his brother. "Did I say Tommaso was my friend?"

Zabarella shook his head. "No. You didn't."

"Of course I didn't." Marco turned to Sebastian. "Why would I call a man who overcharges for shoddy work my friend?"

"You shouldn't," Sebastian said placatingly. "Anyway, this

other photographer is obviously using older technology. He must be making his own negatives using homemade gelatin, because the new stuff *Brennerei und Chemiefabrik Schwarza* is making is good for one-sixtieth-of-a-second exposures in good light."

Marco pursed his lips. "Is that good?"

"Is that good?" Sebastian demanded. "It's not just good, it's brilliant. Just you wait until I develop the shots I took earlier."

"And when will you be doing that?" Marco asked.

"I can do it now if you like. I just need to access my equipment."

Diana was in the kitchen of the Rovarini house. She was stripping down and cleaning her collection of lithotrites. There might have only been one client today, and one currently scheduled for tomorrow, but it never hurt to have everything ready on the off chance someone turned up asking for a quick transurethral lithotripsy.

A knock on the door had her glancing at Paola, the lady of the house. Paola shrugged her lack of knowledge at Diana's unasked question and got to her feet. Diana returned to reassembling a lithotrite while Paola saw to whoever was at the door.

"It's your friend, *Signore* Jones," Paola called.

"He's not my friend," Diana muttered to herself as she laid down the lithotrite and got to her feet.

Sebastian was introducing Paola to his companions when Diana made it to the entry hall. She recognized Paolo, but the other, very rough-looking, men were unfamiliar.

Sebastian saw her. "Hi," he said. "You know Paolo. The others are Marco and Zabarella Loschi."

"*Signora!*" Marco gave Diana an elaborate bow.

Not to be outdone, Zabarella elbowed his brother aside. "I am Zabarella Loschi. This," he said gesturing to Marco, "is my brother. And you are?"

"Diana Cheng," Diana said. As Zabarella took possession of her hand and bent to kiss it, she shot Sebastian a questioning look.

"Marco and Zabarella work at the theater on the *Prato della Valle*."

"We were there earlier, *signora*," Paolo explained. "There was some mock combat and Sebastian took some photographs."

Diana rolled her eyes. "You mean, Sebastian made a nuisance of himself getting in the way while he took some photographs."

"Yes."

"Hey!" Sebastian protested. "I didn't get in anyone's way. I'm very good at not getting in the way. You could say that I'm an expert at not getting in the way."

"If you didn't get in the way, why are they here?" Diana gestured to Marco and Zabarella.

"Because he almost got in the way." Marco glared at Sebastian, as if daring him to contest the charge.

"And because *Signore* Jones took some photographs," Zabarella added.

"I need to develop the film and make some prints," Sebastian said.

"Need?" Diana switched from looking at Sebastian to looking at Paolo. The Venetian was usually a more reliable source of information.

Paolo gestured to the Loschi brothers. "Their boss is interested in hiring Sebastian to take some promotional photographs of his show."

"But first, he wants to see what *Signore* Jones is capable of," Marco said.

Diana turned back to Sebastian.

"They're only familiar with what a local guy can do with a primitive camera obscura," Sebastian said.

"*Signore* Jones claims that he can photograph live action," Marco said. "He has brought us here to watch him process the photographs he took today."

Diana's brows rose. Sebastian had a well-earned reputation for the *perfect* timing of his shots. Or at least, the shots that got shown to the public revealed perfect timing. "You get anything interesting?"

Sebastian nodded. "I think so. Could you entertain everyone while I set up my gear?" Sebastian did not wait for an answer as he disappeared back outside.

Diana stood staring at the door he had disappeared through. Vaguely, she was aware of Paola taking up her role as hostess and leading everyone into the kitchen. Diana followed, just in time to be handed some plates. She distributed the plates around the table while Paola gathered suitable refreshments.

"My apologies, *Signora* Cheng," Paolo said. "You were busy when we turned up?"

She sighed. "Yes." She shook her head. "Sebastian's got the life expectancy of a mayfly."

"*Signora* Cheng. What is that?" Marco asked.

She turned to see what Marco was talking about. "That's a lithotrite." Marco's blank look brought a smile to her face. "It's a medical instrument used to crush bladder stones in a procedure called a transurethral lithotripsy." She passed one of the devices to him.

"That is the operation *Dottore* Gribbleflotz performed on the doge?" Paolo asked.

Diana nodded.

"How does it work?" Marco asked as he squeezed the trigger a couple of times.

Diana smiled. It was not an evil smile, but it was close. "You thread it through the urethra into the bladder and palpate with your hands until you find a bladder stone. You then fish around a bit until you can get the jaws around the stone, and then squeeze."

"Urethra?"

Paolo muttered into Marco's ear, and Marco hastily put the lithotrite back on the table and took a couple of steps back.

The sound of labored footsteps down the hall signaled the return of Sebastian. Paolo hastened to help him with his heavy work chest. They surveyed the kitchen table and Sebastian sent a look of puppylike appeal at Paola. "Please?" he asked.

Paola looked skyward, and then sighed. She grabbed a cloth and wiped down the table, causing everyone to grab their plates as she did so. "Just don't spill anything on it," she said.

"I won't," Sebastian promised.

Paola settled her hands on her hips and glared at Sebastian. "You'd better not." She switched her gaze to Diana. "Make sure he cleans up his mess."

"Oh, I will," she promised.

Sometime later

Sebastian was proud of his photographs. Unfortunately, because he did not have an enlarger, he was only able to print contact prints—that is, prints made by holding the negatives in contact with the photosensitive printout paper with a sheet of glass. This meant the printed images were the same size as the negatives.

"They're a bit small," Marco said as he examined the strip of 35mm photographs of the jousting.

"They can be enlarged."

"Really? How big?"

"As big as you like," Sebastian said. "The movie screen at the Magdeburg opera house is about forty-five feet by twenty feet."

Marco blinked a few times. "You can make photographs that big?"

"In theory," Sebastian said.

"But you'd have a heck of a job handling a piece of photographic paper that size," Diana said.

"What she said," Sebastian said. "The biggest prints I've made are thirty-two inches by twenty-four." He roughly described the sizes with his hands as he said them.

Zabarella gestured to the contact prints. "Could you print all of these that size?"

Sebastian looked at the contact prints. The shots from his Speed Graphic had been printed two to a piece of paper while the 35mm film had been cut into strips so he could print twelve per sheet of paper. There were a lot of negatives. "Even if I had an enlarger, that'd be getting extremely expensive," he warned. "And I don't have any paper that size with me. The largest I have is ten by twelve inch."

"But you said you had printed much bigger," Zabarella said.

"Sure. Back in Grantville. Where I had access to a fully equipped darkroom."

"Marianna's friend from the Society of Aural Investigators is probably set up to process large Kilian images," Diana suggested.

"Yes!" Sebastian's eyes lit up. "And if he doesn't have the larger-sized paper, he probably knows where to get hold of some."

Zabarella and Marco looked at each other, then they looked at Sebastian. "So, you can do it?"

"Maybe," Sebastian said. "If Marianna's friend has the necessary equipment. If he has an enlarger, how about I run off some ten by twelves for your boss. If he's happy, then we can look at printing some larger ones."

Chapter 19

Early evening, Vicenza, Republic of Venice

A horseback journey of twenty-six miles in less than ten hours is entirely possible if you tick all the right boxes. Dr. Gribbleflotz (age forty-two) and Dr. Stone (age fifty-three) ticked none. Neither of them was particularly fit nor young. This would not have been an issue if they'd managed to tick the box marked "experienced rider." However, Phillip had last ridden a horse regularly six or seven years ago while Tom's familiarity with horses was such that he could reliably pick a horse out from a selection of mules, horses, and donkeys nine times out of ten. This meant a compulsory stop in the planned journey to Verona, another twenty-five miles away, as they attempted to regain the use of their legs. Stephan Böhm, on the other hand, had ticked all the right boxes. It was he who was carrying not only his baggage but also that of Drs. Stone and Gribbleflotz as well. While he waited for Phillip to open the door to their room, he took the time to display the kind and caring attitude that would serve him so well in his future career as a physician.

"I warned you that pushing on to Vicenza so quickly would be painful."

Phillip and Tom both shot glares at Stephan before Phillip turned to Tom. "I have some of my special ointment in my baggage. You're welcome to have some."

"Thanks," Tom said. He shot Stephan another glare before turning back to Phillip. "What's in it?"

"A topical anesthetic."

"Oh? What did you use?"

"A combination of clove oil and lavender."

Stephan rolled his eyes at the two men he had come to Italy expecting that he would have to keep from killing each other. While they continued their amicable chat on the best things to use in various ointments, Stephan pushed past and dumped their baggage in the room they had taken for the night. "While you two self-medicate, I'll round up dinner."

Next morning, Vicenza

Drs. Stone and Gribbleflotz were still amongst the walking wounded, even if walking was the last thing they wanted to do. However, they did manage to stagger down for breakfast. Stephan looked them up and down. "In my professional opinion, I think we should delay our departure until you're both a little steadier on your feet."

That earned him a couple of rude looks. "You're too kind," Tom Stone muttered as he adjusted his position in his seat for the sixth time in a little over a minute.

Stephan grinned. "While you two loosen up, I think I'll have a look around the city. See if maybe The Magnificent Ponzi has turned up."

"He's in Verona," Tom said.

Stephan shook his head. "He was last seen in Verona. But we don't know how long he intended staying there, nor where he might head next."

Phillip waved a hand. "If he's putting on a show here, see about getting tickets. Do you have any money?"

The question from Dr. Gribbleflotz was almost immediately followed by a tossed drawstring purse. "Thanks," Stephan said as he caught it. It would not be appropriate to count the contents there and then, so he waited until he'd shut the door on them before he looked. The purse contained at least two ducats. It was not a lot by the standards of what he imagined Dr. Gribbleflotz was used to, but it was more than he normally earned in a week.

A simple query about theaters sent Stephan walking north from their inn. His journey took him along the *Strada di Angeli* toward the *Ponte degli Angeli*, the only bridge across the Bacchiglione River into the northern part of the city. His destination was just beyond the gothic-style Church of Santa Corona, on this, the southern side of the river.

When he reached the river, he looked around. There was nothing that looked like a theater, let alone the Roman theater upon which he had been told the *Teatro Olimpico* was modeled.

Stephan walked around looking for a friendly face, or at least someone who looked as if they had time to help a lost stranger. He spotted a man—actually, there were three tidily dressed elderly men sitting at a table. They were talking amongst themselves over a few drinks. He walked over to them.

"*Scusami*," he said to attract their attention. That brought immediate raised brows. His atrocious accent had probably warned them that he was a foreigner. He held out his hands and shook his head to indicate confusion, and asked, "*Teatro Olimpico*?"

The men all grinned, showing remarkably good teeth for their age—Stephan was an Advanced Medic. Noticing things like that was an occupational hazard—and pointed to a building back the way he had come.

Stephan stared at the building. He had noticed it in passing but ignored it. Anything less like the Roman-theater-inspired structure he was looking for was hard to imagine. He turned back to the three men and pointed to what he had taken to be a former medieval fortress. "*Teatro Olimpico*?" he asked, just to be sure.

They nodded.

Stephan stared at them for a moment. They seemed convinced that the fortress was the place he was looking for, and the way they were lounging in their seats with their drinks in front of them suggested that they were locals, so he shrugged. "*Grazie*," he said to them.

He realized they had not lied when he saw the wrought-iron letters strung across the open gateway that spelled out TEATRO OLIMPICO. To the right, just inside the courtyard the gateway led to, was a noticeboard giving information about the theater. The exterior was, apparently, built in the Palladian style—whatever that might be—while the interior was fitted out like a classical Roman theater. That answered the question of why the building did not look like a Roman theater.

Stephan read further. Ah! It was the last work of Andrea Palladio, whoever he might be. Stephan nodded to himself. The theater was obviously built in a style easily identified as having been designed by Palladio.

There was, in addition, another, smaller, sign. It had two arrows and a few words. One arrow pointed into the courtyard. If one were to follow the path, one would arrive at the entrance to the theater. The other arrow pointed to the right.

To the right of the gateway was a door. On the door was a sign showing two words—BIGLIETTI, and below that, INFORMAZIONE. With a smile on his face, Stephan opened the door.

There was a man behind a grill. Stephan approached him and asked about The Magnificent Ponzi. To his surprise, the ticket seller nodded vigorously and pointed to a poster pinned to a board on the wall behind Stephan. It was advertising The Magnificent Ponzi and his show. Further reading indicated that there was a performance that evening. And, coincidently, Stephan had sufficient funds with which to purchase tickets or, as the sign said, *biglietti*. He approached the ticket seller and held up three fingers while pointing to the poster.

That evening, Vicenza

Stephan Böhm trailed a little behind as the usher led their little group to the seats he'd booked. They were walking on the lowest terrace of the *cavea*. To his left was the orchestra pit. It was about eight feet below the wooden terrace he was walking on. It was also about four feet below the stage. At the equivalent of ten dollars a seat, the pit offered the cheapest seats in the house. The next cheapest were at the ends of the thirteen terraces of the *cavea*, where walls interrupted the sightlines of the stage. As Dr. Gribbleflotz was paying, Stephan had bought some of the most expensive seats in the house. Three seats to the left of the central aisle in the front row.

From their seats—which was a bit of a misnomer because they were sitting on a not particularly comfortable wooden terrace—they had an uninterrupted view of the stage.

"It's not much of a stage," Stephan muttered to Dr. Gribbleflotz. "Where's the proscenium arch?"

"There isn't one," Phillip said. "This is a Classical theater.

The closest thing to a proscenium arch is the *porta regia* in the middle of the *scaenae frons*."

Stephan had been looking at the magnificent three-tier facade that decorated the back of the stage. Now he examined the middle one of the three openings in the *scaenae frons*. Beyond it was a long street scene, or at least it looked like a long street. "That street looks a bit long."

"It's a trick of perspective," Phillip explained. "The theater is quite famous for it. And the *Accademia Olimpica* is so pleased with it that they haven't changed it in the fifty years since it was first presented to the world."

Stephan had another look at the area beyond the stage. He was not impressed. "They'll never make this place a paying proposition. Not unless they create a proper proscenium arch and clear out that old scenery."

"It doesn't have to be profitable," Phillip said. "The membership of the *Accademia Olimpica* includes some very wealthy men, and they are quite happy to keep it as it is."

"It's nice to have money," Stephan muttered. He noticed a strange smell and looked around. He sniffed again. He might be in the USE Medical Department, but he was still a soldier with a soldier's attention to the important things in life. "I smell food," he said as he got to his feet.

With the advantage of the added height, Stephan was able to locate a young woman with a large wicker tray suspended in front of her selling food to members of the audience. He waited until she looked his way and held up a hand. A short exchange of expressions had her rushing over.

"I like the service the expensive seats get," he said to Dr. Gribbleflotz.

Phillip looked up. "What?"

"The woman selling food. A simple wave of my hand and she came running, ignoring the attempts of others to catch her attention. That doesn't happen in the seats I usually get."

Phillip grinned. "Then you'd best make sure her efforts don't go unrewarded. Do you have money?"

"I still have some of the money you gave me earlier."

"Good. Good."

"What can I offer you?" the young woman asked when she arrived.

"What do you have?"

"Snacks that the people from the City from the Future like," the woman answered. "Hard bread twists they call pretzels, salted peanuts, roasted almonds, and sunflower seeds."

"Dr. Stone, Dr. Gribbleflotz, would you like anything?"

"Pretzels for me," Tom called.

"The same for me, please, Stephan," Phillip said.

Stephan handed over some coins. "Three helpings of pretzels, please."

The woman skillfully assembled vine-leaf containers and loaded them with small pretzels and passed them to Tom, Phillip, and Stephan before moving on.

"Why the vine leaf?" Tom asked. "Why not serve them in a paper bag or cone?"

"Paper's expensive, Dr. Stone," Stephan answered. "Vine leaves can be had free for the picking."

"They're very salty," Phillip said.

Stephan nibbled on one of his pretzels. It was, as Phillip had said, very salty. "I thought they were on the cheap side for theater food. I expect they'll send a couple of girls round selling overpriced drinks soon."

Music sounded. Stephan immediately realized that it was canned music, but most of the audience probably didn't even know that such a thing existed and looked around avidly trying to work out where the organ and other instruments and their players were hidden.

There was a buzzing sound and then the front of the stage was lit by beams of brilliant white light. Stephan swung around to locate the spotlights. There were two of them. Each one positioned above the columns of the curved wall at the top of the *cavea*. He could not see much of the spotlights, but he had a fair idea what they were. He edged closer to Dr. Gribbleflotz. "The navy will be interested to hear where their missing arc lights got to, and I bet their missing diesel generator is providing the electricity."

"Shush!" someone from behind them hissed.

Stephan turned his attention back to the stage where two men passed through the *porta regia* and took up positions either side of the entrance. And then they started to sing.

Stephan stared at them. Gio Fasolo and Edith Lynch had commented about how good The Magnificent Ponzi's singers were, but he had not expected them to be this good. He shuffled a little trying to find a comfortable way to sit on the wooden terrace and settled back to enjoy the performance.

Bill Franklin checked that Bernardo was ready to go on when Crescenzo and Angelo finished their introductory number. A nod from Bernardo had Bill carefully moving the edge of the white curtain that hung across the *porta regia* that acted as a backdrop for Bernardo's performance and put an eye to the gap he had made. The white backdrop reflected a lot of the light from the arc lights. This gave Bernardo an almost otherworldly appearance. It also provided a lot of light within the auditorium. More than enough light for Bill to identify Tom Stone in the front row of the *cavea* not more than forty feet away.

"Shit!" he said forcefully as he backed away. "Fuck! Shit! Fucking shit!"

"What's the matter?" Brent Little demanded.

Bill pointed. "Fucking Stoner's out there. In the front row."

Brent hurried over to the curtain and peeked through. Moments later he shot back. "What the fuck is he doing here?" he demanded.

"How the hell should I know?" Bill demanded.

"We need to warn Elisabetta."

"What about Bernardo?" Brent asked.

"She can tell him," Bill muttered as he fished his walkie-talkie out of a pocket and keyed the send button. "Elisabetta. We have a problem."

"What kind of problem?" Elisabetta demanded. "Is there something wrong with Bernardo's flashing light costume?"

"No. It's worse than that. Tom Stone is in the audience."

"Who?"

"Dr. Thomas Stone."

"Where?" Elisabetta demanded.

"Front and center. He's the third man in on your left."

"Why is he here?"

Bill rolled his eyes. "How should I know? But he is, and when he sees the show the shit is going to hit the fan."

He released the send button and waited for Elisabetta's response. It was a while coming.

"Is he here alone?"

Bill looked to Brent. "Is Stone on his own?"

Brent moved up to the curtain and looked through. He came back shaking his head. "He's chatting to the guy to his right."

"That doesn't prove anything."

"And the guy on the end of the row is wearing Medical Department fatigues."

Bill nodded. It did not actually prove that the three men were together, but the chances that a Medical Department soldier just happened to visit the theater and sit so close to Tom Stone was a bit of a stretch. "Who's the guy in the middle?" Bill asked.

"No idea." Brent shrugged. "Does it matter?"

"Not really," Bill admitted. "The shit's going to hit the fan whoever he is." He keyed the send button and let Elisabetta know what they thought about Tom Stone's companions.

Placing a curved seating arrangement inside a rectangular building left an empty space in the corners. Andrea Palladio's design placed concealed staircases in this otherwise wasted space. Patrons could enter or exit the auditorium through columned porticos atop the last terrace of the *cavea*. The staircases did not end at that level. They also serviced a higher level. That higher level was where the two carbon-arc spotlights had been set up. It was also where Elisabetta Garivaghi was standing.

Even if she stood at the balustrade that ringed that highest level, she would have had difficulty seeing anyone seated on the top few terraces of the *cavea*. However, her view of the front row of the *cavea* was uninterrupted. Elisabetta looked down at the first three seats to the left of the central flight of step that divided the *cavea*. They had their backs to her, so she couldn't identify them, but she could see one of the food-and-drink sellers walking back up the steps. Elisabetta held out her hand and snapped her fingers.

When there was no immediate response, she snapped them again, and again.

Magno, a local youth employed for the evening, eventually answered her summons. "Send that girl up to me!"

Magno looked over the edge. "Brigitta?"

Elisabetta glared at the youth. "If that is the name of the food seller."

Magno nodded.

"Well, what are you waiting for? Go and get her. I need to talk to her."

Magno sped off, to return barely a minute later with an obviously worried Brigitta.

"You wanted to see me, *signora*?" she asked hesitantly.

"Yes," Elisabetta said briskly. "There are three men in the front row of the *cavea*." She gestured for Brigitta to follow her to the balustrade. Once there, she pointed. "On the left of the center aisle. I want you to find out who they are." She held up a couple of *soldi* as encouragement.

Brigitta smiled and reached out for the coins. "The one on the end: they called him Stephan. The one in the middle is called *Dottore* Gribbleflotz, and the third man is called *Dottore* Stone."

Elisabetta dropped the coins into Brigitta's outstretched hand. While the girl hastily secured her bounty in a hidden purse, Elisabetta stared into the distance. A smile grew on her face.

Elisabetta shook the images of riches from her head and turned her attention back to Brigitta. "You know my cousin?"

Brigitta winced.

That was more than enough to assure Elisabetta that the girl knew Alessandro. "Find him and tell him I need to speak with him. Urgently."

The girl seemed unwilling to approach her cousin, as any vaguely intelligent female of her class would, so she stooped to bribery. She gave Brigitta another couple of *soldi* with a promise of more when she delivered her cousin. Still hesitant, the girl made her way to the staircase at the back of the landing and stomped her way down.

Elisabetta returned to the balustrade. From her position behind one of the many classical statues set on the plinths along the barrier she looked down upon the audience, concentrating on two men in the front row. Two of the richest men in the USE. And here they were, with just a single bodyguard between them. She smiled. It was not a particularly pleasant smile.

Brigitta reappeared a few minutes later with Alessandro. He was a heavyset man of middle years. Probably about thirty-five. He had good teeth and had only a few pox scars on his face. He looked like a friendly guy. A normal person might look at him and wonder why Brigitta had not wanted to go and fetch him. Which just went to show how much smarter than a normal person Brigitta was.

Brigitta edged around Alessandro to collect the money Elisabetta held out to her. She snatched it and ran.

Alessandro laughed as she disappeared down the stairs. "The girl said you wanted to see me urgently?"

Elisabetta nodded and gestured for Alessandro to follow her to the balustrade. "There are three men in the front row, on the left side of the aisle."

He looked down. "What about them?"

"They are two of the richest men in the USE. The man in the aisle seat is their bodyguard."

Alessandro, Elisabetta was pleased to see, was suddenly staring at the men intensely. "Who are they?"

"*Dottori* Stone and Gribbleflotz. We talked about them earlier today."

"I remember," Alessandro said. He turned his attention back to the men in question. "What is so urgent about them being here?"

"They could cause problems for our little show."

Alessandro smiled at Elisabetta. It was the kind of smile that confirmed Brigitta's fear of the man. It simply oozed a total lack of sympathy. "And you would like me to do something about them?"

"Yes."

"And what do you want out of this?"

"A finder's fee would be nice. But I'll be happy if you'll just get them out of our hair while we extend our tour to Padua and Venice."

"I'll see what I can do."

"I need you to do more than just see what you can do. I need *Dottore* Stone and his companions taken care of tonight."

Alessandro sighed. "That means taking them from the theater. Can you get them a sleeping drought?"

Elisabetta nodded. "They have bought snacks." When Alessandro raised his brows in question, she explained. "The snacks are heavily salted. If you provide me with a drought, I will see that it is added to any drink they buy."

"Good," Alessandro said. "Then I will get everything else underway."

Chapter 20

North of Vicenza

Cold toes woke Stephan. He tried to reach for the blanket to pull it over them, but he discovered that his arms were tied. That discovery increased his level of situation awareness enormously. He had a headache. Not a bad one. Not one that suggested he had been rendered unconscious from a blow to the head. At least, based on his work as a military medic, he did not think so. That left being drugged.

If he had been drugged, then it must have been something he drank at the theater. There was no reason for anyone to kidnap him, which meant he had probably been part of a package deal. He opened his eyes and looked around.

It was early morning. Just after sunrise. At this latitude, in November, that put the time at around six in the morning. He was on a wagon, heading north. Beside him, wrapped up in blankets, were two other humans. He assumed they were Drs. Stone and Gribbleflotz. He nudged the person nearest to him.

"Huh! What?"

That was Dr. Gribbleflotz. Clearly the other person would be Dr. Stone.

Phillip wriggled until his head emerged from under the blanket. A cloud of condensation rose as he spoke. "What's happened. Where are we?"

"Somewhere north of Vicenza. We've been kidnapped."

"Oh." Phillip pursed his lips. "What do we do?"

"There's nothing we can do until we know more. I'd suggest trying to get some rest and sleep off whatever drug they used." Stephan put his words into action by using his feet to adjust his blanket so that it covered his toes. He then snuggled back into the sacks he was lying among and tried to go back to sleep.

"Wakey-wakey!"

The words were convivial. The way they were spoken was not. Nor, once Stephan got a look at the man, was the expression on the speaker's face. He looked malicious. The broken nose, missing teeth, and disfiguring smallpox scars just added to the impression.

"Right you three. Off and help with the unloading."

Stephan shuffled to the back of the wagon and slid off. It was awkward with his arms tied behind his back, but he managed to get his feet on the ground without falling over.

Someone grabbed his arms and fiddled with the bindings. They fell free and he was turned to face the wagon.

"Grab a sack and carry it into the storeroom. You can grab a pair of clogs on the way back."

Stephan dutifully grabbed a sack—of flour he noted—and hefted it onto his shoulder. He then turned and followed a man carrying another sack toward an open door. Just outside the door were a selection of roughly carved wooden clogs. Behind him, he could hear Drs. Stone and Gribbleflotz being untied and loaded.

He kept his wits about him and his eyes open. He had no idea what was going to happen, but if they ever had an opportunity to escape the more information they had the better.

The building was, he assessed, a relatively new two-level farmhouse. No more than two, at a pinch three hundred years old. The walls were covered in cream-colored plaster and it was clearly built with security in mind, with iron bars over the narrow ground-floor windows. The roof was, naturally, terracotta tiles.

It was dark inside. That might have been an artifact of the time of day. With the sun still low in the eastern sky, not much sunlight was hitting the windows on this side of the villa. The narrowness of the windows and their multiple small panes of glass probably did not help.

Stephan managed to follow the man in front without tripping over anything, even as his feet turned numb from the cold. Not just the cold of a late autumn day, but also the cold of stone floors.

Once in the storeroom, Stephan was directed where to dump the sack he was carrying. He took the opportunity to have a look around. This was the dry goods store. A cellar in fact. There was no window. The only light being provided by a couple of simple oil lamps. He glanced from them to the sack of flour he'd just brought in and thought about Dr. Gribbleflotz's demonstration of a dust bomb in the laboratory in Padua.

"Move it!"

The command was accompanied by a boot administered to his buttocks. It hurt, but not badly. Stephan took the hint and moved.

He paused on leaving the farmhouse to slide his stockinged feet into a pair of clogs. The men watching him gave him time to locate a pair with a reasonable fit before urging him on.

Phillip was upset. Someone had stolen his brand-new emerald green merino wool doublet with the cinnabar red highlights and pearl silk lining, leaving him in just his lime green linen shirt. That was bad enough, but someone had also stolen his favorite orange-pink-and-ruby cowboy-style boots. That left him plodding along on a muddy path in his crimson-orange knitted fine-merino stockings carrying a sack of produce over his shoulder.

Ahead of him, he could see a bootless Stephan Böhm. He followed Stephan into the building and down to the cellar where he surrendered his sack and headed back for more. He paused at the door to copy Stephan and secure a pair of wooden clogs. They were not as nice as his boots, but his feet welcomed the insulation from the nearly frozen ground.

Unloading the wagon was mindless, leaving him plenty of time and cognitive capacity to worry over why he was there. They had been kidnapped. Taken from the theater even before they had seen the psychic-surgery demonstration they had hoped to observe. That was very disappointing. He would have liked to see how psychic surgery was done now that he knew what to look out for. But he had been forced to miss it. He was pretty sure it was the drinks they had been served. Certainly, he did not think that the sleep-inducing agent could have been incorporated with the snacks. Too many other people had been eating them and, even in his drugged state, he had not noticed any of their neighbors dropping off. The question was why?

Obviously, they had been drugged to make the kidnap possible.

But why had they been kidnapped? Phillip could not think of any reason why anyone would want to kidnap him. So, the target must have been someone else. Someone who made the effort worthwhile. That counted Stephan Böhm out. As a Medical Department medic, he did not have access to enough money to make the effort expended kidnapping the three of them worthwhile. That left Dr. Thomas Stone. Everyone knew that Thomas had made a fortune with his fancy new dyes. Phillip nodded. It was all Thomas' fault. He glanced around looking for the man.

He found him easily and wasn't he a sorry sight.

Thomas shivered as he carried a basket of produce into the kidnappers' hideout. He had gone out last night in an old but still perfectly serviceable army surplus parka complete with insulated lining. It had even made a comfortable cushion once the theater had warmed up. And now it was gone. Just like his sneakers and knitted wool hat. At least they had left him his (slightly moth-eaten) ex-army wool pullover sweater.

He paused outside the kidnappers' lair to find a pair of clogs that would fit. Unfortunately, his feet appeared to be larger than those of the locals. The biggest pair he found before he was forcibly moved on for taking too long were still a little on the small side and, unlike leather footwear, wooden clogs were not particularly forgiving. By the time they finished unloading the wagon, his toes were cramping.

Eventually, as things will, they finished unloading the contents of the wagon and moving them into storage. Immediately after that, they were marched into the farmhouse, into a common room. And common was the right adjective. Once, it must have been a magnificent room complete with large niches on each side, but now it looked tired and ill-kept. Along the walls and under tables, men slept huddled in blankets on mattresses filled with straw that were scattered about the floor. At the top of the room was a large fireplace. It was so large that it had probably been used for cooking at some stage. A man was working on the embers, trying to get the fire going again. Sprawled out in front of the fire were a couple of large dogs. Massive dogs in fact. Both rolled their heads around to stare at Phillip and his companions as they were marched into the room.

There was a man sitting in a chair by the fire with a booted foot across his knee and a hand on the raised boot. He was a criminal, an uncouth moral degenerate criminal. Phillip felt justified in making this snap judgment based on the evidence available. It was not just that the man was clearly the one responsible for having them kidnapped. That would have made him merely criminal. However, in addition to kidnapping them, the man was wearing Phillip's brand-new emerald green merino wool doublet, and the boot the man's hand was resting on was one of *his* custom orange-pink-and-ruby cowboy boots. That put him beyond the pale.

"Who are you? Why have you brought us here?"

Phillip winced. The demands from Thomas were in line with what he had learned to expect from Americans. However, this probably was not the best time for him to demonstrate his independent spirit.

The man smiled. All he needed was a white cat on his lap and he would be the complete Bond villain. "*Dottore* Stone. It is I who asks the questions." Alessandro Garivaghi shot to his feet. "You are my prisoners." He pointed at Phillip. "You are the great *Dottore* Gribbleflotz. The World's Greatest Alchemist."

"Don't argue. Just go with the flow," Stephan hissed into Phillip's ear.

Phillip examined his fingernails. They were filthy. Still, one had to be prepared to suffer the consequences when he made a stand. He exhaled onto the nails of his right hand and buffed them on his fine linen shirt. The new dirty marks were almost invisible among those left by the sacks he had helped carry in from the wagon. He looked up and smiled. "I have been called that."

"You know how to make the philosopher's stone and thus how to make gold."

"Agree, but stall," Stephan hissed.

Phillip disagreed with Stephan. He knew what happened to people who claimed to be able to make gold through alchemy. A previous tenant of the tower where he had his laboratory back in Prague had made such a claim. After continual failure to produce results, he had come to a bad end. The renowned English alchemist Edward Kelley had been incarcerated. He died in prison, from injuries sustained whilst trying to escape. That was, as Diana Cheng's brother and his friend David Kitt had told him, a euphemism for an extrajudicial killing or execution. He had no intention of following in Edward Kelly's footsteps.

"I've never actually made the philosopher's stone," Phillip said.

"Don't lie to me," Alessandro said. "I have seen a letter from a witness who saw you make several of the great alchemist Basilius Valentinus' twelve keys."

Phillip shook his head. "That's not possible."

Alessandro stomped his foot. One of the feet encased in one of Phillip's boots. They were not designed for stomping. Not with the raised heels that gave the wearer an extra couple of inches in height. It made Alessandro look ridiculous. Not that Phillip was inclined to laugh.

"The witness was there, in Padua, when you did it. He even reported that you showed a number of the faculty how to make red dragon's blood."

"Ahhh! Padua." Phillip nodded sagely. "I did demonstrate the production of red dragon's blood in Padua recently, but that was the only one of Valentine's keys I demonstrated." He shook his head. "I've never tried to solve the riddles of all twelve."

Stephan pushed forward. "That's not to say that, if he had the right materials, *Dottore* Gribbleflotz wouldn't be able to duplicate all twelve keys and make the philosopher's stone."

"What the hell are you trying to pull?" Thomas demanded in English.

"I'm trying to keep us all alive," Stephan snapped back in the same language.

"SILENCE!"

Alessandro reinforced his demand by drawing the revolver from the leather holster attached to the Sam Browne leather webbing he had also requisitioned from Stephan's unconscious body and waved it around. Everyone in the room fell silent.

Alessandro strode unsteadily over to Dr. Stone and waved the revolver's barrel under his nose. "You are the famous *Dottore* Stone. I have heard that you are a very wealthy man." He nodded. "You, I could hold for ransom."

Alessandro stuck the barrel of the revolver under Thomas' nose and gently forced Thomas' head back. "But I won't." He stepped back, pulling the revolver away as he did so and slid it into its holster. With both hands free, he clapped his hands and walked over to Phillip.

"You," he said as he poked a finger into Phillip's chest, "are *Dottore* Gribbleflotz. You also are known to be a rich man. You also, I could hold for ransom.

"Ransoming someone is fraught with dangers." He paced, waving his hands as he did so. "Will their people pay to have them back? Will they try to trap you when you make the exchange? Will they try and capture you? Will you be identified and have the might of the Council of Ten fall upon your family?" Alessandro shook his head. "Kidnapping for ransom is a fool's game.

"There are easier ways to make one's fortune." Alessandro smiled as he looked at Phillip. It was not a particularly pleasant smile. "You are a great alchemist. You know how to make many of Basilius Valentinus' twelve keys. You will make all twelve keys and create the philosopher's stone for me. Once you have done that, you will show my alchemist how to use it to make gold. Then, I will let you go."

Phillip did not need the stifled snort from Stephan to guess just how likely to happen that last might be. It seemed they were this bandit's prisoners until they died. Or, until they could escape.

"You," Alessandro said as he poked his finger into Thomas' chest, "you are supposed to be a great up-time alchemist. You will help *Dottore* Gribbleflotz create the philosopher's stone."

Alessandro next confronted Stephan. "You, I know nothing about. Why should I allow you to live? You are nothing but a useless bodyguard." With that last word, Alessandro shoved Stephan, causing him to lose his balance.

"*Dottore* Böhm is not a bodyguard," Phillip said emphatically as Stephan fell to the ground. "He is a gifted physician and was part of the surgical team responsible for operating on the doge."

Stephan finished his fall facedown to the ground but, by virtue of his unarmed combat training, without planting his face into the stone floor. He lifted his head to look around and discovered a pair of boots right under his nose. They weren't just any boots. They were his boots. His handmade Calagna and Bauer calf-height lace-up combat boots. The person who had stolen them had not done up the laces. Stephan smiled at that. He assumed it meant they were a little small for the thief's feet.

"You like my new boots?"

Stephan looked up. The man with his boots was the same convivial individual who had dragged him off the wagon earlier. On closer inspection, he could see that the man had lost part of his left ear to a slash with an edged weapon. Judging by the various scars on his hands and arms, Stephan felt sure the injury had occurred during a knife fight. That this guy had received such an injury and was still alive to tell the tale said much about his fighting ability. With knife fights more often than not resulting in the death of at least one of the participants, that meant he had been better than the guy that cut him.

The man edged a boot under Stephan's chin and tilted his head back until they were looking into each other's eyes.

"If you want them, you'll have to fight me for them."

Stephan rolled away and scrambled to his feet. It might come to that, but not yet. Stephan knew he was in no condition to fight anyone at the moment, let alone this man. Maybe, when the effects of the drug they had been given had worn off, and when they knew more about their situation and had time to plan an escape, then he might fight the man for his boots.

Stephan turned, and found himself virtually face-to-face with the brigand leader. He took a step backwards and waited.

"So, you are a *dottore* too." Alessandro looked past Stephan to the man behind him. "We will let you live, for now." He clapped his hands. "They can share accommodations with Luigi. Take them away." He ran his eyes over Phillip, Thomas, and Stephan. "You will start work after we have broken fast."

Men grabbed the three of them and marched them out of the farmhouse to a stone barn. In the barn, they were led to a barred wooden door. One of their escort drew back the heavy deadbolt and hauled open the door. The three of them were then shoved into the room and the door slammed shut and bolted behind them.

Chapter 21

A farm near Cresole, north of Vicenza

Phillip looked around their new quarters. That did not take long. It was a very small room. Probably not much more than ten feet square. There were signs that it had once been a storeroom, but probably not of foodstuffs. Not with the unglazed window opposite the door. There was a mattress on the floor. On it, wrapped in blankets, was a gray-haired man.

Phillip studied the sleeping man for a while. He doubted the man was actually sleeping, not with the noise their guards had made. That thought had him glancing toward the door. Stephan had his hands around the iron bars of the small window set in the door they had entered through and was going through all sorts of contortions to see out. "Are there guards?"

Stephan released the bars and turned, shaking his head. "No sign of any."

"What are the chances of getting out the window?"

The question was aimed at Thomas Stone, who had been looking out the window in much the same way Stephan had been looking out through the opening set into the door. "If we could cut through the bars, maybe we could get out. But it'd be right into a rose bush with some of the most vicious thorns I've ever seen."

"It's no good trying to escape." The man on the mattress pulled back the blankets he had been wrapped in and sat up. The chains attached to his legs clattered as he turned around on the mattress to face Phillip.

Phillip studied the man. Based on the man's thin gray hair rather than any other feature that could be the result of his incarceration, he put the man's age at somewhere in the sixties. He was a fragile-looking man with the classic signs of a not particularly successful alchemist. "Luigi?"

Luigi nodded. "I have been called that. And who might you be?"

They had been speaking German for the simple reason that it was the common language Phillip, Thomas, and Stephan were most comfortable with. Phillip switched to the language Luigi had used, Venetian.

"I am *Dottore* Phillip Gribbleflotz, and these are my companions..."

"*The Dottore* Gribbleflotz? Alessandro Garivaghi claims that you taught the da Porto's nephew to make red dragon's blood." Luigi shook his head. "He hit me. He demanded to know why I couldn't make red dragon's blood when Girolomo could do it."

Phillip winced. He knew all about patrons and their unreasonable demands. "Sorry about that."

"I tried to escape." Luigi nodded emphatically. "I did. But they set the dogs on me, and they caught me." He patted one of the iron cuffs locked around his legs. "They gave me these to stop me trying to run away again."

"How did you escape?" Thomas asked. "The window is out, and the door isn't much better."

"I escaped from the laboratory. They weren't expecting that." Luigi sighed. "But they chased me. I hid, but the dogs found me."

"What kind of laboratory?" Stephan asked. His question was in poor Latin, which bore some resemblance to Venetian.

Luigi stared blankly at Stephan. "An alchemist's laboratory," he explained as if to an idiot.

Stephan smiled. "Does that mean you have oil of vitriol and aqua fortis?"

Luigi glared at Stephan. "No alchemist worthy of the name lacks the means to make oil of vitriol and aqua fortis."

"Why are you asking about the laboratory?" Thomas demanded.

Stephan tapped his nose. "I have a cunning plan."

Padua

Magda Edelmännin (aka Mrs. Thomas Stone) had a soft smile on her face as she looked down upon the sweet little eight-month-old baby boy she was holding. Across the room, seated in a comfortable rocking chair, the baby's mother, Dina Kastenmayer (aka Mrs. Phillip Gribbleflotz) gently rocked the chair as she breastfed his twin sister. Magda looked up and watched Dina for a while. She looked so serene and content. One day, in about six months' time, Magda would be doing that with her own baby. She quickly touched the wooden armrest of the chair she was sitting in. It did not do to count one's chickens, but she had passed the first trimester this time.

The sound of footsteps resonating on the wooden floor had both Magda and Dina looking over their shoulders as Ursula Mittelhausen, Diana Cheng, Lise Gebauer, and Marianna Rovarini walked in.

"Are you doing another operation?" Dina called out.

All four of the women nodded. Ursula had found yet another suitable person (in a word, rich) with a bladder stone problem. She would accompany the others as a chaperone and business agent while they performed the actual operation in the home of the client.

"Poor Corporal Böhm. I'm sure he would rather be helping you than chasing around the countryside with Phillip and Thomas."

"Do you think they're safe?" Magda asked.

"Of course they're safe," Ursula said. "Corporal Böhm is a very sensible young man. He'll keep them out of trouble."

A farm near Cresole, north of Vicenza

Thomas stared at Stephan. "Fight the man for your boots? That's not a plan. That's suicide. The guy will try to kill you."

Stephan shrugged. "That would not be entirely unexpected. It just means I'll have to kill him first."

"And you think you can do that?" Thomas demanded. "Kill a man, I mean. After all, you're a medic."

Stephan looked through Thomas in a thousand-yard stare. "I've killed before. Many times."

Thomas' jaw dropped. That answer had not been expected. He managed to close his jaw as he adjusted his thinking. "What happens if you do kill the guy with your boots? I hardly think Garivaghi is going to be happy if you kill one of his men."

"Please, could you speak in Venetian?" a very agitated Luigi demanded. "I can't understand what you are saying."

Thomas, Phillip, and Stephan exchanged looks. They had been speaking in German for a very good reason. They did not know if they could trust Luigi. "We're discussing how we can escape," Phillip said.

Stephan winced. "Dr. Gribbleflotz..."

"They'll expect us to try to escape," Phillip said. He reverted back to Venetian. "Stephan is thinking of fighting a man to get his boots back."

"Why would he want to do that?" Luigi demanded. "Alessandro's men are killers. He would kill your man."

"Thank you for the vote of confidence," Stephan muttered.

"I'm with Luigi. I think it's a horrible idea to fight the man for your boots."

"Do you have a better idea?" Stephan challenged.

Thomas regretfully shook his head. He looked at Stephan and sighed. "At least you don't have to fight him unless Phillip can make some RDX."

"And a suitable detonator," Phillip muttered. "Although Luigi should have everything I need to make fulminate of mercury."

"I have everything," Luigi protested. "I have a complete Gribbleflotz Advanced Alchemist set, with all the extras."

Luigi looked at his companions. "What is RDX, and what are detonators?"

Chapter 22

Vicenza

The brain trust of The Magnificent Ponzi show held a meeting around the breakfast table. That is, if you consider watching Elisabetta count out the previous day's takings having a meeting. Bill, Brent, and Bernardo seemed quite happy to just sit and watch as Elisabetta counted out stacks of coins and placed them into rows.

When Elisabetta had finished arranging four even rows of coins, Bill reached out and swept a row toward him. "What's the schedule?"

Brent, then Bernardo, and finally Elisabetta swept up their shares. She smiled as she poured her share into a drawstring purse. "Today, Bernardo has two operations and this evening's show. Tomorrow, there are two operations. I want to be on the road to Padua by midday tomorrow."

"Padua? But what about *Dottore* Stone? He is in Padua, and—"

Elisabetta petted Bernardo gently. "Never you mind about *Dottore* Stone." She shot Bill and Brent a conspiratorial wink before turning her attention back to her husband. "I am reliably informed that *Dottore* Stone is not currently in Padua."

Bernardo smiled. "That's good. Do you know how long he'll be away?"

"A while," Elisabetta said. "A long while. I doubt that even *Dottore* Stone knows how long he will be away."

A farm near Cresole, north of Vicenza

They were not brought food. Instead, Phillip, Thomas, Stephan, and Luigi were marched out of their cell back to the farmhouse. They were shoved toward a table and told to sit down. Once seated, they were each given a wooden spoon and bowls of steaming rice with bits of shredded salt fish, and vegetables were placed in front of them.

"Well, eat up," Alessandro ordered. "We don't want you collapsing from a lack of food." He clapped his hands. "Some drinks for our honored guests."

Mugs were distributed, and cheap red wine poured into them. Luigi dug in. The rest quickly followed his lead.

They had not long finished their meal when Phillip heard a clinking of chains from behind him. He looked over his shoulder and saw a heavyset man with three chains hanging round his neck.

"Ah, good. You are here, Fabio," Alessandro said. "Gentlemen, if you'd like to turn around, Fabio here has some special gifts for you."

Phillip, Thomas, and Stephan turned around on the bench they were sitting on. Fabio went down the line attaching a pair of leg irons to each of them in turn. Each man stared at the chain that connected the iron cuffs around each ankle.

Phillip lifted his legs. The weight was not a problem, but the short chain was going to restrict his mobility. He looked over toward Alessandro. "You expect me to work in a laboratory with these things on?"

Alessandro nodded. "It's not that I don't trust you, but I don't trust you." He smiled at his little joke as his men laughed. "Follow Fabio to where you will be working."

The door slammed behind them and they could hear a heavy bolt being slid into place. Thomas immediately sank to the ground and pulled his feet in so he could examine his shackles. Stephan did the same.

"How the heck do these things work?" a clearly frustrated Thomas demanded.

"They use a latchkey," Stephan said.

Thomas stared at him. "What's a latchkey?"

"It's a key-like device for lifting levers on a latch."

Thomas rolled his eyes. "Thanks for nothing." He released

his foot and got back to his feet. "At least with a proper lock, I might have been able to pick it. If I had a suitable tool."

"You can pick a latchkey," Stephan said as he too got back to his feet. "I could do it if I had a couple of nails."

Phillip, Thomas, Stephan, and Luigi all looked around the laboratory. It was a well-put-together structure no more than a couple of hundred years old. Which created a bit of a problem. Carpenters of the time did not use nails, or at least they tended not to. Nails were expensive, and, anyway, there were better and much longer-lasting ways of connecting timbers than by driving a piece of iron through them.

"What about an iron stirring rod?" Phillip asked. He turned to Luigi. "Do you have any?"

"Yes." Luigi scampered off, to return seconds later with a selection of iron stirring rods.

Stephan sat back on the floor and tried each one in turn on the lock of one of his shackles. He shook his head. "It's no good. They're all too big. I need to hammer the ends flat to fit them in the slot."

"If we put the end of one into the fire and heated it up, could you reshape it enough?" Phillip asked.

"Not without some kind of hammer and anvil." Stephan surveyed the laboratory. It was heavy on brick and wood, but rather limited when it came to metal. "There's nothing here suitable."

Phillip sighed. "Then we need to think of how we can get you some nails." He clapped his hands. "Until then, let's get started on something we can do. Thomas, can you show Stephan how to grind up green vitriol? And Luigi, I need to distill some aqua vitae. Do you have some wine or grappa?"

With his instructions given, Phillip turned his attention to the distillation furnace. He had opened the firebox and was looking around for firewood when he noticed Stephan and Thomas hadn't moved. "Why haven't you started grinding green vitriol?"

"What's green vitriol?" Thomas asked.

Phillip could only stare at the best chemist from the future. "You don't know what green vitriol is?"

"It's got vitriol in the name, so I assume it has something to do with oil of vitriol—otherwise known as sulfuric acid, but I don't know what it looks like."

Phillip glanced over at Stephan. He was shaking his head. Not that Phillip was surprised. There was no need for a military medic to know what green vitriol looked like. But for Dr. Thomas Stone to not know... He sighed mightily and walked over to the racks of chemicals. A quick scan found a ceramic jar marked with the alchemical symbol for vitriol—a cross with the left bar missing set in a circle. He checked that it was green rather than blue vitriol and handed the container over to Thomas. "Anything else?"

"No. No," Thomas said as he grabbed the jar and headed over to a workbench.

Phillip watched them start work industriously grinding the green vitriol with a pestle and mortar. Happy that they knew what they were doing, Phillip turned his attention back to setting a fire in the furnace. With the dry wood arranged as he liked, he felt for his GribbleZippo. It did not take him long to realize that, along with his watch, boots, and doublet, someone had stolen his lighter as well. He searched for Luigi. "Luigi," he called, "what do you use to start a fire?"

Luigi pointed. "Matches, in the box, over there."

The labeling on the cardboard box said that it contained safety matches. Phillip extracted one of the three-inch-long matches and got close to his pile of tinder before striking it against the side. He had used safety matches before, and someone had clearly been using this box, so the striking surface was obvious. The match flared and within seconds Phillip had the furnace fire started. A few pumps of a bellows and the fire was soon well established. He placed retorts of water over a couple of fire holes and went in search of Luigi.

A few minutes later, Phillip was able to add two retorts of cheap red wine to the distillation furnace. He wandered over to check the progress Stephan and Thomas were making. "How's it going?"

Stephan paused in the crushing of the green-vitriol crystals. "Slowly. And to think that I could be in Padua with my feet up."

Thomas waved his pestle at Phillip. "Are you going to help?"

Phillip shook his head. "Now I've got the water and aqua vitae going, I need to get started purifying the saltpeter for the aqua fortis."

"But I already have aqua fortis," Luigi protested.

"You may," Phillip agreed, "but I doubt that it is as pure or as strong as the aqua fortis I intend on making."

Chapter 23

A farm near Cresole, north of Vicenza

It was late on the first day of their captivity. Phillip, Thomas, Stephan, and Luigi sat on whatever they could find while they gnawed at a chunk of bread while sipping from a mug of watered wine.

"At least they're feeding us," Stephan said.

Thomas examined the chunk of bread in his hand dubiously. "If you call this food."

Stephan reached out a hand. "If you don't want it . . ."

Thomas snatched his hand back and took another bite out of his chunk.

Luigi swallowed and drank some wine to help the bread down. "They will feed us properly at night." He paused to look at Phillip. "That's when *Signore* Garivaghi will ask about our progress."

"Do we have progress to report?" Thomas asked Phillip.

Phillip shook his head. "I'm still at the making-tools stage." He sighed. "This *Signore* Garivaghi is going to be a tough patron." He passed his eyes over his companions. "Anybody got any suggestions for what we could offer him?"

Thomas tentatively raised a hand. "The philosopher's stone isn't just about making gold, is it? I mean, if we could create something spectacular, that would work, wouldn't it?"

"Define spectacular," Phillip said. "I could make my Candles of the Essence of Light."

"Probably not a good idea," Stephan said. "It's a bit too spectacular, and it would be difficult to relate the reaction to the philosopher's stone."

"You have aluminum?" Thomas asked.

Phillip nodded. "Luigi should have some. It's one of the chemicals supplied with the Gribbleflotz Advanced Alchemist set."

Thomas licked his lips. "What about hydrochloric acid and mercury?"

Luigi turned an appealing gaze upon Phillip. "What's hydrochloric acid?"

"*Acidum salis.*"

Luigi shot an offended look in Thomas' direction. "Of course I have *acidum salis*. How do you expect me to make aqua regia without *acidum salis*?"

Thomas turned an appealing gaze upon Phillip. "Aqua regia?"

Phillip sighed. "Don't you know anything about alchemy?"

Thomas shrugged defensively.

"Aqua regia is a combination of nitric and hydrochloric acid that can dissolve gold. Hence the name."

A pained look appeared on Thomas' face. "Royal water?"

Phillip nodded. That was what the Latin translated as. "Because it can dissolve noble gold."

Thomas shrugged. "Okay, that makes some kind of sense. So, you have some aluminum, hydrochloric acid, and some mercury?"

Phillip glanced over to Luigi, who was nodding. "Yes. What is it you intend making?"

"An amalgam of aluminum and mercury. It might be suitably impressive, but someone else is going to have to come up with an explanation that'll keep *Signore* Garivaghi happy."

Phillip and Luigi exchanged looks. They shrugged at each other, and then walked over to the equipment racks to collect what Thomas had asked for plus some items suitable for handling the chemicals.

Thomas selected a piece of aluminum—probably cut from some aluminum siding from an up-time house—from the jar of aluminum and placed it on a watch glass. He then dribbled some hydrochloric acid into the hole that a nail had once made in the aluminum. He used a rag to mop up the acid before depositing a drop of mercury into the indentation the nail had made and stood back.

Phillip looked from the experiment to Thomas and back. There was no noticeable reaction. He glanced over at Stephan and Luigi. They both appeared less than impressed. "What's supposed to happen?"

"It grows 'hairs,'" Thomas said. "You just have to give it time."

"Hairs." Phillip rolled his eyes. "Let's get back to work."

"*Dottore* Gribbleflotz!" Luigi's voice was almost strangled as he called out. "Quick, come and look."

Phillip carefully replaced the retort he had been checking before turning to see what had Luigi so excited. He found the man bent over the aluminum and mercury experiment Thomas had started. He was the last man to get over to it as both Thomas and Stephan had abandoned their tasks when Luigi cried out.

"Perfect," Thomas proclaimed. He gestured for Phillip to examine the small tower of fine hair that had grown out of the piece of aluminum. "How's that for spectacular?"

Phillip edged closer. He took off his spectacles to polish them before bending close. As a skilled and experienced alchemist, he also held his breath—one never knew how dangerous something might be.

"Be careful," Thomas warned. "It's extremely fragile."

Phillip grabbed a sheet of paper and held it to redirect his breathing as he gazed at the remarkable growth. "What is it? How did it happen?" he demanded of Thomas.

"It's aluminum oxide," Thomas said. "Aluminum oxide forms whenever aluminum comes into contact with oxygen. The acid removes the aluminum's protective oxide layer and the mercury prevents oxygen getting into contact with the aluminum, except on the boundary of the mercury. At the boundary, there is a constant supply of unprotected aluminum that reacts to form aluminum oxide. So it grows.

"Do you think it'll keep what's his face happy?"

Phillip smiled. He glanced over to Luigi, who was also smiling. "Animated Philosophical Mercury and the Philosopher's Tree."

"The what?" Thomas demanded.

"That's the explanation we'll use for what you have created," Phillip explained. "Now, it won't work if you don't treat the aluminum with acid first, right?"

Thomas nodded. "You need to clear away the aluminum oxide, so the mercury can be in direct contact with the aluminum."

Phillip clapped his hands. "Perfect." He turned to Luigi. "Do you think *Signore* Garivaghi will be impressed?"

Luigi sighed. "He will blame me for not discovering it sooner."

Phillip chewed his bottom lip. "We need a way to make it

an unusual event. What happens if we add something else to the mercury? Will it still work?" he asked Thomas.

"It should," Thomas said. "What do you have that you can mix with mercury?"

"The usual suspect is gold," Luigi said.

"Do you have any?"

Luigi shook his head.

There was silence as the four stared at the slowly growing tower of aluminum oxide.

"Phillip," Thomas called out, breaking the silence. "You used the phrase, Animated Philosophical Mercury. What exactly is that?"

Phillip shrugged. "It's not actually well explained in the literature."

"So, you can make up your own explanation and no one will be the wiser?"

Phillip hemmed and hawed for a while before finally conceding that yes, one could pretty much make up one's own explanation and no one would be the wiser.

Thomas muttered something Phillip felt was probably derogatory and aimed at alchemy as a science before he became all-serious again. "I don't suppose Luigi's Gribbleflotz Advanced Alchemist set would have any potassium dichromate?"

"It should. It is a rather important oxidizing agent," Phillip said. "Although he may have used it all."

"I haven't used any of it," Luigi said.

Thomas smiled. "Then prepare to be astounded." He waved at Luigi. "Please get the potassium dichromate."

While Luigi went in search of the potassium dichromate, Thomas collected a petri dish, a beaker, and some of the recently made oil of vitriol. He looked at the acid for a moment before getting some of Phillip's triple-distilled water.

He poured some water into the beaker before carefully adding a few drops of concentrated oil of vitriol. He then dissolved some potassium dichromate in the acid. This created a yellowish solution. He then poured that into the petri dish. "I need a drop of mercury and one of those iron stirring rods."

Thomas placed a large drop of mercury in the petri dish and added his mixture of potassium dichromate and acid until the drop was covered. By the time he had done that, Luigi had returned with an iron stirring rod.

"Prepare to be amazed," Thomas said before he touched the mercury with the tip of the stirring rod. Almost immediately, the drop of mercury, which had become discolored, turned back to the normal mercury color and started to pulsate.

"It lives!" Luigi cried as he bent forward for a better look. "It is beating like a heart. How is this possible?"

Thomas smiled. "That's for the world's greatest alchemist to explain."

A few hours later

The rattling of the bolt preceded the entry of Alessandro Garivaghi and his offsider Giulio Alberti—the congenial gentleman wearing Stephan's boots.

Giulio had his thumbs hooked over his belt and looked menacing as he stomped into the laboratory.

Alessandro appeared much more carefree as he stepped up to the distillation furnace—the only source of warmth in the laboratory—and looked around the laboratory. "What do you have to show me?" he demanded.

"We've only just started," Thomas muttered.

Phillip winced. The up-timers might have words like kowtow, but they never seemed willing to carry out the action when the situation really demanded it. It was obvious from his behavior that Thomas had never served a patron. If he had, he would know the correct way to treat them.

Phillip stepped between Alessandro and Thomas and adopted his most obsequious manner as he bowed to Alessandro. "A couple of our experiments have borne unexpected fruit." Phillip gestured for Alessandro to follow him and he led him over to where they had placed Thomas' mercury and aluminum demonstration.

"This is an example of Animated Philosophical Mercury reacting with the up-time metal aluminum to form a variant of the Philosopher's Tree.

"Be careful. It's very..." Phillip cried out as Giulio reached out for it.

"Fragile," he muttered as Giulio crushed the fragile aluminum oxide tower.

Giulio hastily dropped the rapidly disintegrating mesh of

aluminum oxide fibers and jumped back, brushing at the fragments of aluminum oxide that had fallen onto his sheepskin waistcoat.

Phillip looked mournfully at the wrecked tower. He turned to Alessandro. "We do have something else to show you." He gestured toward the petri dish containing the bead of mercury in the solution of oil of vitriol and potassium dichromate.

"This would work much better if we had a smaller piece of iron, like a nail. However, I will attempt to demonstrate with what we have." Phillip dipped the end of an iron stirring rod into some hydrochloric acid before rinsing it off with distilled water and wiping the tip with a rag. He then carefully held it up to the bead of mercury. A faint touch had the yellowed surface of the mercury change color, and then the mercury started to beat.

"It's alive!" Giulio screamed as he leapt back and crossed himself.

Giulio's scream had Phillip jerking back. The iron stirring rod moved with him and the mercury stopped beating.

Alessandro leaned over the petri dish. "Make it beat again!"

Phillip brought the stirring rod back into contact with the mercury. It started to beat again.

Alessandro stood up. He switched his gaze from Phillip to the beating mercury several times before settling on Phillip. "You have created life."

"Not really," Phillip said as he removed the stirring rod, causing the mercury to stop beating. "It is merely a demonstration of Animated Philosophical Mercury.

"It can be easily explained with Paracelsian Alchemy. You see," Phillip explained, "according to my great-grandfather, the great Paracelsus, all material substances are immediately composed of mercury, salt, and sulfur.

"We have this *tria prima* present in this petri dish. The yellow we see indicates the presence of sulfur. I added a special up-time salt from Luigi's store of precious up-time chemicals to the solution, and of course, there is the bead of mercury.

"However, if we just leave it there, nothing happens. It is only when we touch the mercury with iron that it starts to beat." Phillip touched the mercury with the stirring rod to prove his point. "This raises a problem. Why does the iron have this effect?"

Phillip then proceeded to blind everyone with science. He started with a clarification of the supposed uses of the philosopher's stone, including the pursuit of the elixir of life. From there he detoured into his theories about the invigoration of the *quinta essentia* of the human humors and the use of pyramid power. He paused to lament the problems he'd had with his aluminum pyramid before launching into the virtues of aura interpretation and the science of the Chakras.

"We need to do more research," he added. "That means more experiments. And to conduct more experiments, we are going to need a lot more fuel for the distillation furnace." Phillip stared expectantly at Alessandro. When he did not react, Phillip sighed. "I said we are going to need a lot more firewood."

"Okay. Okay," Alessandro said. "I heard you." He pointed to Stephan. "He can chop wood from the wood pile."

"There are a few other things I need."

"Like what?" Alessandro demanded. "You are supposed to be creating the philosopher's stone so that you can start transmuting lead into gold."

Phillip nodded enthusiastically. "Yes. Yes. Of course. However, to make the philosopher's stone, I am going to need some things." He started ticking off the fingers of his left hand. "I will need some horse manure. Also, some..."

"Horse manure? What do you want with horse manure?"

Phillip gave Alessandro his best "condescending look aimed at a patron." "I need it to produce the *quinta essentia* of the waters of wine," he said as if that explained everything.

Alessandro let loose a frustrated sigh. "Very well, but you and your people have to collect it."

Phillip acknowledged this victory by ticking off the next finger. "I also need a barrel of water. A large barrel. And lots of water—the colder the better."

He ticked off another finger. "I need a kilo—about three *libbra*—of fat. Raw. Cut from a recently butchered animal is best."

Alessandro stared at the as yet unticked fourth finger of Phillip's hand. "And is that all you require?"

"Well," Phillip said tentatively. He knew he was playing with fire, but the more misdirection he could create the better. "At some point in the future I will be needing some gold. Not a lot," he hastened to add. "Just a few grams. Less than a ducat's worth in fact."

Alessandro glared at Phillip. "Just a little? A ducat's worth? You're supposed to be making gold for *me*, not asking me for gold."

"Yes, yes," Phillip agreed. "However, in order to create the philosopher's stone, firstly, I will need to recreate Valentine's third key, which needs gold. And, also, to make the Philosopher's Tree."

Alessandro's gaze shot to the crumbled mess that had been an aluminum oxide tower. He pointed to it. "I thought that was supposed to be the Philosopher's Tree."

"Oh, no." Phillip waved nonchalantly at the remains of the experiment. "That's just the aluminum form. The real Philosopher's Tree uses gold."

"Then what good is it?" Alessandro advanced on Phillip. "Why did you waste your time and my resources making it?"

Phillip shuffled back a couple of steps. Maybe, just maybe, he had pushed Alessandro just a little too much. It was time for a little redirection. "We needed to be sure that Luigi's mercury could be animated. Which it can. As you have seen, we were able to make it beat like a heart."

Alessandro muttered something Phillip did not catch, but the man did stop advancing on him. He considered that a win.

Alessandro pointed toward the beating mercury experiment. "Bring that with you. We are going to the house where you will demonstrate it to my men."

Phillip recognized an order when he heard one. He collected the petri dish, beaker of solution, and an iron stirring rod and followed Alessandro to the house. Thomas, Stephan, and Luigi followed with Giulio bringing up the rear, and bolting the laboratory door after him.

In the main room of the house, Alessandro clapped his hands. "My alchemists have something to show you." He directed Phillip to the table as Alessandro's men gathered around.

Phillip placed the petri dish on the table and topped it up with a little more of the oil of vitriol and potassium dichromate solution. He then poked the bead of mercury with the stirring rod and pulled it back just enough that the pulsating mercury would touch it with each beat.

Alessandro's men were very impressed. They were so impressed that they jumped back and crossed themselves. Alessandro laughed. "It is very impressive, isn't it? I think our guests have earned their dinner this day."

Alessandro indicated that Phillip and company should find somewhere to sit. This, naturally, resulted in the mercury ceasing to beat. While Phillip was waiting for his meal to be served, he kept an eye on the experiment.

A man approached and poked the bead of mercury with a finger. It did not beat. He glared at it, and then he glared at Phillip.

"Try poking it with your knife," Phillip suggested.

The man poked it with the tip of his belt knife. Still the bead refused to beat.

"Push your knife in and then slowly withdraw it. The tip of your knife should just touch the mercury."

The man looked dubiously at Phillip before trying to do what he had suggested. He got two beats before he dropped his knife.

Phillip looked at the knife. It was a well-worn and worn-down knife. The blade had been honed almost to extinction, with the eight-inch blade being less than a third of its original depth. It would, he guessed, make an ideal tool for Stephan to try and pick the locks on their shackles. It was just an idle thought, easily brushed aside when their food was served. It was rice, again. With vegetables and salt fish. He worried about that. If they were eating fish, then that put paid to his hopes of getting the necessary animal fat. And then he remembered. The Republic was Catholic. "Is today Friday?" he asked.

"Yes," was the surly answer from the man seated opposite.

Phillip thanked the man before paying his meal the attention it deserved. Beside him, Luigi was eating like there was no tomorrow, while Thomas was eating in careful controlled motions. Stephan, he could see, was supplementing the rice dish by dipping his bread into a bowl of olive oil. He shuddered at the sight of him munching down on the oil-soaked bread. A little oil with one's bread was quite nice, but Stephan was having bread with his olive oil. That was something else altogether.

Less than twenty minutes later, and several attempts by various members of Alessandro's band of brigands to get the mercury to beat, the meal was over. Phillip and the others were ordered to their feet and led down a corridor. Phillip, Thomas, and Stephan were each given a couple of blankets, a sheepskin waistcoat, and a felt hat to keep their heads warm. That last caused several of Alessandro's men to laugh. Something that left Phillip wondering as he fingered his cap. There did not seem to be anything wrong with it, so why the laughter?

They were marched back to their prison and the door slammed

shut and bolted after them. Phillip dropped his blankets, jacket and hat onto the floor and walked over to the door to check whether guards had been set. They hadn't. He turned to his companions and rubbed his hands together to keep them warm. "That went quite well."

"Well?" Thomas demanded. "You're lucky the man didn't wring your neck."

Phillip smiled. A few times there he had felt that Alessandro might have been tempted to do just that. "But he didn't, and I got what I asked for."

"I can understand the firewood," Stephan said, "but why do you need horse shit?"

"It is very important in the production of the *quinta essentia* of the Waters of Wine.

"It is," Phillip protested in the face of dubious looks from his companions. "You are supposed to cover your flask of five-fold distilled waters of wine in horse manure and leave it for three months before decanting off the clear liquid and repeating the exercise for another three months. You do that four times, and after a year you have extremely pure *quinta essentia* of the Waters of Wine."

"But why do you have to cover the flask with horse droppings?" Stephan asked.

"To protect it from the light," Phillip said. He checked how that went down. Luigi looked as if he believed Phillip. Thomas and Stephan both appeared dubious. "That's what I was told," Phillip said. "Myself, I think it has more to do with protecting the flasks from damage. I mean, you're spending a year preparing something. Surely you want to prevent accidental breakages."

Thomas and Stephan both nodded. "That's much more believable," Thomas said.

"But we aren't planning on hanging around that long, so why do I—and I'm pretty sure it is going to be me who has to go outside in the cold to do it—have to collect horse droppings? How does that help us escape?" Stephan asked.

"Stephan. Stephan. Stephan." Phillip shook his head slowly in mock disappointment. "What do you find around horse droppings?"

"Horses."

Phillip clapped his hands. "Correct.

"And what do horses have that might aid our escape?"

Stephan shrugged. "I don't know. Other than serving as a form of transportation, what do horses have that might aid our escape?"

"They often wear shoes, Stephan. Iron shoes. Shoes that are nailed to their hooves. By my brilliance, I have created a situation whereby you will be able to search for something suitable for picking the latches on our shackles." Phillip rubbed his hands together and smiled. "There's no need to applaud."

That earned him a slow handclap from Stephan and Thomas. Luigi, a little lost and not understanding the significance of the slow handclap, joined in a little more enthusiastically.

"What about the fat?" Thomas asked. "What do you need that for?"

"I intend to make soap."

"Soap? Why the heck do you want to make soap?" Thomas demanded. "How does soap help us escape?"

"Soap is very good for cleanliness."

That earned him a sarcastic raised brow from Thomas.

"It's really the byproduct from soap-making I want."

"Byproduct?" Thomas asked.

"Glycerol."

"Glycerol? What the hell?" Thomas demanded. "You said you were going to make RDX, not..."

Phillip shrugged. "Luigi doesn't have the necessary precursors to make RDX, so I have to make do with what is available."

"But, nitroglycerin?" Thomas shook his head. "Do you know how dangerous that stuff is? It's terribly unstable."

"I have made it before," Phillip said. It had been under duress. His laborants had wanted to see what all the fuss was about, and Phillip had stepped in to make the nitroglycerin himself rather than have half-trained laborants chancing their arms—also fingers, eyes, and even their lives—making the stuff themselves. "It's stability depends on the purity of the ingredients and how fresh it is.

"My ingredients will be as pure as I can make them, and I doubt we will be leaving it for much more than a couple of days before it is used."

Thomas was still shaking his head. "I don't suppose there is any diatomaceous earth?"

Phillip shook his head.

"Sawdust?"

Again, Phillip shook his head.

"There must be something you can add to the nitro to stabilize it."

"I've read that flour works. I just have to think up a reason why we need some."

Thomas let out a sigh of relief.

"And then I have to make a detonator."

Thomas just glared at Phillip. "I think I might help Stephan chop firewood and collect horse droppings."

"I do know what I'm doing," Phillip protested.

Chapter 24

Saturday, 15th November 1636, a farm near Cresole, north of Vicenza

Day two of their captivity started with the rattle of chains close to Phillip's ears. Still wrapped in his blankets, Phillip rolled over to see what was causing the sound. Unfortunately for him, he was on the edge of the straw mattress the four of them had been sleeping on. He fell off. Fortunately, the mattress was lying on the floor, so he did not have far to fall. However, it was enough to bring him fully awake.

He was also nearly nose to nose with Stephan, who was doing press-ups. The sheer energy the younger man was demonstrating was distressing, especially so early in the morning. It was, after all, barely light outside.

Phillip scrambled to his feet. This was made difficult by the way he had wrapped the corners of the blankets around the iron shackles that linked his legs together. That had been done in the interests of self-preservation, or at least comfort. The near freezing overnight temperatures would have bled heat out of his body through the iron shackles like nobody's business if he had not covered them. Wrapping them also prevented the chain from rattling when he moved his feet. And as they had been sleeping top-to-toe, that had been a consideration.

Phillip slipped his stockinged feet into his clogs and he was dressed. He avoided breathing in through his nose. He had not had a proper wash or change of clothes in a couple of days and as for the sheepskin waistcoat he was wearing, not only had it been poorly tanned, it had probably never been washed. That was something he intended to correct as soon as he made some soap.

He pulled off the felt cap he had been wearing to rub an itch. That immediately resulted in another itch. Phillip examined his cap. It was a simple brimless felt cap. He remembered the laughter of the night before and turned to Luigi, who was now standing, still wrapped in his blankets, and held up his cap. "Do you know why they laughed when I was handed this cap?"

"It's a pileus."

Luigi had said that as if it meant something. Phillip glanced to Thomas. He shook his head. He glanced over to Stephan, who was now doing sit-ups. Stephan paused long enough to shake his head. "What's a pileus?" he asked Luigi.

"In Roman times it was a symbol of Libertas, the goddess of liberty. Many slaves were given a pileus when they were freed, and they wore it as a symbol of their free status."

"And we are little better than slaves," Thomas muttered. "Hence the laughter."

Luigi nodded.

Stephan had moved on to a new exercise. He had his forearms flat on the cold stone floor and his back horizontal. He was holding the position even as his body started shaking.

"Do you have to do that so early in the morning?" Thomas asked.

Stephan rolled to one side and held his new position, balanced on the side of his foot and forearm while he held the other arm high above his head. "It gets the muscles warm."

After about a minute, Stephan changed arms. Phillip, Thomas, and Luigi exchanged looks and shook their heads.

It took the rattling of the bolt securing the door to their prison to stop Stephan. He was on his feet and putting on his clogs even before the door was fully open.

The door opened extremely energetically, slamming against the wall with considerable force to reveal a wiry man of average height for the times—about five foot five. Phillip did not recognize the man, but he did recognize the up-time sneakers he was wearing. They had previously graced Thomas Stone's oversized feet. To have been given the sneakers, the man had to be high in the gang's hierarchy.

"Wakey, wakey," the man said as he strode into the cell. He stopped suddenly at the sight of all four prisoners on their feet and ready to move out. "You're already up," he muttered.

There was a lot of disappointment in those few words and Phillip immediately marked the man as a bully. Someone to be avoided.

The bully gestured for everyone to follow and he led the way to the farmhouse dining hall.

Alessandro was waiting for them. He was seated at the table, with the remains of his breakfast beside him and the beating mercury experiment in front of him. "It's stopped working," he said peevishly.

Phillip walked over to have a look. The links of the chain attached to his legs rattled as he dragged them across the tiled floor. Alessandro was poking at the bed of mercury with a horseshoe nail. He held out his hand. When that did not elicit the expected result, Phillip asked to be handed the nail. He got a dirty look from Alessandro, but he was handed the nail.

He poked the mercury. There was, as Alessandro had so clearly demonstrated earlier, no reaction. The mercury was still covered by the solution, so there was no issue of it reacting with the air. However, the solution was now a green color. Clearly there had been a chemical reaction. Probably the one responsible for the beating action of the mercury. That left one likely reason for the reaction to have stopped. Phillip rephrased it for consumption by the less alchemically inclined. "You have used up all the fuel in the solution.

"But that is easy to fix. Where is the beaker of additional solution I brought in last night?"

Alessandro pointed to the man who had collected them from the cell. "Andrea drank it."

Phillip did not have a lot of sympathy for any of their captors, but the thought of ingesting oil of vitriol made him feel ill. He turned on Andrea. "You silly, silly man. Why would you do something so foolish?" he demanded. "When did you drink it? How do you feel? Did you burn your throat?" As he asked the latter, Phillip looked around, looking for something he could use to treat the man.

"It was last night," Alessandro said.

Drinking the solution last night meant that there was no

obvious urgency. Phillip studied Andrea. The man was still breathing and did not appear to be in any pain. "You have been very very very lucky. Very lucky. That solution contained oil of vitriol." He raised his brows. "You do know what that is, don't you?" he asked when Andrea did not react.

Andrea slowly shook his head.

Phillip sighed. "It is a very corrosive acid. It could have burnt your throat and your stomach. You could have been left writhing in pain on the floor."

Andrea's face paled and he shot glares at some of his colleagues.

Phillip, who had some understanding of young men, understood this to mean that the others had somehow induced Andrea to drink the solution—probably in the form of a dare or wager. He took the opportunity offered to inspire more distrust amongst their captors. "And then there is the potassium dichromate." He paused to shake his head slowly. "That's a poison. If the dose is high enough, it is a very deadly poison. You don't even have to ingest it. Just spilling some onto your skin could be sufficient." Phillip knew this because reading Material Safety Data Sheets was something of a hobby—if self-preservation could be considered a hobby. He also knew that, in the concentration used, the potassium dichromate was unlikely to cause much more than mild discomfort. However, he did not have to let their captors know that.

"But, obviously, Andrea is neither writhing in pain on the floor, nor dead," Alessandro said.

Phillip nodded. "He has been very lucky. Is it possible he also ingested a considerable quantity of wine after drinking the solution?"

"Before and after," Alessandro said.

Phillip nodded sagely. "That is probably why it didn't kill him."

"This is all very interesting," Stephan said, "but could it wait until after everyone has eaten? Then we could walk over to the laboratory where *Dottore* Gribbleflotz can demonstrate the destructive power of oil of vitriol and make up a new batch of the solution needed to keep the animated mercury beating."

Alessandro stared at Stephan for a while before clapping his hands. The prisoners were guided to their table and left to be seated while food was brought in.

Chapter 25

Phillip led the way to the laboratory. In his hands he had the petri dish with the now stationary bead of mercury, the now empty beaker, the iron stirring rod, and the nail. He paused at the door to allow it to be unbolted. That reminded him. He turned to Alessandro. "If *Dottore* Böhm is to chop firewood, he's going to be coming in and out of the laboratory."

Alessandro waved away Phillip's concern. "We will worry about that later. I want to see what oil of vitriol does to raw meat."

Phillip shrugged. By now Andrea had opened the door and Phillip led the way in. He deposited the petri dish, flask, and stirring rod on a bench. "Stephan, help Luigi set a fire in the distillation furnace. Thomas, prepare another petri dish and flask of solution for the mercury beating heart."

With everyone else allocated tasks, Phillip collected a flask of oil of vitriol and a measuring pipette and turned to Alessandro. "It would be best if we demonstrate the power of oil of vitriol outside."

"Why?" Alessandro demanded.

"Because the smell of burning meat lingers." Phillip held up the flask of acid and pipette encouragingly. "You have the piece of meat?"

Alessandro gestured toward Andrea.

"Shall we all go outside then?" Phillip suggested.

Alessandro moved to one side to allow Phillip to pass. He entered the courtyard and looked around for a suitable place. Somewhere well ventilated and some distance from their living quarters. He found it next to a heap of horse manure. "This'll do," he announced. He directed Andrea to drop the piece of meat he was carrying while he used the heel of his clogs to dig a small hole in the horse manure. He carefully placed his flask of oil of vitriol into the depression and crouched down over it. He then inserted the pipette into the oily liquid and sucked fifty milliliters of oil of vitriol into the measuring bulb before carefully slipping a finger over the end of the pipette. He then walked over to the piece of meat and, from less than half an inch distance, let the oil of vitriol flow out of the measuring pipette and quickly stepped away.

There was smoke, or at least some kind of vapor. The meat started to change color, and there was the smell of caramel. Soon the smell changed to that of burnt caramel as the meat shriveled up and charred.

"And that's what could have happened to Andrea," Phillip announced.

"Why didn't it?" Alessandro asked. "Why didn't the acid burn Andrea like that?" He pointed to the charred remains of the piece of meat.

"Because the oil of vitriol in the solution Andrea drank had been diluted to less than one part in ten. It was still dangerous, just not as dangerous as that." Phillip pointed to the flask nested in a pile of horse manure. The men watching edged away from Phillip and the flask of oil of vitriol.

"Now, *Dottore* Stone should have the animated beating mercury ready to go, so let's get that out of the way and we can get back to work."

"Yes," Alessandro said. "You can get back to work making me gold."

"Making the philosopher's stone," Phillip corrected. "We can't start making gold until we have created the philosopher's stone."

Thomas had decided to help Stephan collect firewood, leaving Phillip in the laboratory with just Luigi for company. He had just set some acids over the distillation furnace when someone new entered the room, rather forcibly.

The heavy wooden door thudded into the wall and bounced back, to be stopped by the outstretched hand of a man wearing a blood-splattered apron. In his right hand he carried a wooden bucket. He glared at Phillip as he advanced into the laboratory.

"*Signore* Garivaghi says I have to give you some of the trimmings from the animal I just killed." Ambroso Querini held up the bucket. "It is silly. I need the fat with which to make soap and he tells me to give it to you."

Phillip ran his eyes up and down the man. Just looking at the slovenly individual, Phillip would not have thought he had even a nodding acquaintance with soap. Still, maybe he made it for Alessandro. "I only need a little bit—about three *libbra*, and I only want to extract the *quinta essentia*. The fats that are used for soap-making are an unwanted byproduct. You can have them or, if you like, I can make a hard soap out of it for you."

Ambroso stared hard at Phillip. It was obvious he did not believe him. Phillip offered Ambroso one of his best winning smiles. Sadly, he appeared immune. Instead, he just offered Phillip the bucket he was holding.

Phillip removed a double handful of raw fat. "That's all I need."

Ambroso looked from his bucket to the double handful of fat Phillip was holding. He then looked at Phillip. "I want the soap," he said before turning and leaving. He left the door wide open behind him.

Phillip hurried over to the door. Before closing it against the cold, he glanced around outside. Off to one side he could see Stephan and Thomas splitting seasoned firewood—proper control of the distillation fire required smaller pieces than regular heating or cooking fires. He waved to them, which they failed to see, and shut the door. He had things to do.

Phillip put the fat into a glass beaker and placed it in a water bath set over a retort hole on the furnace. It would take a while to render down, leaving Phillip with some empty time. He grabbed a pen and paper and sat down to write comprehensive instructions for Stephan to follow when they finished chopping wood.

Chapter 26

A farm near Cresole, north of Vicenza

Chopping wood was a good way to work up a sweat. Working up a sweat outdoors in late November in Vicenza was *contraindicated.* It was for this reason that Stephan had shed his jacket, his sweater, and finally his shirt as his body warmed up while he chopped firewood. Still, gentle wisps of steam were visible about his lean torso.

"That should be enough," Thomas called.

Stephan looked across to the pile of wood he had chopped. He agreed that it should be enough for now. He adjusted his hold on the axe, letting the handle slip through his fingers until the head was almost at his hand. He tightened his grip and looked around for someone to hand it to—there was no way their captors were going to allow him to walk off with it.

"I'll take that," Giulio said.

Stephan swung around. He saw Giulio, and he saw the way Giulio was looking at him. It wasn't sexual; it was assessing. And Giulio seemed to like what he was seeing. He held out a hand for the axe Stephan was holding.

Stephan handed over the axe and grabbed his shirt. After a quick rubdown he pulled it on, followed by his sweater and sheepskin jacket. As a final touch he put on the felt cap before filling a basket of firewood and heading for the laboratory. At the door, he glanced back. Giulio was still watching him.

With both hands needed to hold the basket of wood Stephan

was reduced to kicking at the door with his booted toe to attract the attention of someone inside. It was opened by Andrea. That came as a bit of a shock, and it was a few seconds before he collected himself enough to step into the laboratory. Alessandro Garivaghi was standing close to the distillation furnace, and not just because it was warm over there. No. Dr. Gribbleflotz was showing him something. "Where do you want the wood?" Stephan asked.

Phillip glanced up, saw Stephan, and pointed to a spot by the stokehole of the furnace. "Just over there, please. And Stephan, I've got something I need you to do."

"What?" he asked as he deposited the basket of wood on the floor.

Phillip made a slight adjustment of a retort before leading Stephan to a bench. Dr. Stone, who had dumped his basket of firewood beside Stephan's, followed.

Phillip handed Stephan a sheet of paper. "Everything you need is on the bench. Please follow the directions exactly."

Stephan checked the sheet of directions. It was written in German which, considering what he was being told to do, was fortunate. He stared at the directions in shock. He glanced from Dr. Gribbleflotz to *Signore* Garivaghi and raised his eyebrows in question. Phillip nodded, confirming that yes, he did expect Stephan to make gunpowder while their captor was in the same room. Stephan shrugged and got to work.

"What about me?" Thomas asked.

"You can help me."

"And what'll you be doing?"

"*Signore* Garivaghi wishes to see red dragon's blood being made. While the solution is being distilled, I intend working over there purifying the *quinta essentia* of the animal fat I have so kindly been given."

Stephan followed the direction Dr. Gribbleflotz pointed. There, standing innocently beside a work surface, was a barrel of water, and it dawned on him what the purified *quinta essentia* of animal fat was going to be. His tongue had to work hard to moisten his lips. He glanced at Dr. Stone to see if he had realized what Dr. Gribbleflotz would be making. He had not. There was no way he could be so nonchalantly willing to help Dr. Gribbleflotz if he had. Stephan decided not to enlighten him.

Padua

"Do we have everything?" Rachel Lynch asked of her companions. A cloud of condensation filled the air around her as she spoke.

Edith Lynch, Luchia, her sister Giulia, and their cousin Giovanna Parini, the wife of Antonio Fossato, all rolled their eyes. Rachel's mother put their thoughts into words. "We all know how important this meeting could be."

"If we can get the contract to supply Gribbleflotz with iodized salt, 'we will be made,'" Giulia said, quoting Rachel at the end.

"But we have to be careful of *Signora* Mittelhausen, because she is 'the very devil to negotiate with.'" Giovanna was also quoting Rachel, but she had gone a step further, changing her voice to try and sound like her as well.

Rachel glared at Giovanna. "I do not sound like that," she protested, "and she *is* the very devil to negotiate with."

"Yes, dear," Edith said.

Rachel transferred her glare to her mother. "I don't have to be placated."

"Of course not, darling. But you are a little on edge about this meeting."

"How much coffee did you drink this morning?" Luchia asked.

Now it was Luchia's turn to be glared at. "Just the one," Rachel said indignantly.

"But how many teaspoons of coffee powder?" Giovanna asked.

Rachel *humphed* extremely loudly and pointedly. There was no use protesting her innocence, not when they had all been there to see her spooning in the instant coffee. It had almost been strong enough for the spoon to stand unaided. Of course, *that* could have been because of all the sugar she had added. She turned her back on her companions and led the way to the front door of the Rovarini residence.

They did not have to wait long after knocking for the door to open. "Come on in," Paola Rovarini said, "everyone is in the kitchen." Left unsaid was, "Where it's warm." It was currently somewhere in the mid to high forties outdoors.

Rachel glanced at her companions before kicking off her outdoor boots and replacing them with a pair of slippers from those stored near the door and hanging up her coat. Then they all traipsed into the kitchen.

The warmth was the first thing that hit them. There was an

iron cooking range, just like the ones being made back in USE. Rachel raised her eyebrows at the sight of the thing, and she stepped closer to investigate. It bore a maker's plate from the Republic of Essen, but that was not the most interesting thing. That was the fact she was not feeling much radiant heat coming from the stove itself. A little exploration found a radiator, with taps, to one side. The radiator was hot.

"*Signora* Mittelhausen recommended that we buy that model years ago," Paola said. "It is fully insulated so that the kitchen doesn't get too hot in summer."

Rachel could well understand the need for that feature. She had only been in Italy a few months, but that had been enough to tell her that it could get hot in the summer, Little Ice Age or no Little Ice Age. She turned her back to the radiator and inspected the competition. There was Paola, Ursula Mittelhausen, the nurse Lise Gebauer, and Diana Cheng. "There is no one representing *Dottore* Stone."

"No," Paola agreed.

Rachel glanced at her companions. They had all been sure that Dr. Stone would be involved. "Why not?" she asked Ursula.

Paola whispered into Ursula's ear. She smiled at Rachel. "Because the license has been granted to *Dottore* Gribbleflotz."

Rachel stared at Ursula. The delay in her response suggested that she didn't understand Italian. Of course, that could just be a negotiating ploy. She wouldn't put anything beyond Frau Mittelhausen. On the other hand, when could she have learned Venetian? Of course, it was not that different from Latin, which Rachel assumed both Diana Cheng and Lise Gebauer, because of their medical studies, were fluent in. "Would it be easier if this discussion was conducted in another language?" she asked.

"German?" Paola suggested in German.

Rachel's brows shot up. "You know German?" She hastily corrected herself. "I mean, you are sufficiently confident in the language to conduct business in German?"

Paola smiled and nodded her head.

Rachel so wanted to ask how that was so and, from the smug smile on her face, it was clear that Paola knew it. However, that was a battle for another day. Right now, they had a deal to hash out. "Very well, German it is. Let's get down to business."

Papers appeared on the kitchen table and were passed around.

✧ ✧ ✧

It had quickly become obvious why the discussion was being held in Paola's kitchen. Or at least, another reason became obvious. The warmth of the room was the first reason, but Paola, Lise, and Diana constantly getting up to stir a pot on the stove or check something in the oven quickly brought home that this was a working kitchen.

Around one o'clock they had to pack away their papers and set the table for the midday meal. They were joined for lunch by Paola's husband, various members of the Rovarini family, and some of his employees and their children. With so many already having lunch in the house, Paola had insisted that Rachel's brood should join them.

One advantage with an Italian family lunch was that there were always spare adults available to keep an eye on the children. Rachel's four-year-old son John was doing his best not to make a mess of his clothes while he ate spaghetti in the proper Italian manner. Six-year-old Diana was chatting with a couple of girls her own age while she ate a bowl of rice risotto. It was William, her eight-year-old, Rachel really had to keep an eye on. He was, to put it mildly, a picky eater. There were things he just would not eat, and Rachel could do without the embarrassment of an all-out tantrum. Fortunately, William had found a new friend in one of Paola's grandchildren and he was willing to eat anything Marcello ate. With peace on the horizon, Rachel was free to supervise Edith, her two-year-old daughter, while also eating heartily herself.

She was busy wiping Edith's face and hands clean—never underestimate the ability of a child to get messy when eating—when William popped up beside her.

"Mom, can I go with Marcello to see the jousting?"

Rachel was taken aback. Jousting was something that had happened in the dark ages. She looked over to Marcello. "Jousting?"

Marcello nodded. "At the *Prato della Valle*. Not that they will be competing today, but they should be practicing."

"Can I go, Mom? Please?"

Rachel was not proof against the pleading look her son was sending her way, but she stood her ground as she thought about it. Marcello was a couple of years older than William. "Are your parents okay with you going?" she asked.

Marcello nodded.

Rachel turned back to William. "Do you have your whistle?"

William threaded a thumb through the ribbon around his neck and pulled it up until an up-time–style pea-whistle appeared. Rachel insisted her children always carry one because they made a noise more penetrating and attention-seeking than mere screaming or yelling. She nodded permission. "Okay, off you go, but be sure to be home before dinner." She turned to Marcello. He saw the unspoken request that he look after William and nodded.

"Can I take Gran's gun?" William asked.

Rachel's first instinct was to give a unilateral "No!" but a little thought had her tempering that reaction. Experience had taught her that a more reasoned response yielded better results. It was not that William could be reasoned with because, like most children his age, reason came a poor second to "I want." No, he had to convince himself that a choice was right. "Why do you need a gun?" she asked.

"Because . . ."

Rachel raised her brows. A clear indication that she was waiting for more in the way of an argument.

"I need it for protection."

Rachel slowly shook her head. "If you need to carry a gun for protection, then obviously it is too dangerous for you to go and watch the jousting without an adult to accompany you."

"Oh, no. It's not that dangerous," William protested. "The *Prato della Valle* is quite safe. Isn't it, Marcello?"

"It is quite safe, *Signora* Lynch."

Rachel looked expectantly at William. "If it is quite safe, then you won't be needing a gun, will you?"

William sighed and shook his head.

"Right, off you go then." Rachel waved the boys off.

She watched William disappear and sighed. "Am I a bad mother?" she asked the others.

"For not letting your eight-year-old walk around with a loaded gun?" Diana asked. She shook her head. "That was being smart. I certainly wouldn't have trusted my brother with a gun at eight."

"He misses his father."

Edith snorted. It could have been a picture, so well did it illustrate her opinion of Rachel's comment. "He doesn't miss him. He just feels that he has to be the man of the household."

Rachel sighed. There was, unfortunately, a lot of truth in that. "Let's get back to discussing Gribbleflotz's Iodized Salt."

A farm near Cresole, north of Vicenza

"It's changed back to gold."

Stephan looked around from the hollow length of straw he was packing with fine gunpowder. The leader of the gang that had kidnapped them did not look happy. Dr. Gribbleflotz, though, did not seem to have a care in the world. And as he was currently making nitroglycerin, he had to be acting.

"Then I will dissolve it again and set the retort to distill off the acid again." Phillip followed his words with action. He handed the flask he was holding to Thomas, who, Stephan judged by his less than happy expression, now knew just what he was being handed, and walked over to the retort Alessandro was staring at. He examined the contents of the retort before grabbing some padded gloves and after removing the top of the retort, poured the distillate from the receiver vessel back into the retort and swirled it around until the gold had dissolved again. He then put the top back on and set the retort back on the furnace with the spout directly over the receiver beaker.

"How many times do you have to do this?" Alessandro demanded.

Phillip shrugged. "As many as it takes. There is no fixed number. We just perform the cohobation until we get the desired result."

"We will get the desired result, won't we?" Alessandro demanded.

Phillip reared back on his high horse. "I am *Dottore* Phillip Gribbleflotz. Great-grandson of Paracelsus, the greatest alchemist of his time. I never fail to make something I have made previously." Phillip gave Alessandro a less than gracious nod before walking back to the barrel of water where Thomas was still carefully swirling the flask of acid and the *quinta essentia* of animal fat in the cold water.

"And what is that you are making?" Alessandro demanded as he followed Phillip across the room.

Phillip held out his hand out for the flask and raised it, while still swirling the thick oily contents. "This," he said, holding the flask of clear liquid almost under Alessandro's nose, "will soon be purified *quinta essentia* of animal fat.

"When it is ready, I will be happy to demonstrate its power.

"Now, if you don't mind..." Phillip turned his back on Alessandro and walked over to Thomas. He placed the flask in the cold water and added another few drops of glycerin to the solution. He also used a mercury thermometer to check the temperature.

Sometime later

Phillip held up the flask of purified *quinta essentia* of animal fat. It was a nice clear oily liquid. He had added fifty milliliters of glycerin to the acids, which meant he had about one hundred twenty-three grams of nitroglycerin, or a little over a quarter of a pound. That should, according to Stephan, be enough to disperse the contents of a twenty-pound sack of flour throughout the main room in the farmhouse. He looked across to where Alessandro was sitting impatiently. Phillip smiled. He might benefit from a little excitement.

"Thomas, could you find a ceramic tile and place it on the bench?"

"What're you planning?"

"A simple demonstration for *Signore* Garivaghi."

Alessandro leapt to his feet. "What? What do you have to show me?"

Phillip held up the flask of nitroglycerin. "I am going to put a single drop of this magic liquid on that tile and see what happens if I ignite it."

Phillip did exactly that. He dipped a glass pipette into the nitroglycerin and allowed a small amount to enter it. He then placed a single drop in the middle of the ceramic tile before returning the flask to the barrel of water. He also rinsed the pipette in the cold water. With everything in place, he took a thin wood spill and lit it from the fire. He touched the lit spill to the drop of nitroglycerin.

Nothing happened immediately, but then, less than a second later, a strong and tall flame shot up from the tile. Phillip smiled at Alessandro. "That looks very good. I think we have a very good sample of high-purity *quinta essentia* of animal fat."

"Do it again!"

Phillip repeated the exercise. This time using two drops. Again, the nitroglycerin burned in a bright and towering flare.

When the flame died down, Phillip looked questioningly at Alessandro. "Again?"

Alessandro sighed. "No. I have wasted too much time here already." His eyes drifted over to the retort Luigi was tending. "I wish to be informed when the dragon's blood forms."

"Of course, *Signore* Garivaghi."

"I wasn't talking to you." Alessandro turned to Andrea. "Stay here and keep an eye on them."

Andrea grumbled a reply and Alessandro left.

Andrea found somewhere to sit and plonked himself down. "Do you have anything to drink?"

Phillip smiled. "I have some triple-distilled essence of the waters of wine."

"What is that?"

"It's like grappa, but stronger. Isn't that right, Luigi?"

Luigi nodded vigorously. "It is so strong that it needs to be diluted with distilled water." He splashed some triple-distilled alcohol into a mug and added some water and offered it to Andrea.

Andrea looked at the mug suspiciously. "I want to see you drink it first."

Luigi shrugged and took a large sip. He immediately lowered the mug and shook his head. He whistled. "It's still a bit strong. I'll just add some more water."

"No!" Andrea held out a hand. "I'll take it."

"Sip it," Phillip warned.

"You think I can't hold my wine?" Andrea demanded. He glared at Phillip as he took a swig of 150-proof white spirits.

Luigi rescued the mug as Andrea fought for breath. It took about thirty seconds before Andrea, with tears running down his face, was able to breathe properly again. He immediately held his hand out for the mug. This time, however, he just took a sip. "That is stronger than any grappa I've ever had."

Phillip nodded. "As I said, it is the triple-distilled essence of the waters of wine. It's probably as much as five times stronger than any grappa you have ever drunk."

Andrea took another sip. "I like it. Why can't we always drink it?"

"It is expensive to make," Phillip said.

Andrea sighed. He returned to his seat close to the distillation furnace and made himself comfortable. He took another sip.

Padua

William Lane Franklin Jr. was not sure exactly what he had been expecting to see, but the *Prato della Valle* was not it. Instead of colorful tents arranged around a tiltyard, the theater where mock fighting and tilting took place was within a fenced enclosure. He looked around the rest of the meadow, or *prato*, in which the arena was set. Judging by the areas of swampy ground, it was set in a bit of a valley-like depression, so there was some truth in advertising, but he was still a little disappointed.

William let Marcello lead him up to the fence around the arena. There were some gaps at about the right height for him to look through and, with a little judicious use of their elbows, he and Marcello managed to find spots from which they could survey what was going on inside the arena.

It was just like in the pictures in his illustrated *Ivanhoe*, although not as colorful. William put that down to the fighters practicing rather than performing. There was a tilt barrier—the fence that separated two charging knights as they attempted to skewer each other with their lances. Except that people seemed to be dismantling it. Maybe they were going to rehearse a mock battle. They would certainly need a lot of room to practice mass combat.

Moments later, they were bumped from their places by bigger boys. William stared at their backs and thought how different things would be if he had his grandmother's Beretta Bobcat. Instead, all he could do was sigh and turn to Marcello. "I don't suppose there's any chance we can get inside?"

"Maybe," Marcello said. "It depends on who is at the gate."

William's eyes lit up. "Then what are we waiting for?"

The two boys followed the fence around to the front entrance. As they rounded the last corner, they spied two men pasting up a poster. They slowed down, as it would be pointless to arrive before they had it up so it could be read.

"They're up-timers."

William shot Marcello a questioning glance.

"Look at their clothes."

William did so and realized that Marcello was correct. He studied the men as he and Marcello approached. Maybe he knew them, and besides, something about the one on the left was niggling at him.

The closer they got the more William felt he should know the man. There was something about him that was familiar. And then the man took a pose William remembered. "Dad?"

He had not said it loud enough for even Marcello to have heard. He stared at the man as they got closer. With each step he became more and more convinced that the man was his father. Finally, it all got too much for him and he ran forward, screaming out at the top of his voice as he ran.

"Dad! Dad! Dad!"

The two men stopped what they were doing and turned to look at William as he ran toward them.

The look of disbelief on his father's face had William slowing down rather than running straight up to his father and hugging him. "Dad?

"It's me.

"William.

"Your son."

William "Bill" Lane Franklin held up the broom he had been using to paste up a poster defensively. "William? What are you doing here?"

William stuttered to a complete halt. This was not the greeting he had dreamed of. "I'm here with Marcello." He gestured to his companion.

Bill shook his head. "No. You should be back in Grantville. Not here in Padua."

William shrugged. "When you went away, Mom had to find a job. She got one with the Sanitation Commission." A smile blossomed. "Now we travel all around teaching people all about proper sanitation and stuff like that."

Bill's eyes widened. "Your mother's here in Padua?"

William nodded.

Bill took a step backwards. "You can't tell her I'm here. Promise me you won't tell anyone I'm here."

William did not like keeping secrets from his mother, but this was his dad. "I promise." He looked past his father at the poster he had helped put up. "What are you doing here?"

Bill moved close to William and crouched down to his eye height. "I'm doing something top secret. For the army."

"The USE Army?"

Bill nodded. "Shouldn't you be in school?"

"I'm being homeschooled." William grimaced. "According to the Grantville silly-bus." He did not approve of that. There were lots more interesting things to learn than social studies and English. "But Gio is also teaching me Latin, Greek, and music."

"Who's Gio? Has your mother found herself a new man? Is she sleeping with him?"

The questions came quick-fire. Too fast for William to get a word in if had wanted to. He stared at his father, not really understanding much beyond the first question. "Gio is Luchia's husband."

"Ah. Okay." Bill stood up. "What are you doing here anyway?"

"We hoped to get inside to watch the performers rehearsing for the joust."

Bill shook his head. "I can't let you in. I don't work here."

"Then what are you doing here?" William let his eyes move past his father to the poster he had been pasting up. He read it, and then looked at his father. Something strange was going on here. Something he had to tell his mother about. He let his shoulders slump. "I guess that means we might as well go home." He did not sob. That would have been taking it too far.

"I'm sorry, son."

"Bye, Dad."

"Bye, William. And remember, don't tell anyone that I'm here or what I'm working on. Promise!"

"I won't. I promise." William turned to leave. "Come on, Marcello."

"Did you see that poster?" Marcello asked once they were far enough away that William's father and his colleague would not hear.

William nodded.

"The Magnificent Ponzi will be performing at the *Prato della Valle* next weekend. Isn't that the show *dottori* Stone and Gribbleflotz went to see in Verona?"

Again, William nodded.

Marcello glared at him. "Is that all you're going to do, nod at me?"

Once more, William nodded. He had a wry smile on his face as he quickly skipped clear of the hand Marcello raised to clap him over the ear. "I promised I wouldn't tell anyone."

"But people have to know that The Magnificent Ponzi is here in Padua."

Once more, taking his life into his own hands, William nodded. Before Marcello could say or do anything, he held up a hand. "You didn't promise not to tell anyone what we saw." There was no smile on his face as he said it. He was weaseling out of his promise to his father, but he knew his mother had to be told that his father and The Magnificent Ponzi were here in Padua.

"Sneaky. Your father probably didn't think that I would understand English."

William's father had spoken to him in English, probably for exactly that reason, so he nodded. Marcello raised his hand again as if to clip him across the ear, and William suddenly smiled. "Come on, I'll race you home. You've got a message to pass on to my mom."

William did not burst into Paola Rovarini's home. He was too well trained to do such a thing. Besides, he had Marcello with him. Marcello opened the door and quietly closed it after letting them both in. The sound of adults talking drew them to the kitchen.

William looked around, his eyes wide and attentive, his nose quivering. "Is there anything to eat? I'm hungry." He saw his mother looking at him. "Marcello's hungry too. Aren't you?" he asked Marcello.

"What're you doing back so soon?" Rachel asked. "I thought you were going to the theater at the *Prato della Valle* to watch the fighters practicing."

William pouted. He had really been looking forward to seeing them, but some things were more important than what he wanted. "We got a spot at the fence, but some bigger boys pushed us aside."

Rachel enveloped William in her arms. "And you were so looking forward to seeing them. I'm sorry."

Silence reigned in the kitchen.

To be broken by Marcello. "The Magnificent Ponzi will be performing at the *Prato della Valle* next weekend."

There were bombshells, and then there was what Marcello had just said.

"What?" was the communal roar of more than a dozen adults.

Which, naturally, caused every baby in the room to wake up and start crying.

Rather than wait for the babies to settle down, their mothers removed their respective noise sources from the room, secure in the knowledge that someone would fill them in on anything they might miss later.

"William's father and another up-timer were putting up a poster advertising the coming attraction at the *Prato della Valle*," Marcello said.

Rachel pushed William far enough away that she could look down into his eyes. "Your father? He's here in Padua?"

William gave Marcello a pleading look.

"His father made him promise not to tell anyone that he was in Padua."

Rachel looked down at William. "You made a promise to your father?"

William was torn. Would admitting that mean he had broken his promise? He settled for a nod of his head. It was not really telling anyone anything.

"What the heck's he doing in Padua?" she asked the room in general.

The room in general chose not to reply.

"Putting up posters promoting The Magnificent Ponzi," Paola suggested when it became obvious no one else was going to say anything.

"But why?" Rachel wondered.

"Either he's working for the theater, or he's working for Ponzi," Edith said. "And I doubt he's working for the theater. Sebastian would have told us if he'd run into any Americans during his visits to the theater."

"Yes," Rachel muttered. She reached out and patted William gently on the shoulder. "You did right, William." She smiled. "Now why don't you and Marcello see if Diana can find you something to eat?"

Both boys hurried over to Diana, who soon had some bread, butter and jam prepared for them. With a mug of watered wine as something to drink. Milk would have been better, but who had fresh milk in November? Rachel turned her attention back to the adults gathered around the table. "We need to do something about Ponzi."

"Why?" Luchia asked. "He isn't doing anything illegal."

"He's propagating psychic surgery," Rachel said.

"But *dottori* Stone and Gribbleflotz have surely asked them not to include it in their performance."

"That doesn't mean they won't," Rachel said. "We need to shut him down. Before he causes trouble."

"Paolo. Sebastian's friend. Is an official with the *Provveditori alla Sanità*," Diana said as she returned to the table. "If we told him the situation, maybe he could have a few words with Ponzi?"

"How do you know that he is an official with the *Provveditori alla Sanità*?" Giovanna asked.

"He was instrumental in us gaining the necessary licenses to perform transurethral lithotripsies in the Republic," Ursula said. "However, I think everyone is missing an important point. Where are *dottori* Gribbleflotz and Stone, and Stephan Böhm? If they have spoken with Ponzi, then surely, they should have returned by now. And if they have not, then how does Ponzi know that they aren't here in Padua?"

As the significance of what Ursula had said sank in, everyone sat and stared at her.

"Look," Ursula said defensively, "what I'm saying is, from what Rachel and the rest of the Sanitation Commission mission have said, they have to know *Dottore* Stone would expose them as frauds and charlatans. So, why would they come to Padua? They have to know he lives here."

"Something must have happened to them," Paola said. She looked around for the boys. Both William and Marcello were sitting on the floor by the radiator. "You two. Do you know Sebastian Jones?"

William nodded. "The one with the cameras."

"Yes, him," Paola agreed. "I need you to go and find him, and his companion..."

"Paolo," Diana offered. "Paolo Molin."

"Yes. Right. Sebastian and Paolo Molin. You need to go and find them. Tell them it is urgent they come here."

William and Marcello exchanged looks before getting to their feet. "Where should we start looking?" William asked.

"The *Palazzo della Ragione*," Paola said. "If he's not there, try the *Basilica di Sant'Antonio*."

"There'll be a lot of people there," Marcello said. "How will we find him?"

Diana snorted. "Sebastian will have his cameras, which means he'll have attracted a crowd. Just check out any crowd you see."

Marcello nodded. He turned to William and jerked his head. They made for the door at a moderately paced walk. After they exited the house, the sound of running footsteps could be heard.

It took a while for William and Marcello to run Sebastian and Paolo to ground. They finally found them outside the *Basilica di Sant'Antonio*, where Sebastian was busy taking photographs of locals and processing them on the spot. For that reason, they had to wait for the latest prints to dry before Sebastian was willing to pack up and follow them home.

Things did not develop as Rachel would have liked once they explained the situation to Paolo.

"I can't order them shut down. They aren't doing anything illegal."

Rachel glared at Paolo. "They may be planning on putting on a demonstration of faith healing and psychic surgery."

"Theatrical performances are not illegal. If Ponzi was doing something illegal, then the informer reports of his events would have mentioned it and the *Inquisitori di Stato* would have sent someone out to deal with it."

"Informer reports?"

Paolo nodded. "Reports from informers. You don't think the Republic will just allow groups like yours and Ponzi's to wander around holding events that can attract hundreds of people without checking up on you?"

Rachel stared at him. "There are informers reporting about our activities?"

"Of course. However, there is no need for concern. When I reported to my superiors that *Dottore* Gribbleflotz was in contact with your group, he said that your group's activities were of no concern."

Rachel was not completely mollified. "What are they saying about Ponzi?" she demanded.

Paolo gave Rachel a wry smile. "Nothing of import," he said with a shrug. "He doesn't even try and peddle remedies of dubious worth to the people who attend his performances. That means he is not of interest to the *Sanità*."

"Hang on," Rachel said. "The Sanitation Commission had to get permission for us to operate in the Republic..."

"And," Paolo interrupted, "no doubt Ponzi has suitable papers. Otherwise he wouldn't have been able to book the theater in the *Prato della Valle*."

Rachel glared at Paolo. "They're probably forgeries," she muttered.

Paolo just shrugged. "If they are, it is a matter for the *Inquisitori di Stato*, not the *Sanità*."

"But what about Filippo?" Paola asked. "He left for Verona with *Dottore* Stone and *Signore* Böhm to find these people. Yet they are here in Padua and Filippo is nowhere to be seen."

Paolo sighed. "What is it you want me to do? Go to Verona and find them?"

"Yes."

Paolo rolled his eyes. "I was being sarcastic," he said.

"Would fifty ducats change your mind?" Ursula Mittelhausen asked.

Paolo's jaw dropped. "Are you trying to bribe me? An official with the *Provveditori alla Sanità*?"

"Of course not," Paola said. "She is trying to hire you to do a job."

"Oh, well. That's alright then."

"Good," Rachel said. "When can you leave?"

"I was being sarcastic," Paolo said.

"I'll go," Sebastian said. "You only want to let them know that The Magnificent Ponzi is here in Padua. Don't you."

Paolo swung around. "You? You're not safe out on your own in a city. Who knows what trouble you'll get yourself into in the countryside? There are brigands out there."

Sebastian patted a bulge under his jacket. "I've got a gun."

Paolo raised his eyes heavenward. "He's got a gun," he muttered. Paolo shook his head. "Do you even know what a brigand looks like?"

"We need you to leave as soon as possible," Rachel said.

"That's not a problem." Sebastian smiled at Paolo. "If you're so worried about my safety..."

Paolo ground his teeth.

"Maybe this will make it more palatable for you," Ursula Mittelhausen said.

Paolo looked toward her and discovered that the clicking sound he had sort of been aware of had been her laying out coins on the table. Gold coins. Golden ducats. In rows of ten. She was midway through a third row and still placing down coins. As he watched, Ursula finished the third row and started on a fourth row, and then a fifth row. Paolo swallowed and licked suddenly dry lips. There, laid out on the table, and being added to even as he watched, was a sum in excess of his annual salary. However, it was not the nearly fifty ducats laid out on the table in front of him that really got to him. It was the casual way the woman was still randomly pulling coins from a leather drawstring purse—a purse that was still the size of his fist—suggested that it was full of gold ducats. That suggested real wealth. Wealth on par with that of the heads of the Molin family.

She looked up after placing down the fiftieth gold ducat. "Will you go?"

Paolo stared at the coins. It represented a better apartment in Venice and a few luxuries. "That's a lot of money just to fetch a couple of wanderers."

"There might have been foul play. Ponzi and his team wouldn't come to Padua if they thought *Dottore* Stone was in town. The fact they are here suggests they know he isn't."

"That doesn't necessarily mean anything has happened to them. Ponzi might have just recognized them riding past on the road." Silence and raised eyebrows were the response Paolo's statement got and, he accepted, deserved. "It's a possibility," he protested half-heartedly.

"A very small possibility," Ursula said. "And also, even if they did see them on the road, they won't have any idea when they are due back." She shook her head. "No. There is no way they would be here planning on putting on a show next weekend if they did not know the way would be clear. Obviously, they know that something has happened to *dottori* Stone and Gribbleflotz."

Paolo held his arms up signifying surrender. "Very well. Have it your own way. Something has maybe happened to *dottori* Stone and Gribbleflotz, and you want me to go and rescue them."

"And Stephan," Diana added. "If they've taken him out as well... Well, you better go loaded for bear."

Paolo stared at Diana. He was pretty sure that she had just given him an up-timer expression translated into Latin. He just was not sure what it meant. *Loaded for bear?* "I should arm myself to fight a bear?" he asked.

Diana grinned. "Close enough. It's an American idiom I butchered into Latin. It means go prepared for a hard fight."

Paolo nodded as he muttered the phrase over and over to himself. He might find an opportunity to use it himself one day. He turned to Sebastian. "I have a pump-action 12-gauge shotgun and a pump action .50-100 rifle. Which would you prefer?"

"The shotgun," Sebastian said. "Do you have buckshot?"

"Naturally. I also have slugs." Paolo turned to Paola. "We'll need horses. Good horses. And good saddles."

Paola turned to the boys. "Marcello. Run over to the stables and tell your cousin we need two of his best riding horses saddled up and ready to go as soon as possible."

"I need to get my gear. I'll meet everyone here in a few minutes." Paolo gave a bow to the company and ran off.

"I need to get my gear together too," Sebastian said before he too ran off.

With the kitchen to themselves again, the women looked at each other. "Do we tell Magda and Dina what we fear?" Paola asked.

"No," Edith said.

Rachel agreed. "There's no need to have them worried, especially not Magda. She's got enough to worry about with her pregnancy."

Within half an hour both Paolo and Sebastian were back with their gear. They slung saddlebags over the rumps of their horses and tied them to the saddles. Paolo tied a sheathed rifle to his saddle and handed another sheathed weapon to Sebastian. He also handed him a belt of shotgun cartridges. "The solid slugs are red, and the buckshot are blue."

"Thanks," Sebastian said as he slung the belt bandolier-style across his chest. "How is it you have these guns? Is it normal for officials in the *Provveditori alla Sanità* to go about so armed?"

"No, it's not normal. A contact of my brother-in-law made them available when he learned that I would be venturing out of Venice with *Dottore* Gribbleflotz's party."

"Someone hoping to interest the rich foreigners in their merchandise," Sebastian suggested as he secured the sheathed shotgun to his saddle.

"Yes. But it is fortuitous that we have such weapons if, as *Signora* Cheng suggested, we need to be 'loaded for bear.'" He turned his attention to Ursula, who was approaching them.

Ursula handed Paolo two purses. "This is your payment, and this is for expenses." She clasped her hands over Paolo's. "Bring them back. Bring all three of them back."

"I'll do my best," Paolo said as he first secured the heavy bag containing his payment in a hidden pocket before checking the contents of the other. It was a mishmash of *soldi* and *piccolo*—the sort of impure silver coin most people were used to being paid in. He stashed that in a slightly more accessible pouch on his belt. He glanced up at the sky in order to estimate the time before turning to Sebastian. "I hope you know what you've let yourself in for. We've got about five hours before dusk, and then it'll be a while before the moon is high enough to give us enough light to ride."

"I'll be okay," Sebastian said. "I just about lived in the saddle when I rode with General Stearns' Third Division last year."

Paolo shrugged. "On your backside be it."

Chapter 27

A farm near Cresole, north of Vicenza

Phillip smiled as the gold in the retort turned red. "Andrea, you need to go and get *Signore* Garivaghi."

Andrea crowded up close to have a look. "That is red dragon's blood?"

Phillip nodded. "Now, off you go."

Andrea paused to have one last look at the blood-red crystals forming in the retort before hurrying off. Leaving the door open as he went.

Phillip sighed and waved toward the door. "Thomas, could you . . ."

Thomas closed the door and walked over to look at the retort. "It took longer this time."

"Well, of course it did," Phillip said with a smile. "Our lives depend on making the task last as long as possible."

Thomas stared at Phillip. "You mean you know how it's happening?"

Phillip shook his head. "All I'm doing is letting the retort breathe a little between cohobations."

"Breathe . . ." Thomas stared at the retort. A smile grew upon his face. "It's gold chloride. Normally it would decompose back to gold, but the repeated cohobation fills the retort up with chlorine gas, which prevents the decomposition. Hence the red dragon's blood." He clapped Phillip on the shoulder. "That's brilliant."

Phillip graciously accepted the compliment as his due.

"What is brilliant?" Alessandro demanded from the door.

"*Dottore* Gribbleflotz has made red dragon's blood."

Alessandro hurried over to the retort they were all gathered around. He spent some time staring at it. Eventually he looked up. "What happens now?"

"Now," Phillip said, "I need to distill the essence of the red dragon's blood." He followed his words by changing the receiver flask for a clean one and resetting the red dragon's blood over the furnace.

"What about my gold?" Alessandro demanded.

"As soon as I have extracted the essence of the red dragon's blood, I will attempt to reconstitute your gold."

Alessandro stared at Phillip. He looked less than happy. "Attempt? I want you to do more than attempt to get me my gold back."

"Of course, *Signore* Garivaghi."

"Be sure you do." Alessandro gave Phillip, Thomas, Stephan, and Luigi a telling glare before turning. "Andrea, with me," he said before stalking out of the laboratory. Andrea followed, leaving the door open behind him.

Thomas advanced on the door. "Was everyone born in a tent?" he demanded as he slammed it closed.

"Tent?" Phillip asked.

Thomas grinned. "It's something my mother used to say whenever one of us forgot to shut the door behind us. When you enter or leave a tent, you push your way past the tent flap, which falls back into place after you pass. Sort of like a modern spring door is self-closing.

"So, what do we do now?"

Phillip pointed to the red dragon's blood retort. "I wait for that to finish before reconstituting the gold so that I can hand it back to Alessandro with all due pomp and ceremony."

"Why're you going to do that?" Thomas asked. "That's just more distilled aqua regia, isn't it?"

Phillip stood up straight and attempted to stare down his nose at Thomas. He noticed there was a smear on his spectacles and took them off to clean them. Once they were back on, he returned to looking down his nose at Thomas. "I'll have you know that I will be collecting the essence of red dragon's blood. An important ingredient in the production of the philosopher's stone."

"Seriously?" Thomas asked.

Phillip grinned. "Of course not. There's no such thing as the philosopher's stone, but we won't be telling *Signore* Garivaghi that."

Phillip held the flask up to the light and tapped it a few times.

Thomas joined him in examining the small amount of fluid in the flask. "There's not a lot to show for your efforts."

"It is all one could expect to get when distilling our sample of red dragon's blood."

"Will it be enough to make the philosopher's stone?" Luigi asked.

Phillip shot Thomas a look telling him to stay silent before turning to answer Luigi. "It will be enough to make a small example of the philosopher's stone."

Luigi looked at Phillip in awe. He transferred his gaze to the contents of the flask in Phillip's hand. If anything, his level of awe increased. "Essence of red dragon's blood. I thought it was nothing but a myth," he muttered reverently.

Phillip could feel Thomas was about to say something, so he accidentally on purpose swung the elbow of his free hand into his ribs. He was, naturally, immediately contrite and apologetic. "I'm sorry, I didn't know you were so close."

Phillip passed the flask containing the extracted essence of red dragon's blood to Luigi, who could barely contain himself as he took responsibility for the almost mythical liquid, and guided Thomas to the seat Stephan was preparing for him.

"You knew I was there," Thomas protested as he was helped to sit down.

Phillip shot a glance Luigi's way. He appeared totally entranced with the flask he was holding. "If Luigi believes, then he can more easily convince *Signore* Garivaghi that we are working on the philosopher's stone," he whispered.

Thomas took a big breath, and then slowly released it. "I think I'll live." He settled more comfortably in his seat. "What are you going to do now?"

"Reconstitute *Signore* Garivaghi's gold."

"And then what?"

"By the time the gold is cooled down, it will be time for them to collect us for supper."

✧ ✧ ✧

The door opened and a man they had seen before but whose name they hadn't heard stepped in. "All right, pack everything up and get out of here."

Phillip, Thomas, and Stephan did some "make work" to make it appear as if they had been busy. Luigi finished preparing the furnace for the next day. The man—identified as Roberto—waited impatiently for him to finish before marching everyone out of the laboratory, bolting the door closed behind him.

"Move," Roberto said as he pushed Luigi into the back of Thomas.

Both stumbled and would have fallen but for the quick action of Stephan to catch them. That seemed to inspire Roberto to pick on Stephan as he regularly poked him as they shuffled across the courtyard to the farmhouse.

There was an audience waiting for them. Giulio was standing, slouched against one of the veranda's supports. Other men leaned on other surfaces. They all had mugs in their hands. Giulio pushed off from the veranda support and strode toward them. He concentrated his gaze on Stephan. When he got close enough, he emptied the dregs of his mug in Stephan's face and stared at him, waiting for a response.

Stephan did not do anything. He did not even raise an arm to wipe the cheap red wine from his face. He just stood there watching.

"What?" Giulio demanded. "You're just going to take an insult?" He snorted and turned to his colleagues. "He's too scared to fight me."

"It'd hardly be a fair fight when his legs are chained together."

Giulio glared at Phillip. He waved a hand and called for Fabio to come and free Stephan.

"*Signore* Garivaghi will not be happy," Fabio said as he approached Stephan and crouched to unlock his shackles.

"*Signore* Garivaghi isn't here." Giulio looked at Stephan. "Now will you fight?"

"For my boots?"

Giulio smiled. "For your life."

Chapter 28

A farm near Cresole, north of Vicenza

Stephan bent his knees and moved his weight onto his toes as he studied Giulio. The man appeared about fifteen to twenty years older than Stephan. They were about the same height, but that was where the physical similarities ended. Where Stephan was lean and slight, Giulio was barrel chested and solidly built. He also had at least thirty pounds on Stephan's one hundred thirty-five pounds. Most of it in the upper body, and most of it muscle. His various scars suggested he was an experienced knife fighter. He also had a knife in a sheath belted to his waist. That was bad. Even a highly skilled martial artist—and Stephan knew he was not even close to being one—was at a significant disadvantage against a skilled fighter with a knife. His first job was to get rid of the knife. "What are the rules?"

Giulio sniggered. "There are no rules."

"So, you can use your knife?"

Giulio drew his knife. It was a pretty standard belt knife with a blade about eight inches long. Evidenced by the way repeated honing had worn away the blade, it was either very old or the steel was poor quality. "This knife?" Giulio asked. He laughed. "I don't need this knife to kill you." He looked past Stephan and threw the knife at the farmhouse door.

It hit at a bad angle and bounced off the door.

Stephan's eyes started to follow the thrown knife before his brain kicked into gear. The knife had been a distraction and he had fallen for it. He tautened his body, ready for impact.

The impact came in the form of a shin-slam to the ribs. Stephan was staggered by the blow and hurt. Hurt badly.

At best, Stephan had a cracked rib or two. At worst, he had a couple of broken ribs. He breathed carefully, trying to assess the damage without broadcasting how badly he was hurt to his opponent.

On the other hand, there was nothing in the rules that said he could not exaggerate how badly hurt he was. He moved back, wincing as he moved. Just for display purposes, he quickly mopped his forehead with his shirt sleeve. Then he lowered himself into a fighter's stance, deliberately favoring his left side, and started to shuffle around, trying to get into a position from which he could strike back.

Giulio laughed and stood straighter. Stephan took a chance and went in with a round kick to the side of Giulio's knee. He missed the knee, contacting the calf with the pointed toe of his wooden clog instead as Giulio hastily backpedaled, stumbling a little as he put weight onto his left leg.

Stephan followed up. A palm strike hit Giulio in the nose, sending him falling backwards.

Giulio rolled and was back to his feet before Stephan could jump on him. He came up smiling. It was not a friendly smile.

It took Stephan valuable time to work out why Giulio was smiling. Then he saw the knife. The same knife Giulio had thrown at the door earlier.

Giulio moved forward, favoring his left leg as he did so, thrusting with the knife. Stephan skipped backwards, keeping clear of the sharp steel blade.

Giulio was keeping the knife close to him, not overextending his reach as he moved it from side to side. That was a bit of a nuisance as one of the knife counters Stephan had been taught took advantage of that kind of behavior. He was going to have to do something much more dangerous.

Stephan reached out his right hand toward Giulio's knife hand as he swung the knife to Stephan's left. Immediately, Giulio reversed its direction. Stephan pulled back his right hand and Giulio's knife hand followed it. He swung his left hand at Giulio's arm. He contacted the forearm, forcing Giulio's knife hand across his body.

Stephan grabbed at Giulio's wrist with his right hand. He

wrapped his hand around Giulio's wrist and twisted it clockwise. It didn't cause Giulio to drop the knife, but it did force his arm to straighten. Stephan had intended to do a forearm strike along the triceps tendon, causing the elbow to dislocate. However, with his right arm engaged Giulio stumbled. His left leg almost folding as he put weight onto it. This left him momentarily vulnerable, and Stephan saw a better target. A target that would finish the fight quickly. He swung his left fist with everything he could put behind it. He did not aim for Giulio's ribs. Stephan had a much better target in his sights. He was not going for Giulio's head either. He knew better than to risk breaking the bones in his hand by doing something like that. No, Stephan struck at a point on Giulio's neck. With the precision of the surgeon he hoped one day to be, his fist contacted the carotid sinus, rendering Giulio almost immediately unconscious. Giulio collapsed like a limp rag, his head making a dull thud as it hit the cobblestones. The knife spilling from his hand.

Stephan's next act would have filled his Close Quarters Battle instructors with pride. Obeying one of the golden rules of those upstanding exponents of the art of street fighting—lance corporals Fabricius and Dinckeler of the 1st Marine Reconnaissance Company: it's not over until it's over—he dropped knees first onto Giulio's abdomen. There was an eruption of air from Giulio, but nothing more. Not that Stephan was paying that much attention. He was too busy carrying on the fight. With his knees on Giulio's abdomen, he dropped his weight forward and stuck Giulio with a power-palm strike to the base of the jaw.

Giulio's head went back, but there was no sound other than the dull thud of the head contacting the cobbles. The rest of the world started to penetrate as Stephan realized Giulio was beaten. Really beaten. As in, nearly dead. The man was not breathing, and his lips were already turning blue.

Stephan felt for a carotid pulse; there was one. A weak one. A faint and irregular one. With his hand on Giulio's throat, Stephan learned something else. The brute force with which he had hit Giulio had not only knocked him out, it had also crushed his larynx. That explained the blue tinge. Swelling of the damaged trachea was impeding the free flow of air to Giulio's lungs. Giulio needed an immediate tracheotomy if he were to live much longer. Something Stephan felt disinclined to do even if he had

had the necessary equipment, which he would have if they had not stolen his medical kit. There was a grim smile on his face as he crawled around to Giulio's feet and removed his boots.

"What in God's name has been happening here?" Alessandro Garivaghi demanded.

Chapter 29

A farm near Cresole, north of Vicenza

Phillip Gribbleflotz had, like everyone else, been concentrating on the fight and failed to observe the arrival of six mounted men. He, like everyone else, only became aware of them when Alessandro Garivaghi spoke out.

"Your man challenged *Dottore* Böhm to a fight. He lost."

Alessandro swung his leg over his horse's withers and slid to the ground. He walked over to Giulio. "What's wrong with him?" he asked as he looked down upon Giulio.

Stephan stood up, tying the laces of his recently recovered boots together so he could hang them over his neck as he did so. "Crushed trachea."

Phillip walked over to stand beside Alessandro. Giulio was lying unresponsive on the ground. Phillip dropped down to his knees and explored Giulio's throat with his hand. He felt the damage and looked up at Alessandro. "He is suffocating. He needs an immediate tracheotomy if he is to live. I could attempt that if I had a very sharp knife and a suitable tube."

"There were scalpels and a plastic tracheal tube in the medical kit I was carrying when we were kidnapped," Stephan said.

Phillip looked expectantly at Alessandro. When he did not immediately act, he prompted him. "I may be able to save this man if I have access to *Dottore* Böhm's medical kit. The canvas bag with the red cross on it that he was carrying when we were kidnapped."

Alessandro gestured to one of the men who had arrived with him. "The bag hanging from my saddle. Bring it here." He turned his attention back to Phillip. "If it is *Dottore* Böhm's medical kit, shouldn't he be the one to tend to Giulio?"

Phillip shook his head. "Your man just tried to kill him. It is probably better that *Dottore* Böhm not be responsible for attempting to save his life.

"And besides, I doubt he has ever performed the procedure. Whereas I have.

"Successfully," he added for good measure.

Alessandro nodded. "Fair enough." He gestured to the man who had collected the medical kit. "Give it to *Dottore* Gribbleflotz."

Phillip accepted the satchel and got down to his knees near the head of Giulio before opening it. A shadow loomed above him. It was Stephan. "Can you help?"

"What do you want me to do?"

"Just hold him steady."

Phillip unrolled the kit inside the satchel and smiled. There was more than enough equipment to do the job. He selected a scalpel and a plastic-wrapped tracheal tube. He offered the tracheal tube to Stephan, indicating that he should break it out of its wrapping while he made the necessary incision.

Phillip looked up at Alessandro. "Now, fair warning, it is going to look like I am cutting his throat. I will be, but only enough to make a hole through which I can insert the tracheal tube."

"What does that do?" Alessandro asked.

"I'll be making a hole to bypass the blockage at the larynx. The tracheal tube is there to keep the improvised airway open, so your man can breathe." Having said that, Phillip palpated Giulio's throat to locate the cricoid cartilage just below the larynx and cut into the flesh. Moments later, there was a hissing of air through the opening he had made. He spread the gap between the tracheal rings and threaded the end of the tracheal tube through the opening. He fed about an inch into Giulio's throat. Now to tie it in place. He lifted a free hand to Stephan, who had the supplied ribbon used to secure the tracheal tube ready. With the tracheal tube in place and Giulio breathing, Phillip got back to his feet.

"He's going to need bed rest and nursing until the swelling recedes."

Alessandro snorted and turned to his men. “Take him to his room.”

“Be careful not to dislodge the tracheal tube,” Phillip warned. “If that comes out before the swelling recedes, he will suffocate.”

Alessandro looked at Phillip. “You will accompany Giulio and continue to care for him.” He nodded as if confirming the instruction in his own mind before moving his gaze to Stephan. He looked at him for a while before gesturing to one of his men. “Take the others to their cell and lock them in.”

“What about dinner?” Stephan demanded. “We haven’t been fed yet.”

Alessandro opened his eyes wide. “And what have you done to earn the right to be fed?”

“*Dottore* Gribbleflotz has been able to isolate the essence of the red dragon’s blood,” Luigi said.

“You have?” Alessandro asked Phillip.

He nodded and felt in a pocket. “I have also finished with your gold,” he said as he offered Alessandro the bead of gold he’d made by melting the decomposed residue of the red dragon’s blood after he’d distilled off the essence.

Alessandro stared at the bead of gold. “You have finished with the gold? You are ready to make the philosopher’s stone.”

Phillip shook his head. “I’ve no need for your gold until I complete the philosopher’s stone, and I’m not ready to make it yet. I still have nine keys to work through.”

Alessandro sighed. He waved a hand. “Be off with you. Go and look after Giulio.” He looked at Thomas and company. “And you, go to your cell. Food and wine will be brought over shortly.” He spared everyone a final glance before returning to his horse and leading it into the stable.

“Well, this is fucking marvelous,” Thomas Stone muttered the moment the prison door was shut and bolted behind them.

Stephan staggered over to the straw mattress and collapsed. He winced audibly as the impact moved his cracked ribs. He gently lay back and started feeling about inside his boots.

Thomas walked over to stand over him. “I thought you were planning on killing the guy.”

“He’d be dead if it wasn’t for Dr. Gribbleflotz,” Stephan pointed out. “And he’ll probably die soon anyway.”

"From his wounds?" Thomas asked.

"That too." Stephan beamed as he pulled his hand out of the boot. In it was a greased loop of wire. "We escape tonight."

"What about Phillip?" Thomas demanded. "He's a prisoner in the farmhouse."

Stephan nodded as he unwound the wire saw and checked it for damage. "We'll just have to get him out of there." He turned to Luigi. "Do you know what room *Dottore* Gribbleflotz will be in?"

"Giulio's," Luigi answered. "On the first floor."

Stephan turned back to Thomas. "There you are. That's sorted. Luigi can get Dr. Gribbleflotz out while we place the dust bomb in the dining hall."

"But you don't have the detonators. Phillip made the nitro, but he didn't get around to making anything to set it off."

"What do you think I was doing?"

"You were making fuses."

"And suitable detonators," Stephan said.

"Impossible. You didn't go near the mercury or acids."

Stephan smiled smugly. "You don't need fulminate of mercury detonators to set off nitroglycerin, Dr. Stone. Simple black-powder firecrackers are more than adequate."

Thomas stared disbelievingly at Stephan. "You're sure?"

Stephan nodded. "Been there, done that."

Thomas released a sigh of relief. "So, everything is ready for an escape attempt tonight?"

"Not an attempt, a successful escape," Stephan said as he carefully wound the wire saw around his left bicep.

Thomas watched him for a few seconds. "Why are you doing that?" he asked.

Stephan finished securing the wire saw to his arm and adjusting his shirt to cover it before answering. "Just in case they come back for my boots." He dived into his other boot and surfaced with a small rectangle of folded paper. He slipped that inside the sock on his right foot.

"What was that?" Thomas asked.

"A single-edged razor blade." Stephan examined his boots. After a period of contemplation, he pulled them on. "If I'm wearing them, they're less likely to think of taking them." Having said that, Stephan carefully lay down on the mattress and pulled a blanket over him. "Wake me when they bring in the food."

"You're just going to sleep? What about our escape?"

Stephan opened one eye and contemplated Thomas. "We can't do anything until they settle for the night."

Thomas glared at Stephan. He smiled back, and then he closed his eyes. As an experienced soldier, he was soon asleep.

Chapter 30

A farm near Cresole, north of Vicenza

Phillip finished the meal he had been left and placed the empty bowl outside by the door, just like he'd been told to do. As he stood, he checked the corridor. At the end, by the stairs, one of Alessandro's men watched him. The guard at the stairway meant that was not a likely escape route. Phillip waved and reentered Giulio's room.

It was not a very big room. There was space for a narrow bed, a chest of drawers, and a freestanding wardrobe. The floor was wood, with a large rug made up of sheepskins sewn together. There was a blanket on the rug, indicating that it was where Phillip was expected to sleep. And then there was the window. It had multiple panes of glass, indicating that the farmhouse was very upmarket, or at least that it had been at one time. He undid the latch and discovered that the window opened easily. He poked his head out to have a look around. There were shutters on either side. Their presence explained why the window opened—there was no other way to easily open or close them. He glanced down, and immediately wished he hadn't. It was a long vertical drop to the ground below. Phillip hastily pulled his head back and shut the window.

A change in Giulio's breathing drew Phillip over to his patient. Giulio was still breathing. Something he was sure Stephan would be less than impressed with, even if he was supposed to be an advanced medic dedicated to the preservation of life.

Giulio's breathing was not as labored as it had been a couple of hours ago, but it was still very weak. He ran his fingers lightly over Giulio's throat to check on the damage Stephan's blow had caused. The swelling of the trachea appeared worse. It seemed that Stephan had done so much damage that Giulio was going to have difficulty eating and drinking. Not that Phillip thought that would be a problem for long. If he weren't killed when Stephan detonated the dust bomb, infection would probably take care of him before he starved to death.

Yes. Phillip fully expected Stephan and Thomas to attempt to escape. He also expected them to use the nitroglycerin he had made. He hoped they would help him escape too, and with that thought in mind, he sat on the sheepskin rug and opened Stephan's medical kit. It had been left with him because he had claimed he might need some of its contents. He had not been lying. It wasn't his fault if they assumed that he needed the contents to treat Giulio. In reality, he hoped to use one of the probes to unlock the shackles around his legs. If nothing else, the attempts would help pass the time.

Stephan waited until the door was shut and bolted behind the man who'd delivered their dinner before sliding out from under the blanket. He had deliberately kept his legs covered so that no one would notice he was wearing his boots and, more importantly, that he wasn't wearing the leg shackles. Neither the loss of his boots or the reattachment of the leg shackles would have significantly changed their plans. However, having his boots and not having his legs shackled made everything that little bit easier.

The first order of business was to eat dinner.

Thomas glared at Stephan as he ate. "Shouldn't we be working on our escape?" he demanded in a quiet whisper.

Stephan paused, the next spoonful of rice and vegetables ready to enter his mouth, to shake his head. That done, he went straight back to eating. While he chewed, he pointed at Thomas' bowl and indicated that he should eat too.

"We have to get Phillip free before you detonate the nitro."

"First things first." Stephan gestured toward Luigi, who was shoveling food into his mouth. "Luigi's got the right idea, Dr. Stone. We're going to need energy to survive if we get away. We can plan how to get Dr. Gribbleflotz out while I cut you free."

"So you do plan to get us out of these?" Thomas asked, pointing at his leg chains.

Stephan contemplated them. "It'll probably be quicker to just saw through a link in the chain."

Thomas glared at Stephan once more before sitting on the floor and picking up his bowl and spoon.

Stephan laid his empty bowl and spoon on the floor and walked over to the window. He stood there assessing the branches of the rose bush. He needed a branch about twice as long as his wire saw. He carefully unwound the saw from around his arm and looped it around a likely looking branch and started sawing. Getting the cut branch into their prison presented a few difficulties. In the end, he took off his sheepskin waistcoat and wrapped that around the thorny stem and simply pulled. Of course, not wanting to attract attention, he pulled very slowly. Therefore, the whole exercise took a while.

He handed the sheepskin-wrapped branch to Luigi, who had joined him. And with Luigi pulling on the branch, Stephan measured off the desired length, plus a little more, and sawed through the branch a second time. He stuffed the wire saw into his waistband and walked back to the mattress, where he sat down and started removing rose thorns.

With the branch clear of thorns, Stephan had Luigi hold it in both hands while he cut off a three-inch length. He used the single-edged razor blade to cut a slit into the short length and set the razor blade into it. He then used his new tool to cut notches in the longer piece of rose wood and strung the wire saw across it as if it was a bow. Which it was. A bow saw.

He now had a saw, and a rather dangerous knife. Stephan returned to the window and cut off another length of wood. He cleared it of thorns and pressed the exposed blade into it. It wasn't a great sheath, but it would prevent him cutting himself on the tool. With everything ready, Stephan returned to the mattress. "Who's first?" he asked.

Thomas volunteered, and soon Stephan was sawing away at a link of the chain close to the shackle on Dr. Stone's right leg.

Click.

Phillip stared blankly at the shackle. He had been working on it for what seemed hours with no result, but suddenly, it was open. He stared at it in shock. He had not really expected that he'd be able to pick the lock. But he had. He looked at the other shackle. He shrugged. He had nothing better to do until either the bomb went off, or the others contacted him. He set to work.

Chapter 31

A farm near Cresole, north of Vicenza

It did not take Stephan too long to cut through the links of the chains on Thomas' and Luigi's leg-irons. Two-hundred-year-old forged iron had not stood a chance against the late twentieth century spiral-cut hardened-steel wire saw supplied courtesy of Tracy Kubiak's military outfitting company's stock of up-time military surplus bits and pieces. The saw had not cut through like a hot knife through butter, but in less than twenty minutes Stephan was able to cut both of their chains free. They were going to have to tie the remaining length of chain to something to keep it out of the way, but at least their legs were no longer hobbled together.

With part one of their escape complete, Stephan left the others to cut up the canvas mattress cover with the single-edged razor blade while he set to cutting one of the iron bars set in their prison-door window. He started at the top, cutting at a very oblique angle.

Even with the branch holding the wire taut, it was fatiguing work. After a few minutes sawing, Stephan called Thomas over to take a turn.

Thomas looked at the angle Stephan was cutting and asked why.

"Once the bar is free, I hope to make it into a weapon. Cutting at a shallow angle means it'll have some sort of point."

"Makes sense," Thomas muttered as he started sawing.

With the three of them taking turns, it took less than twenty minutes to complete the cut. In between turns sawing, the three of them rolled up their blankets and used strips cut from the canvas mattress cover to tie them across their chests. It was cold outside, and they had no idea how long it might take to get to safety. It was better to be sure than sorry.

Stephan then started cutting the bar at the bottom. This time it was a perpendicular crosscut. Taking turns, it took less than five minutes to cut the bar free.

Stephan passed Luigi the bar and told him to wrap canvas from the mattress around it to form a handgrip before reaching his arm through the opening and trying to move the bolt securing the door. He could not reach.

All was not lost. Stephan had not really expected he'd be able to reach. He backed away and invited Thomas, who was a few inches taller, to have a go while he collected three strips of canvas from the mattress and started plaiting them.

"Can't quite reach," Thomas announced. "Do you have something I can try to loop around the handle?"

Stephan passed Thomas his plaited canvas cord.

A couple of minutes later, Thomas turned his back to the door and shook his head. "Still can't do it."

"We didn't expect it to be easy," Stephan said as he moved over to the door and tried to loop the fabric cord over the handle of the bolt. Unfortunately, the handle was hanging straight down, making it virtually impossible to hook the loop around it. He pulled back and described the problem. "Any ideas?"

"What about using the bow saw to place the cord?" Luigi suggested.

Stephan and Thomas looked at each other. Both going a little red in the face before Stephan approached the door with cord and bow saw.

It was not easy but, after a dozen tries, he managed to hook the cord under the handle and pull it up to the point where it could be slid open. Next, he tried to pull the bolt back using the bow saw, but he could not get enough leverage. He described his problem to Thomas and Luigi.

"Use the cord from the far edge of the window and try and pull the bolt," Thomas suggested.

"While also using the saw," Stephan agreed. "That should give us enough leverage."

They immediately put the plan into action. Things didn't go

smoothly but after several attempts failed because the upward tension on the cord caused the cord to lift the lever and slip free, judicious use of the saw to keep the lever from flipping up finally resulted in the bolt being drawn.

Stephan passed Thomas the braided cord and bow saw and held his hand out for the iron bar that Luigi had wrapped with canvas. It made a reasonable, but not great, dagger. It was certainly better than nothing.

Stephan signaled to Thomas and Luigi to keep quiet before slowly opening the door. It creaked. There was nothing they could do about that. The hinges were outside their prison cell, otherwise he might have tried smuggling in some of the fat Dr. Gribbleflotz had been working with. As it was, they just had to move slowly and hope no one heard them.

They stepped out of their prison and carefully shut and bolted the door. There was no sign of any guards, which was not too surprising given it was mid-November and the temperature was in the low forties. Not even the dogs wanted to be outside.

As quietly as they could, they made their way to the laboratory. The door was bolted, but not locked. It was a simple matter to draw the bolt and slip through the door.

"*Dottore* Stone, you get the nitro," Stephan directed as he moved over to the bench he had been working at. "I'll get the fuses and matches."

"What about me?" Luigi asked.

"You can start planning how you're going to get *Dottore* Gribbleflotz out of the farmhouse before we blow it up."

Luigi looked around, and then he collected a wicker basket and partially filled it with straw before placing several flasks into it.

"What're you doing?" Thomas asked.

"I want a weapon," Luigi explained. "These are flasks of *Dottore* Gribbleflotz's best acids."

Thomas whistled silently as he stared at the basket. "Nasty," he muttered.

Stephan could only agree. The acids Dr. Gribbleflotz had made were highly concentrated. Anyone being splattered by the contents was in for a heap of hurt. "You got the nitro?" Thomas held up the flask. "You sure that's the right one?"

Thomas turned the flask in the moonlight so Stephan could see the label stuck to the flask. It said, "*Quinta essentia* of animal fat."

"Then, if everyone is ready, let's get this show on the road." Stephan led them out of the laboratory, shutting and bolting the door after Thomas and Luigi. He then sped across the cobbles to the back door of the farmhouse. Once there, he paused to listen. When he was sure he had not been heard, he signaled for the others to join him.

Luigi was first. He wasn't as quick as Stephan. His wooden clogs lacked the traction of Stephan's rubber-soled boots on the icy cobbles. Thomas was slower still, probably because he was being ultra-careful with the flask of nitroglycerin he was carrying.

Stephan carefully opened the door. He looked in, listening. There was not a sound. He gripped his expedient dagger and stepped into the corridor. He glanced over his shoulder to check that Thomas and Luigi were behind him. "Close the door," he ordered. An open door would attract attention.

Slowly, Stephan made his way to the storeroom. He found the flour easily. It was right where he had helped stack it a couple of days ago. He grabbed a sack and rejoined Thomas and Luigi. He signaled for them to follow him. Almost immediately, he signaled for them to stop.

"Your clogs are making too much noise. You'll have to take them off."

Neither man protested, and soon they were following Stephan in stockinged feet, their clogs held snugly under their sheepskin tops.

They were approaching the stairs when they saw the flickering light of a candle coming down them. Stephan waved the others up against the wall while he gently lowered the sack of flour he had been carrying. He slipped the blade of his expedient dagger down his waistband and approached the stairs. From the shadows, Stephan took a quick look to see who was coming down the stairs. It was Andrea, the man who had stolen Dr. Stone's sneakers.

Stephan slid up alongside the stairs and waited for Andrea to reach the floor before he pounced. The thumb and fingers of his left hand pinched Andrea's nose while the palm of the same hand covered Andrea's mouth. Stephan pulled back, taking Andrea off balance as he quickly took him to ground while his right hand grabbed for the candle.

Andrea abandoned his hold on the candleholder and clawed at the hand blocking his mouth and nose.

Stephan turned the candle in his hand and slammed it burning-wick-end-first into Andrea's carotid sinus. Andrea's struggles slackened as Stephan continued to press the candle against his carotid sinus, cutting off the flow of blood to his brain. Seconds later, Andrea stopped struggling and Stephan lowered him gently to the floor.

Stephan tentatively removed his hand from Andrea's mouth. There was no attempt to cry out, so he undid Andrea's belt and offered it and the attached belt-knife to Luigi before sending him up the stairs. Meanwhile, Thomas was furiously working on the laces of the sneakers Andrea was wearing.

Stephan waited for Thomas to put on his sneakers before picking up the sack of flour and carefully crossed the hall to the door of the main room where most of Alessandro's men slept. At the door, he sat the sack of flour onto the floor and used the razor to cut an opening. He held out a hand to Thomas for the flask of nitro and carefully placed it through the hole into the flour. Then he carefully inserted his collection of detonators—he could have used just one, but their lives depended on the nitro exploding, so he had gone for multiple redundancy and made half a dozen. Each with a couple of fuses. He struck a match and lit the fuses.

He signaled for Thomas to open the door. The moment it was open, they realized they need not have to be as quiet as they had been. The room was reverberating from the snores of a dozen men. If they could sleep with that noise, then they could sleep through just about anything.

Stephan carefully slid the dust bomb into the room. He pushed it to one side of the doorway and crawled back out of the room. Together, he and Thomas closed the door. There was a dull *click* as the door latched. There was a muted woof from one of the dogs. Both froze, scared that one of the dogs was about to raise the alarm. But the dogs remained silent.

Stephan and Thomas looked at each other, and then toward the stairs. Both shrugged. Dr. Gribbleflotz and Luigi were on their own. Stephan and Thomas made their escape.

Upstairs, Luigi carefully opened the door to Giulio's room. He slipped in, closing it behind him, and called out in a whisper. "*Dottore* Gribbleflotz. It is me, Luigi."

Phillip hastily removed the leg shackles. He had managed to open the locks on both, but he'd kept them on just in case someone had come to check him. It had been fortunate that he had done that, because Andrea had been in just minutes ago to check on Giulio.

"We're escaping?"

"Yes," Luigi said. "We don't have time to cut your shackles, so I'll have to carry you."

"I managed to pick the locks with tools from Stephan's medical kit."

There was a sigh of relief from Luigi. "That is good. Grab the medical kit and stuff your clogs under your jacket. Then take a couple of these."

"What are 'these'?" Phillip asked as he adjusted the clogs under his jacket.

"Flasks of acid."

Phillip slung Stephan's medical kit over his shoulder before randomly selecting two flasks from Luigi's basket. He checked the labels he had stuck on them in the moonlight. He had one each of oil of vitriol and aqua fortis. "How are we escaping?" he asked.

"The same way I came in. Down the stairs and out the back door."

Phillip grimaced. "What if we're caught?"

"Throw the flasks at them."

"Okay," Phillip muttered. It was not much of an escape plan, but it had the virtue of being simple. "You lead."

They made it down the stairs without raising the alarm. They were just stepping past the recumbent body of Andrea when the door to the main hall opened and a man with a candle in a holder stepped into the corridor.

There was a moment of stunned silence as the man stared at Phillip and Luigi while they stared at him. Then, as one, they regained their wits.

"They're escaping!" the man with the candle yelled.

Luigi threw a flask at the man's feet. It shattered on the floor sending broken glass and concentrated acid everywhere, including onto the brigand's stockinged feet.

The man screamed.

Luigi threw another flask at the floor before turning and running.

Phillip ran after him.

Luigi got to the door first and hauled it open. He stepped through and held it for Phillip. Phillip glanced behind him. There were dogs. He threw both of his flasks at the floor, shattering them and spreading acid over the width of the corridor. Then he passed through the door and both of them started running as fast as their legs could carry them.

The brigands were starting to exit the farmhouse in pursuit when the nitroglycerin exploded. Less than a second later the flour ignited, blowing out windows and doors and sending a wall of flame out the door they'd escaped through.

Vicenza

Paolo Molin and Sebastian Jones were young, fit, and experienced riders on equally young, fit, and experienced—and thus expensive to hire—horses. As such, they made the twenty-six-mile ride from Padua to Vicenza in less than eight hours. They would have arrived sooner, but they had run out of daylight. They had been reduced to a snail's pace between sunset and the moon rising. However, the last full moon had only been three or four days ago, so there was plenty of light once the moon appeared.

They were stopped at the gate by the guard, who were unwilling to let them in until Paolo successfully identified himself as an official with the *Provveditori alla Sanità* on an important mission and slipped them a small gratuity. From that moment on, the guards could not do too much for them.

Paolo asked them if they had seen *dottori* Stone and Gribbleflotz, and Böhm. They asked for a description.

"I've got photographs," Sebastian said as he dug into the satchel he had slung across his chest.

"Here, have you seen any of these men?" Sebastian asked as he passed the photographs to the senior guard.

The senior guard looked at the photos one by one, passing them onto his men as he finished with them. In the light of a fiery torch, the guards examined the photos. One man seemed to have recognized something.

"You've seen one of them?" Paolo asked.

The man shook his head and turned the photo he had been

looking at for Paolo to see. "Not the men, but these boots. They look familiar."

Paolo stared at Sebastian. "Boots? You gave them photographs of boots?"

Sebastian gave him a wry smile and shrugged. "*Dottore* Gribbleflotz's boots are pretty unique and memorable, so I thought I'd include a shot of them in all their glory."

Paolo had seen the boots in question and had to agree: there were unlikely to be two pairs like that in Italy. "But he didn't recognize *Dottore* Gribbleflotz." Paolo turned to the guard. "You recognize the boots, but you didn't recognize *Dottore* Gribbleflotz. How is that possible?"

The guard paled and stepped back from Paolo. "The man wearing the boots was *Signore* Garivaghi. *Signore* Alessandro Garivaghi. A cousin of the da Porto."

Paolo whistled. Things were potentially about to become interesting. Very interesting. Maybe too interesting. He turned to Sebastian. "Would *Dottore* Gribbleflotz have sold someone his boots?"

Sebastian shook his head. "I can't see it happening. He loves those boots. And anyway, why would he do it? It's not as if he's short of money."

"There is no good reason," Paolo conceded. "So why would Alessandro Garivaghi be wearing them?"

Sebastian shrugged.

Paolo sighed. He looked at his horse. Prime animal it might be, but the trip had taken a toll on the beast. "Where might we find *Signore* Garivaghi?" Paolo asked the guard, hoping that it would be somewhere close by.

"*Signore* Garivaghi has a farm near Cresole."

Paolo sighed again. He would have preferred he be somewhere in Vicenza. "How far away is the farm?"

The senior guard pointed to the north. "About four miles that way."

Suddenly, in the direction the guard was pointing, there was a flash of light in the distance.

Paolo stared in the direction of the flash and started counting seconds. He got to seventeen before he heard the sound of an explosion. "About four miles, in that direction?" he asked the guard.

They all studied the skyline where a fiery glow was now visible. "Yes," the guard answered.

"I think that might have been our missing individuals," Sebastian said.

"What makes you say that?" Paolo asked.

"Who else is going to be playing with explosives at night?"

"It could be anyone, but we had better investigate," Paolo said before remounting.

Sebastian also remounted his horse. As a pair, they set off. Not galloping but moving faster than was really safe on the road surface in the moonlight.

Chapter 32

A farm near Cresole, north of Vicenza

"Over here!" Stephan called out and waved when he saw Dr. Gribbleflotz and Luigi exit the farmhouse. Moments later, the nitroglycerin went off. "Get down!" he yelled. The nitroglycerin charge was only supposed to be enough to disperse the flour. It was the flour being set off when particles reached the glowing coals of the fire used to heat the room that was supposed to do the real damage.

Dr. Gribbleflotz was already going to ground as Stephan called and Luigi quickly followed. The brigands, those that had not been knocked down by the initial blast, were milling about when the flour ignited.

The shutters over the windows were sent flying as the fireball blew out the windows. A fraction of a second later, the fireball erupted through the open door, illuminating the courtyard, and enveloping several unfortunates who'd been standing in its path. Their clothes caught fire and they fell to the ground screaming as they tried to put out the flames.

Stephan tugged at Dr. Stone's shoulder and sent him on his way, heading generally south, toward Vicenza, while he ran forward to get Dr. Gribbleflotz and Luigi.

"Either of you hurt?" he demanded as he dragged them in pursuit of Dr. Stone.

"No," Dr. Gribbleflotz muttered.

"I'm okay," Luigi said.

"Good. We need to get away before they set the dogs on us." Stephan glanced behind him, checking on what the brigands were doing. Mostly it looked like they were attending to their fallen or trying to put the fires out. However, he heard the howl of dogs. He returned to running away with a renewed effort, exhorting Dr. Gribbleflotz and Luigi to run faster.

The baying of a dog grew closer. Stephan looked over his shoulder. It was just the one dog. That was good. However, it was a big dog. Something like a mastiff. That was not so good. He yelled at Phillip and Luigi to keep running while he stopped and turned.

Stephan unslung his blanket and wrapped it around his left arm. He then drew the iron-bar dagger and waited.

The dog slowed as it got closer. Probably it was more used to running down prey than being confronted by it. Still, that did not stop it from approaching. Stephan held out his blanket-wrapped arm, inviting it to bite him.

The dog duly took Stephan up on his offer and clamped its jaws around Stephan's arm. Even through the layers of blanket, Stephan could feel the bite. With his left arm in the dog's mouth, he swung his right arm upwards.

The expedient dagger was not very sharp, but brute force reinforced by desperation and adrenaline powered the blunt point through the thin skin of the lower jaw and up into the base of the brain. The dog barely whimpered before it slumped to the ground.

Stephan kept an eye out for brigands as he hauled the dagger out. That the animal did not react he accepted as proof positive that it was dead. After a final sad caress of the dead dog's head, Stephan turned and ran to join the others.

Drs. Stone and Gribbleflotz, and Luigi were standing on the road looking back at the farmhouse when Stephan caught up with them. He looked back. There were flames coming from the farmhouse and someone was trying to guide the brigands to fight the fire. Others were running toward them.

"Move it," Stephan ordered. "Get off the road and head south."

They ran.

Chapter 33

Running across farmland in wooden clogs was difficult at the best of times. Doing it in the dark was an invitation to a broken or twisted ankle. Still, with the sounds of men in pursuit, they did the best they could with Stephan and Dr. Stone supporting Dr. Gribbleflotz and Luigi.

They came to a hedge and, as the others battled through, Stephan took the opportunity to check out the pursuit. In the distance he counted six fiery torches milling around, probably looking for tracks. That implied no dogs. Not that Stephan was willing to stake his life on that. Still, the pursuit was some distance away. Maybe they could lose them. He pushed through the hedge after the others.

The hedge had bordered a road, or at least what passed for road in this part of rural Italy. It might be little more than a muddy track, but at least they would not get lost following it. Unfortunately, it would also be easy for their pursuers to follow them. "Cross the road," Stephan told the others.

"Why don't we follow the road?" Thomas asked in a whisper. "It goes south."

"We will follow the road, but first we have to lay a false trail. Now, everyone, cross the road and break through the hedge on the other side."

Stephan directed the others on how he wanted the damage to the hedge on the other side of the road to appear. It had to look like they had passed through, but it could not be too obvious. He stepped back, into a muddy puddle, and surveyed the gap they had made. He advanced and moved a few branches.

"Right. That's enough. Walk on the firm ground on the edge. Single file. And try to step in the footprints of the person in front of you."

Stephan followed, walking backwards as he did his best to disguise that they had come this way.

Eventually, the natural variations of the road took them out of sight of the point at which they had joined the road. Stephan urged the others to greater speed.

They were virtually running as they rounded a corner, right into two oncoming horsemen. They skidded to a halt. These could not be any of Alessandro's men. They would surely have heard if horses had joined the pursuit. And besides, how could the horses have got in front of them.

Thomas made an executive decision before Stephan could stop him. He ran toward the horsemen calling out to them to help.

"Dr. Stone. Is that you?"

Stephan had been trotting up behind Dr. Stone when he heard the challenge. He stared at the man who had spoken. "Sebastian? Is that you, Sebastian Jones? What in God's name are you doing here?"

"Looking for you and Drs. Stone and Gribbleflotz," Sebastian answered. "More importantly, what are you all doing here?"

Stephan glanced over his shoulder. "We don't have time to explain. We need to keep running. There are people chasing us."

"Who?" the other horseman asked.

"There are at least half a dozen brigands behind us," Stephan said.

"What weapons?" the horseman asked.

Stephan shrugged. He had been too intent on escaping to worry about what weapons the brigands might have. "Whatever the local brigands have, I suppose."

Stephan saw a flash of white as the man smiled. "Then we should let them catch us." The man dismounted, dropping the reins to the ground while he drew a weapon from a sheath attached to the saddle. The man looked at Sebastian. "Will you join me?"

Sebastian dismounted, and he too drew a weapon from a sheath attached to his saddle. He held it out to Stephan. "Do you know how to use a pump-action shotgun?"

Stephan reached for the weapon. "A Model 97," he said as he ran his hands over it. "With the twenty-inch barrel. And the bayonet lug," he added. "Cool."

Sebastian grinned. "I guess that means you know how to use it. Here, you'll be wanting these," he said as he handed over the bandolier of cartridges. "The red are solid slugs while the blue are buckshot."

Stephan snorted as he accepted the ammunition. In the moonlight, it was virtually impossible to tell the different colors apart. Instead, he felt the tips. The slugs felt significantly different from the buckshot.

Stephan checked the shotgun was unloaded. Then he squeezed the trigger. Nothing happened. That was good, and totally expected. With the trigger still pulled back, he slid the slide forward. Just as it reached the front stop, there was a ping of the firing pin being released. Stephan smiled as he loaded the weapon with five rounds of buckshot. He then worked the action to chamber a round before inserting a sixth round. Then he started walking down the road, toward the torches he could see in the distance.

"Just a minute. Where are you going?" Sebastian's companion demanded as he hurried after Stephan.

Sebastian grabbed some of his camera gear from a saddlebag and hurried off in pursuit.

Thomas, Phillip, and Luigi stood and watched the others hurry toward the brigands. They turned to look at each other and shrugged their shoulders.

Stephan walked along the edge of the road, near the hedges that bordered it, as he headed back up the road toward the farmhouse they had only recently escaped from. He scanned ahead, looking for the torches the brigands pursuing them had been carrying.

A couple of minutes later, he saw the flaming torches. The brigands were on the road and approaching. Stephan glanced behind him. Sebastian and his companion were close behind. He gestured for them to take cover in the hedges as he moved into the hedge on the side of the road. And there he crouched and waited.

He did not have to wait long before he could see all six torches and discover that there were seven men heading his way. They were clumped together, making an ideal ambush target. He squinted in the moonlight as he tried to identify what weapons they had. He could make out at least two muskets of some description and three spears. Probably boar spears, he thought as he watched them. He could not make out what weapons the other two were carrying.

He checked the safety was off and the hammer cocked as he watched them. The effective range of a twenty-inch Model 97 firing buckshot was about twenty-five yards. Closer was better. So, he let them get closer.

He was just about to take aim when a hand landed on his shoulder. He shot the owner a dirty look. "What the hell?"

"I need to offer them the chance to surrender," Paolo said. He patted Stephan on the shoulder and stepped out onto the road, but he was careful not to step into Stephan's line of fire.

"*Signore* Alessandro Garivaghi. In the name of the Council of Ten, I call upon you and your men to lay down your weapons and surrender."

The response from the brigands was immediate. Two muskets came up and fired while someone brought up a handgun and fired.

"I want him alive!" Paolo screamed from the cover he had dived for the moment the men brought their muskets up to fire.

A third shot from the hand-gunner identified the man as Alessandro—Stephan could not believe the brigand leader would let anyone else use his stolen revolver and nothing else was likely to be able to fire more than twice. That made him a prime target, and not just because he still had three live rounds in the cylinder. However, the guy from the Council of Ten—and even Stephan knew that made him someone important—had said he wanted the brigand leader alive. That was a constraint Stephan could have done without. He raised his shotgun and looked for a nonlethal target.

At twenty yards the shot dispersal of double-aught buckshot is about ten inches. That was with eight pellets. It meant a shot at the gun-hand had a low probability of a hit. Stephan lowered his aim and fired.

The muzzle flash from the shotgun was impressive. It also temporarily blinded Stephan so that he did not see why Alessandro fell. He just saw him land facedown in the mud, the revolver he had been holding spilling from his hand as he hit the road.

Stephan did not have time to worry about Alessandro just now. There were more important things to worry about, such as the six brigands headed his way. He pumped another round into the shotgun and shot the leading spearman. He had not been told to try and keep Alessandro's men alive, so that shot was to the center of mass. Quickly pumping another round into the chamber, Stephan shot another man. Then another, and another, and another.

A total of six shots later, there was one man left standing and Stephan was out of ammo.

Boom! A shot from across the road, where Paolo had taken cover, rang out and the last man fell to the ground.

Stephan stood and reloaded his shotgun as he surveyed the carnage. There were seven men on the ground, and six spluttering torches. He walked toward the bodies.

He crouched down to pick up the revolver and shoved it into his waistband before rolling Alessandro over. He was examining the extent of Alessandro's injuries when Paolo came up beside him.

"I wanted the bastard alive," he cursed loudly.

"Then you'd better run back and get *Dottore* Gribbleflotz, because he's still alive. For now."

"What?"

"I shot him in the leg. I need proper equipment to treat him and *Dottore* Gribbleflotz has my medical kit."

There was a flash of light, and Stephan glared through blinded eyes at Sebastian. "Did you have to do that?" he demanded.

Sebastian glanced down at the camera in his hands, and then back at the scene in front of him. He nodded. "Yes. It should make a marvelous photo."

"A man could be dying here and all you can see is a marvelous photo opportunity?"

Sebastian pouted. "It sounds bad when you put it that way. Is there anything I can do to help?"

Stephan nodded. "Gather up the torches and try and stand them up around Alessandro so I can see what I'm doing." He glanced at the other man. "You, go and get *Dottore* Gribbleflotz."

Sebastian gathered the torches and arranged them in two self-supporting tripods either side of Alessandro. "You could have been more polite to Paolo," he told Stephan.

"I could have," Stephan agreed. "However, your Paolo insisted he wanted this guy taken alive." He gestured to Alessandro. "So he gets to do his bit to help make it happen."

Sebastian looked down at the now whimpering Alessandro. "How bad is it?"

"I hit his leg with buckshot. How bad do you think it is?" Stephan demanded as he tied the braided cord he had made back in their prison loosely around Alessandro's leg and used a bit of branch he found under the hedge to twist it tight.

Sebastian winced. "Is he going to lose the leg?"

Stephan shrugged as he stared at Alessandro's wounds. "Probably. We need more light."

"There aren't any more torches."

"I know that," Stephan muttered. He looked in the direction of the burning farmhouse. It was not going to be a good place to treat Alessandro, but there were horses there and, he hoped, the wagon that had carried them there from Vicenza. "Where's Gribbleflotz?" he demanded, looking back along the road.

"Coming," Phillip called as he strode quickly along the edge of the muddy road.

Phillip handed Stephan the medical kit the moment he was close enough. He then looked down at the patient. "First things first. I think we need to remove the boots."

Stephan snorted. The boots in question were Dr. Gribbleflotz's, and no doubt he wanted them back. If nothing else, they were probably a lot more comfortable than the clogs he was wearing. "Let's give the man some morphine before you start mauling him."

"Yes. Yes. Of course," Phillip said as he stood back out of Stephan's way.

Stephan used scissors from his medical kit to cut open Alessandro's leggings and then inject the contents of a syrette into Alessandro's thigh. After doing that, he removed the leather Sam Browne webbing Alessandro was wearing and put it on as he regained his feet. "It'll take a few minutes for it to start to work," Stephan said as he pulled the revolver out from his waistband. After a brief examination, he reloaded the revolver using one of the speed-loaders still in their pouch on the belt of the Sam Browne webbing and holstered it. He then picked up the shotgun. "Dr. Gribbleflotz, we're going to have to move the patient. I intend going back to the farm to see if I can get a wagon. Will you be able to manage the patient?"

"Yes, yes," Phillip said. "Thomas can help me."

"Good." Stephan looked over to Paolo. He was standing beside Luigi, who held the reins of two horses. "Shall we go?" he asked.

Paolo nodded and mounted one of the horses.

"Hey, what about me?" Sebastian protested.

"We only have two horses," Paolo said.

Stephan grinned. "Let him have the horse. I'll travel on foot. You should be able to keep up." With the shotgun at port arms, Stephan set off. He had learned on the Marine Advanced Reconnaissance School course that, in a foot race over distances of more than two miles, in warm to hot conditions, he could outrun most dogs. He was pretty sure that he could give the horses a run for their money, especially given their dislike of traveling at night.

Stephan started to overheat before he had covered half a mile. However, unlike dogs, which could only lose excess heat by panting, humans had evolved the ability to shed excess heat by sweating—a much more efficient method of cooling. That little factoid had been the explanation of why he had been able to outrun the dogs during escape and evasion training. Of course, air flow over the sweating body made the cooling system even more efficient.

He unbuttoned the jacket and tried to open it. That proved awkward given he was wearing the Sam Browne webbing and bandolier of shotgun cartridges over it. He also learned something else as he pushed and tugged at the jacket to open it: running with cracked ribs was no fun at all. It seemed the adrenaline that had been flooding through his body had been consumed, taking its anesthetizing effect with it. It was not debilitatingly painful. Certainly, Stephan had endured greater levels of pain while attending the Marine Advanced Reconnaissance School. However, he was now very aware of his damaged ribs.

Stephan rounded a hedge to find a gateway leading to the burning farmhouse. He held up a hand to signal his companions to stop. There was a gentle clip-clop of horse's hooves as Sebastian and Paolo closed on him.

"What's the holdup?" Paolo asked.

"Alessandro's gang is made up of more than just the six men we've already taken out. I don't know how many were killed when the bomb went off, but I'm sure we haven't accounted for all of them."

"Bomb?" Paolo asked as he dismounted.

"*Dottore* Gribbleflotz made up some nitroglycerin and we made a dust bomb. That's what started the fire."

"Do I want to know what nitroglycerin is?" Paolo asked as he tied his horse's reins to a branch before drawing his rifle from its sheath.

"It's a high explosive. I'll tell you more later," Stephan said.

Paolo nodded. "I will be interested to hear. Now, you seem to know what you're doing, so you can take the lead." He turned to Sebastian. "And you. No more photographs. The flash will give us away."

"What if I don't use the flash?" Sebastian asked. "Would that be okay?"

Paolo and Stephan exchanged looks. They could not see it, but they both rolled their eyes. "Just don't use the flash," Paolo warned Sebastian.

Stephan brandished his shotgun. "If you give us away, you'll catch the first round."

"I won't. See," Sebastian said as he hastily unplugged the lead from the camera to his electronic flash, "I've disconnected the flash."

"See that you don't reconnect it," Stephan warned.

"Not even once the shooting starts?" Sebastian asked.

Stephan sighed. "You can use the flash after the shooting starts," he conceded. "Now, follow me, and be careful where you place your feet."

They approached the stables in an arrow formation. Stephan in the front, Sebastian to his left, and Paolo to his right. Stephan noticed the door was open and waved the other two back. He chambered a round and topped up the magazine before creeping forward.

Three men burst through the partially open door and charged Stephan. At a range of less than five yards, he opened fire.

Boom. Boom. Boom. Boom. Boom. Boom.

As fast as he could cycle the action, Stephan fired at the oncoming men. He turned away after the last pump of the slide did not result in a discharge—signifying that the magazine was empty. He had been more intent on cycling the action as quickly as possible rather than counting shots. He remedied the situation, reloading the magazine once more. This time, however, he was reduced to using solid slugs. He had fired off all the buckshot on the bandolier he'd been given.

With the shotgun reloaded, Stephan advanced on the three men on the ground.

Sebastian walked up beside him. "Was that 'slam fire'?"

Stephan nodded before he crouched down beside one of the brigands. The man was as good as dead. He had been hit in the chest and abdomen with buckshot at five yards. The dispersal of the shot that hit his chest was, well, Stephan's clenched fist covered all the hits. He moved on to the next man. The hits were lower, basically disemboweling him.

"Where did you learn to do it?"

Stephan looked up and met Sebastian's eyes. "I was with Heinrich Schmidt's shotgun company until the end of September '31. Rate of fire was our god, and slam fire is nearly twice as fast as normal fire." He moved his arm. The run had not done his ribs any favors, neither had firing a pump-action shotgun. Using it in slam-fire mode had just added to his woes.

"Are you hurt?" Sebastian asked.

"Cracked ribs," Stephan admitted. "I had to fight Alessandro Garivaghi's chief lieutenant for my boots and he got a good shot in."

"What?" Paolo demanded. "You fought with Giulio Alberti?"

"Alessandro just called him Giulio," Stephan said apologetically.

"About your height. Older and heavily built. Had part of his left ear sliced off."

Stephan nodded. "That sounds like the guy."

Paolo whistled. "You wouldn't be here if you hadn't been able to defeat him. How did you manage that? Many very good fighters have gone up against him in the past and not survived."

Stephan shrugged. "Just lucky, I guess."

Paolo snorted. "That takes more than luck. Where did you learn to fight?"

"I associate with a number of dubious characters."

"I told you before, Paolo. Stephan's with 1st Marine Reconnaissance Company."

"There is a whole company of people like you?"

Stephan grinned. "Yeah. All six of us."

"Six?" Paolo stared at Stephan is if he did not believe what he was hearing. "How can there be a company with only six men?"

"The plan was for a full company, with the six of us as the training cadre, but with the Marines not being involved in a lot of fighting, the extra slots in the company haven't been funded."

"Training cadre? That means you can train more men like yourself? Very interesting." Paolo nodded to himself. "Let us get the wagon and on the way back to Alessandro, you can tell me more about the 1st Marine Reconnaissance Company and explain to me why you had to fight Giulio for your boots."

Chapter 34

Sunday, 16th November 1636, Vicenza

Simone da Porto paced the room aggressively. Standing against the wall, trying to make himself as small and insignificant as possible, stood the poor unfortunate individual who'd drawn the short straw. Littering the floor near him were the shattered remains of a crystal brandy decanter and two formerly near-priceless fifteenth-century Barovier *cristallo* glasses.

Simone stopped pacing and glared at the messenger. "What was the fool thinking of?"

"I don't know," Gentullio Campagnolo said.

"Of course you don't know," Simone muttered angrily. "I doubt even Alessandro really knows what he was thinking." He took a deep breath and slowly released it. "Be seated," he said to Gentullio as he slumped into a chair. "Now, how can we get out of this mess with the minimum of fuss?"

Gentullio sat on the edge of the chair he had selected. "Paolo Molin has already started proceedings to confiscate the properties of Alessandro Garivaghi."

Simone's head jerked up. "MOLIN!" he shouted. "What is one of Contarini's secretaries doing in Vicenza?"

"From what I've heard..." Gentullio paused, just in case the da Porto was not interested in what he might have heard.

Simone gestured for him to continue. "Come on, spit it out. What have you heard?"

Gentullio licked dry lips and shuffled on his chair. "Paolo Molin is not Contarini's man. He works for the *Provveditori alla Sanità* and was assigned to follow *Dottore* Gribbleflotz and his party. He and the American, Sebastian Jones, were passing through Vicenza in search of *dottori* Stone, Gribbleflotz, and Böhm, who had failed to return as expected from a trip to Verona. He discovered that they had been kidnapped and immediately rode to their rescue."

Simone stared at the unfortunate Gentullio. "Alessandro kidnapped *Dottore* Stone, the wealthy American industrialist?"

Gentullio nodded.

"And *Dottore* Gribbleflotz, the man who operated on His Serenity?"

Again, Gentullio nodded.

Simone threw himself back in his chair and screamed out to the gods above. "Why me?"

A quick shake of the head and Simone was all business once more. "Who is *Dottore* Böhm?"

"He assisted *Dottore* Gribbleflotz when he operated on His Serenity."

Simone desperately wanted to throw something, but his wife was already going to have words with him over the destruction of the highly decorative *cristallo* glasses. He settled for slumping in his chair and glaring at Gentullio. The man was innocent of any offense other than being the messenger, but right now, Simone was prepared to consider even that offensive. "There are plenty of other less important but still wealthy people Alessandro could have kidnapped. Why did he have to pick on those three?"

"They weren't kidnapped for ransom, *Signore* da Porto. It is my understanding that he put them to work creating the philosopher's stone."

Simone screamed and slammed his fists down on the drinks table, causing the glasses to jump. He managed to save them before they fell to the floor, but that just aggravated his anger. "I'll kill him," he muttered furiously. Part of his anger was aimed at himself. He had told Alessandro about *Dottore* Gribbleflotz making Basil Valentine's third key. He'd virtually primed and pointed Alessandro at the man.

"Killing *Signore* Garivaghi will be a job for the hangman, *Signore* da Porto. However, it is most likely he will only be exiled." Gentullio was a lawyer and the action to correct one's client's apparent misunderstanding of the legalities was automatic.

"If he is exiled, then he better start running, and never stop running, because when I catch him, he'll wish he'd been executed by the state's executioner." Simone smiled. Even just the thought of what he wanted to do to Alessandro made him feel better. "Has Molin sent a messenger to Venice yet?"

Gentullio nodded. "One was sent shortly after he arrived this morning. He also requisitioned pigeons for both Venice and Padua."

Simone sighed. Carrier pigeons could make the forty-mile trip from Vicenza to Venice in under an hour. He glanced at the clock on the mantel above the roaring fire. "Contarini and his pack of vultures are probably already on their way."

"The *Inquisitori di Stato* are not vultures," Gentullio protested.

Simone raised an eyebrow.

"Saying that," Gentullio hastily added, "they will pick over the surviving residue of *Signore* Garivaghi's property very much as vultures are said to pick over the carcass of a dead beast."

"Vultures," Simone reaffirmed. "How much is it going to cost to recover the property they confiscate?"

"Well." Gentullio's tongue darted out to moisten his lips. "None of the persons offended against are really suitable candidates to have the land enfeoffed upon them..."

Simone nodded his agreement. Enfeoffment was an exchange of land for a pledge of service. Something none of the foreigners were likely to offer. "So, the simple payment of a sum of money could be sufficient for the confiscation to be reversed?"

"I wouldn't call it a simple payment," Gentullio prevaricated. "It is likely to take a considerable amount of money to overcome the offense perpetrated upon such important individuals."

"Try and keep it under three thousand ducats."

Gentullio's eyes boggled. He jabbed his thumb into his chest repeatedly. "You want me to negotiate the compensation?"

"If it is beyond your capabilities..."

"Oh, no. No, *Signore* da Porto. I am quite capable of running the negotiations." He paused. His tongue shot out and glided across dry lips. "The property was assessed at the time of the banishment of *Conte* Ludovico da Porto in 1584 as being worth not less than eleven thousand ducats."

Simone arched a speaking eyebrow.

Gentullio got the message. "Of course, that was many years ago and the property has deteriorated a lot since then. Also, the principal residence on the property has recently been damaged by fire. Together, these factors will greatly reduce the current value..."

Simone smiled. "Keep thinking like that.

"You may go."

Gentullio gathered his papers and backed away, bowing intermittently as he did so, until he reached the door. Then he turned, opened the door, and scampered through, closing it gently once he was safely on the other side.

Simone stared at the closed door. It would, he thought, be interesting to see if the young lawyer could make a deal for as little as three thousand ducats. If he could even keep the settlement under five thousand, it would be a sign that he was someone with promise.

Dr. Gribbleflotz and Stephan Böhm were admiring their handiwork when Paolo Molin joined them.

Paolo looked at the man sleeping in the bed. "I am happy to see that you have managed to keep him alive."

"It was touch and go for a while," Phillip said. "If it hadn't been for the ether Stephan had in his medical kit, the trauma of the amputation might have killed him."

Paolo's brows rose as he looked at Stephan. "You just happened to have ether in your medical kit?"

Stephan nodded.

"Is that normal?" Paolo turned to Phillip. "Do people normally carry ether in their medical kit? Do you carry ether in your medical kit?"

"No, I don't," Phillip said.

Paolo turned back to Stephan. "Do you normally carry around such a comprehensive medical kit?"

"You never know when you might need something. And it was fortunate that I had it in my kit. Otherwise our patient might not have survived."

Paolo looked down on the sleeping Alessandro. "For which I am extremely grateful."

"Would it have been a problem if he'd died?" Phillip asked.

Paolo shrugged. "It would have been awkward. Besides, there are questions that need to be asked, and dead men tell no tales."

Phillip and Stephan glanced down upon Alessandro. "What sort of questions?"

"Who else was involved in your kidnapping? What is the

connection between Alessandro and The Magnificent Ponzi? Questions like that."

"I thought he just wanted me because he'd heard I could make Valentine's third key," Phillip said.

"And how did he learn that?" Paolo asked.

Stephan and Phillip responded with silence.

Paolo grinned. "It is a very good question, isn't it?

"Answers to that and many other questions are why it is good that Alessandro will live to have his day in court."

"So, what happens now?" Stephan asked.

"We wait for my cousin Domenico to respond to the messages I sent to Venice."

"How long will that take?"

"If my cousin acts immediately when my news reaches him, he should be here late tomorrow."

"So we have two days to fill until your cousin gets here," Stephan muttered. "Can't we return to Padua? You'll be heading there later, won't you?"

"Domenico will want to speak with all of you before he questions *Signore* Garivaghi and any of the surviving brigands."

"Were there any surviving brigands?" Phillip asked.

"I don't know," Paolo admitted. "That is why I will shortly be heading over to the *Signore* Garivaghi's farm to check."

"I'll go with you," Stephan said.

"What about your ribs?" Paolo asked.

"*Dottore* Gribbleflotz has strapped them."

Paolo rolled his eyes. "Do you want the shotgun?"

Stephan smiled. "Please."

"Is it okay with you if Corporal Böhm accompanies me?" Paolo asked Phillip.

"It's not a problem," Phillip said. "He'll probably want to take his medical kit along, just in case."

"Definitely," Stephan agreed.

Venice

Carlo Contarini was happily engrossed in his correspondence when a knock on the door disturbed his peace. He looked up and glared at the door. "Enter!"

Domenico Molin swung in, closing the door firmly behind him. "Paolo has sent a message by carrier pigeon from Vicenza..."

"What's he doing in Vicenza? He was supposed to attach himself to *Dottore* Gribbleflotz's party and they are in Padua."

Domenico nodded enthusiastically. "He has arrested Alessandro Garivaghi for kidnapping *dottori* Stone, Gribbleflotz, and Böhm."

"Kidnapping?" Carlo held out a hand for the message Domenico was holding. "Why would Garivaghi do such a foolish thing, and to those three of all people?"

Domenico shrugged. "Who knows?"

Carlo studied the flimsy piece of paper. "Paolo could have sent more information." He sighed. "I will have to travel to Vicenza."

"Alvise is already making preparations."

Carlo's brows rose. "You are getting above yourself. What if I had decided not to go to Vicenza?" he asked.

Domenico smiled. "And miss the opportunity to stick it to *Conte* Simone da Porto and his family in person?"

Carlo sighed. "You know me too well.

"Who do we have in Vicenza whom we can trust?"

"Zacharias Valier is the new *podestà* there, sir. He has been in the city for a few months now."

Carlo nodded. "Of course. Zacharias is a good man. Can the others be trusted though?"

Domenico shook his head. "Depends. Maybe. Simone da Porto wields considerable power in the region. But..." He left unsaid that even Simone could not go against the will of the Ten. His family tried that in the past and they were still, decades later, paying the price.

"Indeed," Carlo muttered. "Are we likely to face a rescue attempt?"

"It depends on how many men Alessandro has."

Carlo considered that. He nodded. "Borrow half a dozen soldiers. Ones that can ride," he added. "We will leave for Vicenza as soon as everyone can assemble."

Padua

Paola looked up from the message that had just been delivered to the attentive faces around her sitting room. "Paolo Molin says that he has located *dottori* Stone and Gribbleflotz, and Stephan Böhm in Vicenza."

Magda Edelmännin turned to Dina Kastenmayer. "What can they have been doing in Vicenza?"

Dina shrugged and looked appealingly at Paola.

Paola waved the message. "It doesn't say. All Paolo says is that he has found your missing husbands and Corporal Böhm, and that everyone is well." She read a little more. "It will be at least three days before they will be free to return to Padua." She looked up after saying that. "Why wouldn't they be free to immediately return to Padua if they are unhurt?" she asked the room.

"Maybe it has something to do with The Magnificent Ponzi," Rachel Lynch suggested.

"But The Magnificent Ponzi is here in Padua. Why would he have anything to do with the men having to stay in Vicenza for another three days?" Edith Lynch asked.

"I have no idea," Paola said. "No doubt the men will explain in the fullness of time."

"Meanwhile, what do we do about The Magnificent Ponzi?" Rachel asked. "He has a performance scheduled this weekend and who knows what will happen if it goes ahead."

"We need to collect evidence of wrongdoing," Paola said. "I will get some of the children to keep an eye on what is happening at the *Prato della Valle*."

"William's going to want to be involved with that," Rachel muttered.

"I'm not sure that's a good idea," Edith said. "His father is bound to notice him hanging around and ask questions."

"Surely the father will expect his son to try and be around him?" Magda asked.

Rachel nodded. "But Bill would also interrogate William. It would put a lot of pressure on William I don't want him to be under."

"But it would also distract Bill," Edith pointed out. "He might even show William around, giving him plenty of opportunity to learn what is going on."

"And he'd be making William promise not to tell anyone about what he sees."

"So he takes Marcello with him again," Paola said. "The boys will imagine themselves as spies. They'll probably enjoy it immensely."

Rachel slowly shook her head. "I don't like it. It'll probably end up putting William in an invidious position where he has to lie either to me or to his father."

"How about we ask William and Marcello what they would be willing to do?" Edith suggested.

Rachel signaled her disagreement by shaking her head.

Paola clapped her hands. "If Rachel isn't happy to send William to spy on The Magnificent Ponzi, I have plenty of other cousins, nephews, and nieces who will be willing."

"Well, if William isn't to go, then I guess that is the only alternative," Edith said.

Chapter 35

Tuesday, 18th November 1636, Podestà's Palace, Vicenza

Carlo Contarini arrived late in the day in the town. He noted the sorry state of the city walls—a scandal if one considered the monies expended on their construction only a few years ago—for future attention and headed directly to the *podestà*'s palace.

Carlo was accompanied by Domenico and Alvise Molin, and six soldiers. Passing through the narrow streets of the city he saw the effect his entourage had on the good people of Vicenza. Men crossed themselves, women grabbed their children from the street, and all stared at them as if they saw a ghost. Maybe it was the good horses they rode. Maybe the golden cuirasses of the soldiers or the austere robes worn by Domenico and Alvise denoting their status as secretaries. Or perhaps it was the scarlet robe of his office that he wore.

Carlo smiled. Let the guilty be fearful. *Il Rosso*, the red inquisitor, was in Vicenza to dispense justice.

A small group of people awaited them at the entrance of the palace. Carlo recognized Zacharias Valier. Apart from the servants and a man Domenico pointed out as Paolo Molin, there was also a middle-aged man in a black robe. That should be, in accordance with the message requesting his presence that Carlo had sent ahead, the magistrate responsible for the investigation into the kidnapping and rescue of *dottori* Stone and Gribbleflotz, and Corporal Böhm.

They halted in front of the entrance. Servants rushed forward to hold the horses of Carlo, Domenico, and Alvise. "Domenico, with me!" Carlo slowly swung his leg over his horse's back and slowly lowered himself to the ground. "I'm getting too old for this," he muttered as he turned to his senior secretary. Carlo was fifty-six.

Domenico had the bad manners to grin. "I'm sure they'll have a room ready if you'd like to *freshen up*."

Carlo heard the subtle message in the last two words and glared at his man. "I would like to wash the dust off, and to visit a garderobe where I can sit down properly. I am sick of squatting behind a bush."

This time, Domenico managed to maintain a straight face. "Of course, Your Excellency."

"Proper food. Hot food. And something to drink," Carlo added.

"Which is ready to be served upon your command, Your Excellency," Zacharias called out from the palace's steps.

Carlo looked past Domenico to the man by the door to the house. "Zacharias, old friend. How's Vicenza treating you?" he asked.

"It would be better, Carlo," the *podestà* said, "if we didn't have this unfortunate incident." He turned and signed to the black-robed man to step forward. "Your Excellency," he said, "allow me to introduce you to Julio Trissino, the investigating magistrate in charge of the case against Alessandro Garivaghi."

Carlo nodded in acknowledgement. "Judge Trissino, I am sorry that such a burden has been placed upon you." He meant it. Being the investigating magistrate in a case against a member of the da Porto family was not likely to be life-enhancing.

"It is not as bad as it might be, Your Excellency," Julio said. "*Conte* Simone da Porto seems to have washed his hands of his cousin." He shrugged. "Da Porto has provided a lawyer, as one must. However, the man seems more concerned with preventing confiscation of *Signore* Garivaghi's property than defending the man from the consequences of his crimes."

"Still, that can wait," the *podestà* interrupted. "I'm sure His Excellency wishes to wash and change into something more comfortable. We can talk when you are refreshed."

Carlo nodded in acceptance before he turned around and instructed Alvise and the soldiers to follow the servants around to the palace's stables.

✧ ✧ ✧

A couple of hours later, after Carlo had the opportunity to freshen up and eat a late lunch, they settled in the *podestà*'s office. Carlo took possession of the chair behind a desk, which stood clean, almost barren. To his right Zacharias sat on a smaller chair. To the left Domenico, acting as the only secretary to the meeting, used a small low table to take notes. Opposite Carlo sat Paolo and Julio.

Carlo lounged back in his wooden armchair. "Let us begin," he said and nodded to Domenico.

"By the order of the Council of Ten," Domenico started in a clear, officious manner, "His Excellency, *Signore* Carlo Contarini, acting in his capacity as a member of the *Supremo Tribunale*, tasked to investigate and confirm judgment as necessary on the matter of the kidnapping of *dottori* Stone and Gribbleflotz, and Corporal Böhm by *Signore* Alessandro Garivaghi and his associates. Documents regarding the said affair were presented by *Signore* Julio Trissino, acting in his capacity as *Giudico* of the *Podestà* of Vicenza."

He presented the said documents to Julio. "Is this your signature?" he asked.

"*Si*," the judge replied.

Domenico nodded and proceeded with the list of documents.

Carlo followed this procedure with mild disinterest. He would review all the aforementioned documents during the inquest, but it was always best to complete the secretarial matters first. A report of this meeting would be produced eventually, with all the supporting documents including affidavits, sworn testimonies and such, and then filed accordingly. He was pretty much sure that this affair would not be of such importance as to be filed in the archives of the *Deputato alla Segreta*, the secretary of The Ten. In fact, if not for the persons involved, such a case would normally be judged at a lower level. True, the Ten might become involved, but at a later stage, acting as a court of last resort.

But this case was his. And his judgment would be final. Neither the Senate nor His Serenity, the doge himself, could counteract him. It was the law. But it was only prudent to keep good records.

"Your Excellency?" Domenico broke his reverie.

Carlo looked at the magistrate. "Are you satisfied with Alessandro Garivaghi's guilt?" he asked.

Julio nodded. "I have interviewed *dottori* Stone and Gribbleflotz, Corporal Böhm, as well as their fellow prisoner, the alchemist Luigi Boscolo. Their stories are consistent. And with the added information from your man Paolo and the American, Sebastian Jones, there is more than enough evidence to support charges of kidnapping and unlawful imprisonment." He paused to moisten his lips. "Any charges for attempted murder are a little more difficult to substantiate."

Carlo's brows rose. "Who did he try to murder?"

Paolo held up a hand. "When I challenged him to surrender, he responded by shooting at me."

"That's one." Julio had said charges, so there had to be more than one. Carlo raised a brow inviting Paolo to identify any others.

"Giulio Alberti fought with Corporal Böhm."

Carlo stared at Paolo. He knew Alberti by reputation. He turned back to Julio. "You said you had interviewed Corporal Böhm?"

Julio smiled. "I see you have heard of Giulio Alberti."

"He is a killer. Responsible for more than a dozen deaths that I know of."

"Oh, I'm sure there are many more than a single dozen," Julio said. "However, it seems he met his match with Corporal Böhm. I have seen the body. Not that Corporal Böhm actually killed Alberti," he hastened to add.

"It wasn't through any lack of trying," Paolo said. "He busted Alberti's larynx. If it hadn't been for *Dottore* Gribbleflotz performing an emergency tracheotomy on him, he would have suffocated where he fell. As it is, I am told that Alberti died of smoke inhalation when the farmhouse caught fire."

"Corporal Böhm is a most impressive man," Julio observed. "Not only did he kill eight men and a dog, he was also able to help *Dottore* Gribbleflotz save Alessandro Garivaghi's life."

"I told Böhm that I wanted Garivaghi alive, otherwise it would have been nine men and a dog. And it was a rather large Cane Corso," Paolo added. "He killed it with a sharpened length of iron bar he cut from the prison when they escaped.

"He stabbed it through the soft skin under the jaw," Paolo added, pointing to the point on his own jaw. "He says it went straight up into the dog's brain."

"You sound awfully impressed by the man," Zacharias said.

Paolo nodded. "I am." He turned to Carlo. "And there are

more men just as capable back in the USE. The 1st Marine Reconnaissance Company." Paolo pulled some papers from a satchel at his feet and passed them over to Carlo. "I have written a report."

Carlo glanced down at the wad of papers he had been given. "Indeed, you have. I will read it when I have time." He put the papers to one side and turned his attention to Julio. "Can I see the evidence you have against Alessandro Garivaghi?"

"Of course." Julio started placing papers on the table. "These are the affidavits of seven witnesses who remember seeing Alessandro's men carry three men out of the *Teatro Olimpico* on the night *dottori* Stone and Gribbleflotz, and Corporal Böhm claim they were kidnapped."

Carlo stared at the papers. "A competent lawyer could argue mistaken identity."

"Of course," Julio admitted. "However, I also have the affidavits of *dottori* Stone and Gribbleflotz, and Corporal Böhm, and much of their stories mesh with the stories of the other witnesses."

"*Dottori* Stone and Gribbleflotz might carry some weight, but a simple corporal against the might of the da Portos?" Carlo shook his head.

Julio smiled. "I also have sworn affidavits from members of the Vicenza watch that connect Alessandro with *Dottore* Gribbleflotz's very unique boots. Three of them are members of the Capra family."

Carlo looked at him. "Interesting," he said.

He knew the history. The da Portos might be the most powerful family around Vicenza, but the Capras were not that far behind them. There had been a long feud between them, resulting in a number of deaths. Peace was only declared between the families after *Conte* Ludovico da Porto was condemned to twenty-two years' exile and the confiscation of his free property fifty years ago. Which is not to say the families are not above trying to stab each other in the back every chance they got. He was sure that the Capras were connected to Lucillo Cereda and more recently his heirs as they fought to retain the property that had been enfeoffed upon Lucillo after it was confiscated from *Conte* Ludovico da Porto.

"Won't that cast doubts on their evidence?" Alvise asked.

"Normally, it would. Or at least, could," Julio said. "However, thanks to Paolo Molin's friend, we have photographic evidence."

Paolo nodded vigorously. "Sebastian took lots and lots of

photographs. Some connecting *Signore* Garivaghi directly to *Dottore* Gribbleflotz's boots . . ." He picked one and slid it across the table to Carlo.

Carlo looked at it. And then he stared at it. He looked up. "Is that *Dottore* Gribbleflotz stealing Alessandro's boots?"

"No!" Paolo shook his head vigorously. "*Dottore* Gribbleflotz is merely recovering his boots, which *Signore* Garivaghi had stolen from him." He passed over another photograph. "And this one shows *Dottore* Gribbleflotz pulling on said boots. The boots *Signore* Garivaghi was seen wearing by a member of Vicenza's watch have *Dottore* Gribbleflotz's name branded on them."

"There are also photographs showing Corporal Böhm recovering his revolver and webbing from *Signore* Garivaghi while he lay wounded," Julio added.

"And if those photographs aren't enough," Paolo said, "we also have the evidence collected from the farm in Cresole. The various chemicals *dottori* Stone and Gribbleflotz produced, with their fingerprints all over everything. And then there is the body of Giulio Alberti, complete with the tracheal tube *Dottore* Gribbleflotz inserted into his throat still in place. There cannot be many plastic tracheal tubes in the Republic, so there should be little difficulty connecting the one found in Giulio's throat to the one Corporal Böhm brought with him from the USE.

"And of course, *Signore* Jones was on the scene to record everything with his camera. Including all the locals who turned up to fight the fire."

"*Signore* Jones seems to have been extremely helpful." Carlo looked pointedly at Paolo. "What did you promise him?"

"He insisted on taking photographs, Your Excellency," Paolo said. "In fact, we couldn't stop him taking them. He hopes to sell them to various newspapers back in the USE."

"That is good to hear." Carlo sat back in his chair. "Is there anything that needs immediate attention?"

"Well," Paolo said tentatively.

"What?" Carlo asked. "What needs immediate attention?"

"It doesn't exactly need immediate attention, but The Magnificent Ponzi has a performance scheduled for Saturday night at the theater in the *Prato della Valle*, and *dottori* Stone and Gribbleflotz want to be there so they can check whether or not Ponzi really does perform the fake surgery."

"Fake surgery?" Julio asked.

Paolo nodded. "Apparently, as part of his performance, Ponzi is supposed to remove diseased organs and even bladder stones from patients on stage. He uses just his hands, and although there is lots of blood, there is no scar."

"You say he fakes this surgery?" Julio asked.

Paolo nodded.

"He doesn't actually remove any diseased organs or bladder stones?"

Again, Paolo nodded. "*Dottori* Stone and Gribbleflotz say that although it may appear real, it is indeed faked."

Julio licked his lips and turned to Carlo. "This is very serious."

"What? Fake surgery in a theatrical performance?" Carlo asked.

"It wasn't part of a theatrical performance," Julio said. "A colleague paid The Magnificent Ponzi one hundred ducats to remove bladder stones in a private operation in his home. If, as *Signore* Paolo Molin says, the operation is a fake..."

"Have *Dottore* Gribbleflotz examine your colleague," Paolo suggested. "He will be able to tell if the stones have been removed."

Chapter 36

Wednesday, 19th November 1636, Vicenza

Dr. Phillip Gribbleflotz palpated Judge Flavio Scamozzi's abdomen. "You still have bladder stones," he said. "If I had my equipment and surgical team, I could sort them out in less than an hour." He shrugged. "But I don't. However, if you are willing to travel to Padua, I'm sure we can schedule you for immediate surgery."

"I paid a hundred ducats to have them removed by The Magnificent Ponzi." Flavio glared at Phillip. "Are you saying I have been defrauded?"

Phillip nodded. "If you paid to have the stones removed, then yes."

"But he showed them to me," Flavio protested.

"Props. Were they bloodied?"

Flavio nodded.

"They shouldn't have been. They should have been clean and smelling of urine."

Flavio stared at Phillip. "They didn't smell."

"Then they were mere props." Phillip shook his head gently. "I am afraid, Judge Scamozzi, that you have been tricked by a practiced fraudster." He glanced at the rest of his audience—Carlo Contarini and Judge Julio Trissino. "And he is now in Padua planning to repeat his fraud on any number of unsuspecting innocents."

"Well, something has to be done to prevent that happening," Julio said. "Padua is outside my jurisdiction, but not yours, Your Excellency." He looked pointedly at Carlo.

Carlo sighed. "Very well. We will make for Padua as soon as possible."

"I will accompany you," Flavio said. He smiled at Phillip. "I wish to take you up on your offer, and if you do remove my bladder stones, they can be used as evidence of Ponzi's fraud."

Padua

It was late on Wednesday when sixteen men rode into Padua. There was no foolishness from the guards at the gate about not letting them in. The guards did not even try to stop them. They just opened the gates to let them ride straight in. Having the senior member of the *Tre Inquisitori di Stato* in your party, complete with soldiers carrying his personal standard, was good for something. They dropped Judge Flavio Scamozzi off at a colleague's house before continuing along to Thomas Stone's apartment in the central city. Leaving him in the tender embrace of his wife, they then moved on to the Rovarini compound off to the east of the city, inside the outer city wall.

"Phillip!" Dina cried out the moment she saw him before charging up to him and throwing herself into his arms.

Phillip did what came naturally. He caught her and kissed her. Soundly.

Sebastian Jones also did what came naturally. He took a photograph of the emotional reunion.

Stephan Böhm laid hands on Sebastian and advised him, in a quiet and controlled manner, to leave the happy couple alone or face having his camera and all of his film suffer a truly catastrophic accident. He accompanied his words with the kind of smile that Sebastian found incredibly convincing. He hastily put away his camera.

Diana walked around the happy couple and wandered up to Stephan. "Who're your new friends?"

"What? No 'I'm glad to see you'?"

"I'm glad to see you," Diana parroted deadpan. And then she grinned and hugged Stephan.

Stephan winced. Diana was not a small girl even by up-timer standards. She was taller than him for a start, and she was no ninety-pound weakling. The compression of his chest hurt.

Diana was instantly contrite. "Are you alright?"

"Cracked ribs," Stephan explained. He lifted his shoulders a couple of times to settle everything before gesturing to the rest of their party. "These are Paolo's boss and his retinue."

Diana studied the men. The scarlet robe of Paolo's boss was especially noticeable. "I thought you said Paolo was an official with the *Provveditori alla Sanità*," she muttered.

"Working under the direct supervision of *Il Rosso*, Carlo Contarini."

"*Il Rosso* is the most important of the three Inquisitors of the State. That makes him very important. So, what's he doing in Padua?"

Stephan smiled. "He's here to arrest The Magnificent Ponzi."

Diana's brows rose. "On what charge? When we asked Paolo to do something before he headed out to find and bring you guys back, he said that Ponzi wasn't doing anything illegal."

"Ponzi might not have been doing anything illegal in Padua, but while he was in Vicenza, he charged a judge one hundred ducats to remove bladder stones."

"One hundred?" Diana winced. "I'm going to have words with Frau Mittelhausen. We're obviously not charging enough." She looked at Stephan. "He faked it?"

Stephan nodded. "Dr. Gribbleflotz confirmed that the judge still had bladder stones earlier today."

Diana whistled. "Defrauding a judge. What kind of fool does that?" she asked.

"Ponzi and company, obviously."

Diana grinned. "True. So, when does it happen? When do Ponzi and his team get arrested?"

"Tomorrow sometime."

"I want to be there," Diana said.

Chapter 37

Thursday, 20th November 1636, Vicenza

The sun was still debating the merits of creeping above the horizon when Carlo Contarini, Domenico, Alvise, and Paolo staggered bleary-eyed into Paola Rovarini's lantern-illuminated kitchen. A few minutes later, Judge Flavio Scamozzi and his Padua colleague, Judge Cesare Valentini, arrived.

"Why do we have to be here so early?" Flavio asked. "You won't be arresting Ponzi until all his people have arrived at the theater."

"We need to collect evidence of a crime before we can arrest Ponzi and his people," Carlo said. "That means that *Dottore* Gribbleflotz has to remove your bladder stones."

Flavio sulked. "But the sun isn't even up yet."

"Judge Scamozzi," Phillip said in his most patron-placating tone of voice, "you will need time in which to recover from the surgery. If you truly wish to be present when the arrests are made, we need to conduct the operation as soon as possible."

"Who will be performing the operation?" Cesare asked.

Flavio looked at Cesare as if his mind were wandering. "*Dottore* Gribbleflotz, of course."

Cesare shrugged. "It's just that I have heard good things about *Signora* Cheng." He gestured to Diana. "I understand she has done the operation over a dozen times since she arrived in Padua."

Diana responded to the recommendation with a modest bow of her head.

Flavio's eyes ran over Diana. "I'm not having a strange woman touch me there."

"You would be in good hands if you did allow *Signora* Cheng to perform the operation," Stephan Böhm said.

Flavio snorted. "I am already having my doubts about putting my life in your hands. I'm certainly not going to let some unqualified individual stick strange mechanical devices down my penis."

"*Signora* Cheng is properly qualified," Phillip said. "She is certified to not only perform a transurethral lithotripsy; she is also certified to teach others how to perform the procedure.

"So, who is it to be?" Phillip asked. "I'm quite happy to stand aside and let *Signora* Cheng perform the operation. As Judge Valentini said, she has performed over a dozen since arriving in Padua." He grinned. "That means she has more experience with the procedure than I do."

Flavio gave Diana a distrusting glance. "More experience than you?"

Phillip nodded.

"And fully qualified to perform the procedure?"

Phillip nodded. "Taught and certified to perform the procedure by none other than the head of surgery at Leahy Medical Center in Grantville, *Dottore* Johannes Schultes himself."

Flavio's tongue shot out and moistened his lips. "I have heard of *Dottore* Schultes." He released a set-upon sigh. "Very well, she can perform my operation. It's not going to hurt, is it?"

Phillip shook his head. "The procedure is performed under a general anesthetic. That means you will be sound asleep. You won't feel a thing."

"Although there may be some tenderness when you wake up," Diana warned. "Still, you should be up on your feet inside a couple of hours."

"Very well. Get on with it."

"If you feel here," Diana told Judge Valentini, "you should be able to feel the bladder stone."

Cesare felt the area he had been directed to. "I can feel something. A lump."

"Right." Diana manipulated the lithotrite. "Can you feel that?" she asked.

"Something just grabbed the lump."

Diana smiled behind her surgical mask. "Now, if you'd like to take the trigger of the lithotrite, you can crush the stone."

"Me?" Cesare pointed to himself.

"As long as all you do is squeeze the trigger, there's nothing that can go wrong."

A little tentatively, Cesare put his hand around the lithotrite's trigger system and squeezed. There was significant resistance, so he put in more effort. His knuckles were showing white when there was an audible crack.

Cesare stared at Flavio's tincture-of-iodine-painted abdomen. A smile started to blossom. "I did it. I broke a bladder stone."

Diana took back possession of the lithotrite. "Of course, it is still too big to pass through the urethra, so I'll just break it down some more." She spent several minutes nibbling away at the bladder stone until it was reduced to sufficiently small fragments. She then checked the bladder for more stones. There were a few smaller ones. She dealt with those in the same manner before withdrawing the lithotrite. "And now to aspirate some of the evidence." Diana accepted a tube with a deflated rubber bladder from Lise Gebauer, who was back serving in her normal role of theater nurse. Diana carefully threaded the tube down Judge Scamozzi's urethra and then, by careful manipulation of a screw valve, sucked up as many of the fragments as she could. When the bladder was full, she removed it and emptied it through a fine-mesh sieve into a chamber pot.

Cesare pointed to the fine gravel collected in the sieve. "Is that all from Flavio's bladder stones?"

"It won't be all of it," Diana said, "just the bulk of it. The rest should pass with normal urination." She looked down at her patient. "He's going to need to drink more fluids if he doesn't want to have a recurrence of the problem."

Cesare grinned. "I'm sure Flavio will be only too happy to drink more."

Diana smiled back but shook her head. "I don't mean he should drink more alcohol. He needs to increase his hydration levels. That means drinking plenty of water, or at least very watered-down wine."

Cesare winced. "Watered wine? You don't add water to fine wine."

"He doesn't have to drink watered wine; just add some non-alcoholic beverages to his diet. Such as herbal tea or fruit juice. Orange juice would be good. I've read that drinking at least a glass of orange juice a day can reduce the risk of recurrence of bladder and kidney stones."

"Ah." Cesare smiled. "That is different. I'm sure Flavio can be persuaded to add orange juice to his beverage list. Especially if it means he doesn't have to suffer the pain of bladder stones again."

Planning for the raid on the theater at *Prato della Valle* was well underway when Flavio Scamozzi made his way into the salon nearly ninety minutes after the completion of his surgery. Nurse Gebauer followed, a less than happy look on her face. Everyone was gathered around a cleared area where children's building blocks had been used to create a model of the theater and surrounding streets.

"How do you feel?" Cesare asked when he saw Flavio.

Flavio shrugged and kneaded his abdomen with his fingers. "Better, I think."

"You seem to be moving better," Cesare observed.

Flavio nodded. "But my groin is brown. Why is that?"

"That's the tincture of iodine," Stephan said. "We used it to disinfect the operation site to reduce the risk of infection."

"It should fade over the next few days," Diana said. "If it fades too quickly, we'll want to check you for iodine deficiency."

Flavio nodded, obviously having no real idea what Diana was talking about. Instead, he concentrated on the children's building blocks set up on the floor. "What is this?" he asked.

"It is Corporal Böhm's idea. We have created a representation of the layout of the theater at *Prato della Valle* to assist in our planning.

"It is a very good idea. It makes planning so much easier. As does having proper maps." Carlo held up the sheet of paper he was holding so Flavio could see it. It was clearly an annotated map of the layout of the theater.

"Where did you get the map?" Flavio asked.

Carlo gestured toward Paola and Rachel. "They have had spies watching the theater and Ponzi since early Monday morning.

"Now, where were we?" Carlo referred to a sheet of paper in his hand as he pointed out the various points of entry, or more importantly for them, egress. "My soldiers will guard the exits while the rest of us go in the front door."

"Will we be armed?" Stephan asked.

"Weapons will be carried." Carlo cast his eyes over his men. "However, there will be no shooting unless I give the word."

"What if they shoot at us?" Alvise asked. All six soldiers nodded their heads in agreement.

"Self-defense will be permitted, but it better be in self-defense. I don't want to find anyone shot in the back."

"Shoot someone in the back?" Alvise sounded outraged. "We wouldn't do a thing like that, would we?" he asked the soldiers.

They all dutifully shook their heads while denying that they would ever think of shooting someone in the back.

Carlo just looked at them, clearly not taken in by their protestations. "See that you don't, or I will have you charged with murder. Also, convicted and executed."

That had the soldiers and Molins standing straight and nodding their heads. "We understand," they said.

"I'm sure you do," Carlo said. "Now, back to the raid..."

Planning took another half hour, followed by an hour for lunch. After checking their equipment one last time, they set off for the *Prato della Valle*. The plan was to hit Ponzi and his people when they sat down for their own lunch. The schedule for which Paola's spies had noted and recorded.

Chapter 38

They did not approach the theater in one large mob. That would have attracted attention. Not that Carlo and the judges in their formal robes did not attract attention. However, the addition of six heavily armed soldiers would have attracted unwanted attention. Someone might guess their destination and hurry ahead to warn the people at the theater. So they had split up. Alvise and the soldiers had headed out in a circuitous route under the guidance of Marcello Rovarini and William Franklin. Meanwhile, Carlo and the judges, with Domenico, Paolo, Stephan, and Sebastian accompanying them, headed straight for the main gate into the theater. Behind them came the rest—Drs. Stone and Gribbleflotz, Rachel and Edith Lynch, and last but not least, Ursula Mittelhausen, Diana Cheng, and Lise Gebauer. Paola, for reasons of her own, had chosen to remain at home in her nice warm kitchen with Dina and Magda.

They halted at the gate blocking the main entrance and Carlo directed Domenico to pull the bellpull while he checked out his companions.

Judges Flavio Scamozzi and Cesare Valentini were clad in their formal robes. They did not carry any weapons, but then, their formal robes sort of negated the need. Paolo had a repeating rifle, Corporal Böhm had a repeating shotgun, and the American Sebastian Jones had his cameras. Of all the weaponry on display, Carlo thought those last were the most powerful.

"Go away. We're not open," a voice called through the heavy wooden gate.

Domenico exchanged a look with Carlo. Carlo nodded. "Open in the name of the Ten!" Domenico called out.

There was a rattling, and then the small hatch in the gate opened and a head appeared. Marco Loschi took one look at the robes being worn by Carlo and the judges and reared back, hitting his head on the frame with a resounding thud before slamming the hatch closed. Moments later there was the sound of heavy timbers being moved, and then the gate opened.

Marco stood white-faced and shaking as Carlo and his retinue approached. "Your Excellency, how may I be of service?"

"I seek Bernardo Ponzi, otherwise known as The Magnificent Ponzi. Where is he?"

Marco gulped a couple of times before answering. "I can lead you to him."

Carlo nodded. He had not really expected anything less. "Good." He waved a hand for Marco to lead the way.

They entered the theater's auditorium, for lack of a better term. The theater was more akin to an old Roman amphitheater, like the famous Colosseum in Rome, than a modern theater. It was a place designed more for mock battles than artistic performances, with plenty of seating and walls that prevented people sneaking in without paying.

There had been changes put in place for Ponzi's performance. Whereas the mock battles used the arena, Ponzi's performance needed a much smaller stage. A small raised platform had been built at one end of the arena. The rest of the arena had been filled with bench seating, more than doubling the theater's normal capacity.

As they proceeded in silence up the central aisle toward the raised stage people started to take notice. A silence fell over the theater.

Bernardo Ponzi noticed the silence and looked up. He saw Carlo in his scarlet robe and paled. *Il Rosso* was coming toward him, in the company of *dottori* Stone and Gribbleflotz. His eyes widened, and his jaw dropped as he took unintentional steps backwards. He bumped into a chair, knocking it over, entangling his legs with those of the chair. He fell, still staring in disbelief at *dottori* Stone and Gribbleflotz. Bernardo scrambled to his feet and took off.

Carlo raised a hand. He snapped his fingers a couple of times before pointing at the rapidly receding Ponzi.

Paolo shared a smile with Stephan and they both set off in pursuit.

Bill Franklin stomped his way onto the stage. "What the hell's going on? Who are these people, Marco?"

"Hello, Bill," Rachel Lynch called out.

"What the fuck? What're you doing here?" Bill demanded as he made his way across the stage toward Rachel and the others.

Rachel gestured to Carlo and Cesare. "These charming men are here to arrest The Magnificent Ponzi."

Bill glanced toward Carlo and Cesare. "On what charge? We haven't done anything wrong."

Cesare stepped up. "Bernardo Ponzi, also known as Bernardino Ponzi, is charged with defrauding Judge Flavio Scamozzi of one hundred ducats, being the fee he charged to perform surgery upon Judge Scamozzi to remove bladder stones."

Bill approached the end of the stage and looked down upon Cesare and the others. "Well, if Bernardo accepted money to perform the surgery, I'm sure he did it."

"He said he did it," Flavio said. "However, *Dottore* Cheng performed a transurethral lithotripsy upon me this morning, and I have seen the fragments she removed from my bladder. There is no way Bernardo Ponzi could have removed stones from my bladder and left that volume of fragments behind."

"Also," Cesare said, "under *Signora* Cheng's supervision, I was able to feel a large stone in Judge Scamozzi's bladder. A stone larger than my thumb. A stone so big that there is no way Bernardo Ponzi should have been able to miss it when he operated on Judge Scamozzi. I also felt *Signora* Cheng grab the stone with a lithotrite. And"—he paused dramatically before continuing—"I used the lithotrite to break a piece off the stone in Judge Scamozzi's bladder." He looked hard at Bill. "I am satisfied that Bernardo Ponzi faked the surgery, using various props to make it appear that he reached into Judge Scamozzi's bladder and removed a number of stones. A surgery for which Bernardo Ponzi charged one hundred ducats."

Bill's eyes started darting around.

"It's no good running, Bill," Rachel said. "They have this place surrounded."

Bill stilled. "Why would I run?" he asked. "I haven't done anything wrong. I just work for the guy."

✧ ✧ ✧

Bernardo Ponzi, full name Bernardo Carlo Pietro Giovanni Guglielmo Tebaldo Ponzi, was a talented and experienced conman in his early thirties. One of his talents was fleetness of foot, and he was putting it to good use as he attempted to get away from Paolo and Stephan.

Paolo was in his early thirties and had never been particularly fleet of foot. There was no way he could have caught Bernardo even if he'd tried. Stephan was in his early twenties and was fleet of foot. He could easily have run down Bernardo, but he didn't even try. Instead he jogged along beside Paolo, going just fast enough to keep their prey in view.

The pre-raid planning session had concluded that there was a high probability that Bernardo would bolt when he saw Drs. Stone and Gribbleflotz. They could have left them behind, but Carlo had felt the potential for a public display of guilt—which running would be—was worth the inconvenience of having to give chase. Of course, Carlo was not going to be one of the people required to chase Ponzi, so it was easy to see why he had seen merit in the idea.

Bernardo made it to an exit. He glanced over his shoulder as he tore at the bolt securing the gate, trying to move it.

Paolo and Stephan continued approaching at a steady jog. They could have sprinted to catch Bernardo before he got the gate open, but this was a known exit. If Alvise and the soldiers had dispersed themselves according to the plan, there should be at least one soldier waiting at the gate with their bayonet fitted to their musket.

Bernardo's look of desperation turned to elation as the bolt slid free and the gate started to open. He gave Paolo and Stephan the local equivalent of a one-finger salute and hauled the gate open. His intention to jump through the open gate came to a screaming halt when confronted by two soldiers with bayonet-equipped muskets aimed at his midsection.

Bernardo looked at the points of the bayonets, which were actually a couple of feet away from him, and then he looked over his shoulder. Paolo and Stephan had slowed to a walk.

"Bernardo Ponzi, you are under arrest," Paolo said.

"What for?" Bernardo protested. "I haven't done anything wrong."

Stephan put a hand on Paolo's shoulder to stop him saying anything. "How about conspiracy to kidnap *dottori* Stone and

Gribbleflotz and myself in the *Teatro Olimpico* in Vicenza on Thursday, the thirteenth of November?"

Bernardo stood tall. "I have absolutely no idea what you are talking about."

Stephan smiled. "Then why did you run when you saw *dottori* Stone and Gribbleflotz?"

Bernardo clenched his teeth and glared at Stephan.

"Secure the prisoner," Paolo told the two soldiers. "We will take him back to His Excellency."

Stephan snuck in while Bernardo was concentrating his attention on Paolo and the two soldiers and applied a simple follow-me hold. "Lead the way."

Paolo observed the way Bernardo was wincing as he tried to fight Stephan's hold and smiled. "There is no need to be too gentle with him."

Bill Franklin and Brent Little were vigorously protesting their innocence when Paolo and Stephan fronted up with Bernardo. Stephan, for one, was dubious about their claims. He let the soldiers take charge of Bernardo and wandered closer.

"The bastard's going to weasel his way out of it," a feminine voice muttered.

Stephan looked around and saw the speaker had been Rachel Lynch. That explained the *bastard* reference. Bill Franklin was her ex-husband. He had walked out on her and the children while she was pregnant with their fourth child. Personally, he would have added a few more colorful adjectives. He leaned forward. "What do you mean, he's going to get away with it?"

Rachel looked over her shoulder at Stephan. "They don't have anything to hold him on," she muttered bitterly. "He claims he was just hired to run the electrics."

"Is he an electrician?"

Rachel laughed. "Bill? No. He's a technician-grade radio ham, with his own rig. He got a job with the USE Signals Corps and was assigned to the navy in Magdeburg."

Stephan's eyes lit up. "Magdeburg? About when did he leave to join Ponzi?"

"Late '34. Why?"

"Because in late '34 someone stole a portable diesel generator, a couple of electric arc spotlights, cabling, and other supplies.

"Did you know that The Magnificent Ponzi uses a couple of electric arc spotlights to illuminate his act?"

"He had them at Verona. Do you think... Nah." Rachel shook her head. "Bill probably bought the generator and spotlights with the money he got mortgaging his half of the house."

"If they are the navy's generator and spotlights, then he would still be guilty of receiving stolen goods."

Rachel turned to stare at Bill. She sighed. "I guess that's better than nothing. How do we prove it?"

"I look at the generator and spotlights. They should have 'Property of the USE Navy' stamped or engraved on them somewhere. There should also be a military item number."

"Then let's check them out." She grabbed Stephan and pushed her way up to Bill and Brent.

"Hey, Bill. Where're the generator and spotlights you had in Verona? Stephan here would like to have a look at them." Her smile was sweet, in the same way a cat's smile was sweet as it played with a mouse.

Bill stared at Rachel. "The generator and spotlights?" His eyes became shifty, darting left and right. "Why do you want to look at the generator and spotlights?" he asked Stephan.

"I'm wondering if perhaps they might be the generator and spotlights that were stolen from the navy storeroom in Magdeburg a couple of years ago."

"I can show you," one of the other prisoners said.

"Crescenzo!" Bill shouted accusingly.

Crescenzo looked at Bill. "Why shouldn't I show the man the generator and spotlights? You said you bought them."

Bill wiped his sleeve across his forehead. Stephan saw the action and considered it a sign of probable guilt. It was mid-November and it was not hot enough for anyone not doing physical activity to be sweating for any other reason.

"What's going on?" Carlo demanded as he approached.

Stephan pointed to Crescenzo. "This man is willing to show me the generator and spotlights that are used in The Magnificent Ponzi's act."

Carlo glanced at Crescenzo, and then across to Bill. "What's so special about the generator and spotlights?"

"Someone stole a portable diesel generator and electric arc spotlights from the USE Navy back in late '34. I'm sure the navy would like them back."

Carlo smiled. He gestured for Paolo to join Crescenzo and Stephan.

"Wait for me," Sebastian called as he hurried after them.

Edith Lynch stepped up beside her daughter. "William Lane Franklin?"

Bill glared at his ex-mother-in-law. "You know who I am."

She smiled as she handed Bill several envelopes in heavy bond paper. "You've been served," she said as he accepted the envelopes.

"What the hell?" Bill demanded. He looked from Edith to the envelopes. "What the hell are these?"

"A summons for nonpayment of court-imposed child support for the last two years, and a foreclosure notice for your half of the family home."

"Foreclosure? How did that happen?"

"How the hell do you think it happened, you moron?" Rachel shouted. "You took the money and haven't even been paying the interest. Of course they foreclosed."

Bill turned to Rachel. "You lost the house?"

"What do you think?" Rachel demanded. "I had four children, three under the age of five. There was no way I could earn enough to service a mortgage for over a quarter of a million dollars."

"Oh!"

"Is that all you can say?" Rachel asked. She stared at the man she had married and sighed. He just wasn't worth her anger. "Come on, Mom."

"Just a moment," Edith said. "Here comes Stephan, and he looks happy."

Rachel looked in the direction her mother was pointing. Stephan was returning, and he did look extremely happy. She glanced at Bill. He was looking at Stephan too, and he did not look particularly happy. That made Rachel happy. She grabbed her mother's hand and set off to join the group that included Stephan's likely target, Carlo Contarini.

Stephan handed Carlo a sheet of paper torn from the notebook he kept in his medical kit. "If you radio those to Magdeburg, they'll be able to compare them with the numbers for the missing generator and spotlights."

Carlo raised his brows. "Using what for a radio? Any radios

we can get are currently being distributed throughout the *Stato da Màr*—the venetian possessions in the Adriatic and eastern Mediterranean. The *Terraferma*, the mainland territories, have to wait their turn."

Stephan pointed to Rachel, who had just arrived behind Carlo with her mother in tow. "She has a radio able to reach the USE embassy in Venice. They can relay the message to Magdeburg."

"Actually," Rachel said, "if Bill still has his rig, that might be better."

"Rig? Better?" Carlo's eyes darted between Rachel and Stephan.

Rachel smiled. "Bill had an up-time radio transceiver. That means it can do voice."

Carlo looked across the arena to where Bill was watching them. "Will your husband be willing to operate it for me?"

"Ex-husband," Rachel said with some heat. She shook herself. "Sorry about that. It's a sore point. And you don't need Bill. I might not have sat the exams, but I know how to operate his rig." She smiled smugly. "Probably better than he does."

Carlo turned to Paolo. "See that the evidence is secured," he instructed before heading back to the stage where the prisoners were assembled.

They were almost there when a heavyset and richly clothed man arrived with Marco trailing in behind.

"What's happening?" the man demanded. "Why are you arresting The Magnificent Ponzi? When can he be released? He has a performance scheduled for Saturday." He looked skyward. "Why are you doing this to me?" he pleaded.

Chapter 39

Carlo approached the man. "What seems to be the problem?"

Benito Ragazzoni pointed to the soldiers gathered around Bernardo Ponzi and his team. "That is the problem. Marco here"—he used his thumb to point—"tells me you are arresting The Magnificent Ponzi."

Carlo nodded.

"But you can't," Benito pleaded. "I cancelled the regular jousts so that Ponzi could put on his performance." He pointed to the seats in the arena. "I have added extra seating for the show."

"You've spent money?" Carlo suggested.

"Yes, I've spent money. Money I will have to account for to the shareholders. Money I was expecting to recoup from Ponzi's performance."

"I'm afraid I can't help you," Carlo said. "Bernardo Ponzi has been arrested for defrauding a magistrate and being a party to a kidnapping."

Benito's eyes widened. He looked over toward Ponzi and spat in his direction. "I am ruined," he proclaimed with animated hand-waving.

"Maybe I can offer a solution," Rachel suggested.

"Who're you?" Benito demanded.

"Rachel Lynch," Rachel said as she handed Benito a card. "Of the Grantville Traveling Roadshow. We have a standard performance demonstrating marvels from the City from the Future."

Benito stared at Rachel, his tongue running over his lips. "Marvels from the City from the Future, you say?"

Rachel politely pointed to the card she had handed Benito. "And I'm sure that we can persuade *Dottore* Gribbleflotz to demonstrate some of the wonders of modern alchemy while *Dottore* Stone can demonstrate the Science of the Chakras."

"You can get *dottori* Stone and Gribbleflotz to perform?"

Rachel reached out and patted Benito on the shoulder. "Let's find somewhere quiet where we can hammer out a satisfactory deal."

Thomas turned to Phillip. "Did that just happen?"

"Frau Lynch promising that we would help put on a show?" Phillip nodded. "I think she did. And I think you should do your presentation of the Science of the Chakras in a costume just like you wore in Prague."

"Unfortunately, I don't have that costume here with me." Thomas' sorrow at the lack was sadly lacking in conviction.

Phillip smiled at Thomas. "Fortunately, I believe The Magnificent Ponzi has a suitable costume he won't be needing."

Thomas visualized the costume The Magnificent Ponzi had worn in those parts of the Vicenza performance he had seen. It made even the outfit he had worn in Prague look positively dowdy. "No way," he protested.

"It is an ideal opportunity to start rewriting the narrative of what happened in Prague."

Thomas glared at Phillip. The bastard was guilt-tripping him. Unfortunately, he was doing a really good job. "If I do this, we're all square?"

Phillip nodded. "We'll be all square."

"I'll be a laughingstock," Thomas muttered.

"No you won't," Phillip said reassuringly. "We'll work out a performance that absolutely reeks of class."

Thomas laughed. "Class? With me wearing an oversized turban?"

Phillip nodded. "With flashing lights. Don't forget the flashing lights."

"Yeah, right. How could I possibly forget the flashing lights?"

"We have to keep our public interested." Phillip laid a hand on Thomas' shoulder. "Come on, let's catch up with Frau Lynch before she makes commitments we can't keep."

Chapter 40

Saturday, 22nd November, Padua

Phillip walked out onto the *Prato della Valle* arm-in-arm with his wife. He paused to take in the scene.

The walls of the theater had been done up with colored bunting. No doubt colored with dyes from Lothlorien Farbenwerke and Pharmaceuticals. There were other, less obvious, items sourced from Grantville on display, and that was just outside the walls.

There was a short queue of people waiting to gain entry at the gate. Phillip led Dina over to it and they took their place at the end of the line.

Spaced along the wall were plywood sheets with posters pasted upon them describing various wonders from the City from the Future, and then there were the ones advertising the evening's performance. Phillip happily spent the time waiting to be let in reading the posters and commenting on them with the people behind and in front of him. Dina was equally happy chatting with a couple of women.

After barely ten minutes in the queue, Phillip and Dina arrived at the front. They had their left sleeves rolled up in accordance with the directions they'd read two or three billboards back.

"*Dottore* Gribbleflotz, *Signora* Kastenmayer, why are you waiting in line?" Benito Ragazzoni said as he tried to usher them through. "You should have come straight up to the gate. My people would have let you straight in."

Phillip looked from Dina to the people they had happily been chatting to and back to Benito. "It was only fair to take a place in the queue." He waved to the people he had been chatting to and passed through the gate with Dina.

Once through the gate, they presented their exposed forearms to the two women on duty. A template with a one-inch-square hole cut in it was placed over their forearms and quickly swabbed with a cloth dipped in tincture of iodine. The iodine was blotted, and they were sent on into the theater proper.

Neither noticed that the queue had bunched up behind them. A man pointed in their direction. "That was the famous *Dottore* Gribbleflotz? The man who is in litigation with the Vicenza da Portos over his kidnapping?"

Benito nodded. "The same. And he will be part of this evening's performance. You should make the effort to be here."

Large swaths of the bench seating that Benito had set out for Ponzi's performance had been removed from the arena so that stalls could be set up. The stage was still in place and two men were currently on stage singing to a crowd that had gathered at their feet. Phillip stared at them through his glasses. He took his glasses off and cleaned them. He looked again. Nothing had changed. "Aren't those Ponzi's men on the stage?"

"Who?"

Phillip remembered that Dina had not been present when they confronted Bernardo Ponzi, so wouldn't recognize the men. "He had a couple of men at his performance in Vicenza. Absolutely marvelous voices. I'm just surprised they are still free."

"They do have very good voices," Dina agreed. They did not have to go up to the stage to hear them because the men's voices were being pumped out for all to hear by loudspeakers.

Phillip cast about for someone who could explain what was going on. His eyes settled upon Edith Lynch watching over an enthralled crowd of mostly men and boys gathered around her stall. "There's someone to ask." He led the way around the edge of the crowd.

"Frau Lynch," he called as he got close enough to touch.

"Dr. Gribbleflotz, Dina, isn't it a wonderful crowd?" She waved her hands to encompass the arena. It was not packed with people, but then, that would not have been wonderful. There were plenty of people milling about, but there was also plenty of room for them to mill about in. People could stop anywhere to look at anything without a tide of humanity pushing them along. It was, as Edith had said, a wonderful crowd. One that was just the right size for the space available.

"It is," Phillip agreed. "I was just wondering. I couldn't help but notice the singers . . ."

"Crescenzo and Angelo." Edith nodded. "Gio knew their choirmaster back in Milan."

"Shouldn't they be in prison with the Ponzis and the up-timers?"

"Gio didn't think so. And neither did Herr Contarini once Gio explained their situation." Edith grinned. "I think Gio backed them because he wanted to add their voices to our performance."

"They'll be singing tonight?"

"Definitely." Edith waved to her stall. "How would you like to buy a Mockbee electric train set for your children?"

"They're a bit young," Dina said.

Edith laughed. "You're never too young for trains." She edged closer and whispered conspiratorially. "Most fathers buy them for themselves, no matter what they claim."

Phillip looked at the metal track as trains chugged around an elaborate circuit. "Aren't they dangerous?"

"You're thinking of the first-generation Fassbinder-Lionel sets. Those were an accident waiting to happen." Edith shook her head. "No. These trains were designed by mothers. It is virtually impossible to get an electric shock from them."

"They seem to be extremely expensive," Dina said, pointing to a price list displayed under glass.

"That they are," Edith admitted. "Still, selling them isn't the prime reason for this display."

"Then what is the purpose of the display?" Phillip asked.

"To promote railroads." Edith pointed to some of the scale models around the track layout. "People can see how much the train can move compared with alternative modes of transport." She smiled. "It makes them think. And, if someone wants to buy a train set, that's just a cherry on top."

"Have you sold many?" Phillip asked.

"Three."

"That's not many," Dina noted.

"Fortunately, Elaine doesn't have to worry about money."

"Elaine?" Phillip asked.

"Elaine Mockbee Pierce." Edith nodded at Phillip's and Dina's raised brows. "Yes, One of the USE Steel Pierces."

"Where are you getting the electricity from?" Phillip asked.

Edith jerked her thumb toward the back of the display. "We have a hot-bulb-powered generator. It's great, but nowhere near as good as the diesel generator Ponzi had." She smiled. "We're hoping to keep it. Possession being nine points of the law."

"I thought it was stolen from the navy?" Phillip said. "And that Corporal Böhm was able to locate the navy's markings on it and the spotlights."

"A mere technicality," Edith said with a casual wave of her hands. "If the navy fights our possession, we'll sic the Grantville Red Cross Sanitation Squad on to them." She grinned. "That'll teach them."

"Is the Grantville Red Cross Sanitation Squad so formidable?" Dina asked.

"Evelyn Paxton, Minnie Frost, and Priscilla Fortney alone are enough to make grown men tremble. If you add the other twenty or so members of the squad, well..."

"Paxton?" Dina rubbed her chin in thought. "Any relation to the Paxtons of Paxton's Revitalizing Cream?"

"Evelyn was the brains behind the revitalizing cream. It's how the Sanitation Squad can afford to support our operation."

Phillip made a deliberate pass with his eyes over the crowds of people at each of the stalls. "You seem to be doing well enough without extra funding."

"Today's a good day," Edith said. "Not all of them are this good. We can't wait until Gribbleflotz Iodized Salt is up and running." She smiled at a private joke. "You have to stop by Ursula Mittelhausen's stall."

"Frau Mittelhausen has a stall?" Phillip asked.

Edith nodded. "Just around the corner. You can't miss it."

Phillip exchanged a look with Dina. They shrugged at each other. "Thank you, we will do that," Phillip told Edith before setting off around the corner.

"Do you know what Frau Mittelhausen has been up to?" Phillip asked Dina.

She shook her head. "I've been spending most of my time with Magda."

They rounded the corner to discover that Ursula Mittelhausen was running a food stall. But it was no ordinary food stall. This one was giving away free samples. Phillip and Dina battled their way through the students who were doing their best to appear nonchalant as they grabbed little bite-sized pieces of salt meat.

On show were samples of meat cured with normal salt and meat cured using Gribbleflotz Iodized Salt. There was also meat cured with saltpeter and salt, giving the meat an unusual (for salt-cured meat) pinkish color.

Ursula was, with the aid of her Italian butcher, extolling the benefits of Gribbleflotz Iodized Salt and how it did not harm the flavor. Phillip looked at it and had to shake his head. "Frau Mittelhausen did say that she would market the difference in the salt meat's color as a selling point."

"She seems to be doing a roaring trade," Dina said.

"They are mostly starving students taking free samples."

"They don't look like they are starving."

Phillip laughed. "Of course they're starving. It's a rule. And few of them would be able to afford meat."

They wandered over to Ursula. "Are you selling the meat or just giving away samples?" Phillip asked.

Ursula spiked a couple of pieces of meat cured with iodized salt with toothpicks and handed one each to Phillip and Dina. "Antonio here has taken plenty of orders for salt meat."

Ursula's butcher friend slithered over. "*Dottore* Gribbleflotz, and *Signora* Kastenmayer, it is a pleasure to meet you." He demonstrated this by cheek-kissing Dina and shaking Phillip's hand. "My Uncle Giovanni has spoken of you."

Phillip stared hard at Antonio as he mentally churned through the names of everyone he knew in Padua. "Giovanni?"

"Giovanni Barbaro. He is a . . ."

"Knacker," Phillip said with confidence. He turned to Dina. "I met Antonio's uncle when I was first in Padua. He sold me some sheep skulls I needed to make cupels with. He also introduced me to blister beetles." He turned back to Antonio. "Is your uncle still about?" Too many of the people he had known in Padua had died in the years since he'd been a student. Some through old age and other causes, but too many of them had succumbed to the plague that swept through northern Italy from 1629 until 1631.

"Still going strong," Antonio said.

Phillip smiled. He was happy to know another old acquaintance had survived. "I must drop by and chat with him. The information he gave me about blister beetles allowed me to save the life of a young bride who'd been accused of murdering her new husband."

Antonio nodded enthusiastically. "Uncle Giovanni would love to hear about that."

"I'll call on him later. Is he still at the same house?"

Antonio nodded.

A digital merry tune emanating from Phillip's pocket stopped them all cold. Phillip dipped his hand into his fob-pocket and drew out his FrankenWatch. The first thing he did was press the button to shut off the alarm. Then he checked the time. "Sorry. Have to go. I'm on next."

"Next?" Antonio asked.

Phillip gestured toward the stage. "I've got a slot scheduled right after the singing stops."

Chapter 41

Phillip mounted the stage and looked out upon the sea of faces. It was not that big a crowd—maybe two hundred at most. A mere fraction of what they hoped to pack into the theater that evening. Right now, his job was to promote the upcoming show and muster interest amongst the paying public. However, first he had something else to do. A sort of public service message. Phillip tapped the microphone he was holding. That sound came out of the speakers on the stage. He smiled and glanced across to where Rachel Lynch was waiting. She claimed that they would be able to record his spiel, which was good, because he was going to be explaining away the events in Prague and when one was lying through one's teeth one needed some way of remembering one's lies.

Rachel held up a hand and signaled a countdown as she folded up her fingers. On zero, she pressed a button on the machine she was standing over and waved Phillip on.

"Good afternoon everyone." That attracted almost no interest from the people not already looking his way.

"I am *Dottore* Phillip Theophrastus Gribbleflotz, although only my mother uses the Theophrastus. Probably because she knows I don't like it." That earned some laughs from the crowd.

"I am in the Republic because His Serenity, the doge of Venice, was suffering from bladder stones and he had recently read an article I wrote in the *Proceedings of the Royal Academy of Bohemia* about an operation to safely and painlessly remove the stones." He smiled as he said that. Samuel would be proud of him for promoting the Royal Academy.

"After successfully operating on His Serenity, I traveled to Padua where I have friends." He smiled. "You see, twenty years ago, I was a student at the university, studying medicine under the great Professor Casseri. I made a number of friends, and I took the opportunity of an all-expenses-paid trip to Venice to visit my friends."

There were titters of laughter and a few more people abandoned the stalls in favor of listening to him.

"That, of course, doesn't explain why I am here today." Phillip smiled. "Some of you might be aware that The Magnificent Ponzi was supposed to be putting on a performance this evening." He looked around his crowd. There was some nodding of heads.

"The Magnificent Ponzi is unable to be here tonight because he has been unavoidably detained.

"He has been arrested for fraud." There were loud murmurings from the crowd. Phillip nodded to confirm that they had heard him correctly. "In his performances, The Magnificent Ponzi would perform acts of *faith healing* and *psychic surgery.* I don't know about the faith healing, but the psychic surgery was faked. He only pretended to thrust his hand into a patient's abdomen and removed diseased organs, and in the case for which he is currently being held, bladder stones.

"Now, you might be asking, why the fuss? A stage performance is just that. One expects to be entertained. One doesn't care if it is real or not." Phillip nodded sagely, and many in his growing audience did likewise.

"However, The Magnificent Ponzi didn't just perform his psychic surgery on the stage, he also performed it in the private homes of people who paid for him to treat them. He charged a magistrate of Vicenza one hundred ducats to remove bladder stones using his psychic surgery."

Phillip nodded to his audience. "Yes. I know what you're thinking. Magistrates are paid way too much." That earned a round of laughter.

"However, consider. When I examined that magistrate several days after Ponzi operated, I discovered a bladder stone the size of my thumb." He held up his hand so everyone could see his thumb. "And, I am most reliably informed, such bladder stones can be excruciatingly painful. So painful that a man would pay almost any fee to have them removed.

"So maybe the magistrate borrowed the money or sold off some assets."

Phillip waited for the laughter that followed that highly unlikely suggestion to quiet down. He was smiling now. The crowd was growing, and he knew he had them in the palm of his hand.

Phillip started pacing the stage. "Now, you're probably wondering why an educated man, and one assumes that a magistrate is an educated man, might be taken in by one such as The Magnificent Ponzi." He stopped to face the audience. "The problem is, Ponzi was extremely convincing, and he claimed to have been taught how to use the power of his mind to perform psychic surgery by none other than *Dottore* Thomas Stone himself." Phillip pointed to Thomas, who was still wearing his master of Akashic Magick and scholar of the Chakras costume.

"He also claimed that his psychic surgery used the same techniques *Dottore* Stone used when he operated on me in Prague.

"This is, of course, a lie. A fabrication. No one has operated on me. However, there was an incident in Prague that might lend some credibility to this claim. If one is unfamiliar with what actually happened."

Phillip started pacing the stage once more as he spoke into the microphone. "I was in the king of Bohemia's quarters, displaying my latest invention—the GribbleChrome color photographic technique—when *Dottore* Stone and his companion Guptah Rai Singh, a gifted practitioner of the science of the Chakras, burst into the room." Phillip stopped pacing to look out at his audience. "I can tell you here and now, I was terrified. In the up-time histories mercenaries burst into the sleeping quarters of the king and assassinated him. I thought that was what was happening. But I was quickly able to identify *Dottore* Stone and his companion.

"Guptah Rai Singh is extremely sensitive to variations in the Chakras and he had felt something wrong with my Chakras from the adjacent room where they had been waiting. After a brief examination, he squeezed part of my abdomen, and something squirted out. It is only after discussing the event with *Dottore* Stone that I now understand what happened.

"Somehow, I became infested with an insect larva. Like a maggot, only bigger. And while most maggots only eat dead flesh, this larva ate living flesh."

Phillip recommenced his pacing. "Now, you might wonder why I didn't feel the larva feeding off my flesh." He paused to shrug his shoulders. Being on stage he exaggerated the action so that the people at the back of the crowd could see. "We have hypothesized that, like a leech, it secretes a painkiller. So that the host doesn't feel anything.

"Or at least, the host isn't consciously aware of anything happening. My Chakras knew something was happening and called for help. Fortunately for me, Guptah Rai Singh heard the call and responded immediately. He located the larva and squeezed it out of my abdomen through its breathing hole. Unfortunately, the larva ruptured on the way out and was disposed of before more reasoned minds could hope to examine it."

Phillip looked out at his audience, which had continued to grow while he was talking. "The Magnificent Ponzi based his psychic surgery on this event. As for the name..." Phillip sighed. "He took that from up-time sources." He nodded. "Yes, the up-timers also had problems with people faking surgery using just their hands. I believe that is where Ponzi got the idea.

"Up-time, in the world the Americans came from, practitioners of psychic surgery prey upon the gullible and the desperate. It is my hope that by speaking out about it now, I can stop psychic surgery from establishing a foothold in alternative medicine."

Phillip lowered the microphone and walked to the middle of the stage. "That was all rather intense, wasn't it? So, on a lighter note, I will describe some of the things that we will be seeing in this evening's performance."

Phillip did not quite stumble down the steps as he abandoned the stage to the next act, but the effort to keep the crowd entertained had been draining. He looked around until he located Dina and headed her way. He was intercepted by two expensively dressed men before he could reach her.

"*Dottore* Gribbleflotz, a moment of your time, if you please."

Phillip did not please. He was hungry and thirsty. However, he had learned not to offend people before he knew what they wanted. "How may I be of assistance?"

"Dr. Johann Vesling, professor of anatomy at the university," the man said in German as he offered Phillip his hand.

Phillip took the hand gingerly and shook it, fortunately without having the life squeezed out of his hand. He looked questioningly at Dr. Vesling's companion.

"Dr. Johann Wirsung, a prosector for Dr. Vesling."

Phillip shook Wirsung's hand. "Ah. I had the same job for Professor Casseri when I was a student. Those were the days."

"In the up-timers' world, Dr. Wirsung gained fame for discovering the pancreatic duct," Dr. Vesling said.

"And I died a year later, in 1643," Wirsung muttered.

Phillip's gaze darted between the two German doctors. He was getting the impression that Vesling resented the fact that his subordinate had a major claim to fame in the up-timer encyclopedias. It seemed that history might be repeating itself at Padua. Phillip well remembered the acrimony between Hieronymus Fabricius ab Aquapendente, the longtime holder of the chair of surgery and anatomy at Padua, and Professor Casseri, his one-time student who proved to be a better teacher. Conflict was something best avoided, so he changed the topic. "You wanted a word with me?" he prompted.

"Yes," Vesling agreed. "Are we to believe that the rumors that Dr. Stone's companion operated on you and removed a growth or diseased organ using just his bare hands is just that, a rumor?"

"I'm afraid so," Phillip confirmed. "Dr. Stone's colleague was called back to his home in India before he could fully explain what he had done and why.

"However, we think we have determined the facts of the matter." Phillip smiled convincingly. He was sure his smile was convincing. He had almost convinced himself.

"So there will be no seminars on how to operate on a patient without the patient feeling any pain?"

"Oh." Phillip waved his hands—being amongst his Italian friends again had brought back the lost art of speaking with his hands. "I wouldn't say that. The up-timers have introduced safe anesthetics. My colleague, Corporal Böhm, is trained and certified to administer ether as an anesthetic. I'm sure he'd be only too happy to demonstrate the specialty."

"Isn't that dangerous?" Wirsung asked.

"All surgery is dangerous," Phillip pointed out. "However, anesthesia makes things a lot easier. Why, just the other day, I had to amputate a leg above the knee. In the old days, before we had reliable anesthetics, I'd have taken maybe thirty seconds to lop it off—while the wide-awake and screaming patient was being held down upon the operating table. And then one would cauterize the stump.

"It was all rather messy, and the survival rate was never that good. However . . ." Phillip's eyes lit up as he remembered working on Alessandro's leg. "With my patient under anesthesia, I was able to take my time. I was able to save more of the leg and create a much better flap. One with plenty of muscle tissue between the bone and the skin.

"Normally, I'd say my patient could look forward to a fine old age. However, the man is being held on charges of kidnapping and banditry, so . . ." Phillip once more let his hands do the talking.

"A waste," Vesling said.

"Would we be able to get the body for an anatomy class?" Wirsung asked hopefully.

"He's in Vicenza."

Wirsung sighed in disappointment. "A pity."

"Yes," Vesling agreed. "A great pity. Almost as great a pity that there is no truth in the stories circulating about the emergency operation performed in the king of Bohemia's bedchamber."

"Well, I'm sorry," Phillip muttered resentfully.

"Yes. Yes. Of course, Dr. Gribbleflotz. Obviously, it is not your fault."

"But it's still a great pity." Phillip was able to let the hint of a smile surface as he realized he was not being blamed. It was just that Vesling's disappointment was so great. "You'd be better served asking my colleagues Frau Cheng and Corporal Böhm to give seminars on the new medicine. They are both extremely knowledgeable about it. They are both in programs that prepare people for the Doctor of Osteopathic Medicine examinations."

"We should learn from a student and a soldier?" Vesling demanded disparagingly.

Phillip nodded. "Don't just take my word for it. Go and ask them. Ask to look at their textbooks and study notes."

Vesling and Wirsung stared at Phillip. After a few seconds they looked at each other. They nodded. "We will," Vesling said.

Phillip watched them walk away.

"What was that all about?" Dina asked.

Phillip started guiltily. He had totally forgotten about his wife being right beside him. "Just a couple of like-minded professionals walking off to their doom." He smiled as he said it. He could almost picture Diana Cheng's reaction to those two men with their, to her, obsolete views on medicine and medical theory questioning her about modern medicine. He almost felt sorry for them. Almost.

Dina's eyes followed Vesling and Wirsung. "Their doom?"

Phillip's smile grew. "I sent them to talk to Diana and Stephan about modern medicine."

Dina whistled meaningfully. "She's going to tell them everything they know is wrong."

"Probably not everything."

Dina looked at Phillip and slowly shook her head. "That was mean. What have those men ever done to you?"

A loud rumble from Phillip's stomach saved him from the necessity of answering. Dina looped her arm through his and started walking. "Come on. Let's find something to soothe the savage beast."

"I'm not a savage beast," Phillip protested as he walked beside her.

"I wasn't talking about you, dear."

Chapter 42

Diana closed her medical textbooks and slid them back into her bag. "That was weird," she said to Stephan Böhm as both watched the two German doctors walk away.

"What was weird?" Sebastian Jones demanded as he joined them at their stall with Paolo Molin in tow. Dr. Stone and his wife followed.

Diana pointed. "Those two. They started talking about the transurethral lithotripsy and had a play with the lithotrites." She gestured to the three instruments on the benchtop of their stall. There was also a container of shells which people could pick apart with them. "And then they started to ask us about modern medicine."

"It was more of an interrogation," Stephan said.

"Did you hold your own?" Thomas Stone asked.

Diana and Stephan exchanged looks. "Yes," Diana said warily. "Who were they? Do you know them?"

"Dr. Johann Vesling, professor of anatomy and surgery, and Dr. Johann Wirsung, a prosector for Dr. Vesling. It is possible that you might be invited to give a course of seminars on up-time medicine."

Stephan's eyes lit up. "How well would it pay?"

"Why're you worried about being paid?" Paolo asked. "You're in line for a generous compensation payout for being kidnapped."

"Yes. Well." Stephan looked down and kicked his toe into the ground. "Frau Mittelhausen has sort of persuaded me to invest that money into the Gribbleflotz Iodized Salt Company."

"She is very persuasive," Thomas agreed. "Still, I'm sure the university would pay a fee."

"But when would this seminar happen?" Stephan asked. "We've been here a bit longer than I expected we would be, and I doubt either the Medical Department or the Marines will consider giving seminars a good enough reason to delay my return to duty."

"All may not be lost," Paolo said. "*Signore* Contarini was so impressed by my report on your 1st Marine Reconnaissance Company that he is hoping to convince the other members of the Council of Ten to request that they be sent to Venice to recruit and train a similar unit for our navy."

Stephan's jaw dropped. Diana lent a finger to help him close his mouth. He smiled. He grinned. He beamed. And his eyes lit up with excitement. "Captain Finck will be all for it. Colonel von Brockenholz and Admiral Simpson will be in favor too." Stephan screwed up his nose. And sighed. "But I'm not so sure about the politicians."

Paolo clapped a hand on Stephan's shoulder. "Let *Signore* Contarini worry about the politicians. How about we walk down to the Beretta stall. They have a shotgun I'm sure you'll love."

"Does it have a pistol grip and folding stock?"

Diana shook her head as she watched the pair walk off. "Boys and their toys," she muttered as she turned around. Her eyes lit onto the way Magda was rubbing the right side of her abdomen. "Are you all right?"

Magda looked up guiltily and stopped rubbing herself. "It's just a little discomfort. The midwife says it's normal."

Diana's tongue shot out and moistened her lips. Her first, instinctive, diagnosis was round ligament pain—where the ligaments that connect the front part of the womb to the groin are strained. However, Magda was barely into the second trimester and the baby clearly wasn't big enough to be stretching the ligaments to the point of its being painful yet. That left her wondering what could be going on.

"Are you sure, dear?" Thomas asked solicitously.

Magda shot Diana a dirty look before smiling brightly at her husband. "Of course, I'm sure." She took a couple of steps without wincing in pain and turned. "See. It was just a momentary discomfort."

To get back into Magda's good graces, Diana set out to distract

Dr. Stone from whatever might be wrong with Magda. "Did you get some photos of Dr. Stone in costume?" she asked Sebastian.

He laughed. "Did I ever. In color too."

Diana almost asked how he could take color photographs, but then she remembered that Sebastian was taking photographs for print media. Actual color photographs still were not possible, but with a three-color camera, one could make three images from which printing plates could be made. Those plates could be used to print color images.

"I'll be a laughingstock," Thomas protested.

Magda moved in to cuddle him. "No you won't."

"Oh, yes I will."

"It's your own fault," Diana said. "You do realize that the Prague Chapter of the Society of Aural Investigators has adopted outfits in the style of the costumes you and Mr. Mundell were wearing as their formal robes?"

Thomas winced. "Why would they want to do a silly thing like that?"

"Because that's what you wore when you did readings for the king, and the great Dr. Stone can't be wrong.

"Of course, most of the time, they just wear a long white lab coat over their normal clothes. Only bringing out the fancy stuff for high-value clients and formal get-togethers."

Thomas slowly shook his head. "I am so glad I'm not in Prague."

"I wouldn't get too complacent," Sebastian said. "Prospero Cristofori wants to introduce them to the Padua Chapter of the Society of Aural Investigators."

Thomas' eyes turned skyward. "Why me?" he implored.

"Because you started it," Diana said without a hint of sympathy. She gathered her books and the lithotrites. "I don't know about everyone else, but I want something to eat before this evening's performance."

"You did have to remind me about that," Thomas muttered.

Chapter 43

Diana turned around in her seat as Prospero Cristofori, president (and only member) of the Padua Chapter of the Society of Aural Investigators, completed his act and high-fived Luchia Odescalchi. Between them they had successfully guided Prospero through an aural investigation using the new all-dancing, all-singing theremin. Or, as Prospero called it, a new and improved Gribbleflotz Magneto-Etheric Aural Aura Detector.

"I really doubted that would work," Rachel Lynch said from behind Diana.

"What could go wrong?" Diana protested as she swung round in her seat. "When my dad makes something, it works."

"That's not what I meant," Rachel said. "I was more worried about the audience reaction. Having someone waving their hands in the air as Cristofori adds and subtracts various metal bracelets and gems isn't very visual. Especially for those way back in the cheap seats."

"Yes," Luchia agreed. "But they can hear the sounds the theremin makes."

"It wouldn't work in Vegas," Diana said, "but people here and now have lower expectations. Heck, just the amount of light we've got is probably new and exciting enough for most of them to go home happy."

"And now it's Tom Stone's turn," Rachel said as she swapped places with Luchia. "How did you manage to persuade him to do a Chakras thing, let alone do it in Ponzi's silly stage outfit?"

Diana looked toward the corner where Stephan was sitting. Their eyes met, and they smiled at each other. "It's similar to what he wore when he did Chakra readings for the king of Bohemia and is now the pattern for the formal robes of the Prague Chapter of the Society of Aural Investigators."

"Is that why Cristofori wanted to wear it for his act?"

"Probably," Diana said. "But we can't have two acts wearing the same costume, so he had to settle for the standard white lab coat they usually wear." She signaled to Stephan. "Let's have the prospects."

Earlier, Diana, Stephan, Lise, and Marianna had mingled with the audience as they lined up to enter the theater. They had talked with them, deliberately eliciting information that could be used in the performance. Stephan, Lise, and Marianna had been going over the notes they'd taken to find likely prospects for Dr. Stone to diagnose on stage. They were not looking for anything complicated. They wanted something straightforward that Dr. Stone could claim his science of the Chakras could diagnose and if possible, that he could treat on stage.

Stephan handed Diana a sheet of paper. "Here's one that looks like it might be simple acid reflux."

Diana checked the notes. They had been taken by Lise, which gave Diana confidence. Marianna was progressing with her training, but Lise was fully trained and had worked at Leahy Medical Center for years. Acid reflux was bound to have been something she'd had to deal with. "That's good. We'll need to get some Gribbleflotz *Sal Aer Fixus* out to Dr. Stone."

"Seriously?" Rachel demanded. "You're going to have Dr. Stone treat someone with Gribbleflotz's baking soda?"

"It's cheap, we have it to hand, and it's the right stuff for the job." Diana met Rachel's stare. "It's not like aspirin, where Lothlorien Farbenwerke make their own version."

Rachel shook her head ruefully. "I'll believe it when I see it."

"Then you'll believe it soon," Diana said. "Just as soon as we locate the subject."

"I see her," Lise said. "Just behind Fraus Edelmännin and Kastenmayer."

Diana grabbed the pair of binoculars that she had sourced for just this purpose and stood up. She scanned the seats behind Magda and Dina. "I need a description. Whereabouts behind?"

"Three in from the aisle. She's wearing a peasant-style top over a white long-sleeve blouse."

"I see someone, but she's got lace trimmings," Diana said.

"That's her."

Diana shot Lise a look. "Peasants don't wear lace."

"I said *peasant style*."

"Okay. I've got her then." Diana made a note of where the woman was sitting and kept an eye on her while she watched Dr. Stone's performance. He was actually quite impressive. Mixing his Chakras in with modern chemistry and lighting effects. She snorted with laughter when he told a story using his hands to cast shadows onto a large sheet of mostly white canvas they had draped over the back of the stage.

It was almost time for Dr. Stone to perform his special party trick. Diana used the binoculars to check the designated patient was still seated in the same place. She was. Movement from just in front of the woman had Diana focusing on Dr. Stone's wife. "Frau Edelmännin's still showing signs of abdominal discomfort."

"Flatulence, distention, bowel cramping, uterine contractions, or round ligament tension?" Stephan asked.

That was a checklist of the most common causes of abdominal discomfort in pregnant women. "Can't say without examining her properly," Diana said.

"Are you worried about Dr. Stone's wife?" Rachel asked.

Both Diana and Stephan nodded.

"I doubt it's uterine contractions. She's not far enough along."

"It could be if it's a precursor to a spontaneous abortion," Stephan said. "She has a history of them."

"Frau Edelmännin's midwife isn't worried, so I doubt it's that," Diana said. "And she's not far enough along for the round ligaments to be stretching enough to hurt."

Rachel snorted. "Shows what you know. I've had four babies, and I've had round ligament pain as early as three months."

"Are you sure?" Diana asked. "I mean, how do you know it was the round ligament?"

"I asked. Dr. Shipley was only too happy to explain what was happening."

"Okay." Diana dragged out the word as she accepted what Rachel had said. If Dr. Shipley said it, it was most likely true.

"But it can't be round ligament pain," Rachel said. "Not if Frau Edelmännin is just sitting there. It usually happens when you move, laugh, sneeze, or cough."

Diana, Stephan, Rachel, and Lise all looked out toward Magda, who was sitting quietly on a bench. "Lise," Diana said, "could you slip out and see if you can attach yourself to Frau Edelmännin's party?"

"Sure. Do you want me to go home with her?"

"Please. Especially if she leaves without Dr. Stone."

"Okay. If you don't need me, I'll slip out now."

Diana waved Lise off and turned her attention back to Dr. Stone's performance. It was time for the healing part.

Tom took a deep breath. Being up here on stage in front of thousands of people was extremely stressful. As such, he was glad he was wearing the outlandish costume. It was a shield.

"Flashing lights in three," Rachel Lynch's voice sounded over the earpiece he was wearing.

Tom took another deep breath to help steady himself. This was the big test. Could he carry it off?

"One."

The spotlights dimmed. This did not scare the audience. The lights had been dimmed several times during the performance. Not least during Gio's act with the microwave oven.

"Two."

Tom exaggerated the movement of his head as he scanned the audience. What light there was reflected from the fine wire woven into the fabric of the turban he was wearing and the large central gem.

"Three."

On Rachel's call, the lights set into the fake gemstone rings he was wearing started to flash, as did the lights behind the gem in his turban.

"We're going with a woman to the right of the aisle seated just behind Magda and Dina. We suspect acid reflux, so this should be easy."

Tom snorted to himself. It was easy for Diana to say that; she wasn't up here on stage. He continued to wave his hands about. "I feel the fluctuations of distressed Chakra energies."

"We're going with a combination of yellow, green, and blue lights. They'll signify a throat-related ailment that causes pain around the heart region due to a stomach issue."

Tom repeated the information, indicating that he felt someone suffering. He did not call it heartburn, but he did relate the symptoms of the problem as Diana dictated them to her.

"Slow your hand-waving. Rachel's going to try and control the colors as your hands pass the prospect."

Tom did as he was told, and lo and behold, as his hands went past where Magda was seated, only the yellow, green, and blue lights showed, and instead of flashing, they stayed on. Slowly, Tom zeroed in on the designated patient. He gave directions to Luchia until she was standing right behind the designated patient. And with her help, he persuaded the young woman to come forward.

Relaying Diana's description of the likely symptoms, Tom gained the trust of the woman as he held his hands and the sometimes flashing yellow, green, or blue rings over her body. He was careful not to touch her. That would have been inappropriate. But he soon zeroed in on the stomach region.

"I think I know what the problem is," he declared. The filters were removed from in front of the spotlights allowing the stage to be flooded with light. "And I can treat it right here and now." He walked to the back of the stage where a table had been set up, and loaded items onto a tray. He then brought the tray over to the microphone stand where he had left the woman.

"Take a small spoonful of this in a cup of water whenever you feel the burning sensation."

"Water?" the woman said with absolute disgust.

"Water that has been treated with several drops of the Ethereal Essence of Common Salt infused in Thrice-Blessed Radiated Water," Tom said. "Or any other suitable drink. Although I'm not sure what it will taste like in wine or beer."

The woman looked at Tom. Then she looked at the paper bag on the tray. She picked it up and examined it. "This?" she protested. "This is Gribbleflotz *Sal Aer Fixus*. It is just cooking powder. I bought a bag at the market earlier today for three *soldi*."

"Well," Tom said as he took the bag from the woman's hands. "If you insist, I can have my assistant measure some into a smaller bag and sell it to you at ten times the price as *Dottore* Stone's Patent Stomach Calming Powder." He passed the bag to Luchia, who stood back, but did not move far away.

The woman stared at Tom for a moment, and then started laughing. Soon the audience joined in.

"Perfect," Diana said over the radio. "Now mix up a dose and have her drink it."

Tom gestured for Luchia to mix a dose and pass it to the woman. "Just drink that down."

She stared suspiciously at him, so he held out a hand to Luchia, who mixed up a second dose. He saluted the woman and the audience with it before drinking it down. The woman hesitantly copied him. Taking small sips to start with before taking larger gulps until the glass was empty. She rubbed her nose. "It tickled."

Tom smiled and invited the audience to give the woman a round of applause as Luchia guided her back to her seat. That was the end of his act. As the spotlights dimmed the lights on his turban and fingers started to flash. They continued to flash for a few seconds after the spotlights were blinkered. And then they too went dark. When the spotlights were unblinkered, Tom had left the stage and been replaced by Dr. Gribbleflotz.

Phillip started with a monologue about the trials and tribulations about being a poor misunderstood alchemist. Hinting on the recent problems in Vicenza.

"Let me tell you, there is no such thing as a philosopher's stone that allows an alchemist to turn base metal into gold." He nodded energetically to reinforce the statement. "If it was possible, the up-timers would have done it, and they hadn't."

He diverged a little. "We, before the coming of the City from the Future, knew of twelve elements: copper, lead, gold, silver, iron, carbon, tin, sulfur, mercury, zinc, arsenic, and antimony. The up-timers, they know of one hundred and twelve." He paused to smile at the audience. "I won't list them all. However, I have personally been able to isolate phosphorus, nickel, hydrogen, oxygen, calcium, iodine, and of course, aluminum.

"No. If there was a way to make gold from base metal, the up-timers would surely have discovered it.

"That is not to say that a person knowledgeable in the art cannot make gold using base materials."

Phillip pulled a lump of coal from a pocket in his white lab coat. "This is a lump of coal. It is ordinary coal that any of you could find. It makes a good fuel when added to a fire. It is, I'm sure you will all agree, a very base material. However, with knowledge of the up-time alchemy, *Dottore* Stone has been able to break it down to produce the dyes for which he is so famous. Color-fast dyes in colors people could only imagine. Color-fast dyes that people are willing to pay a lot of money for." Phillip opened his lab coat so that the audience could see and admire the selection of colors with which his clothes were dyed.

"That is how a person can make gold out of base materials. By learning about the science of alchemy." He gave a wide grin. "You can buy your very own Gribbleflotz Junior, Intermediate, or Advanced Alchemist set from the new *Dottore* Gribbleflotz Emporium of Natural Wonders at the university end of *Piazza delle Erbe*. You can also buy your own copy of any of the Alchemical texts published by HDG Laboratories. Starting with Saltzman, Siebenhorn, and Stolz's *Introductory Alchemy*."

It was product placement at its finest. Phillip was sure Frau Mittelhausen would be proud of him.

"And now for a little light relief, I will demonstrate a few simple experiments. The first we call the Alchemist's Flytrap."

Most of the experiment had been prepared in advance, so Phillip was able to quickly prepare the triiodide, smear it onto the papers, and place the papers onto the holders. With the spotlights, even shining from a distance, it did not take the triiodide long to dry.

"We call it the Alchemist's Flytrap because the moment a fly lands on the triiodide…" Phillip touched the triiodide on the lowest paper with a feather on the end of a long pole. Nothing happened.

Phillip played up to the audience as he wondered privately why it had not gone off. "…the moment a fly lands on it," he said as he touched it again with the feather.

Again, the triiodide did not explode. Phillip looked at his audience and held up his hands apologetically.

Crack!

The triiodide went off in a cloud of purple, which was more than adequately illuminated by the spotlights. "Did anyone see what happened to the fly?" Phillip demanded of the audience. He was not sure what had set it off, but a fly landing on it was what the audience had been primed to expect, so that was what he gave them as a cause. Nobody admitted to seeing the fly, but the explosion did attract a round of applause. Phillip bowed and acknowledged it in his usual modest way—by holding out his hands and asking for greater applause. He got it, and some laughter.

"The purple cloud is iodine. Now, where have we heard of iodine before?" Phillip looked at the experimental equipment and then at his audience. He smiled and undid the cuff of his left arm. "That's right. Everyone here should have had a square inch of their inner forearm painted with tincture of iodine." He examined his still-dark stain. "That painted patch of skin is important. It is an indicator of whether or not you are suffering from iodine deficiency.

"If your stain disappears within the next two days, then you have iodine deficiency. Iodine deficiency is bad for your health, but there is a simple way to ensure you get enough iodine in your diet. Simply replace your normal salt with the new Gribbleflotz Iodized Salt—available from the *Dottore* Gribbleflotz Emporium of Natural Wonders. Because the amount of iodine needed is so small, Gribbleflotz Iodized Salt will be available from the store at the same price as normal salt." Phillip had been surprised that Frau Mittelhausen was prepared to price it the same as regular salt. He had expected her to charge a higher price. However, apparently the markup on regular salt left plenty of room to profit even after iodizing and packaging the salt.

"You could buy someone else's iodized salt, but then, you'd be left wondering, 'How do I know that the salt I have bought is really iodized?' There is a simple test." Phillip stood to one side as stagehands brought up a small table and set the test equipment upon it.

Phillip described his actions as he performed them. "You simply dissolve a few spoonfuls of the suspect salt in warm water, add a little white vinegar and hydrogen peroxide. Stir. And then add a little water in which rice has been boiled."

He held up the glass beaker so all could see. Just to make it easier, he held a white piece of paper up behind the flask. "That blue-purple color indicates the presence of iodine."

Phillip returned everything to the table, which was whisked away. "Test kits, or just the hydrogen peroxide, can be purchased from the *Dottore* Gribbleflotz Emporium of Natural Wonders. Or you can simply ask that an assistant at the shop test your salt for you. They will be happy to do so for a modest charge. Now, for something completely different..."

Phillip grabbed the microphone stand and moved closer to one side of the stage. A table had been set up there. Another table was set up in the middle of the stage. Standing on it was a single candlestick.

"Have you ever blown on a glowing ember to make it burst into flame?" he asked the audience. "Fire needs a gas called oxygen. It is present in the air that we breathe. When you blow on an ember, you are increasing the flow of oxygen to the ember. Of course, for the ember to flare into flame, it needs something called an air-fuel mix. Too much fuel and not enough air and you will not get a flame. An example you may be familiar with is dropping a burning splint into a pool of oil. The oil is more likely to douse the burning splint than to catch fire. But bring the same burning splint up to a wick emerging from the same oil, and the wick will burn.

"So, let us see what happens if I blow some fine gunpowder over a candle."

Phillip walked over the candle and used his GribbleZippo to light the wick before returning to his table. He picked up a folded piece of paper. And advanced toward the candle. He held up his right hand and the lights dimmed. He then blew on the paper, sending a cloud of fine gunpowder out toward the candle. There was enough light for the dust particles to be seen. And then the first part of the dust cloud touched the flame and the dust cloud flashed as it burned.

"That was exciting, wasn't it? Let's try something else." He checked the next paper. "Finely ground rice."

That flashed as well as the gunpowder had.

"Finely ground flour."

That also flashed nicely.

"Finely ground sugar."

That flamed even better than the rice and flour.

"What is happening here?" Phillip asked the audience. "Let us see what happens if I try to set a pile of those same powders alight."

He lit a candle before placing a spoonful of fine gunpowder onto a ceramic tile. He lit the splint. "I think we all know what's going to happen if I touch a burning splint to gunpowder." He touched the gunpowder and it quickly caught fire and flared.

"We were all expecting that to happen, weren't we?" The question elicited a response from some members of the audience.

Phillip spooned rice powder, fine flour, and finely ground sugar onto separate tiles. "So, what do people expect to happen if I touch these with a burning splint? Hands up if you think they will burn." Quite a few hands went up. "And who thinks that nothing will happen?" A few hands were tentatively raised, with most of them taken down when the people saw they were clearly in a minority.

One by one, Phillip introduced the burning splint to the finely ground powders. Each time nothing happened. After finely ground sugar gave a negative result, Phillip moved back to the front center of the stage.

"So why is it that the powders that could flash when blown over a candle wouldn't burn when the flame was held to the powder, and why did the gunpowder ignite regardless?"

Phillip smiled. "That is alchemy at work. Gunpowder is a mixture of compounds. Carbon, sulfur, and saltpeter. The other powders are mostly carbon compounds. Gunpowder catches fire so easily because of the sulfur. It also burns, even when it is in a pile, because the saltpeter contains oxygen. Conversely, the other powders don't contain oxygen and need to get it from the air. As a solid pile of powder, there is too much fuel and not enough oxygen for it to burn.

"If you wish to understand more about fire and oxygen, the Gribbleflotz Junior Alchemist set comes with instructions on how to perform various experiments, a scientific explanation as to what is happening, and complete safety instructions.

"And now for my final demonstration."

Stagehands brought on an empty barrel half, into which they poured a layer of sand. Over which they then poured water. They erected a three-legged stand over the barrel and handed Phillip the front plate of a cavalry cuirass and a ceramic flowerpot.

Phillip held up the flowerpot. "This contains a mixture of finely ground iron oxide and aluminum. The Americans call this mixture *thermite*." He shook his head dramatically. "The names Americans use are so often lacking in suitable drama. I call it the 'Gribbleflotz Candles of the Essence of Light.' A much more satisfying and descriptive name."

He paused to allow the laughter to settle. "Now, the thing about the candles of the essence of light is that, like the sun—the true pure essence of light—it can get extremely hot. Hot enough to burn through steel armor."

He placed the armor on top of the tripod and then set a smaller tripod on top of it. He set the flowerpot of thermite in the tripod and stood back.

Phillip looked at his audience. He glanced over at his experiment and pursed his lips before turning back to his audience. "We need a little drama. Drumroll, please," he called.

A drumroll sounded over the sound system and continued as Phillip added the chemicals necessary to ignite the thermite and stood back. The drumroll continued as the lights dimmed.

A few seconds later the thermite caught fire, drawing *oohs* and *ahhs* from the audience.

The thermite burned brightly, and then a stream of molten iron poured out from the base of the flowerpot. It hit the cuirass. Moments later it dropped through the cuirass into the barrel below. Steam shot up, scattering the light from the still-burning flowerpot of thermite. Slowly it burned out.

Phillip returned to the microphone as the lights came back on, illuminating the stagehands as they dismantled the props and fished some still-hot iron from the barrel of water. One of them brought the iron and armor up to Phillip.

Phillip held up the cuirass. "As you can see, the stream of molten iron was hot enough to melt through this armor." He then exchanged the armor for the misshaped lump of iron from the barrel. It was still hot, so he had to juggle it from hand to hand. "The formerly molten iron is still a bit too hot to handle. So I'll let this man take charge of it." The man in question was wearing blacksmith's gauntlets.

"And that is all we have for you this evening. I hope you all learned something and enjoyed yourselves." Phillip looked back and gestured for his fellow performers to come on stage. They formed up, taking their bows as the crowd applauded.

Sebastian Jones appeared in front of everyone and took a group photograph.

Diana leaned back in her chair. "That all went quite well."

"A very good show," Rachel agreed.

"I can't see Frau Edelmännin," Stephan said.

"What?" Diana stared at Stephan for a moment before grabbing the binoculars and checking the seat Magda had been occupying. Dina Kastenmayer was missing as well. "When did they leave?" she asked.

"No idea," Stephan said.

Diana and Stephan looked to Rachel. She held up her hands. "I wasn't watching her. I was concentrating on the control board."

"Frau Kastenmayer wouldn't have left before Dr. Gribbleflotz's performance ended without a good reason. Frau Edelmännin must be feeling worse." Diana turned to Stephan. "Do you have your medical kit?"

Stephan pointed to where it was hanging. "The rest of our gear is still at the *Palazzo Angeli*."

"It might be an idea to stop and collect it on the way to Dr. Stone's apartment." Diana took in a deep breath. "Right now, I think we need to talk to Dr. Stone."

"Magda is ill?" Tom Stone demanded.

"We don't know," Diana said. "All we know is she had abdominal pains earlier, and that she left before the end of the show."

Tom ran his fingers through his hair. "She said there was nothing wrong. That the midwife said there was nothing to worry about."

"It might just be gas," Diana suggested. "Still, I'd be happier if I could examine her."

"She's not going to like it."

"Frau Edelmännin will like losing her child even less," Stephan pointed out.

"Lose the baby?" Tom looked at Stephan in horror. "Surely it's not that serious."

"Anything is possible until we know otherwise," Diana said. "That's why I need to examine your wife." She sighed. "Dr. Stone, I doubt Frau Edelmännin would have left the performance early just for a little abdominal discomfort. Not without telling you."

Tom slumped. "No. She wouldn't."

"So, it is agreed that we all go around to your apartment and you convince your wife to let me examine her."

"I'll get my coat."

Diana waved for Stephan to follow Dr. Stone.

"It could just be flatulence," Rachel suggested.

"Or bowel cramping," Diana said. "On the other hand, it could be something serious."

"Like what?"

Diana shrugged. "Kidney stones, urinary infection. Maybe even appendicitis."

"Appendicitis would be bad."

Chapter 44

Phillip rode herd on Thomas all the way back to his apartment in the central city. He had managed to calm him down and even talk sense into him. And then they arrived to a wide-open front door. Thomas lost it. He ran into the apartment calling out for his wife.

"Magda! Magda! Are you all right?"

Lise Gebauer appeared in response to his calls. She saw who had accompanied him home and slumped in relief. "You got my message."

"What message?" Thomas demanded.

Lise appealed mutely to Diana.

"We didn't get any message," Phillip said. "When did you send it?"

"Just after the housekeeper insisted on calling in a doctor."

"A doctor?" Thomas wailed. "Where's Magda? What's wrong with Magda? Is Magda all right?"

Lise led the way to Magda's bedroom, where she was lying on the four-poster bed while the midwife and Dina did their best to keep the doctors at bay.

"What's going on?" Thomas demanded.

Dr. Johann Vesling turned. "You wife is in pain, and these *women*"—he used the word scornfully, gesturing to Dina and the midwife—"won't let me examine her."

Thomas pushed through to Magda and wrapped his arms around her. Phillip, meanwhile, surveyed the occupants. There was another woman. He guessed that she was the housekeeper.

There were also three doctors: Dr. Vesling, Dr. Wirsung, and a doctor he had not previously met. He introduced himself.

"*Dottore* Gribbleflotz, and you are?"

"*Dottore* Bonaventura Ferrari," the man said as he shook Phillip's hand.

"Could everyone move away while *Signora* Cheng examines *Signora* Edelmännin?" Phillip suggested before herding everyone except his wife and the midwife clear while Diana approached.

Diana drew the curtain of the four-poster to shield Magda from the eyes of all the males and started her examination. She called out the symptoms as she discovered them. After a few minutes she pulled back the curtain.

"What's wrong with Magda?" Thomas demanded.

"Colic," Dr. Wirsung said.

"Urinary infection," Dr. Vesling said.

"It is the simple movement of the baby pressing on sensitive areas," Dr. Ferrari said.

"Diana?" Thomas asked.

"I'd really like to have a white blood cell test to be sure, but I think it's appendicitis."

"Don't listen to her," Dr. Vesling instructed Thomas Stone.

"I could do a rudimentary white blood cell test by spinning a blood sample in a glove to separate the layers," Stephan suggested.

Diana licked her lips. "It'll be crude, but I'll feel more confident of my diagnosis if I can see that there's a heightened level of white blood cells."

"What are white blood cells?" Dr. Ferrari asked.

Diana turned to him. "They are the cells in the body that defend it against infection. If you've ever seen blood separated into layers, the white layer between the yellow and red layers is made up of white blood cells."

"You mean *Phlegm*?"

"If you want to use Hippocrates' four humors of the blood then yes, it is Phlegm."

While Diana had been explaining things to the down-time doctors, Stephan had been working with Dr. Stone and Magda. He drew a syringe of blood from Magda's arm and injected it into a test tube. He then capped the test tube and forced it into a finger in a latex glove, tied a string to the glove, and started swinging it in a circle.

"What about blood-typing?" Diana asked.

"I don't have any antibody reagents, but we could use known blood in plasma," Stephan suggested. "I'm type A positive."

"That's good, because I'm B positive."

"What are they talking about?" Dr. Vesling demanded of Phillip.

"Blood types," he explained. "If we have to operate, it is a good idea to have blood available to replace any the patient loses." Phillip held up a hand to silence the down-time doctors before they could take issue with what he had just said. "Blood transfusions were very common up-time. After early experiments resulted in the deaths of patients, they realized that not all blood was the same. So, they developed tests to ensure that donor and recipient had compatible blood."

While Phillip had been speaking, Diana had raided Stephan's Advanced Medic medical kit for a couple of clean test tubes, a wax crayon, and a couple of sterile lancets. She used the crayon to label the test tubes A and B.

"Whenever you're ready," Diana called out to Stephan.

He gave the test tube of blood a few more whirls before stopping to check. He smiled when he saw the plasma and blood had separated.

He carefully added several drops of plasma to both the A and B test tubes before letting Diana stick his finger with a lancet and squeeze out several drops into the test tube labeled A. Then it was Stephan's turn to use a lancet on Diana and her blood was dripped into the other test tube. They were capped and gently shaken to mix the blood and plasma.

"We have a winner," Diana said holding up the A sample. "Anybody here, other than Corporal Böhm, know if they are type A or type O?"

"I'm O positive," Lise said.

"I am A positive," Dina said.

"That's good," Phillip said. "Stephan, I assume you have the equipment necessary for a blood transfusion." Stephan nodded. "Very well. Then, if we all agree that an operation is necessary..."

"Who is all agreeing?" Dr. Vesling screeched.

Phillip sighed and held his hand out to Stephan. "The separated blood, please."

Stephan handed it over and Phillip held it up to the light. There were four distinct layers. Top to bottom they were yellow, white, red, and black. "*Signora* Cheng, would you say the white layer is significantly thicker than you would expect in a healthy person?"

Diana nodded. "There is definitely an infection somewhere."

"So we must operate." Phillip clapped his hands. "Who and where?"

The down-time doctors stared blankly at Phillip.

"Have none of you ever performed an appendectomy?" Phillip asked.

Three heads moved side to side slowly. That was not promising. Phillip turned to Diana. "*Signora* Cheng..."

"You have more experience performing the procedure."

"But..." Phillip took a deep breath to calm himself down. Or at least to try and calm himself down.

"I can assist." Diana shot a quick glance toward Thomas and Magda.

Phillip thought he understood what Diana was not saying. Someone had to perform the operation, and if his performing the operation once, under the direct supervision of Dr. Schultes, made him the more experienced surgeon, then that someone looked to be him. He turned to Dr. Vesling. "I need an operating room prepared immediately."

"A what?"

"They don't have any operating rooms, *Dottore* Gribbleflotz," Diana said.

"What was that?" Thomas demanded. "There are no operating rooms?"

"Not as we know them," Diana said. "That's why we've been doing the transurethral lithotripsy procedures in private homes and barbers' rooms. Our best bet would be the anatomical theater in the university. We can position the spotlights at the top. That way the heat from the light won't cook the patient."

"I am here," Magda pointed out.

"I'm sorry, *Signora* Edelmännin, but if you do have appendicitis, then your appendix has to come out as soon as possible."

Magda held her hands over her belly defensively. "What about my baby?"

"The surgery shouldn't endanger the baby," Phillip said.

Magda ignored Phillip and kept her eyes on Diana.

"Up-time, appendicitis in pregnant women was quite common.

About one in a thousand to fifteen hundred women need an appendectomy during pregnancy. With proper care, there is no danger to mother or baby."

Magda swallowed and gripped Thomas' hands.

"Won't the baby have pushed the appendix about?" Thomas asked. Phillip nodded. "Then how will you know where to make an incision?"

Phillip glanced hesitantly at Magda.

"Phillip. I must know. Surely you aren't planning on opening Magda up until you find it?"

"At this point in *Signora* Edelmännin's pregnancy, it should be directly above the McBurney's point, about level with the navel," Diana said.

Phillip sent Diana a smile of thanks. He could have announced he knew where to look because he had once dissected a woman at about this stage in her pregnancy, but he didn't think the association with death would be welcomed just now. "What Diana said. We should also be able to confirm the location by palpation."

Thomas gripped Magda's hands in his own. "Do it."

Later that evening, the Anatomy theater, University of Padua

Phillip stepped into the anatomical theater and immediately had a feeling of déjà vu. He knew he had been here before, nearly twenty years ago. But back then, he had been relegated to one of the seven tiers that ringed the dissection table in ever increasing diameters—rather like a funnel.

No. That was not why things felt so familiar. He worried his lip with his teeth as he checked everyone was in place. Stephan was at Magda's head administering ether. Cristofori was standing possessively over the theremin as it spat out the sound of Magda's beating heart.

Nurse Gebauer was tending to the instruments while Diana Cheng stood to one side waiting to assist him. Everyone was wearing a surgical smock made from clean sheets that had been run up on a sewing machine in the short time since the operation had been scheduled. Everyone but Phillip had a surgical mask covering their faces. He would don his after explaining what was about to happen to the audience that had gathered—and for a sudden operation being conducted in the dead of night, a lot of people had dragged themselves out of their beds to watch.

It was standing room only on the tiers surrounding the dissection table except, Phillip noticed, for the area around one man on the second tier. He stared at the silhouette, and then it came to him. It was the spirit of his great mentor, Dr. Giulio Casseri, here to watch him display his skill. Phillip smiled up at his mentor and held out his arms to draw his attention to the body before him.

There was a flash of light.

Chapter 45

Phillip blinked several times as he tried to restore his vision. As he did so, he realized that the light had been Sebastian Jones' flash unit. Still blinking, he looked up again. Yes. It was definitely Sebastian. He smiled ruefully. It had been a silly flight of fantasy that the spirit of his mentor would be here watching over him. He looked up at his audience and started his spiel.

"Tonight, I will be performing an emergency appendectomy on a thirty-nine-year-old woman who is sixteen weeks pregnant. Assisting me will be *Signora* Cheng, a student in the DO program at the University of Jena. Providing anesthesia will be Corporal Böhm of the USE Military Department. Nurse Gebauer is the sterile-theater nurse in charge of instruments while *Signora* Rovarini is the non-sterile nurse. *Signora* Rovarini will be spraying the air with a fine mist of carbolic acid to reduce the risk of the bacteria and viruses you are all breathing out infecting the patient."

Phillip pointed to Cristofori. "We also have *Signore* Cristofori running the heart monitor. The sound you can hear is the patient's heart beating." He nodded to Cristofori, who turned up the volume so that the sound of Magda's slow but regular heartbeat reverberated through the theater.

"The surgical team are all wearing sterile surgical gowns to reduce the risk of infection. The patient is shrouded on sterile sheets with only the operation site exposed for the same reason. We are all wearing surgical masks so that we don't exhale bacteria or viruses onto the patient." Phillip gestured for Marianna to come up and tie his face mask in place before he took his position in front of the patient. "We begin," he announced.

On his words the two carbon-arc spotlights they had borrowed were switched on and bathed Magda and the team with bright white light.

Phillip described everything he did in a clear and confident voice as he operated. So confident did he sound that no one was aware of just how much prompting he was getting from Diana.

The operation proceeded efficiently, and within minutes he was able to cut the inflamed appendix out. He showed the pus-filled organ to the audience while Diana started closing the incision.

"As you can see, the appendix is full of pus. If we hadn't removed it, it would have burst in situ resulting in a life-threatening infection." He placed the organ into a dish Marianna presented for that purpose and turned back to help Diana finish closing the incision.

Phillip waited for Magda to be carried out of the anatomical theater before following. At the door, he turned and had one last look. The audience was disbanding already. Movement from the top tier drew his attention. He wiped his spectacles clean and stared. No. The movement was just a couple of men dismantling the spotlights. He smiled to himself. Obviously, the Grantville Traveling Roadshow people did not trust anyone with their valuable new hardware.

He inhaled deeply through his nose. It was strange. The last time he had been here the smell had been so different. That thought had him smiling. Even in the depths of winter, a human body started to pong after the first three or four days of a dissection. Today the theater smelt of human sweat and caustic soda.

"Dr. Gribbleflotz. Are you okay?" Diana Cheng asked.

He turned and smiled at her. "Just reminiscing over the last time I was here. It smelt different."

Diana raised her brows in question.

"My mentor, Professor Casseri, was conducting his one and only anatomy demonstration in the theater."

"Ah!" Diana nodded knowingly. "The cadaver was a bit ripe?"

"Just a bit."

They both grinned at each other at the understatement.

"The cadavers we used in Gross Anatomy were treated with embalming mixtures that can stop putrification for weeks if there is a suitable cool place to store them."

"It will be something to suggest if they aren't already using them." Phillip held the door open for Diana to pass through. They were met by Thomas Stone.

"They won't let me in to see Magda," he said by way of a greeting.

"Corporal Böhm and Nurse Gebauer?" Phillip asked. "They have orders not to allow anyone to disturb the patient until she wakes up."

"But I'm her husband," Thomas cried plaintively.

"We could let you stand at the door." Phillip looked to Diana for confirmation. She nodded.

"Speaking of doors . . ." Thomas stepped around Phillip and pushed open the door into the anatomical theater. He looked around. "Not much of an operating room," he muttered.

"It's basically all they have."

"They need something better. No one should be operated on in a dissection theater." Thomas turned to Phillip and Diana. "Someone should be doing something about it."

"Hello, Someone," Diana said, looking straight at Thomas.

"Me?" Thomas demanded. "What do I know about operating rooms?"

"You don't have to know anything about operating rooms," Diana said. "You just need the desire to build one and plenty of money. You can hire people who know all about them to design something suitable."

Thomas smiled and offered Diana his hand. "Hi, I'm Someone. I want to build an operating room in Padua."

"That's the spirit," Diana said. "Dr. Schultes in Grantville will know who can help you."

"I'll get onto it right away," Thomas promised.

"Meanwhile, why don't we all go and check on your wife?"

Stephan Böhm was standing at the entrance to the recovery room repelling all-comers. He smiled when he saw Phillip and the others approaching and gestured for the gaggle of doctors trying to get past to look behind them.

"*Dottore* Gribbleflotz, this man won't let us in to check the patient," Dr. Vesling said.

"Corporal Böhm is acting in accordance with my instructions." That was a complete and utter lie. However, if he had imagined the doctors would take it upon themselves to burst into the room where Magda was recovering from the anesthetic, he most certainly would have issued such an instruction.

"How is the patient?" he asked Stephan.

"Doing well, *Dottore* Gribbleflotz. She's sleeping naturally now. I don't want to disturb her because the longer she sleeps the less likely she is to awaken with post-anesthetic nausea or vomiting."

"That is something best avoided," Phillip agreed. He turned to Dr. Vesling. "If you are quiet, I will let you in to watch while I check the patient."

"What about me?" Thomas demanded.

"If *Dottore* Stone wishes to sit quietly with his wife..." Stephan suggested as he moved aside to let people into the recovery room.

"Of course."

"Thomas, if you promise to do as you are told..."

"I promise, Phillip."

"Then, in you go." Phillip gestured for Thomas to precede him. Diana entered right behind him, and the gaggle of doctors followed behind her.

The examination was brief. There really was not much to see. Just an incision that had been closed with over a dozen stitches. Phillip checked Magda's heartbeat and breathing before checking the fetal heartbeat. Everything seemed as it should be. He left Magda in the care of her midwife and husband and ushered everyone else out.

"That went quite well," he proclaimed with satisfaction as he led everyone away from the recovery room.

"The operation was most impressive," Dr. Vesling agreed. "How long will it be before she is ambulatory?"

Phillip looked toward Diana. "Three days?"

"One to three days," Diana said. "She should be back to normal activities in two to four weeks."

"So quickly?" Dr. Ferrari asked.

Phillip nodded. "There were no problems so, yes. It should be that quick."

"But she is pregnant," Dr. Ferrari said.

Phillip smiled. "I'm guessing you don't have any children."

Dr. Ferrari squinted as he looked at Phillip. "No. Why?"

"Because if you did, I'm sure your wife would have informed you that being pregnant is not the same as being ill."

Dr. Ferrari glanced at a couple of the other doctors. They

nodded. Phillip assumed they were fathers. "So *Signora* Edelmännin's pregnancy isn't important?"

"Oh, it's important. Just not a significant factor in her recovery," Phillip said. "We'll have to keep an eye on her, but it won't stop her being back on her feet in a couple of days."

Dr. Ferrari sighed loudly. "You and your companions know so much. It is a pity your companions lack even a licentiate. But for that, they could have presented seminars on the new medical advances from Grantville."

Phillip experienced a brainwave. "The university could grant them *licentia docendi*." He held up his hands to silence any protest at his suggestion that the university grant Diana and Stephan licenses to teach. "In fact, doesn't the university only require the payment of a fee before allowing someone to undertake the examinations for a *doctorate in artibus et medicine*?"

"We do require some proof of medical knowledge sufficient to justify the time and effort of an examination. It does last five days, you know," Vesling said self-importantly.

Phillip did know. Or at least, that had been the duration of the examinations back when he was last in Padua. It was nice to know that had not changed. He glanced at Diana and Stephan. She looked like she might burst if she held back what she wanted to say much longer. Stephan looked like he was only just starting to understand what Phillip was suggesting. That was probably due to his Latin, which might not be up to the task of the examinations. That would be a pity.

Phillip smiled at Vesling. "I believe that you and *Dottore* Wirsung questioned both *Signora* Cheng and Corporal Böhm earlier today." A thought struck him, and he quickly checked the time on his pocket watch. It was nearly three in the morning. "Better make that earlier yesterday. I'm sure they managed to hold their own."

"They did better than hold their own," Dr. Wirsung said.

"There you are then," Phillip said. "If we add their recently demonstrated competence in the operating room, I'm sure everyone will agree that there is ample evidence that they are up to the task of the examinations."

"And, of course, you yourself trained under *Dottore* Casseri for three years," Dr. Ferrari said.

"Yes," Phillip agreed, not too sure what Dr. Ferrari was getting at.

"It is a good idea," Dr. Ferrari said. "However, I doubt we have ever had three candidates for the *doctorate in artibus et medicine* all at the same time before." He shook his head regretfully. "I can't spare fifteen days to cover all three candidates. Not right now."

Several of the other doctors gathered around voiced their agreement with Ferrari's problem.

"*Three* candidates?" Phillip asked.

"But of course, *Dottore* Gribbleflotz. Surely you want to cap off your earlier studies with a *doctorate in artibus et medicine* from the finest medical school in the world?"

Phillip did not have to think long before agreeing. He was sure he could pass the examinations. Hadn't he been taught by Professor Casseri, one of the finest teachers to have ever graced the halls of Padua? Hadn't he spent four years as a military physician? Hadn't he spent two years working with Dr. Gaspard Bauhin, professor of the practice of medicine and professor of anatomy and botany at Basel? Hadn't he worked for several months with Dr. Franz de le Boë, a recent graduate of the Jena-Leahy medical program better known in the up-time histories as Franciscus Sylvius—after whom both the Sylvian fissure and the Sylvian aqueduct were named? "When?" he asked.

Stephan held up his hand and waited until he was noticed. "It's not that I'm not interested," he said, "but I don't think my Latin would be up to it."

Dr. Vesling waved a hand. "Don't let that bother you. I am from Minden in Westphalia and *Dottore* Wirsung is from Augsburg. If necessary, we can translate."

"Then I'm in."

All attention turned to Diana. She smiled. "You have to ask?"

"About *Dottore* Ferrari's concern over time," Dr. Vesling said. "It might be possible to convince the faculty to allow all three of you to be examined at the same time.

"Of course, the whole examination will have to be public, and only one candidate will be allowed in the examination room at a time. But with care and the cooperation of all concerned, I am sure we can do it," Dr. Vesling said to muted exclamations of approval.

Chapter 46

Wednesday, 26th November 1636, Jena, USE

The position of dean of the Jena medical faculty was an unpaid position that took too much time away from more productive tasks. As such, the position was not much sought after. Instead, faculty members had to serve a year in the position by rotation. This year it was the turn of Dr. Zacharias Brendel to occupy the dean's office. For the winter term he was also rector of the whole university. Normally this would be cause for complaint. However, the previous November, measles and influenza had run through the faculty. Several members had not survived, and the others had been forced to take up the slack. Such was the life of an academic.

Zacharias could not help himself as he looked at the photograph on the front page of the *Grantville Times*. He smiled.

"You're looking frightfully happy," Dr. Dominicus Arumäus, Zacharias' immediate predecessor in the role of rector of the university, said.

Zacharias answered the implied question by showing Dominicus the front page of the newspaper. There was a photograph of Dr. Phillip Gribbleflotz standing behind a patient in the anatomical theater in Padua. The headline read, GRIBBLEFLOTZ PERFORMS LIFE-SAVING OPERATION.

Dominicus' eyes opened wide. "Oh, dear. Werner isn't going to like that."

Zacharias could only agree. Dr. Werner Rolfinck did not approve of Dr. Phillip Gribbleflotz. He felt that Phillip was a charlatan. A very lucky and successful charlatan, but still a charlatan nonetheless.

Seeing Phillip "winning" once more was bound to set him off. And that was not all. "It gets better," he told Dominicus. "I have heard that Dr. Gribbleflotz, Frau Cheng, and Corporal Böhm have all been invited to sit the examinations for the Padua *doctorate in artibus et medicine*."

Dominicus' eyes opened wide. "Years ago, didn't Werner block Gribbleflotz's application to matriculate here?"

Zacharias nodded.

"And now he is a candidate for the Padua *doctorate in artibus et medicine*!" Dominicus smiled "Werner is definitely not going to like that. What are their chances?"

Zacharias gestured to the man seated beside him, Dr. Johannes Schultes, the head of surgery at Leahy Medical Center in Grantville. The man who had made a special early morning train trip, with a collection of morning editions of the Grantville newspapers, just to be here on this auspicious occasion.

"Dr. Schultes?" Dominicus prompted.

Johannes smiled. "Corporal Böhm is one of the best Advanced Combat Medics the program has produced, and Frau Cheng is so far ahead of everyone else in her year group that it is not funny. As for Dr. Gribbleflotz..." He shrugged. "Dr. de la Boë has said good things about him, so he might be up to it."

Dominicus nodded thoughtfully. "I wonder what odds the bookmakers are offering."

"Thinking of placing a bet?" Johannes asked.

"Maybe." Dominicus smiled. "Maybe." He gestured toward the newspaper Zacharias was reading. "May I?"

Zacharias had not finished reading the newspaper yet, but the sound of familiar footfalls reverberating through the corridor just outside the staffroom had him folding it and passing it to Dominicus. He shot Johannes a smile before settling back in his chair and pretending to immerse himself in one of the letters Johannes had received from Padua in last night's mail.

Dr. Werner Rolfinck stormed into the staffroom, the heavy wooden doors bursting open as he powered through the doorway. Once in the staffroom, he stopped and looked around. Zeroed in on Zacharias. And stalked in his direction.

Zacharias kept his head down, even if his eyes were peeking up, and pretended disinterest in anything beyond the letter he was reading. It was a very interesting letter. It had been posted by Diana Cheng on Sunday and arrived on Tuesday. Zacharias' mind wandered a bit as he tried to comprehend mail traveling so far so fast. Barely three days to get from Padua to Grantville. That was modern technology for you.

Zacharias was so involved in his thoughts that he did not have to feign surprise when a newspaper was slapped down on the drinks table between him and Johannes. "What? What? What?" he demanded as he turned his focus onto Werner Rolfinck. He looked down at the folded newspaper Werner had slapped down. It was the *National Inquisitor.* A Grantville newspaper with something of a reputation for sensationalizing stories. He could only wonder what they had done with the Gribbleflotz story. And it was probably the Gribbleflotz story that had upset Werner—they had used what looked like it might be the same photograph as the *Grantville Times* on their front page.

"The *Inquisitor*?" Johannes asked pointedly. "Really, Werner. I thought better of you." The slow shake of his head signaled his disappointment with Werner.

"I didn't buy it," a clearly outraged Werner said. "One of my students was reading it.

"That charlatan has really done it this time," Werner said as he unfolded the newspaper so that Zacharias and Johannes could read the headline: GRIBBLEFLOTZ WOWS PADUA. "Seriously," Werner demanded. "How can they write such drivel?"

"Because it sells," Zacharias suggested, tongue in cheek.

With the bit between his teeth, Werner ignored Zacharias' quip. "And I have heard a rumor that Padua has decided to allow Gribbleflotz to sit the examination for a medical doctorate." He shook his head, his face flushed with anger. "He'll fail of course."

"He might not," Johannes said. "Dr. de la Boë is very impressed with him."

Werner's glare told Johannes how much he valued Dr. de la Boë's opinion. He turned to Zacharias. "You're the Dean of Medicine, what are you going to do about Gribbleflotz?"

Zacharias turned to Johannes. He tilted his head slightly in inquiry. "Offer him an honorary doctorate," he suggested.

Johannes smiled. "Or we could offer him the chance to test out on parts of the D.O. program."

"Test out on the D.O. program? Are you mad?" Werner demanded.

Zacharias stared at Werner in shock. Or at least, he hoped the expression he was putting on looked like he was shocked. "Surely you are not suggesting that we just *give* Dr. Gribbleflotz a Doctorate of Osteopathic Medicine? I mean, a *doctorate in artibus et medicine* from Padua is something very special, but there are limits." That was a bit of a dig. Werner's own doctorate was from Padua while Zacharias' alma mater was the University of Jena.

"You're going to do nothing?" Werner demanded.

"What do you expect me to do? It is up to Padua whether or not they award Dr. Gribbleflotz a *doctorate in artibus et medicine*."

Werner glared at Zacharias. He also glared at Johannes. No one said anything for nearly a minute, and then Werner turned on his heel and stalked out of the staffroom.

The moment the door closed behind him, the staff members, who had been remarkably silent during Werner's confrontation with Zacharias, started muttering amongst themselves.

"What do you really think Dr. Gribbleflotz's chances of passing the Padua examinations are?" Zacharias asked.

"Quite good, actually," Johannes said. "Did I ever tell you about the time I observed him assisting Dr. Casseri while he performed an anatomical demonstration when I was in Padua?"

"No. Tell me more."

Magdeburg, USE

Prime Minister Ed Piazza carefully went through the photographs David Zimmermann had placed on his desk, placing them in rows across the surface of his up-time–style office desk. "How did they manage to get Tom Stone to wear that outrageous costume?" he asked.

David examined the photograph Ed was pointing to. It was a group photograph of the performers taken at the end of Saturday night's performance in Padua while they were taking their bows. Everyone was still in costume, including Dr. Thomas Stone, who was dressed as a master of Akashic Magick and scholar of the Chakras. "I believe they used simple blackmail."

Ed stared at David. "Blackmail?"

"That's what my sources say." David grinned. "You can't see it in those photographs, but the gem in the turban flashes and changes color, as do the rings on Dr. Stone's fingers. I understand that Dr. Stone put on a most impressive performance."

Ed winced for Tom. "Does that mean the incident in Prague is dealt with?"

David nodded emphatically. "Dr. Gribbleflotz and Dr. Stone managed to come up with an explanation for the psychic surgery, and the science of the Chakras has been reduced to a mere diagnostic tool rather than a cure."

"How did they explain the psychic surgery?" Ed asked.

"They said everyone was mistaken, and that Herr Mundell had merely expelled a carnivorous insect larva through its breathing hole. That explained the lack of a scar, and they claimed that it ruptured as it was expelled, hence all the blood."

"So all's well that ends well?" Ed asked.

"Even better than that," David said. "Dr. Gribbleflotz, Frau Cheng, and Corporal Böhm have all been invited to sit the Padua medical doctorate examinations. And," David added, "I have been warned that the Republic of Venice may ask for the 1st Marine Reconnaissance Company to be sent to Venice to help select and train a similar unit for their navy."

"What are the feelings on that?"

"Colonel von Brockenholz and Admiral Simpson are sure to approve, meaning it will be a purely political decision, and there are a number of very good reasons for allowing the deployment."

Prague, Kingdom of Bohemia

Dr. Franz de la Boë could feel Nurse Gertraud Kaufmann breathing over his shoulder as he tried to read the newspaper.

"I see Frau Cheng is sitting the medical examinations in Padua."

"Yes," Franz muttered as he continued reading the story of recent events in Padua. Most of it was aimed at Dr. Gribbleflotz—him being the president of the Royal Academy, but Frau Cheng had rated a mention as one of two colleagues invited to sit the examinations with Dr. Gribbleflotz.

"She'll pass."

"You think so? The Padua medical examinations have the reputation of being the hardest in all Europe."

Gertraud snorted. "This is Frau Cheng we are talking about,

Dr. de la Boë. Her name was always being bandied about when I did my nursing degree in Grantville. She was taking nursing courses while she was still at school. Of course she'll pass. She probably knows more about medicine than most of the teachers at Padua."

Padua, Republic of Venice

Phillip and Stephan were seated awaiting their turn before the examiners. Seated opposite, with a book in his hand, was Giuseppe Veracini, a licentiate in the theology faculty. His job was to make sure that the candidate coming out of the examination room did not give away what sort of questions were being asked. He had been reading, but the loud noises coming from the examination room had caught even his attention.

The door opened to allow Diana to exit the examination room. It was shut smartly the moment she was clear. She turned to glare at it before heading over to where Stephan and Phillip were seated.

"Imbeciles," she muttered. "Complete and utter imbeciles."

"Who are imbeciles?" Stephan asked.

"They are," Diana answered with a flick of her hand toward the examination room. "Some fool suggested that the purpose of the lungs was to cool the blood."

Phillip smiled. "But you put him right?"

"You bet I did," Diana muttered as she found a chair and dragged it over. "I described the respiratory system and tried to beat gas-exchange theory into their closed minds." She sighed. "I hope it won't be used against me when they decide whether or not to award me the doctorate."

"Was this *imbecile* one of the examiners?" Giuseppe asked.

All eyes locked on Giuseppe. "No," Diana said. "It was a member of the audience."

"And how did the examiners react to your explanation?"

"They just asked more questions."

Giuseppe steepled his hands and smiled over the tips of his fingers. "Then I wouldn't worry."

Diana's response was preempted by the door to the examination room opening. An usher appeared. "*Signore* Stephan Böhm, please."

Stephan got to his feet and shook out his clothes. "Wish me luck."

"Good luck," both Phillip and Diana said.

Prospero Cesare Giulio Cristofori, president of the Padua Chapter of the Society of Aural Investigators, fingered the brass pin he'd added to the lapel of his white lab coat that marked him as qualified to operate the new Gribbleflotz Magneto-Etheric Aural Aura Detector as he continued to hold the detector's microphone over his client's heart.

He glanced at his glamorous assistant. Marianna Rovarini was concentrating on the ribbon of paper coming out of the detector as she pumped the pedal that powered the device. She looked almost as worried as he felt. The client's heart just sounded wrong. It was skipping and fluttering.

"Is something wrong?" their client asked.

Prospero glanced at Marianna again. She nodded to his unasked question. "Your Oskaloosa appears unstable," he said. "I would like your permission to consult with *Dottore* Stone about possible treatment."

Giovanni Valpi stared at Prospero. "*The Dottore* Stone? From the City from the Future?"

Prospero nodded. "He is an expert on the science of the Chakras."

Giovanni took a deep breath, his hand going to his chest as he did so. "You have my permission."

Prospero laid the paper trace from the Gribbleflotz Magneto-Etheric Aural Aura Detector out on Dr. Stone's desk. "You can see that the heart is beating irregularly."

Thomas studied the graphical description of Giovanni's heartbeat. It was a phonocardiogram rather than an electrocardiogram, but the information was there if you knew how to read the graphs. There were oscillations for the lub-dub of the heartbeat followed by a gap before the next lub-dub. With the aid of a measuring rule, Thomas was able to confirm what he thought he could see. The gap between the lub-dubs was inconsistent. "Atrial fibrillation," he announced. "Or at least, that's what it looks like."

"Can you treat it?" Marianna asked.

Thomas nodded. "Digitalis should do the trick. But I'm not willing to prescribe it without checking your patient personally."

"Client," Prospero corrected.

Tom was taken aback by the correction. In his book, someone receiving medical services was a patient. He stared at Prospero. He saw a handsome young man in his early to mid-twenties in a white lab coat with a number of small badges on the lapel. Pinned to the breast pocket of the lab coat was a large badge identifying him as a member of the Padua Chapter of the Society of Aural Investigators. That was the reason for the disconnect. Aural investigators were not medical professionals.

But they could be. Tom started smiling. Finally, he could see a light at the end of the tunnel. A road to redemption. A way to assuage his guilty conscience over his part of the conspiracy that was foistering New Age mumbo jumbo as a trustworthy science onto an unsuspecting and trusting population. And a way of turning the science of the Chakras and Dr. Gribbleflotz's Society of Aural Investigators into a force for good. He could turn them into a trip wire. They'd need a little training, and Prospero was a perfect example of how a little training could pay dividends. He could turn the Society of Aural Investigators into an army of, not first responders, but rather a group who could spot symptoms and refer patients to suitable professionals for treatment. He would have to put his idea to his co-conspirators, but he was pretty sure that Diana and Stephan, at least, would fully support him. In the meantime, he had a patient to examine.

"Very well, client. So, when can I see *Signore* Valpi?"

"If you give me some suitable times, I will make the arrangements with *Signore* Valpi. Where would you like to see him?" Prospero asked.

"Here, in my rooms."

"We'll get right onto it," Marianna said before dragging Prospero out of Thomas' office.

Chapter 47

Saturday, 29th November 1636, Padua

University notices:

Promoted to the degree of *doctorate in artibus et medicine.*

Gribbleflotz, Phillip Theophrastus M.D. (Amsterdam); M.D. (Prague), M.D. (Olmütz), M.D. (Karolinum)

Cheng, Diana B.S.N. (Jena-Leahy)

Böhm, Stephan

Monday, 1st December 1636, Padua

The celebrations started on Friday. A small group—no more than two hundred people—gathered at the Rovarini compound to welcome home the newly crowned doctors of medicine and celebrate their success. The party had only grown from there. However, it was now Monday morning and the party was over. Everyone had work to do.

Paola shooed off the last of the partygoers and turned to inspect her home. It was spick-and-span. She turned to her worthy lieutenants—Diana Cheng, Stephan Böhm, and Lise Gebauer—they, probably because of their medical training, had been a force to be reckoned with when it came to cleaning the house. Not that they did all the work. No, they delegated. Each of them had taken command of a team of, sometimes unwilling, volunteers and put them to work. A cleanup that might normally have taken all day had been completed before preparations for lunch had to be started. "Thank you for..."

Her statement of thanks was interrupted by the clatter of iron hooves moving at speed on cobbles. All four of them hurried over to the window to see what was going on. The hoofbeats settled into a slower pace and then a mounted man trotted into the Rovarini compound. A youth ran up to take charge of the horse as the man dismounted.

He walked toward the house.

Paola, Diana, Lise, and Stephan looked at each other, and then they hurried toward the door. Paola, as the homeowner, took the lead. She had the door open just as the man was about to knock.

"Yes?" she invited.

The man, breathing heavily, held out a white envelope. "Radiogram from the USE Embassy for *Dottore* Gribbleflotz," he announced.

"Come inside and refresh yourself," Paola ordered. She looked out to the youth holding the horse. "Gabriele, look after the horse. Walk it around until it is cool, rub it down, and then give it a little water."

"I know how to look after a horse, *Zia* Paola."

Paola closed the door and turned around. Diana and Stephan were supporting the messenger as he staggered to the table while Lise was getting a mug of wine. She stared at the back of the messenger. A radiogram meant important news. Important news brought by a nearly exhausted messenger couldn't be good news. "I'll get Filippo," she announced.

She returned a few minutes later with Phillip, Diana, and Ursula Mittelhausen. Phillip gave the man some money and accepted the envelope. He ran a nervous tongue over dry lips as he stared at it.

"Just open it," Ursula said.

Paola offered Phillip a knife. He took it and broke the seal. He handed back the knife before opening the envelope and reading the message. His head dropped. He walked over to Dina and wrapped his arms around her.

Paola got the message. Bad news. She tapped the messenger on the shoulder and indicated that he should follow her. She handed him some bread and olive oil and led him outside.

The moment the door closed behind Paola, Phillip told Dina the bad news. She buried her head in his shoulder and cried.

"What's happened?" Ursula asked.

"Pastor Kastenmayer passed away in his sleep on Saturday night."

"We'll have to leave for Grantville as soon as possible," Ursula said.

"Dina's brother Martin has already arranged seats on Wednesday's flight." Phillip turned to Diana, Lise, and Stephan. "He was only able to book four seats. Dina, Frau Mittelhausen, and I make three. Who would like the remaining seat?"

"You'll probably want it for the children," Lise said. Diana agreed. Stephan reminded everyone that he was still awaiting orders and should stay in Padua until they arrived.

"Thank you," Phillip said. He then led his distraught wife back to their bedroom.

Chapter 48

January 1637, Padua, Republic of Venice

Paolo Molin strode into the large three-story building that housed the *Dottore* Gribbleflotz Emporium of Natural Wonders as if he owned it.

He did not. But he was the manager. Not just of the emporium, but of the whole building. There were some sixty thousand square feet of revenue-generating space in the three-story building set on the half-acre site between the *Via Roma* and the *Piazza delle Erbe*, and it was his job to ensure every square foot earned its keep.

He held the door open for the two porters trailing behind him, each with a portmanteau balanced on their shoulder.

Paolo led them up two flights of stairs and toward the manager's apartment. He unlocked it and held the door open for them. After directing them where to leave his luggage, Paolo paid them off, adding a tip large enough to extract a smile from both men, before showing them out.

With the door shut behind them, Paolo surveyed his apartment. It was too large for a single man but, with the recent improvement in his situation, he could now afford to marry. He advanced to the window at the end of the room and looked out upon the *Piazza delle Erbe*. To his right was the *Palazzo della Ragione*. The large medieval structure, with its three-hundred-foot frontages on both the *Piazza della Frutta* and the *Piazza delle Erbe*, had been *Signora* Mittelhausen's first choice to house the emporium. However, she had been unable to secure a deal and had been forced to accept her second choice.

Paolo shook himself out of his reverie. He had been absent from Padua for nearly three weeks—giving evidence against Alessandro Garivaghi and processing the necessary paperwork for both the Gribbleflotz Iodine Company and the Gribbleflotz Iodized Salt Company—and it was time to check any changes that may have been made to his domain in his absence.

Paolo started on the top floor and worked his way down. There was a lot to see and a lot of people to chat to, so it was almost two hours before he arrived at his last stop, the emporium itself.

"Paolo, wait for me!" Sebastian Jones called as he hurried across the *Piazza delle Erbe*, one hand doing its best to stop his camera bag bouncing about. "Did you . . ."

"Get your supplies?" Paolo nodded. "I sent them ahead on a barge. They should arrive later today, or early tomorrow morning."

"Thanks," Sebastian muttered, and then he smiled. "One of Alberto Rovarini's friends says he knows the house in the tourist brochure." His shoulders slumped. "But he doesn't remember any balcony overlooking the courtyard."

Paolo stared at Sebastian. Sometimes it was hard to understand what he was talking about. Now was one of those times. "House? Balcony?"

"In Verona. Juliet's balcony."

"Ahhh!" Enlightenment struck. "Shakespeare's *Romeo and Juliet*." He smiled. "And what do you intend to do if there is no balcony?"

Sebastian shrugged. "Maybe I can persuade them to build one. It was a major tourist attraction up-time."

Paolo could only laugh at the outrageousness of Sebastian's suggestion. He knew Sebastian was quite capable of creating the tourist attractions the up-timers would expect to find. He was shaking his head slowly as he pushed open the door and entered the emporium.

The *Dottore* Gribbleflotz Emporium of Natural Wonders was more than just a shop. It was an experience of things natural, as seen through the eyes of the up-timers. That meant that the emporium also served as a display case of things modern. Things modern included things new and novel as opposed to just things from Grantville. So there were guns for sale. Modern rifles and pistols that could fire cartridges, like the pump-action rifle and shotgun that had been so useful in rescuing *dottori* Stone and Gribbleflotz. Thinking about guns, and how their recent use had contributed to his improved circumstances, Paolo entered the main hall.

To be met by the dulcet tones of someone's curses reverberating around the main hall of the emporium. He recognized the voice, also the subject matter, and some of the terms aimed at Rachel Lynch's target. Bill Franklin was probably very lucky he was not within her reach. Paolo followed the repeated cursing to Rachel. She had an open letter in her hand.

"Is there something the matter?" Paolo asked. Given the circumstances, the question might be considered superfluous. However, it did provide a suitable opening for him to learn what had upset Rachel.

"It's that useless ex-husband of mine." She waved the papers in front of Paolo. "He's going away, deserting his children again. In fact, the bastard has all but disowned them. He says he has a job with the Venetian Navy." She glared at Paolo.

Paolo held up his hands defensively. "I had nothing to do with that," he protested.

"How come he's free to go?" she demanded.

"There was not enough evidence to charge him in connection with the kidnapping of Drs. Stone, Gribbleflotz, and Böhm."

"Okay," Rachel conceded, "but what about the theft of USE naval equipment? There's plenty of evidence to support that charge. How is it that he's getting off scot-free?"

Paolo smiled. He had always thought that his command of the English language was good, but that was before he was exposed to up-time English. This time, however, he could make a good guess as to the meaning. "I'm sure he didn't get off 'scot-free.' There are sure to have been fines and other penalties imposed."

"A fine?" Edith humphed. "He should be in prison."

"They could be large fines."

"I hope he can't pay them," Rachel muttered as she picked up her last piece of mail. A package rather than just a letter.

She broke the seal and opened it. There was an enclosure. She pulled that out and unrolled it. "A license," she whispered. "To operate as an apothecary here in Padua."

Rachel looked Paolo in the eye. "Is it real?"

Paolo held out a hand. "Let me see."

Rachel passed him the document. A quick glance at the signatures at the bottom was all it took to bring a smile to his face. He looked up at Rachel. "It is signed by my old boss at the *Provveditori alla Sanità* and two of his colleagues. There couldn't be a more real document."

A smile appeared on Rachel's face. Her eyes lit up. Paolo met her smile with one of his own. She reached out her hand. Paolo reached out a hand. They reached out to each other and...

There was a flash of light.

Epilogue

Tuesday, 5th May 1637, Padua

Birth Notices:

Phillipa STONE

STONE, Thomas and Magdalena Edelmännin are pleased to announce the safe arrival of Phillipa Diana Stephane on May 3, 1637, weighing 5 lb., 10 oz. Mother and baby are both well.